EX LIBRIS

VINTAGE **CLASSICS**

ghostly

ALSO BY AUDREY NIFFENEGGER

The Time Traveler's Wife
Her Fearful Symmetry
The Three Incestuous Sisters
The Adventuress
The Night Bookmobile
Raven Girl

ghostly

A Collection of Ghost Stories

Edited, Illustrated and Introduced by

Audrey Niffenegger

VINTAGE

ACKNOWLEDGEMENTS

Every effort has been made to trace and contact all copyright holders. If there are any inadvertent omissions or errors we will be pleased to correct them at the earliest opportunity.

Vintage Classics gratefully acknowledges permission to reprint copyright material as follows:

Audrey Niffenegger: 'Secret Life, With Cats', first published in the *Chicago Tribune* in 2006. Copyright © Audrey Niffenegger 2006.

P. G. Wodehouse: 'Honeysuckle Cottage', first published in the *Saturday Evening Post* in 1925. Copyright by the Trustees of the Wodehouse Estate.

Neil Gaiman: 'Click-Clack the Rattlebag', first published in *Impossible Monsters* in 2013. Copyright © Neil Gaiman 2013.

A. M. Burrage: 'Playmates', first published in *Some Ghost Stories* in 1927. Copyright by the Estate of A. M. Burrage.

A. S. Byatt: 'The July Ghost', first published in *Firebird I* in 1982. Copyright © A. S. Byatt 1982.

Kelly Link: 'The Specialist's Hat', first published in *Event Horizon* in 1998 and reprinted in Kelly Link's *Strange Things Happen* (Small Beer Press) and Kelly Link's *Pretty Monsters* (Viking). Copyright © Kelly Link 1998. Permission granted by the author.

Amy Giacalone: 'Tiny Ghosts', first published in this collection. Copyright © Amy Giacalone 2015.

Rebecca Curtis: 'The Pink House', first published in *The New Yorker* in 2014. Copyright © Rebecca Curtis 2014, used by permission of The Wylie Agency (UK) Limited.

Ray Bradbury: 'August 2026: There Will Come Soft Rains', first published in *Collier's* magazine in 1950. Copyright © Ray Bradbury 1950.

1 3 5 7 9 10 8 6 4 2

Vintage Classics, an imprint of Vintage,
20 Vauxhall Bridge Road,
London SW1V 2SA

Vintage Classics is part of the Penguin Random House group of companies whose addresses can be found at global.penguinrandomhouse.com.

Introductory material and illustrations copyright © Audrey Niffenegger 2015
Anthology copyright © Random House Group Ltd 2015

Audrey Niffenegger has asserted her right to be identified as the author of this Work in accordance with the Copyright, Designs and Patents Act 1988

First published by Vintage Classics in 2015

www.vintage-books.co.uk

A CIP catalogue record for this book is available from the British Library

ISBN 9781784870065

Printed and bound in Great Britain by Clays Ltd, St Ives plc

Penguin Random House is committed to a sustainable future for our business, our readers and our planet. This book is made from Forest Stewardship Council® certified paper.

CONTENTS

INTRODUCTION

Dead is the most alone you can be.

We all wonder about death, but we don't understand it. Ghost stories are speculations, little experiments in death. We try it on for size – it never quite fits. Good, we say, it's nothing to do with us, this death. But what about that other death over there: what's that one about? There are always new deaths to marvel at, deaths that create a shiver of pleasure because they are not ours, not yet.

Ghost stories are a literature of loneliness and longing. Ghost stories can be violent, grotesque, thrilling, repulsive. But the quieter, more desperate stories resonate more intensely. They are powered by grief and loss, separation and finality. Death is a mystery, comfort is scarce, but we will play with our bereavements, we will invent little amusements that explode with sorrow, thus we will armour ourselves against inevitable loss.

The ghost story transcends time and culture; tales of ghosts and haunted places reverberate through the literatures of ancient Greece and Rome, the Old Testament, the *One Thousand and*

One Nights. The *Tale of Genji* includes harrowing ghost stories. Ghosts pervade Shakespeare's plays and John Donne's poetry. The wrongness of the ghost is the same across cultures: something is seriously out of place.

The stories in this collection are English and American and range across more than 170 years. They are not diverse or representative; they are only stories I have chosen because I like them, and what I like about them is their intimacy, their off-kilter matter-of-factness and their vivid evocations of order disrupted, sudden awful knowledge, the human condition as cosmic joke. There are stories here that show their age; in Rudyard Kipling's 'They' there is a complacent acceptance of colonial mores that is jarring to modern hearts and minds. Yet the story's main concern – lost children and grieving parents – is still relevant and powerful. Some of the stories portray antediluvian attitudes towards women, but we can see around the prejudices of these characters and their very badness is what calls forth the ghosts that will punish the malefactors.

Houses, lovers, children, cats: things that are frequently haunted. There are plenty of ghost stories that feature strange ghosts haunting public places, but for this book I have chosen more domestic ghosts, particular ghosts haunting their own families, friends or small objects. Houses, lovers, children, cats: they are so close to us, so familiar and everyday, that they can be more frightening because they were once innocent and beloved.

Houses contain us, we live our lives in them, and it is not surprising that they might continue to shelter us after we die. We are attached to our homes, perhaps so much that we cannot leave, even though we are dead. A haunted house has an emptiness that is filled by the inappropriate or unnatural. A house can lose its soul, a house can go bad. Houses can be monuments to personality, we inflict our tastes upon them, but they can afflict us with their perversity in return. Ghosts can be like vermin – pests to be driven away or exterminated. We are anxious about our houses. Even the most conciliatory, helpful house can become supernaturally burdensome.

Haunting equals attachment equals an odd kind of love, even if that love is unwanted or is unpleasant or dangerous to the loved one. We grieve, but eventually we assert our independence from the dead. A ghost story is often a story of grief gone awry. We let our longing bring our beloved dead back to us, where they should not be. Ghosts are not very comforting. Their companionship does not sate our loneliness. We have to turn back to the company of the living, or die.

Children make excellent ghosts: their stolen, unlived lives echo after they are gone. We are haunted by the ghosts of children who grow up and by those who do not. Children often don't know danger when they see it, and they can be dangerous in their innocence. Children don't differentiate very firmly between possible and impossible. They have empty places in their knowledge of the world that allow pretend to be real, and ghosts can inhabit this emptiness.

Cats are like ghosts. They live with us, but they have their own secretive agendas. Cats are uncanny. They can be provoking, but also glamorous. They seem to know things. They seem slightly out of time. We project emotion onto them, they love us inscrutably, if at all. They have a keen sense of retribution. Cats see us and judge us.

It is not necessary to believe in ghosts to appreciate a good ghost story. We all believe in death. What happens after that is up for grabs, blank space haunted by artists and prophets. We enjoy teasing ourselves with possible afterlives. But if we allow the past to haunt us, or keep our gazes fixed on imaginary future heavens or hells, we fail to pay attention to the present. To be haunted is to turn away from the liveliness of our lives. We become a little dead to ourselves if we pine too much for the dead.

Ghosts are excessive, they persist when they should go away. Ghosts are wanting, they are missing something. We bring ghosts upon ourselves. We stumble onto them, other people's ghosts. They linger. They are like hungry cats – if we feed them, they might make themselves at home. These stories are diversions, but also warnings. Be kind to your cat, disobey the babysitter, do not open mail from dead ladies, pay attention to the seemingly insignificant. Don't get carried away when redecorating your home.

Be kind. Pay attention. Don't get carried away. It sounds reasonable and boring. But in books we can make as many vicarious mistakes as we care to, so go ahead: turn the page and let yourself be haunted.

Edgar Allan Poe

The Black
Cat

'THE BLACK CAT'

EDGAR ALLAN POE (AMERICAN, 1809–1849)

First published in the 19 August 1843 issue of the *Saturday Evening Post*.

Edgar Allan Poe is the greatest American master of the uncanny, and *The Black Cat* is the quintessential Poe story, gleefully perverse, driven by guilt and revenge. It is especially satisfying to consider the cat as an agent of justice and scourge of bullies. Poe is known to have owned a black cat.

2

THE BLACK CAT
Edgar Allan Poe

For the most wild yet most homely narrative which I am about to pen, I neither expect nor solicit belief. Mad indeed would I be to expect it, in a case where my very senses reject their own evidence. Yet, mad am I not – and very surely do I not dream. But tomorrow I die, and today I would unburden my soul. My immediate purpose is to place before the world, plainly, succinctly, and without comment, a series of mere household events. In their consequences, these events have terrified – have tortured – have destroyed me. Yet I will not attempt to expound them. To me, they have presented little but horror – to many they will seem less terrible than *baroques*. Hereafter, perhaps, some intellect may be found which will reduce my phantasm to the commonplace – some intellect more calm, more logical, and far less excitable than my own, which will perceive, in the circumstances I detail with awe, nothing more than an ordinary succession of very natural causes and effects.

From my infancy I was noted for the docility and humanity of

3

my disposition. My tenderness of heart was even so conspicuous as to make me the jest of my companions. I was especially fond of animals, and was indulged by my parents with a great variety of pets. With these I spent most of my time, and never was so happy as when feeding and caressing them. This peculiarity of character grew with my growth, and, in my manhood, I derived from it one of my principal sources of pleasure. To those who have cherished an affection for a faithful and sagacious dog, I need hardly be at the trouble of explaining the nature or the intensity of the gratification thus derivable. There is something in the unselfish and self-sacrificing love of a brute, which goes directly to the heart of him who has had frequent occasion to test the paltry friendship and gossamer fidelity of mere *Man*.

I married early, and was happy to find in my wife a disposition not uncongenial with my own. Observing my partiality for domestic pets, she lost no opportunity of procuring those of the most agreeable kind. We had birds, gold-fish, a fine dog, rabbits, a small monkey, and a *cat*.

This latter was a remarkably large and beautiful animal, entirely black, and sagacious to an astonishing degree. In speaking of his intelligence, my wife, who at heart was not a little tinctured with superstition, made frequent allusion to the ancient popular notion, which regarded all black cats as witches in disguise. Not that she was ever *serious* upon this point – and I mention the matter at all for no better reason than that it happens, just now, to be remembered.

Pluto – this was the cat's name – was my favorite pet and

playmate. I alone fed him, and he attended me wherever I went about the house. It was even with difficulty that I could prevent him from following me through the streets.

Our friendship lasted, in this manner, for several years, during which my general temperament and character – through the instrumentality of the Fiend Intemperance – had (I blush to confess it) experienced a radical alteration for the worse. I grew, day by day, more moody, more irritable, more regardless of the feelings of others. I suffered myself to use intemperate language to my wife. At length, I even offered her personal violence. My pets, of course, were made to feel the change in my disposition. I not only neglected, but ill-used them. For Pluto, however, I still retained sufficient regard to restrain me from maltreating him, as I made no scruple of maltreating the rabbits, the monkey, or even the dog, when, by accident, or through affection, they came in my way. But my disease grew upon me – for what disease is like Alcohol! – and at length even Pluto, who was now becoming old, and consequently somewhat peevish – even Pluto began to experience the effects of my ill temper.

One night, returning home, much intoxicated, from one of my haunts about town, I fancied that the cat avoided my presence. I seized him; when, in his fright at my violence, he inflicted a slight wound upon my hand with his teeth. The fury of a demon instantly possessed me. I knew myself no longer. My original soul seemed, at once, to take its flight from my body; and a more than fiendish malevolence, gin-nurtured, thrilled every fibre of my frame. I took from my waistcoat pocket a penknife, opened it, grasped the poor beast by the throat, and deliberately cut one of its eyes from the socket! I blush, I burn, I shudder, while I pen the damnable atrocity.

When reason returned with the morning – when I had slept off the fumes of the night's debauch – I experienced a sentiment half of horror, half of remorse, for the crime of which I had been guilty; but it was, at best, a feeble and equivocal feeling, and the soul remained untouched. I again plunged into excess, and soon drowned in wine all memory of the deed.

In the meantime the cat slowly recovered. The socket of the lost eye presented, it is true, a frightful appearance, but he no longer appeared to suffer any pain. He went about the house as usual, but, as might be expected, fled in extreme terror at my approach. I had so much of my old heart left, as to be at first grieved by this evident dislike on the part of a creature which had once so loved me. But this feeling soon gave place to irritation. And then came, as if to my final and irrevocable overthrow, the spirit of PERVERSENESS. Of this spirit philosophy takes no account. Yet I am not more sure that my soul lives, than I am that perverseness is one of the primitive impulses of the human heart – one of the indivisible primary faculties, or sentiments, which give direction to the character of Man. Who has not, a hundred times, found himself committing a vile or a stupid action, for no other reason than because he knows he should *not*? Have we not a perpetual inclination, in the teeth of our best judgment, to violate that which is *Law*, merely because we understand it to be such? This spirit of perverseness, I say, came to my final overthrow. It was this unfathomable longing of the soul *to vex itself* – to offer violence to its own nature – to do wrong for the wrong's sake only – that urged me to continue and finally to consummate the injury I had inflicted upon the unoffending brute. One morning, in cold blood, I slipped a noose about its neck and hung it to the limb of a tree; – hung it with the tears streaming from my eyes, and with the bitterest remorse at my heart; – hung it *because* I knew that it had loved me, and *because* I felt it had given me no reason of offence; – hung it *because* I knew that in so doing I was committing a sin – a deadly sin that would so jeopardize my immortal soul as to place it – if such a thing were possible – even beyond the reach of the infinite mercy of the Most Merciful and Most Terrible God.

On the night of the day on which this most cruel deed was done, I was aroused from sleep by the cry of fire. The curtains of my bed were in flames. The whole house was blazing. It was with great difficulty that my wife, a servant, and myself, made our escape from the conflagration. The destruction was complete. My entire worldly wealth was swallowed up, and I resigned myself thenceforward to despair.

I am above the weakness of seeking to establish a sequence of cause and effect, between the disaster and the atrocity. But I am detailing a chain of facts – and wish not to leave even a possible link imperfect. On the day succeeding the fire, I visited the ruins. The walls, with one exception, had fallen in. This exception was found in a compartment wall, not very thick, which stood about the middle of the house, and against which had rested the head of my bed. The plastering had here, in great measure, resisted the action of the fire – a fact which I attributed to its having been recently spread. About this wall a dense crowd were collected, and many persons seemed to be examining a particular portion of it with very minute and eager attention. The words 'strange!' 'singular!' and other similar expressions, excited my curiosity. I approached and saw, as if graven in *bas-relief* upon the white surface, the figure of a gigantic *cat*. The impression was given with an accuracy truly marvellous. There was a rope about the animal's neck.

When I first beheld this apparition – for I could scarcely regard it as less – my wonder and my terror were extreme. But at length reflection came to my aid. The cat, I remembered, had been hung in a garden adjacent to the house. Upon the alarm of fire, this garden had been immediately filled by the crowd – by some one of whom the animal must have been cut from the tree and thrown, through an open window, into my chamber. This had probably been done with the view of arousing me from sleep. The falling of other walls had compressed the victim of my cruelty into the substance of the freshly spread plaster; the lime of which, with the flames, and the *ammonia* from the carcass, had then accomplished the portraiture as I saw it.

Although I thus readily accounted to my reason, if not altogether to my conscience, for the startling fact just detailed, it did not the less fail to make a deep impression upon my fancy. For months I could not rid myself of the phantasm of the cat; and, during this period, there came back into my spirit a half-sentiment that seemed, but was not, remorse. I went so far as to regret the loss of the animal, and to look about me, among the vile haunts which I now habitually frequented, for another pet of the same species, and of somewhat similar appearance, with which to supply its place.

One night as I sat, half stupefied, in a den of more than infamy, my attention was suddenly drawn to some black object, reposing upon the head of one of the immense hogsheads of gin, or of rum, which constituted the chief furniture of the apartment. I had been looking steadily at the top of this hogshead for some minutes, and what now caused me surprise was the fact that I had not sooner perceived the object thereupon. I approached it, and touched it with my hand. It was a black cat – a very large one – fully as large as Pluto, and closely resembling him in every respect but one. Pluto had not a white hair upon any portion of his body; but this cat had a large, although indefinite splotch of white, covering nearly the whole region of the breast.

Upon my touching him, he immediately arose, purred loudly, rubbed against my hand, and appeared delighted with my notice. This, then, was the very creature of which I was in search. I at once offered to purchase it of the landlord; but this person made no claim to it – knew nothing of it – had never seen it before.

I continued my caresses, and when I prepared to go home, the animal evinced a disposition to accompany me. I permitted it to do so; occasionally stooping and patting it as I proceeded. When it reached the house it domesticated itself at once, and became immediately a great favorite with my wife.

For my own part, I soon found a dislike to it arising within me. This was just the reverse of what I had anticipated; but – I know not how or why it was – its evident fondness for myself rather disgusted and annoyed me. By slow degrees these feelings of disgust and annoyance rose into the bitterness of hatred. I avoided the creature; a certain sense of shame, and the remembrance of my former deed of cruelty, preventing me from physically abusing it. I did not, for some weeks, strike, or otherwise violently ill use it; but gradually – very gradually – I came to look upon it with unutterable loathing, and to flee silently from its odious presence, as from the breath of a pestilence.

What added, no doubt, to my hatred of the beast, was the discovery, on the morning after I brought it home, that, like Pluto, it also had been deprived of one of its eyes. This circumstance, however, only endeared it to my wife, who, as I have already said, possessed, in a high degree, that humanity of feeling which had once been my distinguishing trait, and the source of many of my simplest and purest pleasures.

With my aversion to this cat, however, its partiality for myself seemed to increase. It followed my footsteps with a pertinacity which it would be difficult to make the reader comprehend. Whenever I sat, it would crouch beneath my chair, or spring upon my knees, covering me with its loathsome caresses. If I arose to walk it would get between my feet and thus nearly throw me down, or, fastening its long and sharp claws in my dress, clamber, in this manner, to my breast. At such times, although I longed to destroy it with a blow, I was yet withheld from so doing, partly by a memory of my former crime, but chiefly – let me confess it at once – by absolute *dread* of the beast.

This dread was not exactly a dread of physical evil – and yet I should be at a loss how otherwise to define it. I am almost ashamed to own – yes, even in this felon's cell, I am almost ashamed to own – that the terror and horror with which the animal inspired me, had been heightened by one of the merest chimeras it would be possible to conceive. My wife had called my attention, more than once, to the character of the mark of white hair, of which I have spoken, and which constituted the sole visible difference between the strange beast and the one I had destroyed. The reader will remember that this mark, although large, had been originally very indefinite; but, by slow degrees – degrees nearly imperceptible, and which for a long time my reason struggled to reject as fanciful – it had, at length, assumed a rigorous distinctness of outline. It was now the representation of an object that I shudder to name – and for this, above all, I loathed, and dreaded, and would have rid myself of the monster *had I dared* – it was now, I say, the image of a hideous – of a ghastly thing – of the GALLOWS! – oh, mournful and terrible engine of Horror and of Crime – of Agony and of Death!

And now was I indeed wretched beyond the wretchedness of mere Humanity. And *a brute beast* – whose fellow I had contemptuously destroyed – *a brute beast* to work out for *me* – for me, a man fashioned in the image of the High God – so much of insufferable woe! Alas! neither by day nor by night knew I the blessing of rest any more! During the former the creature left me no moment alone, and in the latter I started hourly from dreams of unutterable fear to find the hot breath of *the thing* upon my face, and its vast weight – an incarnate nightmare that I had no power to shake off – incumbent eternally upon my *heart*!

Beneath the pressure of torments such as these the feeble remnant of the good within me succumbed. Evil thoughts became my sole intimates – the darkest and most evil of thoughts. The moodiness of my usual temper increased to hatred of all things and of all mankind; while from the sudden, frequent, and ungovernable outbursts of a fury to which I now blindly abandoned myself, my uncomplaining wife, alas, was the most usual and the most patient of sufferers.

One day she accompanied me, upon some household errand, into the cellar of the old building which our poverty compelled us to inhabit. The cat followed me down the steep stairs, and, nearly throwing me headlong, exasperated me to madness. Uplifting an axe, and forgetting in my wrath the childish dread which had hitherto stayed my hand, I aimed a blow at the animal, which, of course, would have proved instantly fatal had it descended as I wished. But this blow was arrested by the hand of my wife. Goaded by the interference into a rage more than demoniacal, I withdrew my arm from her grasp and buried the axe in her brain. She fell dead upon the spot without a groan.

This hideous murder accomplished, I set myself forthwith, and with entire deliberation, to the task of concealing the body. I knew that I could not remove it from the house, either by day or by night, without the risk of being observed by the neighbors. Many projects entered my mind. At one period I thought of cutting the corpse into minute fragments, and destroying them by fire. At another, I resolved to dig a grave for it in the floor of the cellar. Again, I deliberated about casting it in the well in the yard – about packing it in a box, as if merchandise, with the usual arrangements, and so getting a porter to take it from the house. Finally I hit upon what I considered a far better expedient than either of these. I determined to wall it up in the cellar, as the monks of the Middle Ages are recorded to have walled up their victims.

For a purpose such as this the cellar was well adapted. Its walls were loosely constructed, and had lately been plastered throughout with a rough plaster, which the dampness of the atmosphere had prevented from hardening. Moreover, in one of the walls was a projection, caused by a false chimney, or fireplace, that had been filled up and made to resemble the rest of the cellar. I made no doubt that I could readily displace the bricks at this point, insert the corpse, and wall the whole up as before, so that no eye could detect any thing suspicious.

And in this calculation I was not deceived. By means of a crowbar I easily dislodged the bricks, and, having carefully deposited the body against the inner wall, I propped it in that position, while with little trouble I relaid the whole structure as it originally stood. Having procured mortar, sand, and hair, with every possible precaution, I prepared a plaster which could not be distinguished from the old, and with this I very carefully went over the new brick-work. When I had finished, I felt satisfied that all was right. The wall did not present the slightest appearance of having been disturbed. The rubbish on the floor was picked up with the minutest care. I looked around triumphantly, and said to myself: 'Here at least, then, my labor has not been in vain.'

My next step was to look for the beast which had been the cause of so much wretchedness; for I had, at length, firmly resolved to put it to death. Had I been able to meet with it at the moment, there could have been no doubt of its fate; but it appeared that the crafty animal had been alarmed at the violence of my previous anger, and forbore to present itself in my present mood. It is impossible to describe or to imagine the deep, the blissful sense of relief which the absence of the detested creature occasioned in my bosom. It did not make its appearance during the night; and thus for one night, at least, since its introduction into the house, I soundly and tranquilly slept; aye, *slept* even with the burden of murder upon my soul.

The second and the third day passed, and still my tormentor came not. Once again I breathed as a freeman. The monster, in terror, had fled the premises for ever! I should behold it no more! My happiness was supreme! The guilt of my dark deed disturbed me but little. Some few inquiries had been made, but these had been readily answered. Even a search had been instituted – but of course nothing was to be discovered. I looked upon my future felicity as secured.

Upon the fourth day of the assassination, a party of the police came, very unexpectedly, into the house, and proceeded again to make rigorous investigation of the premises. Secure, however, in the inscrutability of my place of concealment, I felt no embarrassment whatever. The officers bade me accompany them in their search. They left no nook or corner unexplored. At length, for the third or fourth time, they descended into the cellar. I quivered not in a muscle. My heart beat calmly as that of one who slumbers in innocence. I walked the cellar from end to end. I folded my arms upon my bosom, and roamed easily to and fro. The police were thoroughly satisfied and prepared to depart. The glee at my heart was too strong to be restrained. I burned to say if but one word, by way of triumph, and to render doubly sure their assurance of my guiltlessness.

'Gentlemen,' I said at last, as the party ascended the steps, 'I delight to have allayed your suspicions. I wish you all health and a little more courtesy. By the bye, gentlemen, this – this is a very well-constructed house,' (in the rabid desire to say something easily, I scarcely knew what I uttered at all), – 'I may say an *excellently* well-constructed house. These walls – are you going, gentlemen? – these walls are solidly put together'; and here, through the mere frenzy of bravado, I rapped heavily with a cane which I held in my hand, upon that very portion of the brick-work behind which stood the corpse of the wife of my bosom.

But may God shield and deliver me from the fangs of the Arch-Fiend! No sooner had the reverberation of my blows sunk into silence, than I was answered by a voice from within the tomb! – by a cry, at first muffled and broken, like the sobbing of a child, and then quickly swelling into one long, loud, and continuous scream, utterly anomalous and inhuman – a howl – a wailing shriek, half of horror and half of triumph, such as might have arisen only out of hell, conjointly from the throats of the damned in their agony and of the demons that exult in the damnation.

Of my own thoughts it is folly to speak. Swooning, I staggered to the opposite wall. For one instant the party on the stairs remained motionless, through extremity of terror and awe. In the next a dozen stout arms were toiling at the wall. It fell bodily. The corpse, already greatly decayed and clotted with gore, stood erect before the eyes of the spectators. Upon its head, with red extended mouth and solitary eye of fire, sat the hideous beast whose craft had seduced me into murder, and whose informing voice had consigned me to the hangman. I had walled the monster up within the tomb.

secret
life
with
cats

Audrey Niffenegger

'SECRET LIFE, WITH CATS'

AUDREY NIFFENEGGER (AMERICAN, 1963–)

First published in the *Chicago Tribune* in 2006.

Over the years I have adopted five cats, though I've never had more than two at once; it would be a mistake to get carried away. I wrote this story after spending a little time hanging out at a cat shelter, eavesdropping on the volunteers while trying to choose a cat. I had recently lost a close friend (I did not know why then, and still don't; she simply stopped speaking to me) and my favourite cat had just died. So this story was prompted by absence. There all resemblance to reality ends, thank goodness.

SECRET LIFE, WITH CATS
Audrey Niffenegger

I don't know why Ruth left me her house, with all its attendant complications. Perhaps she sensed that I longed for change, for an adventure. Perhaps she pitied me. Maybe she knew what I would do with such a gift, though I did not know myself.

You might think that I was an unlikely heiress. I was forty-two years old, married, no kids. My husband, Jim, was older than me. He was a real estate agent and spent his days stalking through other people's homes, extolling their bathrooms and evaluating their roofs. Houses meant money to Jim. When I met him he was a tenure-track professor in the Anthropology department at Northwestern University. He was thirty-five and I was twenty. I sat in the front row of Methodologies of Urban Ethnography, entranced by his easy, confident lectures, his Brooks Brothers suits, his longish brown hair and sensual green eyes. He was studiously pale in those days, and his hands had never held a hammer, much less a pneumatic staple gun. He gave me a B+ for the semester and asked me out on the last day of class.

I am not a terribly practical person. I was not an asset as a faculty wife: I was too shy, pretty, and had a knack for blurting out non sequiturs to full professors. In the third year of our marriage Jim was denied tenure, and a year later, after our health insurance was gone, I was diagnosed with ovarian cancer. Debt piled up. Jim taught part-time at Chicago City Colleges and began selling real estate.

At first real estate was a stop-gap. I would lie on the couch in our tiny south Evanston apartment, bald from chemo and ravenous from steroids, and Jim would sit with my bloated feet on his lap, wearing his Century 21 vomit-yellow jacket. He'd tell me stories. There was the two-flat with the racing pigeon empire on the roof, the illegal apartment in the basement of a house full of Haitian tenants who followed Jim and his buyer from room to room but never spoke a word. Jim began every story the same way: 'Beatrice, you've never seen anything like it.' The possessions of the sellers, their bad taste, bad habits, their misconceived notions of what might attract buyers: these fascinated Jim in much the same way that the subjects of his ethnographies once had. He sold his first house and we gloated over the commission; even though it went directly toward hospital bills Jim was as hooked as any gambler. He stopped teaching, and sold real estate full-time. Every house sold was a triumph.

I got well. We became solvent, and then we became well-off. At the time that Ruth bequeathed me her house, Jim and I had been living in a spacious Victorian on Judson Avenue for ten years. We had relentlessly improved it. We'd remodeled the kitchen and the bathrooms, rewired, re-roofed, added a gazebo and a family room, moved and expanded closets, punched new doorways through old walls. Sometimes when I got up in the night to go to the toilet I got lost. The house was Jim's baby. It was beautiful and ravenous, and he tended to it with the same solicitude he had once lavished on me. The houses he sold fed the house we lived in.

As our house became sleek and lovely I began to fade away. I have aged as pretty blonde girls do: my pink cheeks are too red, my hair is shot with gray, my blue eyes are pale and watery. My skin is chamois-soft and there are lines in my face from frowning; my hips have spread and veins have made dark spots on my legs. When Ruth left me her house all these things were only beginning to happen, and now they are well on their way. Now I don't mind, but at that time I was unhappy, because I knew Jim hardly saw me when he looked at me. I couldn't be the mother of his children, and so I had become the mother of his house.

I was in charge of keeping the house. I washed its windows, vacuumed its floors, waxed it and painted it and helped choose wallpaper for it. Jim made a point of consulting me about the house. Would I like stainless steel appliances? Overstuffed Crate & Barrel leather chairs? Chinese or Persian carpets? Rosewood shoe racks? I didn't really care, and I noticed that Jim tended to wind up doing whatever he wanted anyway. I kept it all clean. Then we hired a cleaning service and I didn't even do that anymore.

★　　★　　★

I met Ruth at the Happy Cat Home. I realize that this is ironic. Jim was allergic to cats, and I began to volunteer at this no-kill shelter in Rogers Park just to have something alive to care for.

Ruth had been a volunteer for years. She was the first person I met there. The reception room was cinderblock-ugly and clean. It was full of scratching posts and carpeted cat perches. There was a desk, a folding chair, a bank of filing cabinets, and a chintz couch. There was one cat in the room, asleep on the couch. He was a Siamese named Reginald who lived at the shelter. Ruth sat at the desk and filled out paperwork with me. I drank coffee out of a Styrofoam cup and looked at her while she asked me questions.

'You have cats at home?'

'Actually, no; my husband's allergic. I had a cat when I was a child.'

Ruth was small, sharp, and quick. Her face was heart-shaped and her eyes were dark. She seemed to me like a silent movie starlet who had become careless with her looks. She must have been in her seventies then, and her clothes often sported safety pins; her shoes were always on the verge of splitting from the soles, and there were usually stains on her sleeves. She always had a cup of coffee in hand. She drank it almost white, more milk than coffee. Ruth had an educated voice. If I closed my eyes while she was talking I could swear I was listening to NPR.

'What days can you come in?'

'Any day. I'm a housewife.'

Did I imagine it, or did Ruth wince when I called myself a housewife?

'Well, you can work as many hours as you want. We're chronically short of volunteers.'

'What will I be doing?'

'Feeding, scooping out litter pans, running the cats to the vet if you drive. Show them to people, try to find them homes.' Ruth smiled. 'And of course there's the socializing, playing with them and petting them, that's the fun part.'

I smiled back, and perhaps it was then that we began to be friends.

★   ★   ★

I never have had many friends, and I didn't have siblings either. I was so quiet as a girl that other children tended to forget I was there. I liked to lie on my bed and read, or play odd little games with dolls, or watch TV. I had a best friend in high school, but then her family moved to Maryland. In college my few friends seemed to melt away when I started dating Jim. So I was a little intoxicated by Ruth.

It wasn't what she said so much as how she was. She was confident, but she listened. She was compelling. Oh, I'm afraid I'm not doing such a good job of conjuring her up for you. She was like an older sister to me, a clever sister; it was as though we somehow shared a past which there was no need to speak of, about which too much had already been said, even though we'd never talked about it at all.

Ruth had a preternatural ability to divine the desires of the cats, and to command them. They flocked to her and deferred to her. They loved her, and so did I.

Ruth could feed liquid medicines to cats from a spoon. She would hold it out to a sick old cat and coo, 'Drink up, sweetie.' The cat would make a face and lap the nasty stuff up, like a child. Once we had an orange tom named Lump who was dying of kidney failure. He hung on and on; finally the staff decided it was time to put him down. I was getting ready to drive him to the vet when Ruth came in. She sat down next to the panting cat and whispered in his ear. Lump dragged himself onto her lap, closed his eyes, and died.

'What did you say to him?' I asked.

Ruth shook her head. 'It's private,' was all she said.

My own relationship with the cats was more difficult. I was a little frightened of them. I tried not to let Ruth see this, but of course she knew. If a cat hissed at me I froze. When two cats fought I could only stand helplessly by; Ruth would snap her fingers and the combatants would slink apart apologetically. The other volunteers sprayed them with squirt guns.

I slowly developed a rapport with certain cats. My favorites were Lucky, an earless, balding thing who loved to sit in my lap for hours; Madge, a tortoiseshell who bit everyone but me; and Elvis, a fat blond cat who followed me everywhere and enjoyed chewing on my wristwatch band. I loved the kittens, but everyone loves kittens. They never stayed around long enough to be memorable.

Ruth and I would sit in the lunch room and play cards, each with a cat on our laps and more curled around our ankles. We played simple games like Hearts and Crazy Eights. Ruth never told me anything about her life outside the shelter, and I didn't talk about Jim or real estate or our house. One Monday morning I came to work with a black eye.

'What happened?' Ruth asked.

'I walked into a door.' This was the truth; I had gotten up in the middle of the night, thirsty and sleep-fuddled, and had collided with one of the recently relocated doors in my search for the bathroom. I could see that Ruth was drawing her own conclusions.

'No, really. I do that a lot.'

Ruth now looked extremely skeptical. 'You don't do it here.'

'Yes, well, my husband isn't remodeling the Happy Cat Home. He has an insatiable urge to make closets where no closets were before.' That was all we said about it. I admit that I felt a little glamorous. Without doing a thing Jim had incurred Ruth's dislike. No one else at the shelter asked me about the black eye, and I imagined Ruth telling them my closet story, which was not even a story but actually true. That night Jim came home with steaks. I put one on my eye for a while to please him, and then we ate them.

★   ★   ★

Things went along this way for a few years. Cats came and went; the young pretty ones tended to go, and the old broken ones tended to stay. I got more relaxed and skillful with them; I could give the diabetic cats insulin and clip claws without getting scratched. Jim continued to put our house through startling transformations, and finally installed a bathroom right off the master bedroom. Ruth and I went to the movies now and then, but mostly we spent our time at the shelter, wrangling cats and playing cards.

Then Ruth died.

I don't know how it happened. One Wednesday in July, she didn't show up for her shift at the shelter. No one answered her phone. Jim and I were on vacation in Nova Scotia, so I heard about it the following Monday from Ellie, the director of the shelter. They had gotten worried; after all, Ruth was old, though she didn't complain about her health. They'd called the emergency number on her volunteer application, but it was disconnected. It had been hot all week, in the upper nineties. They went to Ruth's house and rang the bell. No answer. I had never been to Ruth's house. Ellie said it was a small brick ranch-style place. She went around and looked in all the windows, which were open. No sign of Ruth. The police couldn't find her either. 'Maybe she went on vacation, and just forgot to tell you, Ma'm,' the officer suggested.

Ruth never came back. There was no body, no funeral, no grave.

I worried, and felt spurned. I couldn't imagine Ruth leaving without saying goodbye. Something terrible must have happened to her. But no one knew anything. Jim suggested that she might have amnesia, but he liked to listen to Radio Mystery Theater and I knew that sort of thing only happened in melodramas.

At the end of the summer, I got a registered letter at the shelter. I remember holding it in my hand, the weight of it, the pause before opening it, my puzzlement as to who might send me a letter at work. It was from a downtown law firm, and it informed me that Ruth had died and left me her house and its contents.

I'm ashamed to say that my first response was relief: Ruth hadn't abandoned me, she had only died.

That evening Jim came into the kitchen as I was making dinner and said, 'How was your day?' I opened my mouth to tell him about Ruth, about her house...and I said, 'Just a day. How about you?'

★   ★   ★

Ruth's house was on Pratt, near Ridge Avenue; it was a ten-minute walk from the Happy Cat Home. Jim would have called it a tear-down. The house was small and sat far back on a double lot. It was a single-story brick house, neat and plain, built in the sixties. Elm trees that had somehow eluded Dutch Elm Disease loomed over it. A sprinkler sat unused in the middle of a beige lawn.

I let myself in the front door.

The house itself was silent; a shimmer of cicada singing came in the open windows along with a warm breeze. I stood in the entryway and felt like an intruder. This was Ruth's house. Ruth was a very private person. Standing there looking at her couch, her dinette set, her desk, I felt reluctant. *But she gave it to you. She wanted you to be here.* The thought came into my head as though someone was urging me to accept hospitality. *Come in, come in.* I set my purse on an armchair and began to wander slowly through the rooms.

Ruth must have furnished her house in the 1970s. All the furniture was teak, or covered in nubby off-white fabric. There were batik throw pillows and a beanbag chair. Her dishes were heavy stoneware, the carpeting was brown shag. Everything was somewhat worn.

I opened one of the desk drawers. It was empty. There were circles on the windowsills where plants had been. There was nothing in the kitchen cabinets but curling shelf-paper; nothing in the bathroom except an extra roll of toilet paper. In the bedroom closet I found two dresses that had belonged to Ruth. I leaned in and smelled them. They smelled like the Happy Cat Home.

But what about Ruth's cats? There was no cat hair anywhere. No furniture had been clawed, there was no evidence of a litter box. And yet I remembered Ruth sharing stories of her cats' antics. Perhaps whoever had taken the plants and rest of it had taken the cats, too. What were their names? I couldn't remember.

I sat down on Ruth's bed. The curtains moved in the breeze. I felt watched. 'Thank you,' I said to Ruth, in case she could hear me. Then I felt silly. I got my purse, locked up the house and left.

★ ★ ★

I didn't go back for a week. There was no reason to go. I worked my shifts at the shelter, but without Ruth it seemed dull and sad. I sat down one day to eat by myself in the shelter's squalid lunch room, and suddenly it occurred to me that I could eat at Ruth's house; it was so close. I gathered my food and left.

A bus was letting children off on the corner as I walked toward the house. They stared at me and whispered to each other as I let myself in.

The house was exactly the same. I sat at the dining room table and ate my yogurt and my tuna fish sandwich. When I was done I folded up the zip lock bags and put them in my purse. It seemed wrong to leave any trash behind, even in the garbage can.

I stood in the kitchen looking out at the backyard. There was a small patio with a few old lawn chairs randomly placed, a planter full of dirt. Then I sat on Ruth's bed. I took off my shoes and lay down on top of the bedspread, experimentally. The bed was very soft.

I didn't mean to sleep. Even as I was falling asleep I thought, *no, I must get back to work*, but I knew I was sleeping already. It was the kind of sleep that is like dropping into a hole. Then I was half-awake, and had a curious sensation: there was a weight on the bed, leaning against me, and as I moved in my waking the weight went to the edge of the bed and fell off. It landed with a thud on the floor.

I sat up and looked at the floor, but there was nothing there. I looked at my watch. Only half an hour had gone by. I put on my shoes and went back to the shelter.

★   ★   ★

I came back the next day. I decided to turn on the sprinkler, and watched it fling water in a circle as I ate lunch. When I walked into the bedroom there was a dead sparrow on the bed, neatly centered on the pillow I had used the day before. And somehow I understood.

That evening Jim and I were eating dinner out on our deck. Jim had recently purchased an elaborate gas grill, so we were eating ribs and grilled vegetables. I knew that I would be the one who got to scrub the burnt barbeque sauce off the new grill when dinner was over.

'Jim?'

'Mmm?' He had his mouth full.

'I'm going to Boise tomorrow.' Boise was where my mother lived. 'I'll be back in a week or so.'

'Hmm. Everything okay?'

'Sure; but it's been a while.'

'Well, give her my love.'

'Okay.'

That was the last conversation we had. After twenty-one years of marriage there's not a lot to say.

I left the next morning. I didn't bring many things: a suitcase full of clothing, a few books. I had a checking account Jim didn't know about. I'd been saving my clothing allowance for a long time, not for any particular reason, just to have some money of my own. I took all the evidence of that with me.

I bought some groceries. I bought bath towels and dish soap and a small radio. I drove to Ruth's house, now my house, and put the car in the garage. Now I was invisible. No one knew where I was.

*   ★   *

The first few days were uneventful. I often had the feeling that something was moving at the edge of my vision, a slight blur, a dark shape. I read my books and ate chocolate. I listened to All Things Considered and took long baths.

On the third night I woke up suddenly. A large cat was sitting on the bed, looking at me. Its eyes reflected pale green. I offered my hand to it. It considered this for a moment, then flicked its tail and jumped off the bed. There was a slight thump as it landed, and then silence. I looked all over the room, but didn't find it.

The next day I put a dish of cat food on the kitchen floor. I watched it for a while; nothing happened. A few hours later I checked again and the food was gone.

The days began to blur together. Purring sounds in my ear. Aluminum foil balls rolling of their own volition across the floor. Invisible cat feet making soft dents in the bedspread. I woke up close to dawn and saw cats swarming around the bedroom, colorless in the half-light, an uncountable number of them. I was afraid then.

A few days later I was vacuuming the living room when I noticed something dark on the white wall. I got down on my knees to look at it. It was writing, small and cramped. It said: *You could probably levitate if you wanted to.* The thing that frightened me and thrilled me was that the words were so low to the ground—just above the baseboard.

I stood up. The house seemed expectant. I didn't know if I

33

wanted to levitate. I had never thought about it. I went outside and stood on the patio. After a while I went back inside. Curtains were moving slightly in the breeze; otherwise the house was still. There was a feeling of disappointment, but I did not know if it was mine or someone else's.

*   *   *

I had been living in the house for two weeks. It was early evening. I was curled up on the couch, reading the newspaper. It was October, and chilly. I had closed all the windows and turned on the heat. I was content.

I had begun to distinguish between aloneness and loneliness. In Ruth's house I was alone; the phantom cats and NPR were company enough. But I wasn't lonely, and I realized only by this how lonely I had been before.

Now I had the familiar sense of being watched. I put down the newspaper. There was a white cat sitting in the armchair. It was very thin, with green eyes and a rather haughty manner. We stared at each other. It seemed to be considering me, judging me.

'Well, come on, then,' it said. It rose, stretched, jumped to the floor and stood looking at me expectantly. When I didn't get up instantly it turned its back and marched off toward the bedroom. I hesitated, then followed it.

The closet stood open. I had hung a few dresses and skirts next to Ruth's; these had been pushed aside and the back of the closet was now another doorway. I couldn't think how I had failed to notice this door. The white cat stalked through it and I followed.

There were stairs, which led down. The house was built on a concrete slab; these stairs had no business being here. There was hardly any light and I felt my way with my hands touching the walls and my feet seeking each step before advancing. The walls and the steps seemed to be made of earth. Sound was deadened. I had no idea if the white cat was still with me. I went down and down. . . finally there were no more stairs. I was in a hallway which led to a door. The white cat sat in front of the door with its tail twitching.

'There you are. You're very slow.' It nudged open the door and disappeared through it. I followed.

The room was big and low-ceilinged. It smelled of earth and unbathed flesh, meat, baby powder, damp wood, old sweaters. The room was full of things, in no order at all, and cats were everywhere. The cats were playing, napping, eating, yawning, fighting, and they were doing all this in the midst of shoes, hats, dresses, books, dead plants, papers, a typewriter, a few small lamps with chewed cords, underwear, knickknacks, a footstool, a child's rocking chair, suitcases, combs, a toothbrush. . . all of the things which had been missing from Ruth's house were here. Some of the cats wore pieces of costume jewelry I remembered seeing on Ruth.

They all ignored me, or pretended to ignore me. The white cat was nowhere to be seen, and I wondered why I'd been brought down here. The disorder was oppressive. I felt large; at first I thought I was the only thing in the room over two feet tall.

'Hello, Beatrice.' Her voice came from a dark corner. I took a step forward and stopped. Where was she?

Ruth was sitting in a metal folding chair, the kind people take to parades. She was wrapped in a blanket. All I could see of her was her face. Ruth looked tired, but otherwise not too different from when I'd seen her last.

'Ruth! I was so worried about you! What are you doing down here? Are you okay?' I was so relieved to see her, and so confused. I edged a little closer.

Ruth chuckled. It was such a familiar sound—it evoked all those games of Crazy Eights in the Happy Cat House lunchroom. 'Well, darling, I don't think I would exactly describe myself as 'okay'; I'm dead, after all, so 'okay' is a little beside the point, don't you think?'

'But—?' I remembered that I had no idea how she'd died.

'It wasn't that big of a deal. I slipped and cracked my head in the bathtub. It was very tidy.' Ruth's voice was kind, but I could tell she thought I was focusing on the wrong thing. *Barking up the wrong tree,* would have been her way of putting it.

'Yes, but Ruth—no one could find you. We checked, we looked for you, but you had just. . .vanished.' I knew I sounded a little petulant, I couldn't help it.

Ruth smiled, as though she was proud of how she'd mystified us all. 'That's right. They couldn't find me, because the cats ate me.'

'Ate you?'

'Yep. Every little bit of me. It's such a cliché, isn't it? But they didn't do it for the usual reasons. They weren't hungry, they weren't locked in the house. They did it to bring me down here, with them. So we could be together.'

The longer I stood here listening to Ruth in this dark, smelly, chaotic room, the more revolted and sad I felt. The cats had gradually stopped milling around. Now they sat silently, listening. Ruth waited for me to respond. Finally I said, 'Won't you come upstairs? We could be together—with the cats, too, of course.' There was a deep stillness among the cats now, as they waited to hear what Ruth would say.

'Oh, Bea. I wish I could, I really do. Remember how much fun we had?' Ruth smiled, and I thought *she is the only person I have ever truly loved.* 'But you see,' she continued, still smiling, 'I can't do that. I belong here now, with my sweeties.' There was an audible hum in the room, all the cats purring. 'Plus, I'm afraid I'm not exactly ambulatory.'

'Why not?' I asked, without thinking.

'Well. . .they are cats, after all. They aren't doctors, or mechanics. I'm afraid they did a rather poor job of reassembling me.' Ruth nodded at her own blanket-wrapped form. The cats looked at her, anxious, loving.

'We tried, Ruth,' said the white cat, who had reappeared and was sitting at her feet.

'I know you did, Thaddeus,' said Ruth in her most gentle voice. The cats began to surge around her, rubbing against her blanket with sorrowful expressions on their faces.

I stood there watching, at a loss. Tears ran down my face. 'Oh, God, Ruth . . . what can I do?'

She looked back at me calmly. 'I don't think there's much you can do, darling. But how are you? How do you like the house? You're living here now, aren't you?'

I had a sudden vision of myself, living in Ruth's house, calmly going about my life upstairs while she was down here, with the cats. . . .

I cried out, turned and stumbled toward the door. Ruth called out, 'Beatrice, wait—' but I ran up the stairs without answering her. I could hear the cats hissing. I reached the closet and slammed the door behind me. Within minutes I was in my car, driving blindly down Pratt, away from Ruth and her house, away from those cats.

★   ★   ★

I sold the house to a developer. It was on the market for two days. A few weeks later Ruth's house was a pile of rubble, and I was driving to New Mexico. I bought a condo in Albuquerque, filed for a divorce, and got a German Shepard puppy named Millie.

I think about Ruth a lot. But it's too late to change anything. And though I've tried to levitate, I can't do it. It's probably just as well.

Edith Wharton

Pomegranate Seed

'POMEGRANATE SEED'*

EDITH WHARTON (AMERICAN, 1862–1937)

First published in the *Ladies' Home Journal* in 1931.

'Pomegranate Seed' is the most restrained, sympathetic ghost story I know of, rivalled perhaps only by A. S. Byatt's 'The July Ghost' for its perfect balance of love and intimate horror. Wharton arouses pity, but the governing emotion is love, excessive love that overthrows the laws of nature. Wharton's own marriage was difficult and ended in divorce long before this story was written. 'Pomegranate Seed' is a late work by an empathetic master.

---

*Persephone, daughter of Demeter, goddess of fertility, was abducted and taken to Hades by Pluto, the god of the underworld. Her mother begged Jupiter to intercede, and he did so. But Persephone had broken her vow of abstinence in Hades by eating some pomegranate seeds. She was therefore required to spend a certain number of months each year – essentially the winter months – with Pluto.

POMEGRANATE SEED
Edith Wharton

I

Charlotte Ashby paused on her doorstep. Dark had descended on
the brilliancy of the March afternoon, and the grinding, rasping
street life of the city was at its highest. She turned her back on
it, standing for a moment in the old-fashioned, marble-flagged
vestibule before she inserted her key in the lock. The sash curtains
drawn across the panes of the inner door softened the light within
to a warm blur through which no details showed. It was the hour
when, in the first months of her marriage to Kenneth Ashby, she
had most liked to return to that quiet house in a street long since
deserted by business and fashion. The contrast between the soul-
less roar of New York, its devouring blaze of lights, the oppression
of its congested traffic, congested houses, lives, minds and this
veiled sanctuary she called home, always stirred her profoundly.
In the very heart of the hurricane she had found her tiny islet –
or thought she had. And now, in the last months, everything was
changed, and she always wavered on the doorstep and had to force
herself to enter.

While she stood there she called up the scene within: the hall hung with old prints, the ladder-like stairs, and on the left her husband's long shabby library, full of books and pipes and worn armchairs inviting to meditation. How she had loved that room! Then, upstairs, her own drawing room, in which, since the death of Kenneth's first wife, neither furniture nor hangings had been changed, because there had never been money enough, but which Charlotte had made her own by moving furniture about and adding more books, another lamp, a table for the new reviews. Even on the occasion of her only visit to the first Mrs Ashby – a distant, self-centred woman, whom she had known very slightly – she had looked about her with an innocent envy, feeling it to be exactly the drawing room she would have liked for herself; and now for more than a year it had been hers to deal with as she chose – the room to which she hastened back at dusk on winter days, where she sat reading by the fire, or answering notes at the pleasant roomy desk, or going over her stepchildren's copy-books, till she heard her husband's step.

Sometimes friends dropped in; sometimes – oftener – she was alone; and she liked that best, since it was another way of being with Kenneth, thinking over what he had said when they parted in the morning, imagining what he would say when he sprang up the stairs, found her by herself and caught her to him.

Now, instead of this, she thought of one thing only – the letter she might or might not find on the hall table. Until she had made sure whether or not it was there, her mind had no room for anything else. The letter was always the same – a square greyish envelope with 'Kenneth Ashby, Esquire', written on it in bold but faint characters. From the first it had struck Charlotte as peculiar that anyone who wrote such a firm hand should trace the letters so lightly; the address was always written as though there were not enough ink in the pen, or the writer's wrist were too weak to bear upon it. Another curious thing was that, in spite of its masculine curves, the writing was so visibly feminine. Some hands are sexless, some masculine, at first glance; the writing on the grey envelope, for all its strength and assurance, was without doubt a woman's. The envelope never bore anything but the recipient's name; no stamp, no address. The letter was presumably delivered by hand – but by whose? No doubt it was slipped into the letter box, whence the parlourmaid, when she closed the shutters and lit the lights, probably extracted it. At any rate, it was always in the evening, after dark, that Charlotte saw it lying there. She thought of the letter in the singular, as 'it', because, though there had been several since her marriage – seven, to be exact – they were so alike in appearance that they had become merged in one another in her mind, become one letter, become 'it'.

The first had come the day after their return from their honeymoon – a journey prolonged to the West Indies, from which they had returned to New York after an absence of more than two months. Re-entering the house with her husband, late on that first evening – they had dined at his mother's – she had seen, alone on the hall table, the grey envelope. Her eye fell on it before Kenneth's, and her first thought was: 'Why, I've seen that writing before'; but where she could not recall. The memory was just definite enough

45

for her to identify the script whenever it looked up at her faintly from the same pale envelope; but on that first day she would have thought no more of the letter if, when her husband's glance lit on it, she had not chanced to be looking at him. It all happened in a flash – his seeing the letter, putting out his hand for it, raising it to his shortsighted eyes to decipher the faint writing, and then abruptly withdrawing the arm he had slipped through Charlotte's, and moving away to the hanging light, his back turned to her. She had waited – waited for a sound, an exclamation; waited for him to open the letter; but he had slipped it into his pocket without a word and followed her into the library. And there they had sat down by the fire and lit their cigarettes, and he had remained silent, his head thrown back broodingly against the armchair, his eyes fixed on the hearth, and presently had passed his hand over his forehead and said: 'Wasn't it unusually hot at my mother's tonight? I've got a splitting head. Mind if I take myself off to bed?'

That was the first time. Since then Charlotte had never been present when he had received the letter. It usually came before he got home from his office, and she had to go upstairs and leave it lying there. But even if she had not seen it, she would have known it had come by the change in his face when he joined her – which, on those evenings, he seldom did before they met for dinner. Evidently, whatever the letter contained, he wanted to be by himself to deal with it; and when he reappeared he looked years older, looked emptied of life and courage, and hardly conscious of her presence. Sometimes he was silent for the rest of the evening; and if he spoke, it was usually to hint some criticism of her household arrangements, suggest some change in the domestic administration, to ask, a little nervously, if she didn't think Joyce's nursery governess was rather young and flighty, or if she herself always saw to it that Peter – whose throat was delicate – was properly wrapped up when he went to school. At such times Charlotte would remember the friendly warnings she had received when she became engaged to Kenneth Ashby: 'Marrying a heartbroken widower! Isn't that rather risky? You know Elsie Ashby absolutely dominated him'; and how she had jokingly replied: 'He may be glad of a little liberty for a change.' And in this respect she had been right. She had needed no one to tell her, during the first months, that her husband was perfectly happy with her. When they came back from their protracted honeymoon the same friends said: 'What have you done to Kenneth? He looks twenty years younger'; and this time she answered with careless joy: 'I suppose I've got him out of his groove.'

But what she noticed after the grey letters began to come was not so much his nervous tentative faultfinding – which always seemed to be uttered against his will – as the look in his eyes when he joined her after receiving one of the letters. The look was not unloving, not even indifferent; it was the look of a man who had been so far away from ordinary events that when he returns to familiar things they seem strange. She minded that more than the faultfinding.

Though she had been sure from the first that the handwriting on the grey envelope was a woman's, it was long before she associated the mysterious letters with any sentimental secret. She

47

was too sure of her husband's love, too confident of filling his life, for such an idea to occur to her. It seemed far more likely that the letters – which certainly did not appear to cause him any sentimental pleasure – were addressed to the busy lawyer than to the private person. Probably they were from some tiresome client – women, he had often told her, were nearly always tiresome as clients – who did not want her letters opened by his secretary and therefore had them carried to his house. Yes; but in that case the unknown female must be unusually troublesome, judging from the effect her letters produced. Then again, though his professional discretion was exemplary, it was odd that he had never uttered an impatient comment, never remarked to Charlotte, in a moment of expansion, that there was a nuisance of a woman who kept badgering him about a case that had gone against her. He had made more than one semiconfidence of the kind – of course without giving names or details; but concerning this mysterious correspondent his lips were sealed,

There was another possibility: what is euphemistically called an 'old entanglement'. Charlotte Ashby was a sophisticated woman. She had few illusions about the intricacies of the human heart; she knew that there were often old entanglements. But when she had married Kenneth Ashby, her friends, instead of hinting at such a possibility, had said: 'You've got your work cut out for you. Marrying a Don Juan is a sinecure to it. Kenneth's never looked at another woman since he first saw Elsie Corder. During all the years of their marriage he was more like an unhappy lover than a comfortably contented husband. He'll never let you move an armchair or change the place of a lamp; and whatever you venture to do, he'll mentally compare with what Elsie would have done in your place.'

Except for an occasional nervous mistrust as to her ability to manage the children – a mistrust gradually dispelled by her good humour and the children's obvious fondness for her – none of these forebodings had come true. The desolate widower, of whom his nearest friends said that only his absorbing professional interests had kept him from suicide after his first wife's death, had fallen in love, two years later, with Charlotte Gorse, and after an impetuous wooing had married her and carried her off on a tropical honeymoon. And ever since he had been as tender and lover-like as during those first radiant weeks. Before asking her to marry him he had spoken to her frankly of his great love for his first wife and his despair after her sudden death; but even then he had assumed no stricken attitude, or implied that life offered no possibility of renewal. He had been perfectly simple and natural, and had confessed to Charlotte that from the beginning he had hoped the future held new gifts for him. And when, after their marriage, they returned to the house where his twelve years with his first wife had been spent, he had told Charlotte at once that he was sorry he couldn't afford to do the place over for her, but that he knew every woman had her own views about furniture and all sorts of household arrangements a man would never notice, and had begged her to make any changes she saw fit without bothering to consult him. As a result, she made as few as possible; but his way of beginning their new life in the old setting was so frank and unembarrassed that it put her immediately at her ease, and she was almost sorry to find that the portrait of Elsie Ashby, which used to hang over the desk in his library, had been transferred in their absence to the children's nursery. Knowing herself to be the indirect cause of this banishment, she spoke of it to her husband; but he answered: 'Oh, I thought they ought to grow up with her looking down on them.' The answer moved Charlotte, and satisfied her; and as time went by she had to confess that she felt more at home in her house, more at ease and in confidence with her husband, since that long coldly beautiful face on the library wall no longer followed her with guarded eyes. It was as if Kenneth's love had penetrated to the secret she hardly acknowledged to her own heart – her passionate need to feel herself the sovereign even of his past.

With all this stored-up happiness to sustain her, it was curious that she had lately found herself yielding to a nervous apprehension. But there the apprehension was; and on this particular afternoon – perhaps because she was more tired than usual, or because of the trouble of finding a new cook or, for some other ridiculously trivial reason, moral or physical – she found herself unable to react against the feeling. Latchkey in hand, she looked back down the silent street to the whirl and illumination of the great thoroughfare beyond, and up at the sky already aflare with the city's nocturnal life. 'Outside there,' she thought, 'skyscrapers, advertisements, telephones, wireless, airplanes, movies, motors, and all the rest of the twentieth century; and on the other side of the door something I can't explain, can't relate to them. Something as old as the world, as mysterious as life ... Nonsense! What am I worrying about? There hasn't been a letter for three months now – not since the day we came back from the country after Christmas ... Queer that they always seem to come after our holidays! ... Why should I imagine there's going to be one tonight!'

No reason why, but that was the worst of it – one of the worst! – that there were days when she would stand there cold and shivering with the premonition of something inexplicable, intolerable, to be faced on the other side of the curtained panes; and when she opened the door and went in, there would be nothing; and on other days when she felt the same premonitory chill, it was justified by the sight of the grey envelope. So that ever since the last had come she had taken to feeling cold and premonitory every evening, because she never opened the door without thinking the letter might be there.

Well, she'd had enough of it: that was certain. She couldn't go on like that. If her husband turned white and had a headache on the days when the letter came, he seemed to recover afterward; but she couldn't. With her the strain had become chronic, and the reason was not far to seek. Her husband knew from whom the letter came and what was in it; he was prepared beforehand for whatever he had to deal with, and master of the situation, however bad; whereas she was shut out in the dark with her conjectures.

'I can't stand it! I can't stand it another day!' she exclaimed aloud, as she put her key in the lock. She turned the key and went in; and there, on the table, lay the letter.

2

She was almost glad of the sight. It seemed to justify everything, to put a seal of definiteness on the whole blurred business. A letter for her husband; a letter from a woman – no doubt another vulgar case of 'old entanglement'. What a fool she had been ever to doubt it, to rack her brains for less obvious explanations! She took up the envelope with a steady contemptuous hand, looked closely at the faint letters, held it against the light and just discerned the outline of the folded sheet within. She knew that now she would have no peace till she found out what was written on that sheet.

Her husband had not come in; he seldom got back from his office before half-past six or seven, and it was not yet six. She would have time to take the letter up to the drawing room, hold it over the tea kettle which at that hour always simmered by the fire in expectation of her return, solve the mystery and replace the letter where she had found it. No one would be the wiser, and her gnawing uncertainty would be over. The alternative, of course, was to question her husband; but to do that seemed even more difficult. She weighed the letter between thumb and finger, looked at it again under the light, started up the stairs with the envelope – and came down again and laid it on the table.

'No, I evidently can't,' she said, disappointed.

What should she do, then? She couldn't go up alone to that warm welcoming room, pour out her tea, look over her correspondence, glance at a book or review – not with that letter lying below and the knowledge that in a little while her husband would come in, open it and turn into the library alone, as he always did on the days when the grey envelope came.

Suddenly she decided. She would wait in the library and see for herself; see what happened between him and the letter when they thought themselves unobserved. She wondered the idea had never occurred to her before. By leaving the door ajar, and sitting in the corner behind it, she could watch him unseen . . . Well, then, she would watch him! She drew a chair into the corner, sat down, her eyes on the crack, and waited.

As far as she could remember, it was the first time she had ever tried to surprise another person's secret, but she was conscious of no compunction. She simply felt as if she were fighting her way through a stifling fog that she must at all costs get out of.

At length she heard Kenneth's latchkey and jumped up. The impulse to rush out and meet him had nearly made her forget why she was there; but she remembered in time and sat down again. From her post she covered the whole range of his movements – saw him enter the hall, draw the key from the door and take off his hat and overcoat. Then he turned to throw his gloves on the hall table, and at that moment he saw the envelope. The light was fall on his face, and what Charlotte first noted there was a look of surprise. Evidently he had not expected the letter – had not thought of the possibility of its being there that day. But though he had not expected it, now that he saw it he knew well enough what it contained. He did not open it immediately, but stood motionless, the colour slowly ebbing from his face. Apparently he could not make up his mind to touch it; but at length he put out his hand, opened the envelope, and moved with it to the light. In doing so he turned his back on Charlotte, and she saw only his bent head and slightly stooping shoulders. Apparently all the writing was on one page, for he did not turn the sheet but continued to stare at it for so long that he must have reread it a dozen times – or so it seemed to the woman breathlessly watching him. At length she saw him move; he raised the letter still closer to his eyes, as though he had not fully deciphered it. Then he lowered his head, and she saw his lips touch the sheet.

'Kenneth!' she exclaimed, and went on out into the hall.

The letter clutched in his hand, her husband turned and looked at her. 'Where were you?' he said, in a low bewildered voice, like a man waked out of his sleep.

'In the library, waiting for you.' She tried to steady her voice: 'What's the matter! What's in that letter? You look ghastly.'

Her agitation seemed to calm him, and he instantly put the envelope into his pocket with a slight laugh. 'Ghastly? I'm sorry. I've had a hard day in the office – one or two complicated cases. I look dog-tired, I suppose.'

'You didn't look tired when you came in. It was only when you opened that letter – '

He had followed her into the library, and they stood gazing at each other. Charlotte noticed how quickly he had regained his self-control; his profession had trained him to rapid mastery of face and voice. She saw at once that she would be at a disadvantage in any attempt to surprise his secret, but at the same moment she lost all desire to manoeuvre, to trick him into betraying anything he wanted to conceal. Her wish was still to penetrate the mystery, but only that she might help him to bear the burden it implied. 'Even if it *is* another woman,' she thought.

'Kenneth,' she said, her heart beating excitedly, 'I waited here on purpose to see you come in. I wanted to watch you while you opened that letter.'

His face, which had paled, turned to dark red; then it paled again. 'That letter? Why especially that letter?'

'Because I've noticed that whenever one of those letters comes it seems to have such a strange effect on you.'

A line of anger she had never seen before came out between his eyes, and she said to herself: 'The upper part of his face is too narrow; this is the first time I ever noticed it.'

She heard him continue, in the cool and faintly ironic tone of the prosecuting lawyer making a point: 'Ah, so you're in the habit of watching people open their letters when they don't know you're there?'

'Not in the habit. I never did such a thing before. But I had to find out what she writes to you, at regular intervals, in those grey envelopes.'

He weighed this for a moment; then: 'The intervals have not been regular,' he said.

'Oh, I dare say you've kept a better account of the dates than I have,' she retorted, her magnanimity vanishing at his tone. 'All I know is that every time that woman writes to you – '

'Why do you assume it's a woman?'

'It's a woman's writing. Do you deny it?'

He smiled. 'No, I don't deny it. I asked only because the writing is generally supposed to look more like a man's.'

Charlotte passed this over impatiently. 'And this woman – what does she write to you about?'

Again he seemed to consider a moment. 'About business.'

'Legal business?'

'In a way, yes. Business in general.'

'You look after her affairs for her?'

'Yes.'

'You've looked after them for a long time?'

'Yes. A very long time.'

'Kenneth, dearest, won't you tell me who she is?'

'No. I can't.' He paused, and brought out, as if with a certain hesitation: 'Professional secrecy.'

The blood rushed from Charlotte's heart to her temples. 'Don't say that – don't!'

'Why not?'

'Because I saw you kiss the letter.'

The effect of the words was so disconcerting that she instantly repented having spoken them. Her husband, who had submitted to her cross-questioning with a sort of contemptuous composure, as though he were humouring an unreasonable child, turned on her a face of terror and distress. For a minute he seemed unable to speak; then, collecting himself, with an effort, he stammered out: 'The writing is very faint; you must have seen me holding the letter close to my eyes to try to decipher it.'

'No; I saw you kissing it.' He was silent. 'Didn't I see you kissing it?'

He sank back into indifference. 'Perhaps.'

'Kenneth! You stand there and say that – to me?'

'What possible difference can it make to you? The letter is on business, as I told you. Do you suppose I'd lie about it? The writer is a very old friend whom I haven't seen for a long time.'

'Men don't kiss business letters, even from women who are very old friends, unless they have been their lovers, and still regret them.'

He shrugged his shoulders slightly and turned away, as if he considered the discussion at an end and were faintly disgusted at the turn it had taken.

'Kenneth!' Charlotte moved toward him and caught hold of his arm.

He paused with a look of weariness and laid his hand over hers. 'Won't you believe me?' he asked gently.

'How can I? I've watched these letters come to you – for months now they've been coming. Ever since we came back from the West Indies – one of them greeted me the very day we arrived. And after each one of them I see their mysterious effect on you, I see you disturbed, unhappy, as if someone were trying to estrange you from me.'

'No, dear; not that. Never!'

She drew back and looked at him with passionate entreaty. 'Well, then, prove it to me, darling. It's so easy!'

He forced a smile. 'It's not easy to prove anything to a woman who's once taken an idea into her head.'

'You've only got to show me the letter.'

His hand slipped from hers and he drew back and shook his head.

'You won't?'

'I can't.'

'Then the woman who wrote it is your mistress.'

'No, dear. No.'

'Not now, perhaps. I suppose she's trying to get you back, and you're struggling, out of pity for me. My poor Kenneth!'

'I swear to you she never was my mistress.'

Charlotte felt the tears rushing to her eyes. 'Ah, that's worse, then – that's hopeless! The prudent ones are the kind that keep their hold on a man. We all know that.' She lifted her hands and hid her face in them.

Her husband remained silent; he offered neither consolation nor denial, and at length, wiping away her tears, she raised her eyes almost timidly to his.

'Kenneth, think! We've been married such a short time. Imagine what you're making me suffer. You say you can't show me this letter. You refuse even to explain it.'

'I've told you the letter is on business. I will swear to that too.'

'A man will swear to anything to screen a woman. If you want me to believe you, at least tell me her name. If you'll do that, I promise you I won't ask to see the letter.'

There was a long interval of suspense, during which she felt her heart beating against her ribs in quick admonitory knocks, as if warning her of the danger she was incurring.

'I can't,' he said at length.

'Not even her name?'

'No.'

'You can't tell me anything more?'

'No.'

Again a pause; this time they seemed both to have reached the end of their arguments and to be helplessly facing each other across a baffling waste of incomprehension.

Charlotte stood breathing rapidly, her hands against her breast. She felt as if she had run a hard race and missed the goal. She had meant to move her husband and had succeeded only in irritating him; and this error of reckoning seemed to change him into a stranger, a mysterious incomprehensible being whom no argument or entreaty of hers could reach. The curious thing was that she was aware in him of no hostility or even impatience, but only of a remoteness, an inaccessibility, far more difficult to overcome. She felt herself excluded, ignored, blotted out of his life. But after a moment or two, looking at him more calmly, she saw that he was suffering as much as she was. His distant guarded face was drawn with pain; the coming of the grey envelope, though it always cast a shadow, had never marked him as deeply as this discussion with his wife.

Charlotte took heart; perhaps, after all, she had not spent her last shaft. She drew nearer and once more laid her hand on his arm. 'Poor Kenneth! If you knew how sorry I am for you – '

She thought he winced slightly at this expression of sympathy, but he took her hand and pressed it.

'I can think of nothing worse than to be incapable of loving long,' she continued, 'to feel the beauty of a great love and to be too unstable to bear its burden.'

He turned on her a look of wistful reproach. 'Oh, don't say that of me. Unstable!'

She felt herself at last on the right tack, and her voice trembled with excitement as she went on: 'Then what about me and this other woman? Haven't you already forgotten Elsie twice within a year?'

She seldom pronounced his first wife's name; it did not come naturally to her tongue. She flung it out now as if she were flinging some dangerous explosive into the open space between them, and drew back a step, waiting to hear the mine go off.

Her husband did not move; his expression grew sadder, but showed no resentment. 'I have never forgotten Elsie,' he said.

Charlotte could not repress a faint laugh. 'Then, you poor dear, between the three of us – '

'There are not – ' he began; and then broke off and put his hand to his forehead.

'Not what?'

'I'm sorry; I don't believe I know what I'm saying. I've got a blinding headache.' He looked wan and furrowed enough for the statement to be true, but she was exasperated by his evasion,

'Ah, yes; the grey envelope headache!'

She saw the surprise in his eyes. 'I'd forgotten how closely I've been watched,' he said coldly. 'If you'll excuse me, I think I'll go up and try an hour in the dark, to see if I can get rid of this neuralgia.'

She wavered; then she said, with desperate resolution: 'I'm

sorry your head aches. But before you go I want to say that sooner or later this question must be settled between us. Someone is trying to separate us, and I don't care what it costs me to find out who it is.' She looked him steadily in the eyes. 'If it costs me your love, I don't care! If I can't have your confidence I don't want anything from you. '

He still looked at her wistfully. 'Give me time.'

'Time for what? It's only a word to say.'

'Time to show you that you haven't lost my love or my confidence.'

'Well, I'm waiting.'

He turned toward the door, and then glanced back hesitatingly. 'Oh, do wait, my love,' he said, and went out of the room.

She heard his tired step on the stairs and the closing of his bedroom door above. Then she dropped into a chair and buried her face in her folded arms. Her first movement was one of compunction; she seemed to herself to have been hard, unhuman, unimaginative. 'Think of telling him that I didn't care if my insistence cost me his love! The lying rubbish!' She started up to follow him and unsay the meaningless words. But she was checked by a reflection. He had had his way, after all; he had eluded all attacks on his secret, and now he was shut up alone in his room, reading that other woman's letter.

3

She was still reflecting on this when the surprised parlourmaid came in and found her. No, Charlotte said, she wasn't going to

dress for dinner; Mr Ashby didn't want to dine. He was very tired
and had gone up to his room to rest; later she would have something brought on a tray to the drawing room. She mounted the
stairs to her bedroom. Her dinner dress was lying on the bed, and
at the sight the quiet routine of her daily life took hold of her
and she began to feel as if the strange talk she had just had with
her husband must have taken place in another world, between
two beings who were not Charlotte Gorse and Kenneth Ashby,
but phantoms projected by her fevered imagination. She recalled
the year since her marriage – her husband's constant devotion;
his persistent, almost too insistent tenderness; the feeling he had
given her at times of being too eagerly dependent on her, too
searchingly close to her, as if there were not air enough between
her soul and his. It seemed preposterous, as she recalled all this,
that a few moments ago she should have been accusing him of an
intrigue with another woman! But, then, what –

Again she was moved by the impulse to go up to him, beg
his pardon and try to laugh away the misunderstanding. But she
was restrained by the fear of forcing herself upon his privacy. He
was troubled and unhappy, oppressed by some grief or fear; and
he had shown her that he wanted to fight out his battle alone. It
would be wiser, as well as more generous, to respect his wish.
Only, how strange, how unbearable, to be there, in the next room
to his, and feel herself at the other end of the world! In her nervous agitation she almost regretted not having had the courage to
open the letter and put it back on the hall table before he came in.
At least she would have known what his secret was, and the bogy

might have been laid. For she was beginning now to think of the mystery as something conscious, malevolent: a secret persecution before which he quailed, yet from which he could not free himself. Once or twice in his evasive eyes she thought she had detected a desire for help, an impulse of confession, instantly restrained and suppressed. It was as if he felt she could have helped him if she had known, and yet had been unable to tell her!

There flashed through her mind the idea of going to his mother. She was very fond of old Mrs Ashby, a firm-fleshed clear-eyed old lady, with an astringent bluntness of speech which responded to the forthright and simple in Charlotte's own nature. There had been a tacit bond between them ever since the day when Mrs Ashby Senior, coming to lunch for the first time with her new daughter-in-law, had been received by Charlotte downstairs in the library, and glancing up at the empty wall above her son's desk, had remarked laconically: 'Elsie gone, eh?' adding, at Charlotte's murmured explanation: 'Nonsense. Don't have her back. Two's company.' Charlotte, at this reading of her thoughts, could hardly refrain from exchanging a smile of complicity with her mother-in-law; and it seemed to her now that Mrs Ashby's almost uncanny directness might pierce to the core of this new mystery. But here again she hesitated, for the idea almost suggested a betrayal. What right had she to call in anyone, even so close a relation, to surprise a secret which her husband was trying to keep from her? 'Perhaps, by and by, he'll talk to his mother of his own accord,' she thought, and then ended: 'But what does it matter? He and I must settle it between us.'

She was still brooding over the problem when there was a knock on the door and her husband came in. He was dressed for dinner and seemed surprised to see her sitting there, with her evening dress lying unheeded on the bed.

'Aren't you coming down?'

'I thought you were not well and had gone to bed,' she faltered.

He forced a smile. 'I'm not particularly well, but we'd better go down.' His face, though still drawn, looked calmer than when he had fled upstairs an hour earlier.

'There it is; he knows what's in the letter and has fought his battle out again, whatever it is,' she reflected, 'while I'm still in darkness.' She rang and gave a hurried order that dinner should be served as soon as possible – just a short meal, whatever could be got ready quickly, as both she and Mr Ashby were rather tired and not very hungry.

Dinner was announced, and they sat down to it. At first neither seemed able to find a word to say; then Ashby began to make conversation with an assumption of ease that was more oppressive than his silence. 'How tired he is! How terribly over-tired!' Charlotte said to herself, pursuing her own thoughts while he rambled on about municipal politics, aviation, an exhibition of modern French painting, the health of an old aunt and the installing of the automatic telephone. 'Good heavens, how tired he is!'

When they dined alone they usually went into the library after dinner, and Charlotte curled herself up on the divan with her knitting while he settled down in his armchair under the lamp and lit a pipe. But this evening, by tacit agreement, they avoided the room in which their strange talk had taken place, and went up to Charlotte's drawing room.

They sat down near the fire, and Charlotte said: 'Your pipe?' after he had put down his hardly tasted coffee.

He shook his head. 'No, not tonight.'

'You must go to bed early; you look terribly tired. I'm sure they overwork you at the office.'

'I suppose we all overwork at times.'

She rose and stood before him with sudden resolution. 'Well, I'm not going to have you use up your strength slaving in that way. It's absurd. I can see you're ill.' She bent over him and laid her hand on his forehead. 'My poor old Kenneth. Prepare to be taken away soon on a long holiday.'

He looked up at her, startled. 'A holiday?'

'Certainly. Didn't you know I was going to carry you off at Easter? We're going to start in a fortnight on a month's voyage to somewhere or other. On any one of the big cruising steamers.' She paused and bent closer, touching his forehead with her lips. 'I'm tired too, Kenneth.'

He seemed to pay no heed to her last words, but sat, his hands on his knees, his head drawn back a little from her caress, and looked up at her with a stare of apprehension. 'Again? My dear, we can't; I can't possibly go away.'

'I don't know why you say "again", Kenneth; we haven't taken a real holiday this year.'

'At Christmas we spent a week with the children in the country.'

'Yes, but this time I mean away from the children, from servants, from the house. From everything that's familiar and fatiguing. Your mother will love to have Joyce and Peter with her.'

He frowned and slowly shook his head. 'No, dear; I can't leave them with my mother.'

'Why, Kenneth, how absurd! She adores them. You didn't hesitate to leave them with her for over two months when we went to the West Indies.'

He drew a deep breath and stood up uneasily. 'That was different.'

'Different? Why?'

'I mean, at that time I didn't realise – ' He broke off as if to choose his words and then went on: 'My mother adores the children, as you say. But she isn't always very judicious. Grandmothers always spoil children. And sometimes she talks before them without thinking.' He turned to his wife with an almost pitiful gesture of entreaty. 'Don't ask me to, dear.'

Charlotte mused. It was true that the elder Mrs Ashby had a fearless tongue, but she was the last woman in the world to say or hint anything before her grandchildren at which the most scrupulous parent could take offence. Charlotte looked at her husband in perplexity.

'I don't understand.'

He continued to turn on her the same troubled and entreating gaze. 'Don't try to,' he muttered.

'Not try to?'

'Not now – not yet.' He put up his hands and pressed them

against his temples. 'Can't you see that there's no use in insisting? I can't go away, no matter how much I might want to.'

Charlotte still scrutinised him gravely. 'The question is, *do* you want to?'

He returned her gaze for a moment; then his lips began to tremble, and he said, hardly above his breath: 'I want – anything you want.'

'And yet – '

'Don't ask me. I can't leave – I can't!'

'You mean that you can't go away out of reach of those letters!'

Her husband had been standing before her in an uneasy half-hesitating attitude; now he turned abruptly away and walked once or twice up and down the length of the room, his head bent, his eyes fixed on the carpet.

Charlotte felt her resentfulness rising with her fears. 'It's that,' she persisted. 'Why not admit it? You can't live without them.'

He continued his troubled pacing of the room; then he stopped short, dropped into a chair and covered his face with his hands. From the shaking of his shoulders, Charlotte saw that he was weeping. She had never seen a man cry, except her father after her mother's death, when she was a little girl; and she remembered still how the sight had frightened her. She was frightened now; she felt that her husband was being dragged away from her into some mysterious bondage, and that she must use up her last atom of strength in the struggle for his freedom, and for hers.

'Kenneth – Kenneth!' she pleaded, kneeling down beside him. 'Won't you listen to me? Won't you try to see what I'm suffering?

I'm not unreasonable, darling, really not. I don't suppose I should ever have noticed the letters if it hadn't been for their effect on you. It's not my way to pry into other people's affairs; and even if the effect had been different – yes, yes, listen to me – if I'd seen that the letters made you happy, that you were watching eagerly for them, counting the days between their coming, that you wanted them, that they gave you something I haven't known how to give – why, Kenneth, I don't say I shouldn't have suffered from that too; but it would have been in a different way, and I should have had the courage to hide what I felt, and the hope that some day you'd come to feel about me as you did about the writer of the letters. But what I can't bear is to see how you dread them, how they make you suffer, and yet how you can't live without them and won't go away lest you should miss one during your absence. Or perhaps,' she added, her voice breaking into a cry of accusation – 'perhaps it's because she's actually forbidden you to leave. Kenneth, you must answer me! Is that the reason? Is it because she's forbidden you that you won't go away with me?'

She continued to kneel at his side, and raising her hands, she drew his gently down. She was ashamed of her persistence, ashamed of uncovering that baffled disordered face, yet resolved that no such scruples should arrest her. His eyes were lowered, the muscles of his face quivered; she was making him suffer even more than she suffered herself. Yet this no longer restrained her.

'Kenneth, is it that? She won't let us go away together?'

Still he did not speak or turn his eyes to her; and a sense of defeat swept over her. After all, she thought, the struggle was a losing one. 'You needn't answer. I see I'm right,' she said.

Suddenly, as she rose, he turned and drew her down again. His hands caught hers and pressed them so tightly that she felt her rings cutting into her flesh. There was something frightened, convulsive in his hold; it was the clutch of a man who felt himself slipping over a precipice. He was staring up at her now as if salvation lay in the face she bent above him. 'Of course we'll go away together. We'll go wherever you want,' he said in a low confused voice; and putting his arm about her, he drew her close and pressed his lips on hers.

4

Charlotte had said to herself: 'I shall sleep tonight', but instead she sat before her fire into the small hours, listening for any sound that came from her husband's room. But he, at any rate, seemed to be resting after the tumult of the evening. Once or twice she stole to the door and in the faint light that came in from the street through his open window she saw him stretched out in heavy sleep – the sleep of weakness and exhaustion. 'He's ill,' she thought – 'he's undoubtedly ill. And it's not overwork; it's this mysterious persecution.'

She drew a breath of relief. She had fought through the weary fight and the victory was hers – at least for the moment. If only they could have started at once – started for anywhere! She knew it would be useless to ask him to leave before the holidays; and meanwhile the secret influence – as to which she was still so completely in the dark – would continue to work against her, and she would have to renew the struggle day after day till they started on their journey. But after that everything would be different. If once she could get her husband away under other skies, and all to herself, she never doubted her power to release him from the evil spell he was under. Lulled to quiet by the thought, she too slept at last.

When she woke, it was long past her usual hour, and she sat up in bed surprised and vexed at having overslept herself. She always liked to be down to share her husband's breakfast by the library fire; but a glance at the clock made it clear that he must have started long since for his office. To make sure, she jumped out of bed and went into his room, but it was empty. No doubt he had looked in on her before leaving, seen that she still slept, and gone downstairs without disturbing her; and their relations were sufficiently lover-like for her to regret having missed their morning hour.

She rang and asked if Mr Ashby had already gone. Yes, nearly an hour ago, the maid said. He had given orders that Mrs Ashby should not be waked and that the children should not come to her till she sent for them . . . Yes, he had gone up to the nursery himself to give the order. All this sounded usual enough, and Charlotte hardly knew why she asked: 'And did Mr Ashby leave no other message?'

Yes, the maid said, he did; she was so sorry she'd forgotten. He'd told her, just as he was leaving, to say to Mrs Ashby that he was going to see about their passages, and would she please be ready to sail tomorrow?

Charlotte echoed the woman's 'Tomorrow', and sat staring at her incredulously. 'Tomorrow – you're sure he said to sail tomorrow?'

'Oh, ever so sure, ma'am. I don't know how I could have forgotten to mention it.'

'Well, it doesn't matter. Draw my bath, please.' Charlotte sprang up, dashed through her dressing, and caught herself singing at her image in the glass as she sat brushing her hair. It made her feel young again to have scored such a victory. The other woman vanished to a speck on the horizon, as this one, who ruled the foreground, smiled back at the reflection of her lips and eyes. He loved her, then – he loved her as passionately as ever. He had divined what she had suffered, had understood that their happiness depended on their getting away at once, and finding each other again after yesterday's desperate groping in the fog. The nature of the influence that had come between them did not much matter to Charlotte now; she had faced the phantom and dispelled it. 'Courage – that's the secret! If only people who are in love weren't always so afraid of risking their happiness by looking it in the eyes.' As she brushed back her light abundant hair it waved electrically above her head, like the palms of victory. Ah, well, some women knew how to manage men, and some didn't – and only the fair – she gaily paraphrased – deserve the brave! Certainly she was looking very pretty.

The morning danced along like a cockleshell on a bright sea – such a sea as they would soon be speeding over. She ordered a particularly good dinner, saw the children off to their classes, had her trunks brought down, consulted with the maid about getting out summer clothes – for of course they would be heading for heat and sunshine – and wondered if she oughtn't to take Kenneth's flannel suits out of camphor. 'But how absurd,' she reflected, 'that I don't yet know where we're going!' She looked at the clock, saw that it was close on noon, and decided to call him up at his office. There was a slight delay; then she heard his secretary's voice saying that Mr Ashby had looked in for a moment early, and left again almost immediately . . . Oh, very well; Charlotte would ring up later. How soon was he likely to be back? The secretary answered that she couldn't tell; all they knew in the office was that when he left he had said he was in a hurry because he had to go out of town.

Out of town! Charlotte hung up the receiver and sat blankly gazing into new darkness. Why had he gone out of town? And where had he gone? And of all days, why should he have chosen the eve of their suddenly planned departure? She felt a faint shiver of apprehension. Of course he had gone to see that woman – no doubt to get her permission to leave. He was as completely in bondage as that; and Charlotte had been fatuous enough to see the palms of victory on her forehead. She burst into a laugh and, walking across the room, sat down again before her mirror. What a different face she saw! The smile on her pale lips seemed to mock the rosy vision of the other Charlotte. But gradually her colour crept back. After all, she had a right to claim the victory, since her husband was doing what she wanted, not what the other woman exacted of him. It was natural enough, in view of his abrupt decision to leave the next day, that he should have arrangements to make, business matters to wind up; it was not even necessary to suppose that his mysterious trip was a visit to the writer of the letters. He might simply have gone to see a client who lived out of town. Of course they would not tell Charlotte at the office; the secretary had hesitated before imparting even such meagre information as the fact of Mr Ashby's absence. Meanwhile she would go on with her joyful preparations, content to learn later in the day to what particular island of the blest she was to be carried.

The hours wore on, or rather were swept forward on a rush of eager preparations. At last the entrance of the maid who came to draw the curtains roused Charlotte from her labours, and she saw to her surprise that the clock marked five. And she did not yet know where they were going the next day! She rang up her husband's office and was told that Mr Ashby had not been there since the early morning. She asked for his partner, but the partner could add nothing to her information, for he himself, his suburban train having been behind time, had reached the office after Ashby had come and gone. Charlotte stood perplexed; then she decided to telephone to her mother-in-law. Of course Kenneth, on the eve of a month's absence, must have gone to see his mother. The mere fact that the children – in spite of his vague objections – would certainly have to be left with old Mrs Ashby, made it obvious that he would have all sorts of matters to decide with her. At another time Charlotte might have felt a little hurt at being excluded from their conference, but nothing mattered now but that she had won the day, that her husband was still hers and not another woman's. Gaily she called up Mrs Ashby, heard her friendly voice, and began: 'Well, did Kenneth's news surprise you? What do you think of our elopement?'

Almost instantly, before Mrs Ashby could answer, Charlotte knew what her reply would be. Mrs Ashby had not seen her son, she had had no word from him and did not know what her daughter-in-law meant. Charlotte stood silent in the intensity of her surprise. 'But then, where *has* he been?' she thought. Then, recovering herself, she explained their sudden decision to Mrs Ashby, and in doing so, gradually regained her own self-confidence, her conviction that nothing could ever again come between Kenneth and herself. Mrs Ashby took the news calmly and approvingly. She, too, had thought that Kenneth looked worried and overtired, and she agreed with her daughter-in-law that in such cases change was the surest remedy. 'I'm always so glad when he gets away. Elsie hated travelling; she was always finding pretexts to prevent his going anywhere. With you, thank goodness, it's different.' Nor was Mrs Ashby surprised at his not having had time to let her know of his departure. He must have been in a rush from the moment the decision was taken; but no doubt he'd drop in before dinner. Five minutes' talk was really all they needed. 'I hope you'll gradually cure Kenneth of his mania for going over and over a question that could be settled in a dozen words. He never used to be like that, and if he carried the habit into his professional work he'd soon lose all his clients . . . Yes, do come in for a minute, dear, if you have time; no doubt he'll turn up while you're here.'

The tonic ring of Mrs Ashby's voice echoed on reassuringly in the silent room while Charlotte continued her preparations.

Toward seven the telephone rang, and she darted to it. Now she would know! But it was only from the conscientious secretary, to say that Mr Ashby hadn't been back, or sent any word, and before the office closed she thought she ought to let Mrs Ashby know. 'Oh, that's all right. Thanks a lot!' Charlotte called out cheerfully, and hung up the receiver with a trembling hand. But perhaps by this time, she reflected, he was at his mother's. She shut her drawers and cupboards, put on her hat and coat and called up to the nursery that she was going out for a minute to see the children's grandmother.

Mrs Ashby lived nearby, and during her brief walk through the cold spring dusk Charlotte imagined that every advancing figure was her husband's. But she did not meet him on the way, and when she entered the house she found her mother-in-law alone. Kenneth had neither telephoned nor come. Old Mrs Ashby sat by her bright fire, her knitting needles flashing steadily through her active old hands, and her mere bodily presence gave reassurance to Charlotte. Yes, it was certainly odd that Kenneth had gone off for the whole day without letting any of them know; but, after all, it was to be expected. A busy lawyer held so many threads in his hands that any sudden change of plan would oblige him to make all sorts of unforeseen arrangements and adjustments. He might have gone to see some client in the suburbs and been detained there; his mother remembered his telling her that he had charge of the legal business of a queer old recluse somewhere in New

Jersey, who was immensely rich but too mean to have a telephone. Very likely Kenneth had been stranded there.

But Charlotte felt her nervousness gaining on her. When Mrs Ashby asked her at what hour they were sailing the next day and she had to say she didn't know – that Kenneth had simply sent her word he was going to take their passages – the uttering of the words again brought home to her the strangeness of the situation. Even Mrs Ashby conceded that it was odd; but she immediately added that it only showed what a rush he was in.

'But, mother, it's nearly eight o'clock! He must realise that I've got to know when we're starting tomorrow.'

'Oh, the boat probably doesn't sail till evening. Sometimes they have to wait till midnight for the tide. Kenneth's probably counting on that. After all, he has a level head.'

Charlotte stood up. 'It's not that. Something has happened to him.'

Mrs Ashby took off her spectacles and rolled up her knitting. 'If you begin to let yourself imagine things – '

'Aren't you in the least anxious?'

'I never am till I have to be. I wish you'd ring for dinner, my dear. You'll stay and dine? He's sure to drop in here on his way home.'

Charlotte called up her own house. No, the maid said, Mr Ashby hadn't come in and hadn't telephoned. She would tell him as soon as he came that Mrs Ashby was dining at his mother's. Charlotte followed her mother-in-law into the dining room and sat with parched throat before her empty plate, while Mrs Ashby dealt calmly and efficiently with a short but carefully prepared repast. 'You'd better eat something, child, or you'll be as bad as Kenneth . . . Yes, a little more asparagus, please, Jane.'

She insisted on Charlotte's drinking a glass of sherry and nibbling a bit of toast; then they returned to the drawing room, where the fire had been made up, and the cushions in Mrs Ashby's armchair shaken out and smoothed. How safe and familiar it all looked; and out there, somewhere in the uncertainty and mystery of the night, lurked the answer to the two women's conjectures, like an indistinguishable figure prowling on the threshold.

At last Charlotte got up and said: 'I'd better go back. At this hour Kenneth will certainly go straight home.'

Mrs Ashby smiled indulgently. 'It's not very late, my dear. It doesn't take two sparrows long to dine.'

'It's after nine.' Charlotte bent down to kiss her. 'The fact is, I can't keep still.'

Mrs Ashby pushed aside her work and rested her two hands on the arms of her chair. 'I'm going with you,' she said, helping herself up.

Charlotte protested that it was too late, that it was not necessary, that she would call up as soon as Kenneth came in, but Mrs Ashby had already rung for her maid. She was slightly lame, and stood resting on her stick while her wraps were brought. 'If Mr Kenneth turns up, tell him he'll find me at his own house,' she instructed the maid as the two women got into the taxi which had been summoned. During the short drive Charlotte gave thanks that she was not returning home alone. There was something warm and substantial in the mere fact of Mrs Ashby's nearness, something that corresponded with the clearness of her eyes and the texture of her fresh firm complexion. As the taxi drew up she laid her hand encouragingly on Charlotte's. 'You'll see; there'll be a message.'

The door opened at Charlotte's ring and the two entered. Charlotte's heart beat excitedly; the stimulus of her mother-in-law's confidence was beginning to flow through her veins.

'You'll see – you'll see,' Mrs Ashby repeated.

The maid who opened the door said no, Mr Ashby had not come in, and there had been no message from him.

'You're sure the telephone's not out of order?' his mother suggested; and the maid said, well, it certainly wasn't half an hour ago; but she'd just go and ring up to make sure. She disappeared, and Charlotte turned to take off her hat and cloak. As she did so her eyes lit on the hall table, and there lay a grey envelope, her husband's name faintly traced on it. 'Oh!' she cried out, suddenly aware that for the first time in months she had entered her house without wondering if one of the grey letters would be there.

'What is it, my dear?' Mrs Ashby asked with a glance of surprise.

Charlotte did not answer. She took up the envelope and stood staring at it as if she could force her gaze to penetrate to what was within. Then an idea occurred to her. She turned and held out the envelope to her mother-in-law.

'Do you know that writing?' she asked.

Mrs Ashby took the letter. She had to feel with her other hand for her eyeglasses, and when she had adjusted them she lifted the envelope to the light. 'Why!' she exclaimed; and then stopped. Charlotte noticed that the letter shook in her usually firm hand. 'But this is addressed to Kenneth,' Mrs Ashby said at length, in a low voice. Her tone seemed to imply that she felt her daughter-in-law's question to be slightly indiscreet.

'Yes, but no matter,' Charlotte spoke with sudden decision. 'I want to know – do you know the writing?'

Mrs Ashby handed back the letter. 'No,' she said distinctly.

The two women had turned into the library. Charlotte switched on the electric light and shut the door. She still held the envelope in her hand.

'I'm going to open it,' she announced.

She caught her mother-in-law's startled glance. 'But, dearest – a letter not addressed to you? My dear, you can't!'

'As if I cared about that – now!' She continued to look intently at Mrs Ashby. 'This letter may tell me where Kenneth is.'

Mrs Ashby's glossy bloom was effaced by a quick pallor; her firm cheeks seemed to shrink and wither. 'Why should it? What makes you believe – It can't possibly – '

Charlotte held her eyes steadily on that altered face. 'Ah, then you *do* know the writing?' she flashed back.

'Know the writing? How should I? With all my son's correspondents...What I do know is – ' Mrs Ashby broke off and looked at her daughter-in-law entreatingly, almost timidly.

Charlotte caught her by the wrist. 'Mother! What do you know? Tell me! You must!'

'That I don't believe any good ever came of a woman's opening her husband's letters behind his back.'

The words sounded to Charlotte's irritated ears as flat as a phrase culled from a book of moral axioms. She laughed impatiently and dropped her mother-in-law's wrist. 'Is that all? No good can come of this letter, opened or unopened. I know that well enough. But whatever ill comes, I mean to find out what's in it.' Her hands had been trembling as they held the envelope, but now they grew firm, and her voice also. She still gazed intently at Mrs Ashby. 'This is the ninth letter addressed in the same hand that has come for Kenneth since we've been married. Always these same grey envelopes. I've kept count of them because after each one he has been like a man who has had some dreadful shock. It takes him hours to shake off their effect. I've told him so. I've told him I must know from whom they come, because I can see they're killing him. He won't answer my questions; he says he can't tell me anything about the letters; but last night he promised to go away with me – to get away from them.'

Mrs Ashby, with shaking steps, had gone to one of the armchairs and sat down in it, her head drooping forward on her breast. 'Ah,' she murmured.

'So now you understand – '

'Did he tell you it was to get away from them?'

'He said, to get away – to get away. He was sobbing so that he could hardly speak. But I told him I knew that was why.'

'And what did he say?'

'He took me in his arms and said he'd go wherever I wanted.'

'Ah, thank God!' said Mrs Ashby. There was a silence, during which she continued to sit with bowed head, and eyes averted from her daughter-in-law. At last she looked up and spoke. 'Are you sure there have been as many as nine?'

'Perfectly. This is the ninth. I've kept count.'

'And he has absolutely refused to explain?'

'Absolutely.'

Mrs Ashby spoke through pale contracted lips. 'When did they begin to come? Do you remember?'

Charlotte laughed again. 'Remember? The first one came the night we got back from our honeymoon.'

'All that time?' Mrs Ashby lifted her head and spoke with sudden energy. 'Then – yes, open it.'

The words were so unexpected that Charlotte felt the blood in her temples, and her hands began to tremble again. She tried to slip her finger under the flap of the envelope, but it was so tightly stuck that she had to hunt on her husband's writing table for his ivory letter opener. As she pushed about the familiar objects his own hands had so lately touched, they sent through her the icy chill emanating from the little personal effects of someone newly dead. In the deep silence of the room the tearing of the paper as she slit the envelope sounded like a human cry. She drew out the sheet and carried it to the lamp.

'Well?' Mrs Ashby asked below her breath.

Charlotte did not move or answer. She was bending over the page with wrinkled brows, holding it nearer and nearer to the light. Her sight must be blurred, or else dazzled by the reflection of the lamplight on the smooth surface of the paper, for, strain her eyes as she would, she could discern only a few faint strokes, so faint and faltering as to be nearly undecipherable.

'I can't make it out,' she said.

'What do you mean, dear?'

'The writing's too indistinct ... Wait.'

She went back to the table and, sitting down close to Kenneth's reading lamp, slipped the letter under a magnifying glass. All this time she was aware that her mother-in-law was watching her intently.

'Well?' Mrs Ashby breathed.

'Well, it's no clearer. I can't read it.'

'You mean the paper is an absolute blank?'

'No, not quite. There is writing on it. I can make out something like "mine" – oh, and "come". It might be "come".'

Mrs Ashby stood up abruptly. Her face was even paler than before. She advanced to the table and, resting her two hands on it, drew a deep breath. 'Let me see,' she said, as if forcing herself to a hateful effort.

Charlotte felt the contagion of her whiteness. 'She knows,' she thought. She pushed the letter across the table. Her mother-in-law lowered her head over it in silence, but without touching it with her pale wrinkled hands.

Charlotte stood watching her as she herself, when she had tried to read the letter, had been watched by Mrs Ashby. The latter fumbled for her glasses, held them to her eyes, and bent still closer to the outspread page, in order, as it seemed, to avoid touching it. The light of the lamp fell directly on her old face, and Charlotte reflected what depths of the unknown may lurk under the clearest and most candid lineaments. She had never seen her mother-in-law's features express any but simple and sound emotions – cordiality, amusement, a kindly sympathy; now and again a flash of wholesome anger. Now they seemed to wear a look of fear and hatred, of incredulous dismay and almost cringing defiance. It was as if the spirits warring within her had distorted her face to their own likeness. At length she raised her head. 'I can't – I can't,' she said in a voice of childish distress.

'You can't make it out either?'

She shook her head, and Charlotte saw two tears roll down her cheeks.

'Familiar as the writing is to you?' Charlotte insisted with twitching lips.

Mrs Ashby did not take up the challenge. 'I can make out nothing – nothing.'

'But you do know the writing?'

Mrs Ashby lifted her head timidly; her anxious eyes stole with a glance of apprehension around the quiet familiar room. 'How can I tell? I was startled at first. . . '

'Startled by the resemblance?'

'Well, I thought – '

'You'd better say it out, mother! You knew at once it was *her* writing?'

'Oh, wait, my dear – wait.'

'Wait for what?'

Mrs Ashby looked up; her eyes, travelling slowly past Charlotte, were lifted to the blank wall behind her son's writing table.

Charlotte, following the glance, burst into a shrill laugh of accusation. 'I needn't wait any longer! You've answered me now! You're looking straight at the wall where her picture used to hang!'

Mrs Ashby lifted her hand with a murmur of warning. 'Sh-h.'

'Oh, you needn't imagine that anything can ever frighten me again!' Charlotte cried.

Her mother-in-law still leaned against the table. Her lips moved plaintively. 'But we're going mad – we're both going mad. We both know such things are impossible.'

Her daughter-in-law looked at her with a pitying stare. 'I've known for a long time now that everything was possible.'

'Even this?'

'Yes, exactly this.'

'But this letter – after all, there's nothing in this letter – '

'Perhaps there would be to him. How can I tell? I remember his saying to me once that if you were used to a handwriting the faintest stroke of it became legible. Now I see what he meant. He *was* used to it.'

'But the few strokes that I can make out are so pale. No one could possibly read that letter.'

Charlotte laughed again. 'I suppose everything's pale about a ghost,' she said stridently.

'Oh, my child – my child – don't say it!'

'Why shouldn't I say it, when even the bare walls cry it out?

84

What difference does it make if her letters are illegible to you and me? If even you can see her face on that blank wall, why shouldn't he read her writing on this blank paper? Don't you see that she's everywhere in this house, and the closer to him because to everyone else she's become invisible?' Charlotte dropped into a chair and covered her face with her hands. A turmoil of sobbing shook her from head to foot. At length a touch on her shoulder made her look up, and she saw her mother-in-law bending over her. Mrs Ashby's face seemed to have grown still smaller and more wasted, but it had resumed its usual quiet look. Through all her tossing anguish, Charlotte felt the impact of that resolute spirit.

'Tomorrow – tomorrow. You'll see. There'll be some explanation tomorrow.'

Charlotte cut her short. 'An explanation? Who's going to give it, I wonder?'

Mrs Ashby drew back and straightened herself heroically. 'Kenneth himself will,' she cried out in a strong voice. Charlotte said nothing, and the old woman went on: 'But meanwhile we must act; we must notify the police. Now, without a moment's delay. We must do everything – everything.'

Charlotte stood up slowly and stiffly; her joints felt as cramped as an old woman's. 'Exactly as if we thought it could do any good to do anything?'

Resolutely Mrs Ashby cried: 'Yes!' and Charlotte went up to the telephone and unhooked the receiver.

The Beckoning Fair One

Oliver Onions

'THE BECKONING FAIR ONE'

(GEORGE) OLIVER ONIONS (BRITISH, 1873–1961)

First published in 1911 in the collection *Widdershins*.

Oliver Onions was a fiction writer and a visual artist who trained at the Royal Academy and designed the dust jackets for some of his books' first editions. He is best remembered for his ghost stories, but also wrote a number of morose realistic novels and stories. 'The Beckoning Fair One' can be read as an attentive study of a psychotic breakdown or as a very effective ghost story. It is surely a classic in the literature of writer's block.

THE BECKONING FAIR ONE

Oliver Onions

I

The three or four 'To Let' boards had stood within the low paling as long as the inhabitants of the little triangular 'Square' could remember, and if they had ever been vertical it was a very long time ago. They now overhung the palings each at its own angle, and resembled nothing so much as a row of wooden choppers, ever in the act of falling upon some passer-by, yet never cutting off a tenant for the old house from the stream of his fellows. Not that there was ever any great 'stream' through the square; the stream passed a furlong and more away, beyond the intricacy of tenements and alleys and byways that had sprung up since the old house had been built, hemming it in completely; and probably the house itself was only suffered to stand pending the falling-in of a lease or two, when doubtless a clearance would be made of the whole neighbourhood.

It was of bloomy old red brick, and built into its walls were the crowns and clasped hands and other insignia of insurance companies long since defunct. The children of the secluded square had swung upon the low gate at the end of the entrance-alley until little more than the solid top bar of it remained, and the alley itself ran past boarded basement windows on which tramps had chalked their cryptic marks. The path was washed and worn uneven by the spilling of water from the eaves of the encroaching next house, and cats and dogs had made the approach their own. The chances of a tenant did not seem such as to warrant the keeping of the 'To Let' boards in a state of legibility and repair, and as a matter of fact they were not so kept.

For six months Oleron had passed the old place twice a day or oftener, on his way from his lodgings to the room, ten minutes' walk away, he had taken to work in; and for six months no hatchet-like notice-board had fallen across his path. This might have been due to the fact that he usually took the other side of the square. But he chanced one morning to take the side that ran past the broken gate and the rain-worn entrance-alley, and to pause before one of the inclined boards. The board bore, besides the agent's name, the announcement, written apparently about the time of Oleron's own early youth, that the key was to be had at Number Six.

Now Oleron was already paying, for his separate bedroom and workroom, more than an author who, without private means, habitually disregards his public, can afford; and he was paying in addition a small rent for the storage of the greater part of his grandmother's furniture. Moreover, it invariably happened that the book he wished to read in bed was at his working-quarters half a mile and more away, while the note or letter he had sudden need of during the day was as likely as not to be in the pocket of another coat hanging behind his bedroom door. And there were other inconveniences m having a divided domicile. Therefore Oleron, brought suddenly up by the hatchet-like notice-board, looked first down through some scanty privet-bushes at the boarded basement windows, then up at the blank and grimy windows of the first floor, and so up to the second floor and the flat stone coping of the leads. He stood for a minute thumbing his lean and shaven jaw; then, with another glance at the board, he walked slowly across the square to Number Six.

He knocked, and waited for two or three minutes, but, although the door stood open, received no answer. He was knocking again when a long-nosed man in shirt-sleeves appeared.

'I was arsking a blessing on our food,' he said in severe explanation.

Oleron asked if he might have the key of the old house; and the long-nosed man withdrew again.

Oleron waited for another five minutes on the step; then the man, appearing again and masticating some of the food of which he had spoken, announced that the key was lost.

'But you won't want it,' he said. 'The entrance door isn't closed, and a push'll open any of the others. I'm a agent for it, if you're thinking of taking it –'

Oleron recrossed the square, descended the two steps at the broken gate, passed along the alley, and turned in at the old wide doorway. To the right, immediately within the door, steps descended to the roomy cellars, and the staircase before him had a carved rail, and was broad and handsome and filthy. Oleron ascended it, avoiding contact with the rail and wall, and stopped at the first landing. A door facing him had been boarded up, but he pushed at that on his right hand, and an insecure bolt or staple yielded. He entered the empty first floor.

He spent a quarter of an hour in the place, and then came out again. Without mounting higher, he descended and recrossed the square to the house of the man who had lost the key.

'Can you tell me how much the rent is?' he asked.

The man mentioned a figure, the comparative lowness of which seemed accounted for by the character of the neighbourhood and the abominable state of unrepair of the place.

'Would it be possible to rent a single floor?'

The long-nosed man did not know; they might . . .

'Who are they?'

The man gave Oleron the name of a firm of lawyers in Lincoln's Inn.

'You might mention my name – Barrett,' he added.

Pressure of work prevented Oleron from going down to Lincoln's Inn that afternoon, but he went on the morrow, and was instantly offered the whole house as a purchase for fifty pounds down, the remainder of the purchase-money to remain on mortgage. It took him half an hour to disabuse the lawyer's mind of the idea that he wished anything more of the place than to rent a single floor of it. This made certain hums and haws of a difference, and the lawyer was by no means certain that it lay within his power to do as Oleron suggested; but it was finally extracted from him that, provided the notice-boards were allowed to remain up, and that, provided it was agreed that in the event of the whole house letting, the arrangement should terminate automatically without further notice, something might be done. That the old place should suddenly let over his head seemed to Oleron the slightest of risks to take, and he promised a decision within a week. On the morrow he visited the house again, went through it from top to bottom, and then went home to his lodgings to take a bath.

He was immensely taken with that portion of the house he had already determined should be his own. Scraped clean and repainted, and with that old furniture of Oleron's grandmother's, it ought to be entirely charming. He went to the storage ware-house to refresh his memory of his half-forgotten belongings, and to take measurements; and thence he went to a decorator's. He was very busy with his regular work, and could have wished that the notice-board had caught his attention either a few months earlier or else later in the year; but the quickest way would be to suspend work entirely until after his removal...

A fortnight later his first floor was painted throughout in a tender, elderflower white, the paint was dry, and Oleron was in the middle of his installation. He was animated, delighted; and he rubbed his hands as he polished and made disposals of his grandmother's effects – the tall lattice-paned china cupboard with its Derby and Mason and Spode, the large folding Sheraton table, the long, low bookshelves (he had had two of them 'copied'), the chairs, the Sheffield candlesticks, the riveted rose-bowls. These things he set against his newly painted elder-white walls – walls of wood panelled in the happiest proportions, and moulded and coffered to the low-seated window-recesses in a mood of gaiety and rest that the builders of rooms no longer know. The ceilings were lofty, and faintly painted with an old pattern of stars; even the tapering mouldings of his iron fireplace were as delicately designed as jewellery; and Oleron walked about rubbing his hands, frequently stopping for the mere pleasure of the glimpses from white room to white room...

'Charming, charming!' he said to himself. 'I wonder what Elsie Bengough will think of this!'

He bought a bolt and a Yale lock for his door, and shut off his quarters from the rest of the house. If he now wanted to read in bed, his book could be had for stepping into the next room. All the time, he thought how exceedingly lucky he was to get the place. He put up a hat-rack in the little square hall, and hung up his hats and caps and coats; and passers through the small trian-gular square late at night, looking up over the little serried row of wooden 'To Let' hatchets, could see the light within Oleron's red blinds, or else the sudden darkening of one blind and the illumina-tion of another, as Oleron, candlestick in hand, passed from room to room, making final settlings of his furniture, or preparing to resume the work that his removal had interrupted.

2

As far as the chief business of his life – his writing – was con-cerned, Paul Oleron treated the world a good deal better than he was treated by it; but he seldom took the trouble to strike a balance, or to compute how far, at forty-four years of age, he was behind his points on the handicap. To have done so wouldn't have altered matters, and it might have depressed Oleron. He had chosen his path, and was committed to it beyond possibility of withdrawal. Perhaps he had chosen it in the days when he had been easily swayed by something a little disinterested, a little generous, a little noble; and had he ever thought of questioning himself he would still have held to it that a life without nobility and generosity and disinterestedness was no life for him. Only quite recently, and rarely, had he even vaguely suspected that there was more in it than this; but it was no good anticipating the day when, he supposed, he would reach that maximum point of his powers beyond which he must inevitably decline, and be left face to face with the question whether it would not have profited him better to have ruled his life by less exigent ideals.

In the meantime, his removal into the old house with the insurance marks built into its brick merely interrupted *Romilly Bishop* at the fifteenth chapter.

As this tall man with the lean, ascetic face moved about his new abode, arranging, changing, altering, hardly yet into his working-stride again, he gave the impression of almost spinster-like precision and nicety. For twenty years past, in a score of lodgings, garrets, flats, and rooms furnished and unfurnished, he had been accustomed to do many things for himself, and he had discovered that it saves time and temper to be methodical. He had arranged with the wife of the long-nosed Barrett, a stout Welsh woman with a falsetto voice, the Merionethshire accent of which long residence in London had not perceptibly modified, to come across the square each morning to prepare his breakfast, and also to 'turn the place out' on Saturday mornings; and for the rest, he even welcomed a little housework as a relaxation from the strain of writing.

His kitchen, together with the adjoining strip of an apartment into which a modern bath had been fitted, overlooked the alley at the side of the house; and at one end of it was a large closet with a door, and a square sliding hatch in the upper part of the door. This had been a powder-closet, and through the hatch the elaborately dressed head had been thrust to receive the click and puff of the powder-pistol. Oleron puzzled a little over this closet; then, as its use occurred to him, he smiled faintly, a little moved, he knew not by what... He would have to put it to a very different purpose from its original one; it would probably have to serve as his larder... It was in this closet that he made a discovery. The back of it was shelved, and, rummaging on an upper shelf that ran deeply into the wall, Oleron found a couple of mushroom-shaped old wooden wig-stands. He did not know how they had come to be there. Doubtless the painters had turned them up somewhere or other, and had put them there. But his five rooms, as a whole, were short of cupboard and closet-room; and it was only by the exercise of some ingenuity that he was able to find places for the bestowal of his household linen, his boxes, and his seldom-used but not-to-be-destroyed accumulations of papers.

It was in early spring that Oleron entered on his tenancy, and he was anxious to have *Romilly* ready for publication in the coming autumn. Nevertheless, he did not intend to force its production. Should it demand longer in the doing, so much the worse; he realised its importance, its crucial importance, in his artistic development, and it must have its own length and time. In the workroom he had recently left he had been making excellent progress; *Romilly* had begun, as the saying is, to speak and act of herself; and he did not doubt she would continue to do so the moment the distraction of his removal was over. This distraction was almost over; he told himself it was time he pulled himself together again; and on a March morning he went out, returned again with two great bunches of yellow daffodils, placed one bunch on his mantelpiece between the Sheffield sticks and the other on the table before him, and took out the half-completed manuscript of *Romilly Bishop*.

But before beginning work he went to a small rosewood cabinet and took from a drawer his cheque-book and pass-book. He totted them up, and his monk-like face grew thoughtful. His installation had cost him more than he had intended it should, and his balance was rather less than fifty pounds, with no immediate prospect of more.

'Hm! I'd forgotten rugs and chintz curtains and so forth mounted up so,' said Oleron. 'But it would have been a pity to spoil the place for the want of ten pounds or so... Well, *Romilly* simply *must* be out for the autumn, that's all. So here goes –'

He drew his papers towards him.

But he worked badly; or, rather, he did not work at all. The square outside had its own noises, frequent and new, and Oleron could only hope that he would speedily become accustomed to these. First came hawkers, with their carts and cries; at midday the children, returning from school, trooped into the square and swung on Oleron's gate; and when the children had departed again for afternoon school, an itinerant musician with a mandolin posted himself beneath Oleron's window and began to strum. This was a not unpleasant distraction, and Oleron, pushing up his window, threw the man a penny. Then he returned to his table again...

But it was no good. He came to himself, at long intervals, to find that he had been looking about his room and wondering how it had formerly been furnished – whether a settee in buttercup or petunia satin had stood under the farther window, whether from the centre moulding of the light lofty ceiling had depended a glimmering crystal chandelier, or where the tambour-frame or the picquet-table had stood...No, it was no good; he had far better be frankly doing nothing than getting fruitlessly tired; and he decided that he would take a walk, but, chancing to sit down for a moment, dozed in his chair instead.

'This won't do,' he yawned when he awoke at half-past four in the afternoon; 'I must do better than this tomorrow –'

And he felt so deliciously lazy that for some minutes he even contemplated the breach of an appointment he had for the evening.

The next morning he sat down to work without even permitting himself to answer one of his three letters – two of them tradesmen's accounts, the third a note from Miss Bengough, forwarded from his old address. It was a jolly day of white and blue, with a gay noisy wind and a subtle turn in the colour of growing things; and over and over again, once or twice a minute, his room became suddenly light and then subdued again, as the shining white clouds rolled north-eastwards over the square. The soft fitful illumination was reflected in the polished surface of the table and even in the footworn old floor; and the morning noises had begun again.

Oleron made a pattern of dots on the paper before him, and then broke off to move the jar of daffodils exactly opposite the centre of a creamy panel. Then he wrote a sentence that ran continuously for a couple of lines, after which it broke on into notes and jottings. For a time he succeeded in persuading himself that in making these memoranda he was really working; then he rose and began to pace his room. As he did so, he was struck by an idea. It was that the place might possibly be a little better for more positive colour. It was, perhaps, a thought *too* pale – mild and sweet as a kind old face, but a little devitalised, even wan... Yes, decidedly it would bear a robuster note – more and richer flowers, and possibly some warm and gay stuff for cushions for the window-seats...

'Of course, I really can't afford it,' he muttered, as he went for a two-foot and began to measure the width of the window recesses...

In stooping to measure a recess, his attitude suddenly changed to one of interest and attention. Presently he rose again, rubbing his hands with gentle glee.

'Oho, oho!' he said. 'These look to me very much like

window-boxes, nailed up. We must look into this! Yes, those are boxes, or I'm...oho, this is an adventure!'

On that wall of his sitting-room there were two windows (the third was in another corner), and, beyond the open bedroom door, on the same wall, was another. The seats of all had been painted, repainted, and painted again; and Oleron's investigating finger had barely detected the old nailheads beneath the paint. Under the ledge over which he stooped an old keyhole also had been puttied up. Oleron took out his penknife.

He worked carefully for five minutes, and then went into the kitchen for a hammer and chisel. Driving the chisel cautiously under the seat, he started the whole lid slightly. Again using the penknife, he cut along the hinged edge and outward along the ends; and then he fetched a wedge and a wooden mallet.

'Now for our little mystery –' he said.

The sound of the mallet on the wedge seemed, in that sweet and pale apartment, somehow a little brutal – nay, even shocking. The panelling rang and rattled and vibrated to the blows like a sounding-board. The whole house seemed to echo; from the roomy cellarage to the garrets above a flock of echoes seemed to awake; and the sound got a little on Oleron's nerves. All at once he paused, fetched a duster, and muffled the mallet...When the edge was sufficiently raised he put his fingers under it and lifted. The paint flaked and starred a little; the rusty old nails squeaked and grunted; and the lid came up, laying open the box beneath. Oleron looked into it. Save for a couple of inches of scurf and mould and old cobwebs it was empty.

'No treasure there,' said Oleron, a little amused that he should have fancied there might have been. '*Romilly* will still have to be out by the autumn. Let's have a look at the others.'

He turned to the second window.

The raising of the two remaining seats occupied him until well into the afternoon. That of the bedroom, like the first, was empty; but from the second seat of his sitting-room he drew out something yielding and folded and furred over an inch thick with dust. He carried the object into the kitchen, and having swept it over a bucket, took a duster to it.

It was some sort of a large bag, of an ancient frieze-like material, and when unfolded it occupied the greater part of the small kitchen floor. In shape it was an irregular, a very irregular, triangle, and it had a couple of wide flaps, with the remains of straps and buckles. The patch that had been uppermost in the folding was of a faded yellowish brown; but the rest of it was of shades of crimson that varied according to the exposure of the parts of it.

'Now whatever can that have been?' Oleron mused as he stood surveying it . . . 'I give it up. Whatever it is, it's settled my work for today, I'm afraid –'

He folded the object up carelessly and thrust it into a corner of the kitchen; then, taking pans and brushes and an old knife, he returned to the sitting-room and began to scrape and to wash and to line with paper his newly discovered receptacles. When he had finished, he put his spare boots and books and papers into them; and he closed the lids again, amused with his little adventure, but also a little anxious for the hour to come when he should settle fairly down to his work again.

3

It piqued Oleron a little that his friend, Miss Bengough, should dismiss with a glance the place he himself had found so singularly winning. Indeed she scarcely lifted her eyes to it. But then she had always been more or less like that – a little indifferent to the graces of life, careless of appearances, and perhaps a shade more herself when she ate biscuits from a paper bag than when she dined with greater observance of the convenances. She was an unattached journalist of thirty-four, large, showy, fair as butter, pink as a dog-rose, reminding one of a florist's picked specimen bloom, and given to sudden and ample movements and moist and explosive utterances. She 'pulled a better living out of the pool' (as she expressed it) than Oleron did; and by cunningly disguised puffs of drapers and haberdashers she 'pulled' also the greater part of her very varied wardrobe. She left small whirlwinds of air behind her when she moved, in which her veils and scarves fluttered and spun.

Oleron heard the flurry of her skirts on his staircase and her single loud knock at his door when he had been a month in his new abode. Her garments brought in the outer air, and she flung a bundle of ladies' journals down on a chair.

'Don't knock off for me,' she said across a mouthful of large-headed hatpins as she removed her hat and veil. 'I didn't know whether you were straight yet, so I've brought some sandwiches for lunch. You've got coffee, I suppose? – No, don't get up – I'll find the kitchen –'

'Oh, that's all right, I'll clear these things away. To tell the truth, I'm rather glad to be interrupted,' said Oleron.

He gathered his work together and put it away. She was already in the kitchen; he heard the running of water into the kettle. He joined her, and ten minutes later followed her back to the sitting-room with the coffee and sandwiches on a tray. They sat down, with the tray on a small table between them.

'Well, what do you think of the new place?' Oleron asked as she poured out coffee.

'Hm!...Anybody'd think you were going to get married, Paul.' He laughed.

'Oh no. But it's an improvement on some of them, isn't it?'

'Is it? I suppose it is; I don't know. I liked the last place, in spite of the black ceiling and no water-tap. How's *Romilly*?'

Oleron thumbed his chin.

'Hm! I'm rather ashamed to tell you. The fact is, I've not got on very well with it. But it will be all right on the night, as you used to say.'

'Stuck?'

'Rather stuck.'

'Got any of it you care to read to me?...'

Oleron had long been in the habit of reading portions of his work to Miss Bengough occasionally. Her comments were always quick and practical, sometimes directly useful, sometimes indirectly suggestive. She, in return for his confidence, always kept all mention of her own work sedulously from him. His, she said, was 'real work'; hers merely filled space, not always even grammatically.

'I'm afraid there isn't,' Oleron replied, still meditatively dry-shaving his chin. Then he added, with a little burst of candour, 'The fact is, Elsie, I've not written – not actually written – very much more of it – *any* more of it, in fact. But, of course, that doesn't mean I haven't progressed. I've progressed, in one sense, rather alarmingly. I'm now thinking of reconstructing the whole thing.'

Miss Bengough gave a gasp. 'Reconstructing!'

'Making Romilly herself a different type of woman. Somehow, I've begun to feel that I'm not getting the most out of her. As she stands, I've certainly lost interest in her to some extent.'

'But – but – ' Miss Bengough protested, 'you had her so real, so *living*, Paul!'

Oleron smiled faintly. He had been quite prepared for Miss Bengough's disapproval. He wasn't surprised that she liked Romilly as she at present existed; she would. Whether she real-ised it or not, there was much of herself in his fictitious creation. Naturally Romilly would seem 'real', 'living', to her . . .

'But are you really serious, Paul?' Miss Bengough asked pres-ently, with a round-eyed stare.

'Quite serious.'

'You're really going to scrap those fifteen chapters?'

'I didn't exactly say that.'

'That fine, rich love-scene?'

'I should only do it reluctantly, and for the sake of something I thought better.'

'And that beautiful, *beautiful* description of Romilly on the shore?'

'It wouldn't necessarily be wasted,' he said a little uneasily.

But Miss Bengough made a large and windy gesture, and then let him have it.

'Really, you are *too* trying!' she broke out. 'I do wish sometimes you'd remember you're human, and live in a world! You know I'd be the *last* to wish you to lower your standard one inch, but it wouldn't be lowering it to bring it within human comprehension. Oh, you're sometimes altogether too godlike!... Why, it would be a wicked, criminal waste of your powers to destroy those fifteen chapters! Look at it reasonably, now. You've been working for nearly twenty years; you've now got what you've been working for almost within your grasp; your affairs are at a most critical stage (oh, don't tell me; I know you're about at the end of your money); and here you are, deliberately proposing to withdraw a thing that will probably make your name, and to substitute for it something that ten to one nobody on earth will ever want to read – and small blame to them! Really, you try my patience!'

Oleron had shaken his head slowly as she had talked. It was an old story between them. The noisy, able, practical journalist was an admirable friend – up to a certain point; beyond that... well, each of us knows that point beyond which we stand alone. Elsie Bengough sometimes said that had she had one-tenth part of Oleron's genius there were few things she could not have done

– thus making that genius a quantitatively divisible thing, a sort of ingredient, to be added to or subtracted from in the admixture of his work. That it was a qualitative thing, essential, indivisible, informing, passed her comprehension. Their spirits parted company at that point. Oleron knew it. She did not appear to know it.

'Yes, yes, yes,' he said a little wearily, by and by, 'practically you're quite right, entirely right, and I haven't a word to say. If I could only turn *Romilly* over to you you'd make an enormous success of her. But that can't be, and I, for my part, am seriously doubting whether she's worth my while. You know what that means.'

'What does it mean?' she demanded bluntly.

'Well,' he said, smiling wanly, 'what *does* it mean when you're convinced a thing isn't worth doing? You simply don't do it.'

Miss Bengough's eyes swept the ceiling for assistance against this impossible man.

'What utter rubbish!' she broke out at last. 'Why, when I saw you last you were simply oozing *Romilly,* you were turning her off at the rate of four chapters a week; if you hadn't moved you'd have had her three-parts done by now. What on earth possessed you to move right in the middle of your most important work?'

Oleron tried to put her off with a recital of inconveniences, but she wouldn't have it. Perhaps in her heart she partly suspected the reason. He was simply mortally weary of the narrow circumstances of his life. He had had twenty years of it – twenty years of garrets and roof-chambers and dingy flats and shabby lodgings, and he was tired of dinginess and shabbiness. The reward was as far off as ever – or if it was not, he no longer cared as once he would have cared to put out his hand and take it. It is all very well to tell a man who is at the point of exhaustion that only another effort is required of him; if he cannot make it he is as far off as ever...

'Anyway,' Oleron summed up, 'I'm happier here than I've been for a long time. That's some sort of a justification.'

'And doing no work,' said Miss Bengough pointedly.

At that a trifling petulance that had been gathering in Oleron came to a head.

'And why should I do nothing but work?' he demanded. 'How much happier am I for it? I don't say I don't love my work – when it's done; but I hate doing it. Sometimes it's an intolerable burden that I simply long to be rid of. Once in many weeks it has a moment, one moment, of glow and thrill for me; I remember the days when it was all glow and thrill; and now I'm forty-four, and it's becoming drudgery. Nobody wants it; I'm ceasing to want it myself; and if any ordinary sensible man were to ask me whether I didn't think I was a fool to go on, I think I should agree that I was.'

Miss Bengough's comely pink face was serious.

'But you knew all that, many, many years ago, Paul – and still you chose it,' she said in a low voice.

'Well, and how should I have known?' he demanded. 'I didn't know. I was told so. My heart, if you like, told me so, and I thought I knew. Youth always thinks it knows; then one day it discovers that it is nearly fifty –'

'Forty-four, Paul –'

'– forty-four, then – and it finds that the glamour isn't in front, but behind. Yes, I knew and chose, if *that's* knowing and choosing...but it's a costly choice we're called on to make when we're young!'

Miss Bengough's eyes were on the floor. Without moving them she said, 'You're not regretting it, Paul?'

Am I not?' he took her up. 'Upon my word, I've lately thought I am! What *do* I get in return for it all?'

'You know what you get,' she replied.

He might have known from her tone what else he could have had for the holding up of a finger – herself. She knew, but could not tell him, that he could have done no better thing for himself. Had he, any time these ten years, asked her to marry him, she would have replied quietly, 'Very well; when?' He had never thought of it...

'Yours is the real work,' she continued quietly. 'Without you we jackals couldn't exist. You and a few like you hold everything upon your shoulders.'

For a minute there was a silence. Then it occurred to Oleron that this was common vulgar grumbling. It was not his habit. Suddenly he rose and began to stack cups and plates on the tray.

'Sorry you catch me like this, Elsie,' he said, with a little laugh...'No, I'll take them out; then we'll go for a walk, if you like...'

He carried out the tray, and then began to show Miss Bengough round his flat. She made few comments. In the kitchen she asked what an old faded square of reddish frieze was, that Mrs Barrett used as a cushion for her wooden chair.

'That? I should be glad if you could tell *me* what it is,' Oleron replied as he unfolded the bag and related the story of its finding in the window-seat.

'I think I know what it is,' said Miss Bengough. 'It's been used to wrap up a harp before putting it into its case.'

'By Jove, that's probably just what it was,' said Oleron. 'I could make neither head nor tail of it . . .'

They finished the tour of the flat, and returned to the sitting-room.

'And who lives in the rest of the house?' Miss Bengough asked.

'I dare say a tramp sleeps in the cellar occasionally. Nobody else.'

'Hm! . . . Well, I'll tell you what I think about it, if you like.'

'I should like.'

'You'll never work here.'

'Oh?' said Oleron quickly. 'Why not?'

'You'll never finish *Romilly* here. Why, I don't know, but you won't. I know it. You'll have to leave before you get on with that book.'

He mused for a moment, and then said:

'Isn't that a little – prejudiced, Elsie?'

'Perfectly ridiculous. As an argument it hasn't a leg to stand on. But there it is,' she replied, her mouth once more full of the large-headed hat pins.

Oleron was reaching down his hat and coat. He laughed.

'I can only hope you're entirely wrong,' he said, 'for I shall be in a serious mess if *Romilly* isn't out in the autumn.'

4

As Oleron sat by his fire that evening, pondering Miss Bengough's prognostication that difficulties awaited him in his work, he came to the conclusion that it would have been far better had she kept her beliefs to herself. No man does a thing better for having his confidence damped at the outset, and to speak of difficulties is in a sense to make them. Speech itself becomes a deterrent act, to which other discouragements accrete until the very event of which warning is given is as likely as not to come to pass. He heartily confounded her. An influence hostile to the completion of *Romilly* had been born.

And in some illogical, dogmatic way women seem to have, she had attached this antagonistic influence to his new abode. Was ever anything so absurd! 'You'll never finish *Romilly* here.'... Why not? Was this her idea of the luxury that saps the springs of action and brings a man down to indolence and dropping out of the race? The place was well enough – it was entirely charming, for that matter – but it was not so demoralising as all that! No; Elsie had missed the mark that time...

He moved his chair to look round the room that smiled, positively smiled, in the firelight. He too smiled, as if pity was to be entertained for a maligned apartment. Even that slight lack of robust colour he had remarked was not noticeable in the soft glow. The drawn chintz curtains – they had a flowered and trellised pattern, with baskets and oaten pipes – fell in long quiet folds to the window-seats; the rows of bindings in old bookcases took the light richly; the last trace of sallowness had gone with the

daylight; and, if the truth must be told, it had been Elsie herself
who had seemed a little out of the picture.

That reflection struck him a little, and presently he returned
to it. Yes, the room had, quite accidentally, done Miss Bengough
a disservice that afternoon. It had, in some subtle but unmistakable way, placed her, marked a contrast of qualities. Assuming for
the sake of argument the slightly ridiculous proposition that the
room in which Oleron sat *was* characterised by a certain sparsity
and lack of vigour; so much the worse for Miss Bengough; she
certainly erred on the side of redundancy and general muchness.
And if one must contrast abstract qualities, Oleron inclined to the
austere in taste . . .

Yes, here Oleron had made a distinct discovery; he wondered
he had not made it before. He pictured Miss Bengough again as
she had appeared that afternoon – large, showy, moistly pink, with
that quality of the prize bloom exuding, as it were, from her; and
instantly she suffered in his thought. He even recognised now that
he had noticed something odd at the time, and that unconsciously
his attitude, even while she had been there, had been one of criticism. The mechanism of her was a little obvious; her melting
humidity was the result of analysable processes; and behind her
there had seemed to lurk some dim shape emblematic of mortal-
ity. He had never, during the ten years of their intimacy, dreamed
for a moment of asking her to marry him; none the less, he now
felt for the first time a thankfulness that he had not done so . . .

Then, suddenly and swiftly, his face flamed that he should be
thinking thus of his friend. What! Elsie Bengough, with whom he

had spent weeks and weeks of afternoons – she, the good chum, on whose help he would have counted had all the rest of the world failed him – she, whose loyalty to him would not, he knew, swerve as long as there was breath in her – Elsie to be even in thought dissected thus! He was an ingrate and a cad...

Had she been there in that moment he would have abased himself before her.

For ten minutes and more he sat, still gazing into the fire, with that humiliating red fading slowly from his cheeks. All was still within and without, save for a tiny musical tinkling that came from his kitchen – the dripping of water from an imperfectly turned-off tap into the vessel beneath it. Mechanically he began to beat with his finger to the faintly heard falling of the drops; the tiny regular movement seemed to hasten that shameful withdrawal from his face. He grew cool once more; and when he resumed his meditation he was all unconscious that he took it up again at the same point...

It was not only her florid superfluity of build that he had approached in the attitude of criticism; he was conscious also of the wide differences between her mind and his own. He felt no thankfulness that up to a certain point their natures had ever run companionably side by side; he was now full of questions beyond that point. Their intellects diverged; there was no denying it; and, looking back, he was inclined to doubt whether there had been any real coincidence. True, he had read his writings to her and she had appeared to speak comprehendingly and to the point; but what can a man do who, having assumed that another sees as he does, is suddenly brought up sharp by something that falsifies and discredits all that has gone before? He doubted all now...It did for a moment occur to him that the man who demands of a friend more than can be given to him is in danger of losing that friend, but he put the thought aside.

Again he ceased to think, and again moved his finger to the distant dripping of the tap...

And now (he resumed by and by), if these things were true of Elsie Bengough, they were also true of the creation of which she was the prototype – Romilly Bishop. And since he could say of Romilly what for very shame he could not say of Elsie, he gave his thoughts rein. He did so in that smiling, fire-lighted room, to the accompaniment of the faintly heard tap.

There was no longer any doubt about it; he hated the central character of his novel. Even as he had described her physically she overpowered the senses; she was coarse-fibred, over-coloured, rank. It became true the moment he formulated his thought; Gulliver had described the Brobdingnagian maids-of-honour thus: and mentally and spiritually she corresponded – was unsensitive, limited, common. The model (he closed his eyes for a moment) – the model stuck out through fifteen vulgar and blatant chapters to such a pitch that, without seeing the reason, he had been unable to begin the sixteenth. He marvelled that it had only just dawned upon him.

And *this* was to have been his Beatrice, his vision! As Elsie she was to have gone into the furnace of his art, and she was to have come out the Woman all men desire! Her thoughts were to have been culled

from his own finest, her form from his dearest dreams, and her setting wherever he could find one fit for her worth. He had brooded
long before making the attempt; then one day he had felt her stir
within him as a mother feels a quickening, and he had begun to write;
and so he had added chapter to chapter...

And those fifteen sodden chapters were what he had produced!

Again he sat, softly moving his finger...

Then he bestirred himself.

She must go, all fifteen chapters of her. That was settled. For
what was to take her place his mind was a blank; but one thing at a
time; a man is not excused from taking the wrong course because
the right one is not immediately revealed to him. Better would
come if it was to come; in the meantime –

He rose, fetched the fifteen chapters, and read them over
before he should drop them into the fire.

But instead of putting them into the fire he let them fall from
his hand. He became conscious of the dripping of the tap again. It
had a tinkling gamut of four or five notes, on which it rang irregular changes, and it was foolishly sweet and dulcimer-like. In his
mind Oleron could see the gathering of each drop, its little tremble on the lip of the tap, and the tiny percussion of its fall, 'Plink
– plunk', minimised almost to inaudibility. Following the lowest
note there seemed to be a brief phrase, irregularly repeated; and
presently Oleron found himself waiting for the recurrence of this
phrase. It was quite pretty...

But it did not conduce to wakefulness, and Oleron dozed over
his fire.

When he awoke again the fire had burned low and the flames of the candles were licking the rims of the Sheffield sticks. Sluggishly he rose, yawned, went his nightly round of door-locks and window-fastenings, and passed into his bedroom. Soon he slept soundly.

But a curious little sequel followed on the morrow. Mrs Barrett usually tapped, not at his door, but at the wooden wall beyond which lay Oleron's bed; and then Oleron rose, put on his dressing-gown, and admitted her. He was not conscious that as he did so that morning he hummed an air; but Mrs Barrett lingered with her hand on the door-knob and her face a little averted and smiling.

'De-ar me!' her soft falsetto rose. 'But that will be a very o-ald tune, Mr Oleron! I will not have heard it this forty years!'

'What tune?' Oleron asked.

'The tune, indeed, that you was humming, sir.'

Oleron had his thumb in the flap of a letter. It remained there.

'I was humming? . . . Sing it, Mrs Barrett.'

Mrs Barrett prut-prutted.

'I have no voice for singing, Mr Oleron; it was Ann Pugh was the singer of our family; but the tune will be very o-ald, and it is called "The Beckoning Fair One".'

'Try to sing it,' said Oleron, his thumb still in the envelope; and Mrs Barrett, with much dimpling and confusion, hummed the air.

'They do say it was sung to a harp, Mr Oleron, and it will be very o-ald,' she concluded.

'And I was singing that?'

'Indeed you wass. I would not be likely to tell you lies.'

With a 'Very well – let me have breakfast', Oleron opened his letter; but the trifling circumstance struck him as more odd than he would have admitted to himself. The phrase he had hummed had been that which he had associated with the falling from the tap on the evening before.

5

Even more curious than that the commonplace dripping of an ordinary water-tap should have tallied so closely with an actually existing air was another result it had, namely, that it awakened, or seemed to awaken, in Oleron an abnormal sensitiveness to other noises of the old house. It has been remarked that silence obtains its fullest and most impressive quality when it is broken by some minute sound; and, truth to tell, the place was never still. Perhaps the mildness of the spring air operated on its torpid old timbers; perhaps Oleron's fires caused it to stretch its old anatomy; and certainly a whole world of insect life bored and burrowed in its baulks and joists. At any rate, Oleron had only to sit quiet in his chair and to wait for a minute or two in order to become aware of such a change in the auditory scale as comes upon a man who, conceiving the midsummer woods to be motionless and still, all at once finds his ear sharpened to the crepitation of a myriad insects.

And he smiled to think of man's arbitrary distinction between that which has life and that which has not. Here, quite apart from such recognisable sounds as the scampering of mice, the falling of plaster behind his panelling, and the popping of purses or coffins from his fire, was a whole house talking to him had he but known its language. Beams settled with a tired sigh into their old mortices; creatures ticked in the walls; joints cracked, boards complained; with no palpable stirring of the air window-sashes changed their positions with a soft knock in their frames. And whether the place had life in this sense or not, it had at all events a winsome personality. It needed but an hour of musing for Oleron to conceive the idea that, as his own body stood in friendly relation to his soul, so, by an extension and an attenuation, his habitation might fantastically be supposed to stand in some relation to him-self. He even amused himself with the far-fetched fancy that he might so identify himself with the place that some future tenant, taking possession, might regard it as in a sense haunted. It would be rather a joke if he, a perfectly harmless author, with nothing on his mind worse than a novel he had discovered he must begin again, should turn out to be laying the foundation of a future ghost! . . .

In proportion, however, as he felt this growing attachment to the fabric of his abode, Elsie Bengough, from being merely unat-tracted, began to show a dislike of the place that was more and more marked. And she did not scruple to speak of her aversion.

'It doesn't belong to today at all, and for you especially it's bad,' she said with decision. 'You're only too ready to let go your hold on actual things and to slip into apathy; *you* ought to be in a place with concrete floors and a patent gas-meter and a tradesmen's lift. And it would do you all the good in the world if you had a job that made you scramble and rub elbows with your fellow-men. Now, if I could get you a job, for, say, two or three days a week, one that would allow you heaps of time for your proper work – would you take it?'

Somehow, Oleron resented a little being diagnosed like this. He thanked Miss Bengough, but without a smile.

'Thank you, but I don't think so. After all each of us has his own life to live,' he could not refrain from adding.

'His own life to live!...How long is it since you were out, Paul?'

'About two hours.'

'I don't mean to buy stamps or to post a letter. How long is it since you had anything like a stretch?'

'Oh, some little time perhaps. I don't know.'

'Since I was here last?'

'I haven't been out much.'

'And has *Romilly* progressed much better for your being cooped up?'

'I think she has. I'm laying the foundations of her. I shall begin the actual writing presently.'

It seemed as if Miss Bengough had forgotten their tussle about the first *Romilly*. She frowned, turned half away, and then quickly turned again.

'Ah!...So you've still got that ridiculous idea in your head?'

'If you mean,' said Oleron slowly, 'that I've discarded the old *Romilly*, and am at work on a new one, you're right. I have still got that idea in my head.'

Something uncordial in his tone struck her; but she was a

fighter. His own absurd sensitiveness hardened her. She gave a 'Pshaw!' of impatience.

'Where is the old one?' she demanded abruptly.

'Why?' asked Oleron.

'I want to see it. I want to show some of it to you. I want, if you're not wool-gathering entirely, to bring you back to your senses.'

This time it was he who turned his back. But when he turned round again he spoke more gently.

'It's no good, Elsie. I'm responsible for the way I go, and you must allow me to go it – even if it should seem wrong to you. Believe me, I am giving thought to it... The manuscript? I was on the point of burning it, but I didn't. It's in that window-seat, if you must see it.'

Miss Bengough crossed quickly to the window-seat, and lifted the lid. Suddenly she gave a little exclamation, and put the back of her hand to her mouth. She spoke over her shoulder.

'You ought to knock those nails in, Paul,' she said.

He strode to her side.

'What? What is it? What's the matter?' he asked. 'I did knock them in – or, rather, pulled them out.'

'You left enough to scratch with,' she replied, showing her hand. From the upper wrist to the knuckle of the little finger a welling red wound showed.

'Good – gracious!' Oleron ejaculated... 'Here, come to the bathroom and bathe it quickly –'

He hurried her to the bathroom, turned on warm water, and

bathed and cleansed the bad gash. Then, still holding the hand, he turned cold water on it, uttering broken phrases of astonishment and concern.

'Good Lord, how did that happen! As far as I knew I'd...is this water too cold? Does that hurt? I can't imagine how on earth ...there; that'll do –'

'No – one moment longer – I can bear it,' she murmured, her eyes closed...

Presently he led her back to the sitting-room and bound the hand in one of his handkerchiefs; but his face did not lose its expression of perplexity. He had spent half a day in opening and making serviceable the three window-boxes, and he could not conceive how he had come to leave an inch and a half of rusty nail standing in the wood. He himself had opened the lids of each of them a dozen times and had not noticed any nail; but there it was...

'It shall come out now, at all events,' he muttered, as he went for a pair of pincers. And he made no mistake about it that time.

Elsie Bengough had sunk into a chair, and her face was rather white; but in her hand was the manuscript of *Romilly*. She had not finished with *Romilly* yet. Presently she returned to the charge.

'Oh, Paul, it will be the greatest mistake you ever, ever made if you do not publish this!' she said.

He hung his head, genuinely distressed. He couldn't get that incident of the nail out of his head, and *Romilly* occupied a second place in his thoughts for the moment. But still she insisted; and when presently he spoke it was almost as if he asked her pardon for something.

120

'What can I say, Elsie? I can only hope that when you see the new version, you'll see how right I am. And if in spite of all you *don't* like her, well...' he made a hopeless gesture. 'Don't you see that I *must* be guided by my own lights?'

She was silent.

'Come, Elsie,' he said gently. 'We've got along well so far; don't let us split on this.'

The last words had hardly passed his lips before he regretted them. She had been nursing her injured hand, with her eyes once more closed; but her lips and lids quivered simultaneously. Her voice shook as she spoke.

'I can't help saying it, Paul, but you are so greatly changed.'

'Hush, Elsie,' he murmured soothingly; 'you've had a shock; rest for a while. How could I change?'

'I don't know, but you are. You've not been yourself ever since you came here. I wish you'd never seen the place. It's stopped your work, it's making you into a person I hardly know, and it's made me horribly anxious about you...Oh, how my hand is beginning to throb!'

'Poor child!' he murmured. 'Will you let me take you to a doctor and have it properly dressed?'

'No – I shall be all right presently – I'll keep it raised –'

She put her elbow on the back of her chair, and the bandaged hand rested lightly on his shoulder.

At that touch an entirely new anxiety stirred suddenly within him. Hundreds of times previously, on their jaunts and excursions, she had slipped her hand within his arm as she might have slipped it into the arm of a brother, and he had accepted the little affectionate gesture as a brother might have accepted it. But now, for the first time, there rushed into his mind a hundred startling questions. Her eyes were still closed, and her head had fallen pathetically back; and there was a lost and ineffable smile on her parted lips. The truth broke in upon him. Good God!...And he had never divined it!

And stranger than all was that, now that he did see that she was lost in love of him, there came to him, not sorrow and humility and abasement, but something else that he struggled in vain against – something entirely strange and new, that, had he analysed it, he would have found to be petulance and irritation and resentment and ungentleness. The sudden selfish prompting mastered him before he was aware. He all but gave it words. What was she doing there at all? Why was she not getting on with her own work? Why was she here interfering with his? Who had given her this guardianship over him that lately she had put forward so assertively? – 'Changed?' It was she, not himself, who had changed...

But by the time she had opened her eyes again he had overcome his resentment sufficiently to speak gently, albeit with reserve.

'I wish you would let me take you to a doctor.'

She rose.

'No, thank you, Paul,' she said. 'I'll go now. If I need a dressing I'll get one; take the other hand, please. Goodbye – '

He did not attempt to detain her. He walked with her to the foot of the stairs. Half-way along the narrow alley she turned.

'It would be a long way to come if you happened not to be in,' she said; 'I'll send you a postcard the next time.'

At the gate she turned again.

'Leave here, Paul,' she said, with a mournful look. 'Everything's wrong with this house.'

Then she was gone.

Oleron returned to his room. He crossed straight to the window-box. He opened the lid and stood long looking at it. Then he closed it again and turned away.

'That's rather frightening,' he muttered. 'It's simply not possible that I should not have removed that nail . . .'

6

Oleron knew very well what Elsie had meant when she had said that her next visit would be preceded by a postcard. She, too, had realised that at last, at last he knew – knew, and didn't want her. It gave him a miserable, pitiful pang, therefore, when she came again within a week, knocking at the door unannounced. She spoke from the landing; she did not intend to stay, she said; and he had to press her before she would so much as enter.

Her excuse for calling was that she had heard of an enquiry for short stories that he might be wise to follow up. He thanked her. Then, her business over, she seemed anxious to get away again. Oleron did not seek to detain her; even he saw through the pretext of the stories; and he accompanied her down the stairs.

But Elsie Bengough had no luck whatever in that house. A second accident befell her. Half-way down the staircase there was the sharp sound of splintering wood, and she checked a loud cry. Oleron knew the woodwork to be old, but he himself had ascended and descended frequently enough without mishap . . .

Elsie had put her foot through one of the stairs.

He sprang to her side in alarm. 'Oh, I say! My poor girl!'

She laughed hysterically.

'It's my weight – I know I'm getting fat – '

'Keep still – let me clear these splinters away,' he muttered between his teeth.

She continued to laugh and sob that it was her weight – she was getting fat –

He thrust downwards at the broken boards. The extrication was no easy matter, and her torn boot showed him how badly the foot and ankle within it must be abraded.

'Good God – good God!' he muttered over and over again.

'I shall be too heavy for anything soon,' she sobbed and laughed.

But she refused to reascend and to examine her hurt.

'No, let me go quickly – let me go quickly,' she repeated.

'But it's a frightful gash!'

'No – not so bad – let me get away quickly – I'm – I'm not wanted.'

At her words, that she was not wanted, his head dropped as if she had given him a buffet.

'Elsie!' he choked, brokenly and shocked.

But she too made a quick gesture, as if she put something violently aside.

'Oh, Paul, not *that* – not *you* – of course I do mean that too in a sense – oh, you know what I mean!...But if the other can't be, spare me this now! I – I wouldn't have come, but – but – oh, I did, I *did* try to keep away!'

It was intolerable, heartbreaking; but what could he do – what could he say? He did not love her...

'Let me go – I'm not wanted – let me take away what's left of me –'

'Dear Elsie – you are very dear to me –'

But again she made the gesture, as of putting something violently aside.

'No, not that – not anything less – don't offer me anything less – leave me a little pride –'

'Let me get my hat and coat – let me take you to a doctor,' he muttered.

But she refused. She refused even the support of his arm. She gave another unsteady laugh.

'I'm sorry I broke your stairs, Paul...You will go and see about the short stories, won't you?'

He groaned.

'Then if you won't see a doctor, will you go across the square and let Mrs Barrett look at you? Look, there's Barrett passing now –'

The long-nosed Barrett was looking curiously down the alley, but as Oleron was about to call him he made off without a word. Elsie seemed anxious for nothing so much as to be clear of the place, and finally promised to go straight to a doctor, but insisted on going alone.

'Goodbye,' she said.

And Oleron watched her until she was past the hatchet-like 'To Let' boards, as if he feared that even they might fall upon her and maim her.

That night Oleron did not dine. He had far too much on his mind. He walked from room to room of his flat, as if he could have walked away from Elsie Bengough's haunting cry that still rang in his ears. 'I'm not wanted – don't offer me anything less – let me take away what's left of me – '

Oh, if he could only have persuaded himself that he loved her!

He walked until twilight fell, then, without lighting candles, he stirred up the fire and flung himself into a chair.

Poor, poor Elsie!...

But even while his heart ached for her, it was out of the question. If only he had known! If only he had used common observation! But those walks, those sisterly takings of the arm – what a fool he had been!...Well, it was too late now. It was she, not he, who must now act – act by keeping away. He would help her all he could. He himself would not sit in her presence. If she came, he would hurry her out again as fast as he could...Poor, poor Elsie!

His room grew dark; the fire burned dead; and he continued to sit, wincing from time to time as a fresh tortured phrase rang again in his ears.

Then suddenly, he knew not why, he found himself anxious for her in a new sense – uneasy about her personal safety. A horrible fancy that even then she might be looking over an embankment down into dark water, that she might even now be glancing up at the hook on the door, took him. Women had been known to do those things... Then there would be an inquest, and he himself would be called upon to identify her, and would be asked how she had come by an ill-healed wound on the hand and a bad abrasion of the ankle. Barrett would say that he had seen her leaving his house...

Then he recognised that his thoughts were morbid. By an effort of will he put them aside, and sat for a while listening to the faint creakings and tickings and rappings within his panelling... If only he could have married her!... But he couldn't. Her face had risen before him again as he had seen it on the stairs, drawn with pain and ugly and swollen with tears. Ugly – yes, positively blubbered; if tears were women's weapons, as they were said to be, such tears were weapons turned against themselves... suicide again...

Then all at once he found himself attentively considering her two accidents.

Extraordinary they had been, both of them. He *could not* have left that old nail standing in the wood; why, he had fetched tools specially from the kitchen; and he was convinced that that step that had broken beneath her weight had been as sound as the others. It was inexplicable. If these things could happen, anything could happen. There was not a beam nor a jamb in the place that might not fall without warning, not a plank that might not crash inwards, not a nail that might not become a dagger. The whole place was full of life even now; as he sat there in the dark he heard its crowds of noises as if the house had been one great microphone...

Only half conscious that he did so, he had been sitting for some time identifying these noises, attributing to each crack or creak or knock its material cause; but there was one noise which, again not fully conscious of the omission, he had not sought to account for. It had last come some minutes ago; it came again now – a sort of soft sweeping rustle that seemed to hold an almost inaudibly minute crackling. For half a minute or so it had Oleron's attention; then his heavy thoughts were of Elsie Bengough again.

He was nearer to loving her in that moment than he had ever been. He thought how to some men their loved ones were but the dearer for those poor mortal blemishes that tell us we are but sojourners on earth, with a common fate not far distant that makes it hardly worth while to do anything but love for the time remaining. Strangling sobs, blearing tears, bodies buffeted by sickness, hearts and mind callous and hard with the rubs of the world – how little love there would be were these things a barrier to love! In that sense he did love Elsie Bengough. What her happiness had never moved in him her sorrow almost awoke...

Suddenly his meditation went. His ear had once more become conscious of that soft and repeated noise – the long sweep with the almost inaudible crackle in it. Again and again it came, with a curious insistence and urgency. It quickened a little as he became increasingly attentive... it seemed to Oleron that it grew louder...

All at once he started bolt upright in his chair, tense and

listening. The silky rustle came again; he was trying to attach it to something...

The next moment he had leapt to his feet, unnerved and terrified. His chair hung poised for a moment, and then went over, setting the fire-irons clattering as it fell. There was only one noise in the world like that which had caused him to spring thus to his feet...

The next time it came Oleron felt behind him at the empty air with his hand, and backed slowly until he found himself against the wall.

'God in Heaven!' The ejaculation broke from Oleron's lips. The sound had ceased.

The next moment he had given a high cry.

'What is it? What's there? *Who's* there?'

A sound of scuttling caused his knees to bend under him for a moment; but that, he knew, was a mouse. That was not something that his stomach turned sick and his mind reeled to entertain. That other sound, the like of which was not in the world, had now entirely ceased; and again he called...

He called and continued to call; and then another terror, a terror of the sound of his own voice, seized him. He did not dare to call again. His shaking hand went to his pocket for a match, but found none. He thought there might be matches on the mantelpiece –

He worked his way to the mantelpiece round a little recess, without for a moment leaving the wall. Then his hand encountered the mantelpiece, and groped along it. A box of matches fell to the hearth. He could just see them in the firelight, but his hand could not pick them up until he had cornered them inside the fender.

Then he rose and struck a light.

The room was as usual. He struck a second match. A candle stood on the table. He lighted it, and the flame sank for a moment and then burned up clear. Again he looked round.

There was nothing.

There was nothing; but there had been something, and might still be something. Formerly, Oleron had smiled at the fantastic thought that, by a merging and interplay of identities between himself and his beautiful room, he might be preparing a ghost for the future; it had not occurred to him *that there might have been a similar merging and coalescence in the past.* Yet with this staggering impossibility he was now face to face. Something did persist in the house; it had a tenant other than himself; and that tenant, whatsoever or whosoever, had appalled Oleron's soul by producing the sound of a woman brushing her hair.

7

Without quite knowing how he came to be there Oleron found himself striding over the loose board he had temporarily placed on the step broken by Miss Bengough. He was hatless, and descending the stairs. Not until later did there return to him a hazy memory that he had left the candle burning on the table, had opened the door no wider than was necessary to allow the passage of his body, and had sidled out, closing the door softly behind him. At the foot of the stairs another shock awaited him. Something dashed with a flurry up from the disused cellars and disappeared out of the door. It was only a cat, but Oleron gave a childish sob.

He passed out of the gate, and stood for a moment under the 'To Let' boards, plucking foolishly at his lip and looking up at the glimmer of light behind one of his red blinds. Then, still looking over his shoulder, he moved stumblingly up the square. There was a small public-house round the corner; Oleron had never entered it; but he entered it now, and put down a shilling that missed the counter by inches.

'B-b-bran-brandy,' he said, and then stooped to look for the shilling.

He had the little sawdusted bar to himself; what company there was – carters and labourers and the small tradesmen of the neighbourhood – was gathered in the farther compartment, beyond the space where the white-haired landlady moved among her taps and bottles. Oleron sat down on a hardwood settee with a perforated seat, drank half his brandy, and then, thinking he might as well drink it as spill it, finished it.

Then he fell to wondering which of the men whose voices he heard across the public-house would undertake the removal of his effects on the morrow.

In the meantime he ordered more brandy.

For he did not intend to go back to that room where he had left the candle burning. Oh no! He couldn't have faced even the entry and the staircase with the broken step – certainly not that pith-white, fascinating room. He would go back for the present to his old arrangement, of workroom and separate sleeping-quarters;

he would go to his old landlady at once – presently – when he had finished his brandy – and see if she could put him up for the night. His glass was empty now...

He rose, had it refilled, and sat down again.

And if anybody asked his reason for removing again? Oh, he had reason enough – reason enough! Nails that put themselves back into wood again and gashed people's hands, steps that broke when you trod on them, and women who came into a man's place and brushed their hair in the dark, were reasons enough! He was querulous and injured about it all. He had taken the place for himself, not for invisible women to brush their hair in; that lawyer fellow in Lincoln's Inn should be told so, too, before many hours were out; it was outrageous, letting people in for agreements like that!

A cut-glass partition divided the compartment where Oleron sat from the space where the white-haired landlady moved; but it stopped seven or eight inches above the level of the counter. There was no partition at the farther bar. Presently Oleron, raising his eyes, saw that faces were watching him through the aperture. The faces disappeared when he looked at them.

He moved to a corner where he could not be seen from the other bar; but this brought him into line with the white-haired landlady.

She knew him by sight – had doubtless seen him passing and repassing; and presently she made a remark on the weather. Oleron did not know what he replied, but it sufficed to call forth the further remark that the winter had been a bad one for influenza, but that the spring weather seemed to be coming at last...Even this slight contact with the commonplace steadied Oleron a little; an idle nascent wonder whether the landlady brushed her hair every night, and, if so, whether it gave out those little electric cracklings, was shut down with a snap; and Oleron was better...

With his next glass of brandy he was all for going back to his flat. Not go back? Indeed, he would go back! They should very soon see whether he was to be turned out of his place like that! He began to wonder why he was doing the rather unusual thing he was doing at that moment, unusual for him – sitting hatless, drinking brandy, in a public-house. Suppose he were to tell the white-haired landlady all about it – to tell her that a caller had scratched her hand on a nail, had later had the bad luck to put her foot through a rotten stair, and that he himself, in an old house full of squeaks and creaks and whispers, had heard a minute noise and had bolted from it in fright – what would she think of him? That he was mad, of course...Pshaw! The real truth of the matter was that he hadn't been doing enough work to occupy him. He had been dreaming his days away, filling his head with a lot of moonshine about a new *Romilly* (as if the old one was not good enough), and now he was surprised that the devil should enter an empty head!

Yes, he would go back. He would take a walk in the air first – he hadn't walked enough lately – and then he would take himself in hand, settle the hash of that sixteenth chapter of *Romilly* (fancy, he had actually been fool enough to think of destroying fifteen chapters!) and thenceforward he would remember that he had obligations to his fellow-men and work to do in the world. There was the matter in a nutshell.

He finished his brandy and went out.

He had walked for some time before any other bearing of the matter than that on himself occurred to him. At first, the fresh air had increased the heady effect of the brandy he had drunk; but afterwards his mind grew clearer than it had been since morning. And the clearer it grew, the less final did his boastful self-assurances become, and the firmer his conviction that, when all explanations had been made, there remained something that could not be explained. His hysteria of an hour before had passed; he grew steadily calmer; but the disquieting conviction remained. A deep fear took possession of him. It was a fear for Elsie.

For something in his place was inimical to her safety. Of themselves, her two accidents might not have persuaded him of this; but she herself had said it. '*I'm not wanted here...*' And she had declared that there was something wrong with the place. She had seen it before he had. Well and good. One thing stood out clearly: namely, that if this was so, she must be kept away for quite another reason than that which had so confounded and humiliated Oleron. Luckily she had expressed her intention of staying away; she must be held to that intention. He must see to it.

And he must see to it all the more that he now saw his first impulse, never to set foot in the place again, was absurd. People did not do that kind of thing. With Elsie made secure, he could not with any respect to himself suffer himself to be turned out by a shadow, nor even by a danger merely because it was a danger. He had to live somewhere, and he would live there. He must return.

He mastered the faint chill of fear that came with the decision, and turned in his walk abruptly. Should fear grow on him again he would, perhaps, take one more glass of brandy...

But by the time he reached the short street that led to the square he was too late for more brandy. The little public-house was still lighted, but closed, and one or two men were standing talking on the kerb. Oleron noticed that a sudden silence fell on them as he passed, and he noticed further that the long-nosed Barrett, whom he passed a little lower down, did not return his good-night. He turned in at the broken gate, hesitated merely an instant in the alley, and then mounted his stairs again.

Only an inch of candle remained in the Sheffield stick, and Oleron did not light another one. Deliberately he forced himself to take it up and to make the tour of his five rooms before retiring. It was as he returned from the kitchen across his little hall that he noticed that a letter lay on the floor. He carried it into his sitting-room, and glanced at the envelope before opening it.

It was unstamped, and had been put into the door by hand. Its handwriting was clumsy, and it ran from beginning to end without comma or period. Oleron read the first line, turned to the signature, and then finished the letter.

It was from the man Barrett, and it informed Oleron that he, Barrett, would be obliged if Mr Oleron would make other arrangements for the preparing of his breakfasts and the cleaning-out of his place. The sting lay in the tail, that is to say, the postscript. This consisted of a text of Scripture. It embodied an allusion that could only be to Elsie Bengough...

A seldom-seen frown had cut deeply into Oleron's brow. So! that was it! Very well; they would see about that on the morrow...Forthe rest, this seemed merely another reason why Elsie should keep away...

Then his suppressed rage broke out...

The foul-minded lot! The devil himself could not have given a leer at anything that had ever passed between Paul Oleron and Elsie Bengough, yet this nosing rascal must be prying and talking!...

Oleron crumpled the paper up, held it in the candle flame, and then ground the ashes under his heel.

One useful purpose, however, the letter had served: it had created in Oleron a wrathful blaze that effectually banished pale shadows. Nevertheless, one other puzzling circumstance was to close the day. As he undressed, he chanced to glance at his bed. The coverlets bore an impress as if somebody had lain on them. Oleron could not remember that he himself had lain down during the day – off-hand, he would have said that certainly he had not; but after all he could not be positive. His indignation for Elsie, acting possibly with the residue of the brandy in him, excluded all other considerations; and he put out his candle, lay down, and passed immediately into a deep and dreamless sleep, which, in the absence of Mrs Barrett's morning call, lasted almost once round the clock.

8

To the man who pays heed to that voice within him which warns him that twilight and danger are settling over his soul, terror is apt to appear an absolute thing, against which his heart must be safeguarded in a twink unless there is to take place an alteration in the whole range and scale of his nature. Mercifully, he has never far to look for safeguards. Of the immediate and small and common and momentary things of life, of usages and observances and modes and conventions, he builds up fortifications against the powers of darkness. He is even content that, not terror only, but joy also, should for working purposes be placed in the category of the absolute things; and the last treason he will commit will be that breaking down of terms and limits that strikes, not at one man, but at the welfare of the souls of all.

In his own person, Oleron began to commit this treason. He began to commit it by admitting the inexplicable and horrible to an increasing familiarity. He did it insensibly, unconsciously, by a neglect of the things that he now regarded it as an impertinence in Elsie Bengough to have prescribed. Two months before, the words 'a haunted house', applied to his lovely bemusing dwelling, would have chilled his marrow; now, his scale of sensation becoming depressed, he could ask 'Haunted by what?' and remain unconscious that horror, when it can be proved to be relative, by so much loses its proper quality. He was setting aside the landmarks. Mists and confusion had begun to enwrap him.

And he was conscious of nothing so much as of a voracious inquisitiveness. He wanted *to know*. He was resolved to know.

Nothing but the knowledge would satisfy him; and craftily he cast about for means whereby he might attain it.

He might have spared his craft. The matter was the easiest imaginable. As in time past he had known, in his writing, moments when his thoughts had seemed to rise of themselves and to embody themselves in words not to be altered afterwards, so now the questions he put himself seemed to be answered even in the moment of their asking. There was exhilaration in the swift, easy processes. He had known no so such joy in his own power since the days when his writing had been a daily freshness and a delight to him. It was almost as if the course he must pursue was being dictated to him.

And the first thing he must do, of course, was to define the problem. He defined it in terms of mathematics. Granted that he had not the place to himself; granted that the old house had inexpressibly caught and engaged his spirit; granted that, by virtue of the common denominator of the place, this unknown co-tenant stood in some relation to himself: what next? Clearly, the nature of the other numerator must be ascertained.

And how? Ordinarily this would not have seemed simple, but to Oleron it was now pellucidly clear. The key, *of course*, lay in his half-written novel – or rather, in both *Romillys*, the old and the proposed new one.

A little while before Oleron would have thought himself mad to have embraced such an opinion; now he accepted the dizzying hypothesis without a quiver.

He began to examine the first and second *Romillys*.

From the moment of his doing so the thing advanced by leaps and bounds. Swiftly he reviewed the history of the *Romilly* of the fifteen chapters. He remembered clearly now that he had found her insufficient on the very first morning on which he had sat down to work in his new place. Other instances of his aversion leaped up to confirm his obscure investigation. There had come the night when he had hardly forborne to throw the whole thing into the fire; and the next morning he had begun the planning of the new *Romilly*. It had been on that morning that Mrs Barrett, overhearing him humming a brief phrase that the dripping of a tap the night before had suggested, had informed him that he was singing some air he had never in his life heard before, called 'The Beckoning Fair One' . . .

The Beckoning Fair One! . . .

With scarcely a pause in thought he continued.

The first *Romilly* having been definitely thrown over, the second had instantly fastened herself upon him, clamouring for birth in his brain. He even fancied now, looking back, that there had been something like passion, hate almost, in the supplanting, and that more than once a stray thought given to his discarded creation had – (it was astonishing how credible Oleron found the almost unthinkable idea) – had offended the supplanter.

Yet that a malignancy almost homicidal should be extended to his fiction's poor mortal prototype . . .

In spite of his inuring to a scale in which the horrible was now a thing to be fingered and turned this way and that, a 'Good God!' broke from Oleron.

This intrusion of the first *Romilly's* prototype into his thought again was a factor that for the moment brought his inquiry into the nature of his problem to a termination; the mere thought of Elsie was fatal to anything abstract. For another thing, he could not yet think of that letter of Barrett's, nor of a little scene that had followed it, without a mounting of colour and a quick contraction of the brow. For, wisely or not, he had had that argument out at once. Striding across the square on the following morning, he had bearded Barrett on his own doorstep. Coming back again a few minutes later, he had been strongly of opinion that he had only made matters worse. The man had been vagueness itself. He had not been to be either challenged or browbeaten into anything more definite than a muttered farrago in which the words 'Certain things...Mrs Barrett...respectable house...if the cap fits...proceedings that shall be nameless,' had been constantly repeated.

'Not that I make any charge – ' he had concluded.

'Charge!' Oleron had cried.

'I 'ave my idears of things, as I don't doubt you 'ave yours – '

'Ideas – mine!' Oleron had cried wrathfully, immediately dropping his voice as heads had appeared at windows of the square. 'Look you here, my man; you've an unwholesome mind, which probably you can't help, but a tongue which you can help, and shall! If there is a breath of this repeated...'

'I'll not be talked to on my own doorstep like this by anybody....' Barrett had blustered...

'You shall, and I'm doing it...'

'Don't you forget there's a Gawd above all, Who 'as said...'

140

'You're a low scandalmonger! ...'

And so forth, continuing badly what was already badly begun. Oleron had returned wrathfully to his own house, and thenceforward, looking out of his windows, had seen Barrett's face at odd times, lifting blinds or peering round curtains, as if he sought to put himself in possession of Heaven knew what evidence, in case it should be required of him.

The unfortunate occurrence made certain minor differences in Oleron's domestic arrangements. Barrett's tongue, he gathered, had already been busy; he was looked at askance by the dwellers of the square; and he judged it better, until he should be able to obtain other help, to make his purchases of provisions a little farther afield rather than at the small shops of the immediate neighbourhood. For the rest, housekeeping was no new thing to him, and he would resume his old bachelor habits ...

Besides, he was deep in certain rather abstruse investigations, in which it was better that he should not be disturbed.

He was looking out of his window one midday rather tired, not very well, and glad that it was not very likely he would have to stir out of doors, when he saw Elsie Bengough crossing the square towards his house. The weather had broken; it was a raw and gusty day; and she had to force her way against the wind that set her ample skirts bellying about her opulent figure and her veil spinning and streaming behind her.

Oleron acted swiftly and instinctively. Seizing his hat, he sprang to the door and descended the stairs at a run. A sort of panic had seized him. She must be prevented from setting foot in the place.

As he ran along the alley he was conscious that his eyes went up to the eaves as if something drew them. He did not know that a slate might not accidentally fall ...

He met her at the gate, and spoke with curious volubleness.

'This is really too bad, Elsie! Just as I'm urgently called away! I'm afraid it can't be helped though, and that you'll have to think me an inhospitable beast.' He poured it out just as it came into his head.

She asked if he was going to town.

Yes, yes – to town,' he replied. 'I've got to call on – on Chambers. You know Chambers, don't you? No, I remember you don't; a big man you once saw me with ... I ought to have gone yesterday, and – ' this he felt to be a brilliant effort – 'and he's going out of town this afternoon. To Brighton. I had a letter from him this morning.'

He took her arm and led her up the square. She had to remind him that his way to town lay in the other direction.

'Of course – how stupid of me!' he said, with a little loud laugh. 'I'm so used to going the other way with you – of course; it's the other way to the bus. Will you come along with me? I am so awfully sorry it's happened like this ...'

They took the street to the bus terminus.

This time Elsie bore no signs of having gone through interior struggles. If she detected anything unusual in his manner she made no comment, and he, seeing her calm, began to talk less recklessly through silences. By the time they reached the bus terminus, nobody, seeing the pallid-faced man without an overcoat and the large ample-skirted girl at his side, would have supposed that one of them was ready to sink on his knees for thankfulness that he had, as he believed, saved the other from a wildly unthinkable danger.

They mounted to the top of the bus, Oleron protesting that he should not miss his overcoat, and that he found the day, if anything, rather oppressively hot. They sat down on a front seat.

Now that this meeting was forced upon him, he had something else to say that would make demands upon his tact. It had been on his mind for some time, and was, indeed, peculiarly difficult to put. He revolved it for some minutes, and then, remembering the success of his story of a sudden call to town, cut the knot of his difficulty with another lie.

'I'm thinking of going away for a little while, Elsie,' he said.

She merely said, 'Oh?'

'Somewhere for a change. I need a change. I think I shall go tomorrow, or the day after. Yes, tomorrow, I think.'

'Yes,' she replied.

'I don't quite know how long I shall be,' he continued. 'I shall have to let you know when I am back.'

'Yes, let me know,' she replied in an even tone.

The tone was, for her, suspiciously even. He was a little uneasy.

'You don't ask me where I'm going,' he said, with a little cumbrous effort to rally her.

She was looking straight before her, past the bus-driver.

'I know,' she said.

He was startled. 'How, you know?'

'You're not going anywhere,' she replied.

He found not a word to say. It was a minute or so before she continued, in the same controlled voice she had employed from the start.

'You're not going anywhere. You weren't going out this morning. You only came out because I appeared; don't behave as if we were strangers, Paul.'

A flush of pink had mounted to his cheeks. He noticed that the wind had given her the pink of early rhubarb. Still he found nothing to say.

'Of course, you ought to go away,' she continued. 'I don't know whether you look at yourself often in the glass, but you're rather noticeable. Several people have turned to look at you this morning. So, of course, you ought to go away. But you won't, and I know why.'

He shivered, coughed a little, and then broke silence.

'Then if you know, there's no use in continuing this discussion,' he said curtly.

'Not for me, perhaps, but there is for you,' she replied. 'Shall I tell you what I know?'

'No,' he said in a voice slightly raised.

'No?' she asked, her round eyes earnestly on him.

'No.'

Again he was getting out of patience with her; again he was conscious of the strain. Her devotion and fidelity and love plagued him; she was only humiliating both herself and him. It would have been bad enough had he ever, by word or deed, given her cause for thus fastening herself on him...but there;

that was the worst of that kind of life for a woman. Women such as she, business women, in and out of offices all the time, always, whether they realised it or not, made comradeship a cover for something else. They accepted the unconventional status, came and went freely, as men did, were honestly taken by men at their own valuation – and then it turned out to be the other thing after all, and they went and fell in love. No wonder there was gossip in shops and squares and public-houses! In a sense the gossipers were in the right of it. Independent, yet not efficient; with some of womanhood's graces forgone, and yet with all the woman's hunger and need; half sophisticated, yet not wise; Oleron was tired of it all . . .

And it was time he told her so.

'I suppose,' he said tremblingly, looking down between his knees, 'I suppose the real trouble is in the life women who earn their own living are obliged to lead.'

He could not tell in what sense she took the lame generality; she merely replied, 'I suppose so.'

'It can't be helped,' he continued, 'but you do sacrifice a good deal.'

She agreed: a good deal; and then she added after a moment, 'What, for instance?'

'You may or may not be gradually attaining a new status, but you're in a false position today.'

It was very likely, she said; she hadn't thought of it much in that light –

'And,' he continued desperately, 'you're bound to suffer.

Your most innocent acts are misunderstood; motives you never dreamed of are attributed to you; and in the end it comes to – ' he hesitated a moment and then took the plunge, '– to the sidelong look and the leer.'

She took his meaning with perfect ease. She merely shivered a little as she pronounced the name.

'Barrett?'

His silence told her the rest.

Anything further that was to be said must come from her. It came as the bus stopped at a stage and fresh passengers mounted the stairs.

'You'd better get down here and go back, Paul,' she said. 'I understand perfectly – perfectly. It isn't Barrett. You'd be able to deal with Barrett. It's merely convenient for you to say it's Barrett. I know what it is . . . but you said I wasn't to tell you that. Very well. But before you go let me tell you why I came up this morning.'

In a dull tone he asked her why. Again she looked straight before her as she replied:

'I came to force your hand. Things couldn't go on as they have been going, you know; and now that's all over.'

'All over,' he repeated stupidly.

'All over. I want you now to consider yourself, as far as I'm concerned, perfectly free. I make only one reservation.'

He hardly had the spirit to ask her what that was.

'If *I* merely need *you*,' she said, 'please don't give that a thought; that's nothing; I shan't come near for that. But,' she dropped her voice, 'if *you're* in need of *me*, Paul – I shall know if you are, *and*

you will be – then I shall come at no matter what cost. You understand that?'

He could only groan.

'So that's understood,' she concluded. 'And I think that's all.
Now go back. I should advise you to walk back, for you're shivering – goodbye – '

She gave him a cold hand, and he descended. He turned on the
edge of the kerb as the bus started again. For the first time in all
the years he had known her she parted from him with no smile
and no wave of her long arm.

9

He stood on the kerb plunged in misery, looking after her as long
as she remained in sight; but almost instantly with her disappearance he felt the heaviness lift a little from his spirit. She had given
him his liberty; true, there was a sense in which he had never
parted with it, but now was no time for splitting hairs; he was free
to act, and all was clear ahead. Swiftly the sense of lightness grew
on him: it became a positive rejoicing in his liberty; and before he
was half-way home he had decided what must be done next.

The vicar of the parish in which his dwelling was situated lived
within ten minutes of the square. To his house Oleron turned his
steps. It was necessary that he should have all the information he
could get about this old house with the insurance marks and the
sloping 'To Let' boards, and the vicar was the person most likely
to be able to furnish it. This last preliminary out of the way, and –
aha! Oleron chuckled – things might be expected to happen!

But he gained less information than he had hoped for. The house, the vicar said, was old – but there needed no vicar to tell Oleron that; it was reputed (Oleron pricked up his ears) to be haunted – but there were few old houses about which some such rumour did not circulate among the ignorant; and the deplorable lack of Faith of the modern world, the vicar thought, did not tend to dissipate these superstitions. For the rest, his manner was the soothing manner of one who prefers not to make statements without knowing how they will be taken by his hearer. Oleron smiled as he perceived this.

'You may leave my nerves out of the question,' he said. 'How long has the place been empty?'

'A dozen years, I should say,' the vicar replied.

'And the last tenant – did you know him – or her?' Oleron was conscious of a tingling of his nerves as he offered the vicar the alternative of sex.

'Him,' said the vicar. 'A man. If I remember rightly, his name was Madley; an artist. He was a great recluse; seldom went out of the place and – ' the vicar hesitated and then broke into a little gush of candour '– and since you appear to have come for this information, and since it is better that the truth should be told than that garbled versions should get about, I don't mind saying that this man Madley died there, under somewhat unusual cir-cumstances. It was ascertained at the post-mortem that there was not a particle of food in his stomach, although he was found to be not without money. And his frame was simply worn out. Suicide was spoken of, but you'll agree with me that deliberate starvation is, to say the least, an uncommon form of suicide. An open verdict was returned.'

'Ah!' said Oleron...'Does there happen to be any comprehensive history of this parish?'

'No; partial ones only. I myself am not guiltless of having made a number of notes on its purely ecclesiastical history, its registers and so forth, which I shall be happy to show you if you would care to see them; but it is a large parish, I have only one curate, and my leisure, as you will readily understand...'

The extent of the parish and the scantiness of the vicar's leisure occupied the remainder of the interview, and Oleron thanked the vicar, took his leave, and walked slowly home.

He walked slowly for a reason, twice turning away from the house within a stone's-throw of the gate and taking another turn of twenty minutes or so. He had a very ticklish piece of work now before him; it required the greatest mental concentration; it was nothing less than to bring his mind, if he might, into such a state of unpreoccupation and receptivity that he should see the place as he had seen it on that morning when, his removal accomplished, he had sat down to begin the sixteenth chapter of the first *Romilly*.

For, could he recapture that first impression, he now hoped for far more from it. Formerly, he had carried no end of mental lumber. Before the influence of the place had been able to find him out at all, it had had the inertia of those dreary chapters to overcome. No results had shown. The process had been one of slow saturation, charging, filling up to a brim. But now he was light, unburdened, rid at last both of that *Romilly* and of her prototype.

Now for the new unknown, coy, jealous, bewitching, Beckoning Fair!...

At half-past two of the afternoon he put his key into the Yale lock, entered, and closed the door behind him...

His fantastic attempt was instantly and astonishingly successful He could have shouted with triumph as he entered the room; it was as if he had *escaped* into it. Once more, as in the days when his writing had had a daily freshness and wonder and promise for him, he was conscious of that new ease and mastery and exhilaration and release. The air of the place seemed to hold more oxygen; as if his own specific gravity had changed, his very tread seemed less ponderable. The flowers in the bowls, the fair proportions of the meadowsweet-coloured panels and mouldings, the polished floor, and the lofty and faintly starred ceiling, fairly laughed their welcome. Oleron actually laughed back, and spoke aloud.

'Oh, you're pretty, pretty!' he flattered it.

Then he lay down on his couch.

He spent that afternoon as a convalescent who expected a dear visitor might have spent it – in a delicious vacancy, smiling now and then as if in his sleep, and ever lifting drowsy and contented eyes to his alluring surroundings. He lay thus until darkness came, and, with darkness, the nocturnal noises of the old house...

But if he waited for any specific happening, he waited in vain.

He waited similarly in vain on the morrow, maintaining, though with less ease, that sensitised-plate-like condition of his mind. Nothing occurred to give it an impression. Whatever it was which he so patiently wooed, it seemed to be both shy and exacting.

Then on the third day he thought he understood. A look of gentle drollery and cunning came into his eyes, and he chuckled.

'Oho, oho!... Well, if the wind sits in *that* quarter we must see what else there is to be done. What is there, now?... No, I won't send for Elsie; we don't need a wheel to break the butterfly on; we won't go to those lengths, my butterfly...'

He was standing musing, thumbing his lean jaw, looking aslant; suddenly he crossed to his hall, took down his hat, and went out.

'My lady is coquettish, is she? Well, we'll see what a little neglect will do,' he chuckled as he went down the stairs.

He sought a railway station, got into a train, and spent the rest of the day in the country. Oh, yes: Oleron thought *he* was the man to deal with Fair Ones who beckoned, and invited, and then took refuge in shyness and hanging back!

He did not return until after eleven that night.

'*Now*, my Fair Beckoner!' he murmured as he walked along the alley and felt in his pocket for his keys...

Inside his flat, he was perfectly composed, perfectly deliberate, exceedingly careful not to give himself away. As if to intimate that he intended to retire immediately, he lighted only a single candle; and as he set out with it on his nightly round he affected to yawn. He went first into his kitchen. There was a full moon, and a lozenge of moonlight, almost peacock-blue by contrast with his candle-frame, lay on the floor. The window was uncurtained, and he could see the reflection of the candle, and, faintly, that of his own face, as he moved about. The door of the powder-closet stood a little ajar, and he closed it before sitting down to remove his boots on the chair with the cushion made of the folded harp-bag. From the kitchen he passed to the bathroom. There, another slant of blue moonlight cut the windowsill and lay across the pipes on the wall. He visited his seldom-used study, and stood for a moment gazing at the silvered roofs across the square. Then, walking straight through his sitting-room, his stockinged feet making no noise, he entered his bedroom and put the candle on the chest of drawers. His face all this time wore no expression save that of tiredness. He had never been wilier nor more alert.

His small bedroom fireplace was opposite the chest of drawers on which the mirror stood, and his bed and the window occupied the remaining sides of the room. Oleron drew down his blind, took off his coat, and then stooped to get his slippers from under the bed.

He could have given no reason for the conviction, but that the manifestation that for two days had been withheld was close at hand he never for an instant doubted. Nor, though he could not form the faintest guess of the shape it might take, did he experience fear. Startling or surprising it might be; he was prepared for that; but that was all; his scale of sensation had become depressed. His hand moved this way and that under the bed in search of his slippers...

But for all his caution and method and preparedness, his heart all at once gave a leap and a pause that was almost horrid. His hand had found the slippers, but he was still on his knees; save for this circumstance he would have fallen. The bed was a low one; the groping for the slippers accounted for the turn of his head to one side; and he was careful to keep the attitude until he had partly recovered his self-possession. When presently he rose there was a drop of blood on his lower lip where he had caught at it with his teeth, and his watch had jerked out of the pocket of his waistcoat and was dangling at the end of its short leather guard . . .

Then, before the watch had ceased its little oscillation, he was himself again.

In the middle of his mantelpiece there stood a picture, a portrait of his grandmother; he placed himself before this picture, so that he could see in the glass of it the steady flame of the candle that burned behind him on the chest of drawers. He could see also in the picture-glass the little glancings of light from the bevels and facets of the objects about the mirror and candle. But he could see more. These twinklings and reflections and re-reflections did not change their position; but there was one gleam that had motion. It was fainter than the rest, and it moved up and down through the air. It was the reflection of the candle on Oleron's black vulcanite comb, and each of its downward movements was accompanied by a silky and crackling rustle.

Oleron, watching what went on in the glass of his grandmother's portrait, continued to play his part. He felt for his dangling watch and began slowly to wind it up. Then, for a moment ceasing to watch, he began to empty his trousers pockets and to place methodically in a little row on the mantelpiece the pennies and halfpennies he took from them. The sweeping, minutely electric noise filled the whole bedroom, and had Oleron altered his point of observation he could have brought the dim gleam of the moving comb so into position that it would almost have outlined his grandmother's head.

Any other head of which it might have been following the outline was invisible.

Oleron finished the emptying of his pockets; then, under cover of another simulated yawn, not so much summoning his resolution as overmastered by an exhorbitant curiosity, he swung suddenly round. That which was being combed was still not to be seen, but the comb did not stop. It had altered its angle a little, and had moved a little to the left. It was passing, in fairly regular sweeps, from a point rather more than five feet from the ground, in a direction roughly vertical, to another point a few inches below the level of the chest of drawers.

Oleron continued to act to admiration. He walked to his little washstand in the corner, poured out water, and began to wash his hands. He removed his waistcoat, and continued his preparations for bed. The combing did not cease, and he stood for a moment in thought. Again his eyes twinkled. The next was very cunning -

'Hm! . . . *I think I'll read for a quarter of an hour,*' he said aloud . . .

He passed out of the room.

He was away a couple of minutes; when he returned again the room was suddenly quiet. He glanced at the chest of drawers; the comb lay still, between the collar he had removed and a pair of gloves. Without hesitation Oleron put out his hand and picked it up. It was an ordinary eighteenpenny comb, taken from a card in a chemist's shop, of a substance of a definite specific gravity, and no more capable of rebellion against the Laws by which it existed than are the worlds that keep their orbits through the void. Oleron put it down again; then he glanced at the bundle of papers he held in his hand. What he had gone to fetch had been the fifteen chapters of the original *Romilly*.

Hm! he muttered as he threw the manuscript into a chair... 'As I thought... She's just blindly, ragingly, murderously jealous.'

On the night after that, and on the following night, and for many nights and days, so many that he began to be uncertain about the count of them, Oleron, courting, cajoling, neglecting, threatening, beseeching, eaten out with unappeased curiosity and regardless that his life was becoming one consuming passion and desire, continued his search for the unknown co-numerator of his abode.

10

As time went on, it came to pass that few except the postman mounted Oleron's stairs; and since men who do not write letters receive few, even the postman's tread became so infrequent that it was not heard more than once or twice a week. There came a letter from Oleron's publishers, asking when they might expect to receive the manuscript of his new book; he delayed for some days to answer it, and finally forgot it. A second letter came, which also he failed to answer. He received no third.

The weather grew bright and warm. The privet bushes among the chopper-like notice-boards flowered, and in the streets where Oleron did his shopping the baskets of flower-women lined the kerbs. Oleron purchased flowers daily; his room clamoured for flowers, fresh and continually renewed; and Oleron did not stint its demands. Nevertheless, the necessity for going out to buy them began to irk him more and more, and it was with a greater and ever greater sense of relief that he returned home again. He began to be conscious that again his scale of sensation had suffered a subtle change – a change that was not restoration to its former capacity, but an extension and enlarging that once more included terror. It admitted it in an entirely new form. *Lux Orco, tenebrae Jovi.* The name of this terror was agoraphobia. Oleron had begun to dread air and space and the horror that might pounce upon the unguarded back.

Presently he so contrived it that his food and flowers were delivered daily at his door. He rubbed his hands when he had hit upon this expedient. That was better! Now he could please himself whether he went out or not . . .

Quickly he was confirmed in his choice. It became his pleasure to remain immured.

But he was not happy – or, if he was, his happiness took an extraordinary turn. He fretted discontentedly, could sometimes have wept for mere weakness and misery; and yet he was dimly conscious that he would not have exchanged his sadness for all the noisy mirth of the world outside. And speaking of noise: noise, much noise, now caused him the acutest discomfort. It was hardly more to be endured than that new-born fear that kept him, on the increasingly rare occasions when he did go out, sidling close to walls and feeling friendly railings with his hand. He moved from room to room softly and in slippers, and sometimes stood for many seconds closing a door so gently that not a sound broke the stillness that was in itself a delight. Sunday now became an intolerable day to him, for, since the coming of the fine weather, there had begun to assemble in the square under his windows each Sunday morning certain members of the sect to which the long-nosed Barrett adhered. These came with a great drum and large brass-bellied instruments; men and women uplifted anguished voices, struggling with their God; and Barrett himself, with upraised face and closed eyes and working brows, prayed that the sound of his voice might penetrate the ears of all un-believers – as it certainly did Oleron's. One day, in the middle of one of these rhapsodies, Oleron sprang to his blind and pulled it down, and heard as he did so his own name made the subject of a fresh torrent of outpouring.

And sometimes, but not as expecting a reply, Oleron stood still and called softly. Once or twice he called 'Romilly!' and then waited; but more often his whispering did not take the shape of a name.

There was one spot in particular of his abode that he began to haunt with increasing persistency. This was just within the opening of his bedroom door. He had discovered one day that by opening every door in his place (always excepting the outer one, which he only opened unwillingly) and by placing himself on this particular spot, he could actually see to a greater or less extent into each of his five rooms without changing his position. He could see the whole of his sitting-room, all of his bedroom except the part hidden by the open door, and glimpses of his kitchen, bathroom, and of his rarely used study. He was often in this place, breathless and with his finger on his lip. One day, as he stood there, he suddenly found himself wondering whether this Madley, of whom the vicar had spoken, had ever discovered the strategic importance of the bedroom entry.

Light, moreover, now caused him greater disquietude than did darkness. Direct sunlight, of which, as the sun passed daily round the house, each of his rooms had now its share, was like a flame in his brain; and even diffused light was a dull and numbing ache. He began, at successive hours of the day, one after another, to lower his crimson blinds. He made short and daring excursions in order to do this; but he was ever careful to leave his retreat open, in case he should have sudden need of it. Presently this lowering of the blinds had become a daily methodical exercise, and his rooms, when he had been his round, had the blood-red half-light of a photographer's darkroom.

One day, as he drew down the blind of his little study and backed in good order out of the room again, he broke into a soft laugh.

'*That* bilks Mr Barrett!' he said; and the baffling of Barrett continued to afford him mirth for an hour.

But on another day, soon after, he had a fright that left him trembling also for an hour. He had seized the cord to darken the window over the seat in which he had found the harp-bag, and was standing with his back well protected in the embrasure, when he thought he saw the tail of a black-and-white check skirt disappear round the corner of the house. He could not be sure – had he run to the window of the other wall, which was blinded, the skirt must have been already past – but he was *almost* sure that it was Elsie. He listened in an agony of suspense for her tread on the stairs...

But no tread came, and after three or four minutes he drew a long breath of relief.

'By Jove, but that would have compromised me horribly!' he muttered...

And he continued to mutter from time to time, 'Horribly compromising... *no* woman would stand that... not *any* kind of woman... oh, compromising in the extreme!'

Yet he was not happy. He could not have assigned the cause of the fits of quiet weeping which took him sometimes; they came and went, like the fitful illumination of the clouds that travelled over the square; and perhaps, after all, if he was not happy, he was not unhappy. Before he could be unhappy something must have been withdrawn, and nothing had yet been withdrawn from him, for nothing had been granted. He was waiting for that granting, in that flower-laden, frightfully enticing apartment of his, with the pith-white walls tinged and subdued by the crimson blinds to a blood-like gloom.

He paid no heed to it that his stock of money was running perilously low, nor that he had ceased to work. Ceased to work? He had not ceased to work. They knew very little about it who supposed that Oleron had ceased to work! He was in truth only now beginning to work. He was preparing such a work... such a work... such a Mistress was a-making in the gestation of his

Art...let him but get this period of probation and poignant waiting over and men should see...How *should* men know her, this Fair One of Oleron's, until Oleron himself knew her? Lovely radiant creations are not thrown off like How-d'ye-do's. The men to whom it is committed to father them must weep wretched tears, as Oleron did, must swell with vain presumptuous hopes, as Oleron did, must pursue, as Oleron pursued, the capricious, fair, mocking, slippery, eager Spirit that, ever eluding, ever sees to it that the chase does not slacken. Let Oleron but hunt this Huntress a little longer...he would have her sparkling and panting in his arms yet...Oh no: they were very far from the truth who supposed that Oleron had ceased to work!

And if all else was falling away from Oleron, gladly he was letting it go. So do we all when our Fair Ones beckon. Quite at the beginning we wink, and promise ourselves that we will put Her Ladyship through her paces, neglect her for a day, turn her own jealous wiles against her, flout and ignore her when she comes wheedling; perhaps there lurks within us all the time a heartless sprite who is never fooled; but in the end all falls away. She beckons, beckons, and all goes...

And so Oleron kept his strategic post within the frame of his bedroom door, and watched, and waited, and smiled, with his finger on his lips...It was his duteous service, his worship, his troth-plighting, all that he had ever known of Love. And when he found himself, as he now and then did, hating the dead man Madley, and wishing that he had never lived, he felt that that, too, was an acceptable service...

But as he thus prepared himself, as it were, for a Marriage, moped and chafed more and more that the Bride made no sign, he made a discovery that he ought to have made weeks before.

It was through a thought of the dead Madley that he made it. Since that night when he had thought in his greenness that a little studied neglect would bring the lovely Beckoner to her knees, and had made use of her own jealousy to banish her, he had not set eyes on those fifteen discarded chapters of *Romilly*. He had thrown them back into the window-seat, forgotten their very existence. But his own jealousy of Madley put him in mind of hers of her jilted rival of flesh and blood, and he remembered them...Fool that he had been! Had he, then, expected his Desire to manifest herself while there still existed the evidence of his divided allegiance? What, and she with a passion so fierce and centred that it had not hesitated at the destruction, twice attempted, of her rival? Fool that he had been!...

But if *that* was all the pledge and sacrifice she required she should have it – ah, yes, and quickly!

He took the manuscript from the window-seat, and brought it to the fire.

He kept his fire always burning now; the warmth brought out the last vestige of odour of the flowers with which his room was banked. He did not know what time it was; long since he had allowed his clock to run down – it had seemed a foolish measurer of time in regard to the stupendous things that were happening to Oleron; but he knew it was late. He took the *Romilly* manuscript and knelt before the fire.

But he had not finished removing the fastening that held the sheets together before he suddenly gave a start, turned his head over his shoulder, and listened intently. The sound he had heard had not been loud – it had been, indeed, no more than a tap, twice or thrice repeated – but it had filled Oleron with alarm. His face grew dark as it came again.

He heard a voice outside on his landing.

'Paul!...Paul!...'

It was Elsie's voice.

'Paul!...I know you're in...I want to see you...'

He cursed her under his breath, but kept perfectly still. He did not intend to admit her.

'Paul!...You're in trouble...I believe you're in danger...at least come to the door!...'

Oleron smothered a low laugh. It somehow amused him that she, in such danger herself, should talk to him of *his* danger!...Well, if she was, serve her right; she knew, or said she knew, all about it...

'Paul!...Paul!...'

'*Paul!...Paul!...*' He mimicked her under his breath.

'Oh, Paul, it's *horrible!*...'

Horrible, Was it? thought Oleron. Then let her get away...

'I only want to help you, Paul...I didn't promise not to come if you needed me...'

He was impervious to the pitiful sob that interrupted the low cry. The devil take the woman! Should he shout to her to go away and not come back? No: let her call and knock and sob. She had a gift for sobbing; she mustn't think her sobs would move him. They irritated him, so that he set his teeth and shook his fist at her, but that was all. Let her sob.

'*Paul!...Paul!...*'

With his teeth hard set, he dropped the first page of *Romilly* into the fire. Then he began to drop the rest in, sheet by sheet.

For many minutes the calling behind his door continued; then suddenly it ceased. He heard the sound of feet slowly descending the stairs. He listened for the noise of a fall or a cry or the crash of a piece of the handrail of the upper landing; but none of these things came. She was spared. Apparently her rival suffered her to crawl abject and beaten away. Oleron heard the passing of her steps under his window; then she was gone.

He dropped the last page into the fire, and then, with a low laugh rose. He looked fondly round his room.

'Lucky to get away like that,' he remarked. 'She wouldn't have got away if I'd given her as much as a word or a look! What devils these women are!...But no; I oughtn't to say that; one of 'em showed forbearance...'

Who showed forbearance? And what was forborne? Ah, Oleron knew!...Contempt, no doubt, had been at the bottom of it, but that didn't matter: the pestering creature had been allowed to go unharmed. Yes, she was lucky; Oleron hoped she knew it...

And now, now, now for his reward!

Oleron crossed the room. All his doors were open; his eyes shone as he placed himself within that of his bedroom.

Fool that he had been, not to think of destroying the manuscript sooner!...

How, in a houseful of shadows, should he know his own
Shadow? How, in a houseful of noises, distinguish the summons
he felt to be at hand? Ah, trust him! He would know! The place
was full of a jugglery of dim lights. The blind at his elbow that
allowed the light of a street lamp to struggle vaguely through –
the glimpse of greeny blue moonlight seen through the distant
kitchen door – the sulky glow of the fire under the black ashes
of the burnt manuscript – the glimmering of the tulips and the
moon-daisies and narcissi in the bowls and jugs and jars – these
did not so trick and bewilder his eyes that he would not know
his Own! It was he, not she, who had been delaying the shadowy
Bridal; he hung his head for a moment in mute acknowledgment;
then he bent his eyes on the deceiving, puzzling gloom again. He
would have called her name had he known it – but now he would
not ask her to share even a name with the other...

His own face, within the frame of the door, glimmered white
as the narcissi in the darkness...

A shadow, light as fleece, seemed to take shape in the kitchen
(the time had been when Oleron would have said that a cloud
had passed over the unseen moon). The low illumination on the
blind at his elbow grew dimmer (the time had been when Oleron
would have concluded that the lamplighter going his rounds had
turned low the flame of the lamp). The fire settled, letting down
the black and charred papers; a flower fell from a bowl, and lay
indistinct upon the floor; all was still; and then a stray draught

moved through the old house, passing before Oleron's face...

Suddenly, inclining his head, he withdrew a little from the doorjamb. The wandering draught caused the door to move a little on its hinges. Oleron trembled violently, stood for a moment longer, and then, putting his hand out to the knob, softly drew the door to, sat down on the nearest chair, and waited, as a man might await the calling of his name that should summon him to some weighty, high and privy Audience...

II

One knows not whether there can be human compassion for anaemia of the soul. When the pitch of Life is dropped, and the spirit is so put over and reversed that that only is horrible which before was sweet and worldly and of the day, the human relation disappears. The sane soul turns appalled away, lest not merely itself, but sanity should suffer. We are not gods. We cannot drive out devils. We must see selfishly to it that devils do not enter into ourselves.

And this we must do even though Love so transfuse us that we may well deem our nature to be half divine. We shall but speak of honour and duty in vain. The letter dropped within the dark door will lie unregarded, or, if regarded for a brief instant between two unspeakable lapses, left and forgotten again. The telegram will be undelivered, nor will the whistling messenger (wiselier guided than he knows to whistle) be conscious as he walks away of the drawn blind that is pushed aside an inch by a finger and then fearfully replaced again. No; let the miserable wrestle with his own shadows; let him, if indeed he be so mad, clip and strain and enfold and couch the succubus; but let him do so in a house into which not an air of Heaven penetrates, nor a bright finger of the sun pierces the filthy twilight. The lost must remain lost. Humanity has other business to attend to.

For the handwriting of the two letters that Oleron, stealing noiselessly one June day into his kitchen to rid his sitting-room of an armful of fetid and decaying flowers, had seen on the floor within his door, had had no more meaning for him than if it had belonged to some dim and faraway dream. And at the beating of the telegraph-boy upon the door, within a few feet of the bed where he lay, he had gnashed his teeth and stopped his ears, He had pictured the lad standing there, just beyond his partition, among packets of provisions and bundles of dead and dying flowers. For his outer landing was littered with these. Oleron had feared to open his door to take them in. After a week, the errand lads had reported that there must be some mistake about the order, and had left no more. Inside, in the red twilight, the old flowers turned brown and fell and decayed where they lay.

Gradually his power was draining away. The Abomination fastened on Oleron's power. The steady sapping sometimes left him for many hours of prostration gazing vacantly up at his red-tinged ceiling, idly suffering such fancies as came of themselves to have their way with him. Even the strongest of his memories had no more than a precarious hold upon his attention. Sometimes a flitting half-memory, of a novel to be written, a novel it was important that he should write, tantalised him for a space before vanishing again; and sometimes whole novels, perfect, splendid, established to endure, rose magically before him. And sometimes the memories were absurdly remote and trivial, of garrets he had inhabited and lodgings that had sheltered him, and so forth. Oleron had known a good deal about such things in his time, but all that was now past. He had at last found a place which he did not intend to leave until they fetched him out – a place that some might have thought a little on the green-sick side, that others might have considered to be a little too redolent of long-dead and morbid things for a living man to be mewed up in, but ah, so irresistible, with such an authority of its own, with such an associate of its own, and a place of such delights when once a man had ceased to struggle against its inexorable will! A novel? Somebody ought to write a novel about a place like that! There must be lots to write about in a place like that if one could but get to the bottom of it! It had probably already been painted, by a man called Madley who had lived there . . . but Oleron had not known this Madley – had a strong feeling that he wouldn't have liked him – would rather he had lived somewhere else – really couldn't stand the fellow – hated him Madley, in fact. (Aha! that was a joke!) He seriously doubted whether the man had led the life he ought; Oleron was in two minds sometimes whether he wouldn't tell that long-nosed guardian of the public morals across the way about him; but probably he knew, and had made his praying hullabaloos for him also. That was his line. Why, Oleron himself had had a dust-up with him about something or other . . . some girl or other . . . Elsie Bengough her name was, he remembered . . .

Oleron had moments of deep uneasiness about this Elsie Bengough. Or rather, he was not so much uneasy about her as restless about the things she did. Chief of these was the way in which she persisted in thrusting herself into his thoughts; and, whenever he was quick enough, he sent her packing the moment she made her appearance there. The truth was that she was not merely a bore; she had always been that; it had now come to the pitch when her very presence in his fancy was inimical to the full enjoyment of certain experiences...She had no tact; really ought to have known that people are not at home to the thoughts of everybody all the time; ought in mere politeness to have allowed him certain seasons quite to himself; and was monstrously ignorant of things if she did not know, as she appeared not to know, that there were certain special hours when a man's veins ran with fire and daring and power, in which...well, in which he had a reasonable right to treat folk as he had treated that prying Barrett – to shut them out completely...But no: up she popped, the thought of her, and ruined all. Bright towering fabrics, by the side of which even those perfect, magical novels of which he dreamed were dun and grey, vanished utterly at her intrusion. It was as if a fog should suddenly quench some fair-beaming star, as if at the threshold of some golden portal prepared for Oleron a pit should suddenly gape, as if a bat-like shadow should turn the growing dawn to mirk and darkness again...Therefore, Oleron strove to stifle even the nascent thought of her.

Nevertheless, there came an occasion on which this woman Bengough absolutely refused to be suppressed. Oleron could not have told exactly when this happened; he only knew by the glimmer of the street lamp on his blind that it was some time during the night, and that for some time she had not presented herself.

He had no warning, none, of her coming; she just came – was there. Strive as he would, he could not shake off the thought of her nor the image of her face. She haunted him.

But for her to come at that moment of all moments!...Really, it was past belief! How she could endure it, Oleron could not conceive! Actually, to look on, as it were, at the triumph of a Rival...Good God! It was monstrous! Tact – reticence – he had never credited her with an overwhelming amount of either: but he had never attributed mere – oh, there was no word for it! Monstrous – monstrous! Did she intend thenceforward...Good God! to look on!...

Oleron felt the blood rush up to the roots of his hair with anger against her.

'Damnation take her!' he choked...

But the next moment his heat and resentment had changed to a cold sweat of cowering fear. Panic-stricken, he strove to comprehend what he had done. For though he knew not what, he knew he had done something, something fatal, irreparable, blasting. Anger he had felt, but not *this* blaze of ire that suddenly flooded the twilight of his consciousness with a white infernal light. *That* appalling flash was not his – not his *that* open rift of bright and searing Hell – not his, not his! His had been the hand of a child, preparing a puny blow; but what was *this other* horrific hand that was drawn back to strike in the same place? Had *he* set that in motion? Had *he* provided the spark that had touched off the whole accumulated power of that formidable and relentless place? He did not know. He only knew that that poor igniting particle in himself was blown out, that – Oh, impossible! – a clinging kiss (how else to express it?) had changed on his very lips to a gnashing and a removal, and that for very pity of the awful odds he must cry out to her against whom he had lately raged to guard herself . . . guard herself. . .

'*Look out!*' he shrieked aloud . . .

★ ★ ★

The revulsion was instant. As if a cold slow billow had broken over him, he came to to find that he was lying in his bed, that the mist and horror that had for so long enwrapped him had departed, that he was Paul Oleron, and that he was sick, naked, helpless, and unutterably abandoned and alone. His faculties, though weak, answered at last to his calls upon them; and he knew that it must have been a hideous nightmare that had left him sweating and shaking thus.

Yes, he was himself, Paul Oleron, a tired novelist, already past the summit of his best work, and slipping downhill again empty-handed from it all. He had struck short in his life's aim. He had tried too much, had over-estimated his strength, and was a failure, a failure . . .

It all came to him in the single word, enwrapped and complete; it needed no sequential thought; he was a failure. He had missed . . .

And he had missed not one happiness, but two. He had missed the ease of this world, which men love, and he had missed also that other shining prize for which men forgo ease, the snatching and holding and triumphant bearing up aloft of which is the only justification of the mad adventurer who hazards the enterprise. And there was no second attempt. Fate has no morrow. Oleron's morrow must be to sit down to profitless, ill-done, unrequired work again, and so on the morrow after that, and the morrow after that, and as many morrows as there might be ...

He lay there, weakly yet sanely considering it ...

And since the whole attempt had failed, it was hardly worth while to consider whether a little might not be saved from the general wreck. No good would ever come of that half-finished novel. He had intended that it should appear in the autumn; was under contract that it should appear; no matter; it was better to pay forfeit to his publishers than to waste what days were left. He was spent; age was not far off; and paths of wisdom and sadness were the properest for the remainder of the journey ...

If only he had chosen the wife, the child, the faithful friend at the fireside, and let them follow an *ignis fatuus* – that list! ...

In the meantime it began to puzzle him exceedingly that he should be so weak, that his room should smell so overpoweringly of decaying vegetable matter, and that his hand, chancing to stray to his face in the darkness, should encounter a beard.

'Most extraordinary!' he began to mutter to himself. 'Have I been ill? Am I ill now? And if so, why have they left me alone? ... Extraordinary! ...'

He thought he heard a sound from the kitchen or bathroom. He rose a little on his pillow, and listened . . . Ah! He was not alone, then! It certainly would have been extraordinary if they had left him ill and alone – Alone? Oh no. He would be looked after. He wouldn't be left, ill, to shift for himself If everybody else had forsaken him, he could trust Elsie Bengough, the dearest chum he had, for that . . . bless her faithful heart!

But suddenly; a short, stifled, spluttering cry rang sharply out.

'*Paul!*'

It came from the kitchen.

And in the same moment it flashed upon Oleron, he knew not how, that two, three, five, he knew not how many minutes before, another sound, unmarked at the time but suddenly transfixing his attention now, had striven to reach his intelligence. This sound had been the slight touch of metal on metal – just such a sound as Oleron made when he put his key into the lock.

'Hallo! . . . Who's that?' he called sharply from his bed.

He had no answer.

He called again. 'Hallo! . . . Who's there? . . . Who is it?'

This time he was sure he heard noises, soft and heavy, in the kitchen.

'This is a queer thing altogether,' he muttered. 'By Jove, I'm as weak as a kitten too . . . Hallo, there! Somebody called, didn't they? . . . Elsie! Is that you? . . . '

Then he began to knock with his hand on the wall at the side of his bed.

'Elsie!...Elsie!...You called, didn't you?...Please come here, whoever it is!...'

There was a sound as of a closing door, and then silence. Oleron began to get rather alarmed.

'It may be a nurse,' he muttered; 'Elsie'd have to get me a nurse, of course. She'd sit with me as long as she could spare the time, brave lass, and she'd get a nurse for the rest. . . But it was awfully like her voice...Elsie, or whoever it is!...I can't make this out at all. I must go and see what's the matter...'

He put one leg out of bed. Feeling its feebleness, he reached with his hand for the additional support of the wall...

*   *   *

But before putting out the other leg he stopped and considered, picking at his new-found beard. He was suddenly wondering whether he *dared* go into the kitchen. It was such a frightfully long way; no man knew what horror might not leap and huddle on his shoulders if he went so far; when a man has an overmastering impulse to get back into bed he ought to take heed of the warning and obey it. Besides, why should he go? What was there to go for? If it was that Bengough creature again, let her look after herself; Oleron was not going to have things cramp themselves on his defenceless back for the sake of such a spoilsport as *she*!...If she was in, let her let herself out again, and the sooner the better for her! Oleron simply couldn't be bothered. He had his work to do. On the morrow, he must set about the writing of a novel with a heroine so winsome, capricious, adorable, jealous, wicked, beautiful, inflaming, and altogether evil, that men should stand amazed. She was coming over him now; he knew by the alteration of the very air of the room when she was near him; and that soft thrill of bliss that had begun to stir in him never came unless she was beckoning, beckoning...

He let go the wall and fell back into bed again as – oh, unthinkable! – the other half of that kiss that a gnash had interrupted was placed (how else convey it?) on his lips, robbing him of very breath...

12

In the bright June sunlight a crowd filled the square, and looked up at the windows of the old house with the antique insurance marks in its walls of red brick and the agents' notice-boards hanging like wooden choppers over the paling. Two constables stood at the broken gate of the narrow entrance-alley, keeping folk back. The women kept to the outskirts of the throng, moving now and then as if to see the drawn red blinds of the old house from a new angle, and talking in whispers. The children were in the houses, behind closed doors.

A long-nosed man had a little group about him, and he was telling some story over and over again; and another man, little and fat and wide-eyed, sought to capture the long-nosed man's audience with some relation in which a key figured.

'...and it was revealed to me that there'd been something that very afternoon,' the long-nosed man was saying. 'I was standing there, where Constable Saunders is – or rather, I was passing about my business, when they came out. There was no deceiving me, oh, no deceiving *me*! I saw her face...'

'What was it like, Mr Barrett?' a man asked.

'It was like hers whom our Lord said to, "Woman, doth any man accuse thee?" – white as paper, and no mistake! Don't tell *me*!...And so I walks straight across to Mrs Barrett, and "Jane," I says, "this must stop, and stop at once; we are commanded to avoid evil," I says, "and it must come to an end now; let him get help elsewhere."

'And she says to me, "John," she says, "it's four-and-sixpence a week" – them was her words.

'"Jane," I says, "if it was forty-six thousand pounds it should stop"...and from that day to this she hasn't set foot inside that gate.'

There was a short silence: then, 'Did Mrs Barrett ever...*see* anythink, like?' somebody vaguely enquired.

Barrett turned austerely on the speaker. 'What Mrs Barrett saw and Mrs Barrett didn't see shall not pass these lips; even as it is written, keep thy tongue from speaking evil,' he said.

Another man spoke.

'He was pretty near canned up in the Waggon and Horses that night, weren't he, Jim?'

'Yes, 'e 'adn't 'alf copped it...'

'Not standing treat much, neither; he was in the bar, all on his own...'

'So 'e was; we talked about it...'

The fat, scared-eyed man made another attempt.

'She got the key off of me – she 'ad the number of it – she come into my shop of a Tuesday evening...'

Nobody heeded him.

'Shut your heads,' a heavy labourer commented gruffly, 'she hasn't been found yet. 'Ere's the inspectors; we shall know more in a bit.'

Two inspectors had come up and were talking to the constables who guarded the gate. The little fat man ran eagerly forward, saying that she had bought the key off him. 'I remember the number, because of it's being three one's and three three's – 111333!' he exclaimed excitedly.

An inspector put him aside.

'Nobody's been in?' he asked of one of the constables.

'No, sir.'

'Then you, Brackley, come with us; you, Smith, keep the gate. There's a squad on its way.'

The two inspectors and the constable passed down the alley and entered the house. They mounted the wide carved staircase.

'This don't look as if he'd been out much lately,' one of the inspectors muttered as he kicked aside a litter of dead leaves and paper that lay outside Oleron's door. 'I don't think we need knock – break a pane, Brackley.'

The door had two glazed panels; there was a sound of shattered glass; and Brackley put his hand through the hole his elbow had made and drew back the latch.

'Faugh!'... choked one of the inspectors as they entered. 'Let some light and air in, quick. It stinks like a hearse –'

The assembly out in the square saw the red blinds go up and the windows of the old house flung open.

'That's better,' said one of the inspectors, putting his head out of a window and drawing a deep breath... 'That seems to be the bedroom in there; will you go in, Simms, while I go over the rest?...'

They had drawn up the bedroom blind also, and the waxy-white, emaciated man on the bed had made a blinker of his hand against the torturing flood of brightness. Nor could he believe that his hearing was not playing tricks with him, for there were two policemen in his room, bending over him and asking where 'she' was. He shook his head.

'This woman Bengough...goes by the name of Miss Elsie Bengough...d'ye hear? Where is she?...No good, Brackley; get him up; be careful with him; I'll just shove *my* head out of the window, I think...'

The other inspector had been through Oleron's study and had found nothing, and was now in the kitchen, kicking aside an ankle-deep mass of vegetable refuse that cumbered the floor. The kitchen window had no blind, and was over-shadowed by the blank end of the house across the alley. The kitchen appeared to be empty.

But the inspector, kicking aside the dead flowers, noticed that a shuffling track that was not of his making had been swept to a cupboard in the corner. In the upper part of the door of the cupboard was a square panel that looked as if it slid on runners. The door itself was closed.

The inspector advanced, put out his hand to the little knob, and slid the hatch along its groove.

Then he took an involuntary step back again.

Framed in the aperture, and falling forward a little before it jammed again in its frame, was something that resembled a large lumpy pudding, done up in a pudding-bag of faded browny red frieze.

'Ah!' said the inspector.

To close the hatch again he would have had to thrust that pudding back with his hand; and somehow he did not quite like the idea of touching it. Instead, he turned the handle of the cupboard itself. There was weight behind it, so much weight that, after opening the door three or four inches and peering inside, he had to put his shoulder to it in order to close it again. In closing it he left sticking out, a few inches from the floor, a triangle of black and white check skirt.

He went into the small hall.

'All right!' he called.

They had got Oleron into his clothes. He still used his hands as blinkers, and his brain was very confused. A number of things were happening that he couldn't understand. He couldn't understand the extraordinary mess of dead flowers there seemed to be everywhere; he couldn't understand why there should be police officers in his room; he couldn't understand why one of these should be sent for a four-wheeler and a stretcher; and he couldn't understand what heavy article they seemed to be moving about in the kitchen – his kitchen . . .

'What's the matter?' he muttered sleepily...

Then he heard a murmur in the square, and the stopping of a four-wheeler outside. A police officer was at his elbow again, and Oleron wondered why, when he whispered something to him, he should run off a string of words – something about 'used in evidence against you'. They had lifted him to his feet, and were assisting him towards the door...

No, Oleron couldn't understand it at all.

They got him down the stairs and along the alley. Oleron was aware of confused angry shoutings; he gathered that a number of people wanted to lynch somebody or other. Then his attention became fixed on a little fat frightened-eyed man who appeared to be making a statement that an officer was taking down in a notebook.

'I'd seen her with him...they was often together...she came into my shop and said it was for him...I thought it was all right...111333 the number was,' the man was saying.

The people seemed to be very angry; many police were keeping them back; but one of the inspectors had a voice that Oleron thought quite kind and friendly. He was telling somebody to get somebody else into the cab before something or other was brought out; and Oleron noticed that a four-wheeler was drawn up at the gate. It appeared that it was himself who was to be put into it; and as they lifted him up he saw that the inspector tried to stand between him and something that stood behind the cab, but was not quick enough to prevent Oleron seeing that this something was a hooded stretcher. The angry voices sounded like a sea; something hard, like a stone, hit the back of the cab; and the inspector followed Oleron in and stood with his back to the window nearer the side where the people were. The door they had put Oleron in at remained open, apparently till the other inspector should come; and through the opening Oleron had a glimpse of the hatchet-like 'To Let' boards among the privet-trees. One of them said that the key was at Number Six...

Suddenly the raging of voices was hushed. Along the entrance-alley shuffling steps were heard, and the other inspector appeared at the cab door.

'Right away,' he said to the driver.

He entered, fastened the door after him, and blocked up the second window with his back. Between the two inspectors Oleron slept peacefully. The cab moved down the square, the other vehicle went up the hill. The mortuary lay that way.

M. R.
James

The Mezzotint

'THE MEZZOTINT'

M.R. JAMES (MONTAGUE RHODES JAMES, BRITISH, 1862–1936)

First published in James's 1904 collection *Ghost Stories of an Antiquary*.

M.R. James is one of the greatest writers of ghost stories, and no collection of them would be complete without him. 'The Mezzotint' is a particular favourite of mine because I am a printmaker. James wrote many of his ghost stories to be read aloud; I used to read this one to my printmaking classes on Halloween.

THE MEZZOTINT
M. R. James

Some time ago I believe I had the pleasure of telling you the story of an adventure which happened to a friend of mine by the name of Dennistoun, during his pursuit of objects of art for the museum at Cambridge.

He did not publish his experiences very widely upon his return to England; but they could not fail to become known to a good many of his friends, and among others to the gentleman who at that time presided over an art museum at another University. It was to be expected that the story should make a considerable impression on the mind of a man whose vocation lay in lines similar to Dennistoun's, and that he should be eager to catch at any explanation of the matter which tended to make it seem improbable that he should ever be called upon to deal with so agitating an emergency. It was, indeed, somewhat consoling to him to reflect that he was not expected to acquire ancient MSS for his institution; that was the business of the Shelburnian Library. The authorities of that might, if they pleased, ransack obscure corners of the Continent for such matters. He was glad to be obliged at the moment to confine his attention to enlarging the already unsurpassed collection of English topographical drawings and engravings possessed by his museum. Yet, as it turned out, even a department so homely and familiar as this may have its dark corners, and to one of these Mr Williams was unexpectedly introduced.

Those who have taken even the most limited interest in the acquisition of topographical pictures are aware that there is one London dealer whose aid is indispensable to their researches. Mr J. W. Britnell publishes at short intervals very admirable catalogues of a large and constantly changing stock of engravings, plans, and old sketches of mansions, churches, and towns in England and Wales. These catalogues were, of course, the ABC of his subject to Mr Williams: but as his museum already contained an enormous accumulation of topographical pictures, he was a regular, rather than a copious, buyer; and he rather looked to Mr Britnell to fill up gaps in the rank and file of his collection than to supply him with rarities.

Now, in February of last year there appeared upon Mr Williams's desk at the museum a catalogue from Mr Britnell's emporium, and accompanying it was a typewritten communication from the dealer himself. This latter ran as follows:

Dear Sir, –

We beg to call your attention to No. 978 in our accompanying catalogue, which we shall be glad to send on approval.

Yours faithfully,

J. W. Britnell

To turn to No. 978 in the accompanying catalogue was with Mr Williams (as he observed to himself) the work of a moment, and in the place indicated he found the following entry:

'978. – *Unknown*. Interesting mezzotint: View of a manor-house, early part of the century. 15 by 10 inches; black frame. £2 2s.'

It was not specially exciting, and the price seemed high. However, as Mr Britnell, who knew his business and his customer, seemed to set store by it, Mr Williams wrote a postcard asking for the article to be sent on approval, along with some other engravings and sketches which appeared in the same catalogue. And so he passed without much excitement of anticipation to the ordinary labours of the day.

A parcel of any kind always arrives a day later than you expect it, and that of Mr Britnell proved, as I believe the right phrase goes, no exception to the rule. It was delivered at the museum by the afternoon post of Saturday, after Mr Williams had left his work, and it was accordingly brought round to his rooms in college by the attendant, in order that he might not have to wait over Sunday before looking through it and returning such of the contents as he did not propose to keep. And here he found it when he came in to tea, with a friend.

The only item with which I am concerned was the rather large, black-framed mezzotint of which I have already quoted the short description given in Mr Britnell's catalogue. Some more details of it will have to be given, though I cannot hope to put before you the look of the picture as clearly as it is present to my own eye. Very nearly the exact duplicate of it may be seen in a good many old inn parlours, or in the passages of undisturbed country mansions at the present moment. It was a rather indifferent mezzotint, and an indifferent mezzotint is, perhaps, the worst form of engraving known. It presented a full-faced view of a not very large manor-house of the last century, with three rows of plain sashed windows with rusticated masonry about them, a parapet with balls or vases at the angles, and a small portico in the centre. On either side were trees, and in front a considerable expanse of lawn. The legend 'A. W. F. sculpsit' was engraved on the narrow margin; and there was no further inscription. The whole thing gave the impression that it was the work of an amateur. What in the world Mr Britnell could mean by affixing the price of £2 2s. to such an object was more than Mr Williams could imagine. He turned it over with a good deal of contempt; upon the back was a paper label, the left-hand half of which had been torn off. All that remained were the ends of two lines of writing: the first had the letters —*ngley Hall*; the second, —*ssex*.

It would, perhaps, be just worth while to identify the place represented, which he could easily do with the help of a gazetteer, and then he would send it back to Mr Britnell, with some remarks reflecting upon the judgement of that gentleman.

He lighted the candles, for it was now dark, made the tea, and supplied the friend with whom he had been playing golf (for I believe the authorities of the University I write of indulge in that pursuit by way of relaxation); and tea was taken to the accompaniment of a discussion which golfing persons can imagine for themselves, but which the conscientious writer has no right to inflict upon any non-golfing persons.

The conclusion arrived at was that certain strokes might have been better, and that in certain emergencies neither player had experienced that amount of luck which a human being has a right to expect. It was now that the friend – let us call him Professor Binks – took up the framed engraving, and said:

'What's this place, Williams?'

'Just what I am going to try to find out,' said Williams, going to the shelf for a gazetteer. 'Look at the back. Somethingley Hall, either in Sussex or Essex. Half the name's gone, you see. You don't happen to know it, I suppose?'

'It's from that man Britnell, I suppose, isn't it?' said Binks. 'Is it for the museum?'

'Well, I think I should buy it if the price was five shillings,' said Williams; 'but for some unearthly reason he wants two guineas for it. I can't conceive why. It's a wretched engraving, and there aren't even any figures to give it life.'

'It's not worth two guineas, I should think,' said Binks; 'but I don't think it's so badly done. The moonlight seems rather good to me; and I should have thought there *were* figures, or at least a figure, just on the edge in front.'

'Let's look,' said Williams. 'Well, it's true the light is rather cleverly given. Where's your figure? Oh yes! Just the head, in the very front of the picture.'

And indeed there was – hardly more than a black blot on the extreme edge of the engraving – the head of a man or woman, a good deal muffled up, the back turned to the spectator, and look-ing towards the house.

Williams had not noticed it before.

'Still,' he said, 'though it's a cleverer thing than I thought, I can't spend two guineas of museum money on a picture of a place I don't know.'

Professor Binks had his work to do, and soon went; and very nearly up to Hall time Williams was engaged in a vain attempt to identify the subject of his picture. 'If the vowel before the *ng* had only been left, it would have been easy enough,' he thought; 'but as it is, the name may be anything from Guestingley to Langley, and there are many more names ending like this than I thought; and this rotten book has no index of terminations.'

Hall in Mr Williams's college was at seven. It need not be dwelt upon; the less so as he met there colleagues who had been playing golf during the afternoon, and words with which we have no con-cern were freely bandied across the table – merely golfing words, I would hasten to explain.

I suppose an hour or more to have been spent in what is called common-room after dinner. Later in the evening some few retired to Williams's rooms, and I have little doubt that whist was played and tobacco smoked. During a lull in these operations Williams picked up the mezzotint from the table without looking at it, and handed it to a person mildly interested in art, telling him where it had come from, and the other particulars which we already know.

The gentleman took it carelessly, looked at it, then said, in a tone of some interest:

'It's really a very good piece of work, Williams; it has quite a feeling of the romantic period. The light is admirably managed, it seems to me, and the figure, though it's rather too grotesque, is somehow very impressive.'

'Yes, isn't it?' said Williams, who was just then busy giving whisky-and-soda to others of the company, and was unable to come across the room to look at the view again.

It was by this time rather late in the evening, and the visitors were on the move. After they went Williams was obliged to write a letter or two and clear up some odd bits of work. At last, some time past midnight, he was disposed to turn in, and he put out his lamp after lighting his bedroom candle. The picture lay face upwards on the table where the last man who looked at it had put it, and it caught his eye as he turned the lamp down. What he saw made him very nearly drop the candle on the floor, and he declares now that if he had been left in the dark at that moment he would have had a fit. But, as that did not happen, he was able to put down the light on the table and take a good look at the picture. It was indubitable – rankly impossible, no doubt, but absolutely certain. In the middle of the lawn in front of the unknown house there was a figure where no figure had been at five o'clock that afternoon. It was crawling on all-fours towards the house, and it was muffled in a strange black garment with a white cross on the back.

I do not know what is the ideal course to pursue in a situation of this kind. I can only tell you what Mr Williams did. He took the picture by one corner and carried it across the passage to a second set of rooms which he possessed. There he locked it up in a drawer, sported the doors of both sets of rooms, and retired to bed; but first he wrote out and signed an account of the extraordinary change which the picture had undergone since it had come into his possession.

Sleep visited him rather late; but it was consoling to reflect that the behaviour of the picture did not depend upon his own unsupported testimony. Evidently the man who had looked at it the night before had seen something of the same kind as he had, otherwise he might have been tempted to think that something gravely wrong was happening either to his eyes or his mind. This possibility being fortunately precluded, two matters awaited him on the morrow. He must take stock of the picture very carefully, and call in a witness for the purpose, and he must make a determined effort to ascertain what house it was that was represented. He would therefore ask his neighbour Nisbet to breakfast with him, and he would subsequently spend a morning over the gazetteer.

Nisbet was disengaged, and arrived about 9.30. His host was not quite dressed, I am sorry to say, even at this late hour. During breakfast nothing was said about the mezzotint by Williams, save that he had a picture on which he wished for Nisbet's opinion. But those who are familiar with University life can picture for themselves the wide and delightful range of subjects over which the conversation of two Fellows of Canterbury College is likely to extend during a Sunday morning breakfast. Hardly a topic was left unchallenged, from golf to lawn-tennis. Yet I am bound to say that Williams was rather distraught; for his interest naturally centred in that very strange picture which was now reposing, face downwards, in the drawer in the room opposite.

The morning pipe was at last lighted, and the moment had arrived for which he looked. With very considerable – almost tremulous – excitement, he ran across, unlocked the drawer, and, extracting the picture – still face downwards – ran back, and put it into Nisbet's hands.

'Now,' he said, 'Nisbet, I want you to tell me exactly what you see in that picture. Describe it, if you don't mind, rather minutely. I'll tell you why afterwards.'

'Well,' said Nisbet, 'I have here a view of a country-house – English, I presume – by moonlight.'

'Moonlight? You're sure of that?'

'Certainly. The moon appears to be on the wane, if you wish for details, and there are clouds in the sky.'

'All right. Go on. I'll swear,' added Williams in an aside, 'there was no moon when I saw it first.'

'Well, there's not much more to be said,' Nisbet continued. 'The house has one – two – three rows of windows, five in each row, except at the bottom, where there's a porch instead of the middle one, and —'

'But what about figures?' said Williams, with marked interest.

'There aren't any,' said Nisbet; 'but —'

'What! No figure on the grass in front?'

'Not a thing.'

'You'll swear to that?'

'Certainly I will. But there's just one other thing.'

'What?'

'Why, one of the windows on the ground floor – left of the door – is open.'

'Is it really? My goodness! he must have got in,' said Williams, with great excitement; and he hurried to the back of the sofa on which Nisbet was sitting, and, catching the picture from him, verified the matter for himself

It was quite true. There was no figure, and there was the open window. Williams, after a moment of speechless surprise, went to the writing-table and scribbled for a short time. Then he brought two papers to Nisbet, and asked him first to sign one – it was his own description of the picture, which you have just heard – and then to read the other which was Williams's statement written the night before.

'What can it all mean?' said Nisbet.

'Exactly,' said Williams. 'Well, one thing I must do – or three things, now I think of it. I must find out from Garwood' – this was his last night's visitor – 'what he saw, and then I must get the thing photographed before it goes further, and then I must find out what the place is.'

'I can do the photographing myself,' said Nisbet, 'and I will. But, you know, it looks very much as if we were assisting at the working out of a tragedy somewhere. The question is, Has it happened already, or is it going to come off? You must find out what the place is. Yes,' he said, looking at the picture again, 'I expect you're right: he has got in. And if I don't mistake there'll be the devil to pay in one of the rooms upstairs.'

'I'll tell you what,' said Williams: 'I'll take the picture across to old Green' (this was the senior Fellow of the College, who had been Bursar for many years). 'It's quite likely he'll know it. We have property in Essex and Sussex, and he must have been over the two counties a lot in his time.'

'Quite likely he will,' said Nisbet; 'but just let me take my photograph first. But look here, I rather think Green isn't up today. He wasn't in Hall last night, and I think I heard him say he was going down for the Sunday.'

'That's true, too,' said Williams; 'I know he's gone to Brighton. Well, if you'll photograph it now, I'll go across to Garwood and get his statement, and you keep an eye on it while I'm gone. I'm beginning to think two guineas is not a very exorbitant price for it now.'

In a short time he had returned, and brought Mr Garwood with him. Garwood's statement was to the effect that the figure, when he had seen it, was clear of the edge of the picture, but had not got far across the lawn. He remembered a white mark on the back of its drapery, but could not have been sure it was a cross. A document to this effect was then drawn up and signed, and Nisbet proceeded to photograph the picture.

'Now what do you mean to do?' he said. 'Are you going to sit and watch it all day?'

'Well, no, I think not,' said Williams. 'I rather imagine we're meant to see the whole thing. You see, between the time I saw it last night and this morning there was time for lots of things to happen, but the creature only got into the house. It could easily have got through its business in the time and gone to its own place again; but the fact of the window being open, I think, must mean that it's in there now. So I feel quite easy about leaving it. And, besides, I have a kind of idea that it wouldn't change much, if at all, in the daytime. We might go out for a walk this afternoon, and come in to tea, or whenever it gets dark. I shall leave it out on the table here, and sport the door. My skip can get in, but no one else.'

The three agreed that this would be a good plan; and, further, that if they spent the afternoon together they would be less likely to talk about the business to other people; for any rumour of such a transaction as was going on would bring the whole of the Phasmatological Society about their ears.

We may give them a respite until five o'clock.

At or near the hour the three were entering Williams's staircase. They were at first slightly annoyed to see that the door of his rooms was unsported; but in a moment it was remembered that on Sunday the skips came for orders an hour or so earlier than on week-days. However, a surprise was awaiting them. The first thing they saw was the picture leaning up against a pile of books on the table, as it had been left, and the next thing was Williams's skip, seated on a chair opposite, gazing at it with undisguised horror. How was this? Mr Filcher (the name is not my own invention) was a servant of considerable standing, and set the standard of etiquette to all his own college and to several neighbouring ones, and nothing could be more alien to his practice than to be found sitting on his master's chair, or appearing to take any particular notice of his master's furniture or pictures. Indeed, he seemed to feel this himself. He started violently when the three men came into the room, and got up with a marked effort. Then he said: 'I ask your pardon, sir, for taking such a freedom as to set down.'

'Not at all, Robert,' interposed Mr Williams. 'I was meaning to ask you some time what you thought of that picture.'

'Well, sir, of course I don't set up my opinion again yours, but it ain't the pictur I should 'ang where my little girl could see it, sir.'

'Wouldn't you, Robert? Why not?'

'No, sir. Why, the pore child, I recollect once she see a Door Bible, with pictures not 'alf what that is, and we 'ad to set up with her three or four nights afterwards, if you'll believe me; and if she was to ketch a sight of this skelinton here, or whatever it is, carrying off the pore baby, she would be in a taking. You know 'ow it is with children; 'ow nervish they git with a little thing and all. But what I should say, it don't seem a right pictur to be laying about, sir, not where anyone that's liable to be startled could come on it. Should you be wanting anything this evening, sir? Thank you, sir.'

With these words the excellent man went to continue the round of his masters, and you may be sure the gentlemen whom he left lost no time in gathering round the engraving. There was the house, as before under the waning moon and the drifting clouds. The window that had been open was shut, and the figure was once more on the lawn: but not this time crawling cautiously on hands and knees. Now it was erect and stepping swiftly, with long strides, towards the front of the picture. The moon was behind it, and the black drapery hung down over its face so that only hints of that could be seen, and what was visible made the spectators profoundly thankful that they could see no more than a white dome-like forehead and a few straggling hairs. The head was bent down, and the arms were tightly clasped over an object which could be dimly seen and identified as a child, whether dead or living it was not possible to say. The legs of the appearance alone could be plainly discerned, and they were horribly thin.

From five to seven the three companions sat and watched the picture by turns. But it never changed. They agreed at last that it would be safe to leave it, and that they would return after Hall and await further developments.

When they assembled again, at the earliest possible moment, the engraving was there, but the figure was gone, and the house was quiet under the moonbeams. There was nothing for it but to spend the evening over gazetteers and guide-books. Williams was the lucky one at last, and perhaps he deserved it. At 11.30 p.m. he read from Murray's *Guide to Essex* the following lines:

'16½ miles, *Anningley*. The church has been an interesting building of Norman date, but was extensively classicised in the last century. It contains the tombs of the family of Francis, whose mansion, Anningley Hall, a solid Queen Anne house, stands immediately beyond the churchyard in a park of about 80 acres. The family is now extinct, the last heir having disappeared mysteriously in infancy in the year 1802. The father, Mr Arthur Francis, was locally known as a talented amateur engraver in mezzotint. After his son's disappearance he lived in complete retirement at the Hall, and was found dead in his studio on the third anniversary of the disaster, having just completed an engraving of the house, impressions of which are of considerable rarity.'

This looked like business, and, indeed, Mr Green on his return at once identified the house as Anningley Hall.

'Is there any kind of explanation of the figure, Green?' was the question which Williams naturally asked.

'I don't know, I'm sure, Williams. What used to be said in the place when I first knew it, which was before I came up here, was just this: old Francis was always very much down on these poaching fellows, and whenever he got a chance he used to get a man whom he suspected of it turned off the estate, and by degrees he got rid of them all but one. Squires could do a lot of things then that they daren't think of now. Well, this man that was left was what you find pretty often in that country – the last remains of a very old family. I believe they were Lords of the Manor at one time. I recollect just the same thing in my own parish.'

'What, like the man in *Tess of the D'Urbervilles*?' Williams put in.

'Yes, I dare say; it's not a book I could ever read myself. But this fellow could show a row of tombs in the church there that belonged to his ancestors, and all that went to sour him a bit; but Francis, they said, could never get at him – he always kept just on the right side of the law – until one night the keepers found him at it in a wood right at the end of the estate. I could show you the place now; it marches with some land that used to belong to an uncle of mine. And you can imagine there was a row; and this man Gawdy (that was the name, to be sure – Gawdy; I thought

I should get it – Gawdy), he was unlucky enough, poor chap! to shoot a keeper. Well, that was what Francis wanted, and grand juries – you know what they would have been then – and poor Gawdy was strung up in double-quick time; and I've been shown the place he was buried in, on the north side of the church – you know the way in that part of the world: anyone that's been hanged or made away with themselves, they bury them that side. And the idea was that some friend of Gawdy's – not a relation, because he had none, poor devil! he was the last of his line: kind of *spes ultima gentis* – must have planned to get hold of Francis's boy and put an end to *his* line, too. I don't know – it s rather an out-of-the-way thing for an Essex poacher to think of – but, you know, I should say now it looks more as if old Gawdy had managed the job himself. Booh! I hate to think of it! Have some whisky, Williams!'

The facts were communicated by Williams to Dennistoun, and by him to a mixed company, of which I was one, and the Sadducean Professor of Ophiology another. I am sorry to say that the latter, when asked what he thought of it, only remarked: 'Oh, those Bridgeford people will say anything' – a sentiment which met with the reception it deserved.

I have only to add that the picture is now in the Ashleian Museum; that it has been treated with a view to discovering whether sympathetic ink has been used in it, but without effect; that Mr Britnell knew nothing of it save that he was sure it was uncommon; and that, though carefully watched, it has never been known to change again.

Honeysuckle Cottage

P. G. Wodehouse

‘HONEYSUCKLE COTTAGE’

P. G. WODEHOUSE (SIR PELHAM GRENVILLE WODEHOUSE,

BRITISH, 1881–1975)

First published in the 24 January 1925 issue of the *Saturday Evening Post*.

P. G. Wodehouse is best known for his stories featuring Jeeves and Bertie Wooster, which feature many formidable aunts and intransigent nephews. However, according to his memoir, the philosopher Ludwig Wittgenstein thought 'Honeysuckle Cottage' was the funniest thing he had ever read, and I am obliged to agree.

HONEYSUCKLE COTTAGE

P. G. Wodehouse

'Do you believe in ghosts?' asked Mr Mulliner abruptly.

I weighed the question thoughtfully. I was a little surprised, for nothing in our previous conversation had suggested the topic.

'Well,' I replied, 'I don't like them, if that's what you mean. I was once butted by one as a child.'

'Ghosts. Not goats.'

'Oh, ghosts? Do I believe in ghosts?'

'Exactly.'

'Well, yes – and no.'

'Let me put it another way,' said Mr Mulliner, patiently. 'Do you believe in haunted houses? Do you believe that it is possible for a malign influence to envelop a place and work a spell on all who come within its radius?'

I hesitated.

'Well, no – and yes.'

Mr Mulliner sighed a little. He seemed to be wondering if I was always as bright as this.

'Of course,' I went on, 'one has read stories. Henry James's *Turn of the Screw* . . .'

'I am not talking about fiction.'

'Well, in real life— Well, look here, I once, as a matter of fact, did meet a man who knew a fellow—'

'My distant cousin James Rodman spent some weeks in a haunted house,' said Mr Mulliner, who, if he has a fault, is not a very good listener. 'It cost him five thousand pounds. That is to say, he sacrificed five thousand pounds by not remaining there. Did you ever,' he asked, wandering, it seemed to me, from the subject, 'hear of Leila J. Pinckney?'

Naturally I had heard of Leila J. Pinckney. Her death some years ago has diminished her vogue, but at one time it was impossible to pass a book-shop or a railway bookstall without seeing a long row of her novels. I had never myself actually read any of them, but I knew that in her particular line of literature, the Squashily Sentimental, she had always been regarded by those entitled to judge as pre-eminent. The critics usually headed their reviews of her stories with the words:–

ANOTHER PINCKNEY

or sometimes, more offensively:–

ANOTHER PINCKNEY!!!

And once, dealing with, I think, *The Love Which Prevails*, the literary expert of the *Scrutinizer* had compressed his entire critique into the single phrase 'Oh, God!'

'Of course,' I said. 'But what about her?'

'She was James Rodman's aunt.'

'Yes?'

'And when she died James found that she had left him five thousand pounds and the house in the country where she had lived for the last twenty years of her life.'

'A very nice little legacy.'

'Twenty years,' repeated Mr Mulliner. 'Grasp that, for it has a vital bearing on what follows. Twenty years, mind you, and Miss Pinckney turned out two novels and twelve short stories regularly every year, besides a monthly page of Advice to Young Girls in one of the magazines. That is to say, forty of her novels and no fewer than two hundred and forty of her short stories were written under the roof of Honeysuckle Cottage.'

'A pretty name.'

'A nasty, sloppy name,' said Mr Mulliner severely, 'which should have warned my distant cousin James from the start. Have you a pencil and a piece of paper?' He scribbled for a while, poring frowningly over columns of figures. 'Yes,' he said, looking up, 'if my calculations are correct, Leila J. Pinckney wrote in all a matter of nine million one hundred and forty thousand words of glutinous sentimentality at Honeysuckle Cottage, and it was a condition of her will that James should reside there for six months in every year. Failing to do this, he was to forfeit the five thousand pounds.'

'It must be great fun making a freak will,' I mused. 'I often wish I was rich enough to do it.'

"This was not a freak will. The conditions are perfectly understandable. James Rodman was a writer of sensational mystery stories, and his aunt Leila had always disapproved of his work. She was a great believer in the influence of environment, and the reason why she inserted that clause in her will was that she wished to compel James to move from London to the country. She considered that living in London hardened him and made his outlook on life sordid. She often asked him if he thought it quite nice to harp so much on sudden death and blackmailers with squints. Surely, she said, there were enough squinting blackmailers in the world without writing about them.

'The fact that Literature meant such different things to these two had, I believe, caused something of a coolness between them, and James had never dreamed that he would be remembered in his aunt's will. For he had never concealed his opinion that Leila J. Pinckney's style of writing revolted him, however dear it might be to her enormous public. He held rigid views on the art of the novel, and always maintained that an artist with a true reverence for his craft should not descend to goo-ey love stories, but should stick austerely to revolvers, cries in the night, missing papers, mysterious Chinamen and dead bodies – with or without gash in throat. And not even the thought that his aunt had dandled him on her knee as a baby could induce him to stifle his literary conscience to the extent of pretending to enjoy her work. First, last and all the time, James Rodman had held the opinion – and voiced it fearlessly – that Leila J. Pinckney wrote bilge.

'It was a surprise to him, therefore, to find that he had been left this legacy. A pleasant surprise, of course. James was making quite a decent income out of the three novels and eighteen short stories which he produced annually, but an author can always find a use for five thousand pounds. And, as for the cottage, he had actually been looking about for a little place in the country at the very moment when he received the lawyer's letter. In less than a week he was installed at his new residence.'

★   ★   ★

James's first impressions of Honeysuckle Cottage were, he tells me, wholly favourable. He was delighted with the place. It was a low, rambling, picturesque old house with funny little chimneys and a red roof, placed in the middle of the most charming country. With its oak beams, its trim garden, its trilling birds and its rose-hung porch, it was the ideal spot for a writer. It was just the sort of place, he reflected whimsically, which his aunt had loved to write about in her books. Even the apple-cheeked old housekeeper who attended to his needs might have stepped straight out of one of them.

It seemed to James that his lot had been cast in pleasant places. He had brought down his books, his pipes and his golf- clubs, and was hard at work finishing the best thing he had ever done. *The Secret Nine* was the title of it; and on the beautiful summer afternoon on which this story opens he was in the study, hammering away at his typewriter, at peace with the world. The machine was running sweetly, the new tobacco he had bought the day before was proving admirable, and he was moving on all six cylinders to the end of a chapter.

He shoved in a fresh sheet of paper, chewed his pipe thoughtfully for a moment, then wrote rapidly:

'For an instant Lester Gage thought that he must have been mistaken. Then the noise came again, faint but unmistakable – a soft scratching on the outer panel.

'His mouth set in a grim line. Silently, like a panther, he made one quick step to the desk, noiselessly opened a drawer, drew out his automatic. After that affair of the poisoned needle, he was taking no chances. Still in dead silence, he tiptoed to the door; then, flinging it suddenly open, he stood there, his weapon poised.

'On the mat stood the most beautiful girl he had ever beheld. A veritable child of Faërie. She eyed him for a moment with a saucy smile; then with a pretty, roguish look of reproof shook a dainty fore-finger at him.

'"I believe you've forgotten me, Mr Gage!" she fluted with a mock severity which her eyes belied.'

James stared at the paper dumbly. He was utterly perplexed. He had not had the slightest intention of writing anything like this. To begin with, it was a rule with him, and one which he never broke, to allow no girls to appear in his stories. Sinister landladies, yes, and naturally any amount of adventuresses with foreign accents, but never under any pretext what may be broadly described as girls. A detective story, he maintained, should have no heroine. Heroines only held up the action and tried to flirt with the hero when he should have been busy looking for clues, and then went and let the villain kidnap them by some childishly simple trick. In his writing, James was positively monastic.

And yet here was this creature with her saucy smile and her dainty fore-finger horning in at the most important point in the story. It was uncanny.

He looked once more at his scenario. No, the scenario was all right.

In perfectly plain words it stated that what happened when the door opened was that a dying man fell in and after gasping, 'The beetle! Tell Scotland Yard that the blue beetle is—' expired on the hearth-rug, leaving Lester Gage not unnaturally somewhat mystified. Nothing whatever about any beautiful girls.

In a curious mood of irritation, James scratched out the offending passage, wrote in the necessary corrections and put the cover on the machine. It was at this point that he heard William whining.

The only blot on this paradise which James had so far been able to discover was the infernal dog, William. Belonging nominally to the gardener, on the very first morning he had adopted James by acclamation, and he maddened and infuriated James. He had a habit of coming and whining under the window when James was at work. The latter would ignore this as long as he could; then, when the thing became insupportable, would bound out of his chair, to see the animal standing on the gravel, gazing expectantly up at him with a stone in his mouth. William had a weak-minded passion for chasing stones; and on the first day James, in a rash spirit of camaraderie, had flung one for him. Since then James had thrown no more stones; but he had thrown any number of other solids, and the garden was littered with objects ranging from match boxes to a plaster statuette of the young Joseph prophesying before Pharaoh. And still William came and whined, an optimist to the last.

The whining, coming now at a moment when he felt irritable and unsettled, acted on James much as the scratching on the door had acted on Lester Gage. Silently, like a panther, he made one quick step to the mantelpiece, removed from it a china mug bearing the legend A Present from Clacton-on-Sea, and crept to the window.

And as he did so a voice outside said, 'Go away, sir, go away!' and there followed a short, high-pitched bark which was certainly not William's. William was a mixture of Airedale, setter, bull terrier, and mastiff; and when in vocal mood, favoured the mastiff side of his family.

James peered out. There on the porch stood a girl in blue. She held in her arms a small fluffy white dog, and she was endeavouring to foil the upward movement toward this of the blackguard William. William's mentality had been arrested some years before at the point where he imagined that everything in the world had been created for him to eat. A bone, a boot, a steak, the back wheel of a bicycle – it was all one to William. If it was there he tried to eat it. He had even made a plucky attempt to devour the remains of the young Joseph prophesying before Pharaoh. And it was perfectly plain now that he regarded the curious wriggling object in the girl's arms purely in the light of a snack to keep body and soul together till dinnertime.

'William!' bellowed James.

William looked courteously over his shoulder with eyes that beamed with the pure light of a life's devotion, wagged the whip-like tail which he had inherited from his bull-terrier ancestor and resumed his intent scrutiny of the fluffy dog.

'Oh, please!' cried the girl. 'This great rough dog is frightening poor Toto.'

The man of letters and the man of action do not always go hand in hand, but practice had made James perfect in handling with a swift efficiency any situation that involved William. A moment later that canine moron, having received the present from Clacton in the short ribs, was scuttling round the corner of the house, and James had jumped through the window and was facing the girl.

She was an extraordinarily pretty girl. Very sweet and fragile she looked as she stood there under the honeysuckle with the breeze ruffling a tendril of golden hair that strayed from beneath her coquettish little hat. Her eyes were very big and very blue, her rose-tinted face becomingly flushed. All wasted on James, though. He disliked all girls, and particularly the sweet, droopy type.

'Did you want to see somebody?' he asked stiffly.

'Just the house,' said the girl, 'if it wouldn't be giving any trouble. I do so want to see the room where Miss Pinckney wrote her books. This is where Leila J. Pinckney used to live, isn't it?'

'Yes; I am her nephew. My name is James Rodman.'

'Mine is Rose Maynard.'

James led the way into the house, and she stopped with a cry of delight on the threshold of the morning-room.

'Oh, how too perfect!' she cried. 'So this was her study?'

'Yes.'

'What a wonderful place it would be for you to think in if you were a writer too.'

James held no high opinion of women's literary taste, but nevertheless he was conscious of an unpleasant shock.

'I am a writer,' he said coldly. 'I write detective stories.'

'I – I'm afraid' – she blushed – 'I'm afraid I don't often read detective stories.'

'You no doubt prefer,' said James, still more coldly, 'the sort of thing my aunt used to write.'

'Oh, I love her stories!' cried the girl, clasping her hands ecstatically. 'Don't you?'

'I cannot say that I do.'

'What?'

'They are pure apple sauce,' said James sternly; 'just nasty blobs of sentimentality, thoroughly untrue to life.'

The girl stared.

'Why, that's just what's so wonderful about them, their trueness to life! You feel they might all have happened. I don't understand what you mean.'

They were walking down the garden now. James held the gate open for her and she passed through into the road.

'Well, for one thing,' he said, 'I decline to believe that a marriage between two young people is invariably preceded by some violent and sensational experience in which they both share.'

'Are you thinking of *Scent o' the Blossom*, where Edgar saves Maud from drowning?'

'I am thinking of every single one of my aunt's books.' He looked at her curiously. He had just got the solution of a mystery which had been puzzling him for some time. Almost from the moment he had set eyes on her she had seemed somehow strangely familiar. It now suddenly came to him why it was that he disliked her so much. 'Do you know,' he said, 'you might be one of my aunt's heroines yourself? You're just the sort of girl she used to love to write about.'

Her face lit up.

'Oh, do you really think so?' She hesitated. 'Do you know what I have been feeling ever since I came here? I've been feeling that you are exactly like one of Miss Pinckney's heroes.'

'No, I say, really!' said James, revolted.

'Oh, but you are! When you jumped through that window it gave me quite a start. You were so exactly like Claude Masterson in *Heather o' the Hills*.'

'I have not read *Heather o' the Hills*,' said James, with a shudder.

'He was very strong and quiet, with deep, dark, sad eyes.'

James did not explain that his eyes were sad because her society gave him a pain in the neck. He merely laughed scornfully.

'So now, I suppose,' he said, 'a car will come and knock you down and I shall carry you gently into the house and lay you— Look out!' he cried.

It was too late. She was lying in a little huddled heap at his feet. Round the corner a large automobile had come bowling, keeping with an almost affected precision to the wrong side of the road. It was now receding into the distance, the occupant of the tonneau, a stout red-faced gentleman in a fur coat, leaning out over the back. He had bared his head – not, one fears, as a pretty gesture of respect and regret, but because he was using his hat to hide the number plate.

The dog Toto was unfortunately uninjured.

James carried the girl gently into the house and laid her on the sofa in the morning-room. He rang the bell and the apple-cheeked housekeeper appeared.

'Send for the doctor,' said James. 'There has been an accident.'

The housekeeper bent over the girl.

'Eh, dearie, dearie!' she said. 'Bless her sweet pretty face!'

The gardener, he who technically owned William, was routed out from among the young lettuces and told to fetch Doctor Brady. He separated his bicycle from William, who was making a light meal off the left pedal, and departed on his mission. Doctor Brady arrived and in due course he made his report.

'No bones broken, but a number of nasty bruises. And, of course, the shock. She will have to stay here for some time, Rodman. Can't be moved.'

'Stay here! But she can't! It isn't proper.'

'Your housekeeper will act as a chaperone.'

The doctor sighed. He was a stolid-looking man of middle age with side-whiskers.

'A beautiful girl, that, Rodman,' he said.

'I suppose so,' said James.

'A sweet, beautiful girl. An elfin child.'

'A what?' cried James, starting.

This imagery was very foreign to Doctor Brady as he knew him. On the only previous occasion on which they had had any extended conversation, the doctor had talked exclusively about the effect of too much protein on the gastric juices.

'An elfin child; a tender, fairy creature. When I was looking at her just now, Rodman, I nearly broke down. Her little hand lay on the coverlet like some white lily floating on the surface of a still pool, and her dear, trusting eyes gazed up at me.'

He pottered off down the garden, still babbling, and James stood staring after him blankly. And slowly, like some cloud athwart a summer sky, there crept over James's heart the chill shadow of a nameless fear.

★　★　★

It was about a week later that Mr Andrew McKinnon, the senior partner in the well-known firm of literary agents, McKinnon & Gooch, sat in his office in Chancery Lane, frowning thoughtfully over a telegram. He rang the bell.

'Ask Mr Gooch to step in here.' He resumed his study of the telegram. 'Oh, Gooch,' he said when his partner appeared, 'I've just had a curious wire from young Rodman. He seems to want to see me very urgently.'

Mr Gooch read the telegram.

'Written under the influence of some strong mental excitement,' he agreed. 'I wonder why he doesn't come to the office if he wants to see you so badly.'

'He's working very hard, finishing that novel for Prodder &
Wiggs. Can't leave it, I suppose. Well, it's a nice day. If you will
look after things here I think I'll motor down and let him give me
lunch.'

★   ★   ★

As Mr McKinnon's car reached the crossroads a mile from
Honeysuckle Cottage, he was aware of a gesticulating figure by
the hedge. He stopped the car.

'Morning, Rodman.'

'Thank God, you've come!' said James. It seemed to Mr
McKinnon that the young man looked paler and thinner.

'Would you mind walking the rest of the way? There's something I want to speak to you about.'

Mr McKinnon alighted; and James, as he glanced at him, felt
cheered and encouraged by the very sight of the man. The literary
agent was a grim, hard-bitten person, to whom, when he called at
their offices to arrange terms, editors kept their faces turned so
that they might at least retain their back collar studs. There was
no sentiment in Andrew McKinnon. Editresses of society papers
practised their blandishments on him in vain, and many a pub-
lisher had waked screaming in the night, dreaming that he was
signing a McKinnon contract.

'Well, Rodman,' he said, 'Prodder & Wiggs have agreed to our
terms. I was writing to tell you so when your wire arrived. I had a
lot of trouble with them, but it's fixed at 20 per cent., rising to 25,

and two hundred pounds advance royalties on day of publication.'

'Good!' said James absently. 'Good! McKinnon, do you remember my aunt, Leila J. Pinckney?'

'Remember her? Why, I was her agent all her life.'

'Of course. Then you know the sort of tripe she wrote.'

'No author,' said Mr McKinnon reprovingly, 'who pulls down a steady twenty thousand pounds a year writes tripe.'

'Well anyway, you know her stuff.'

'Who better?'

'When she died she left me five thousand pounds and her house, Honeysuckle Cottage. I'm living there now. McKinnon, do you believe in haunted houses?'

'No.'

'Yet I tell you solemnly that Honeysuckle Cottage is haunted!'

'By your aunt?' said Mr McKinnon, surprised.

'By her influence. There's a malignant spell over the place; a sort of miasma of sentimentalism. Everybody who enters it succumbs.'

'Tut-tut! You mustn't have these fancies.'

'They aren't fancies.'

'You aren't seriously meaning to tell me—'

'Well, how do you account for this? That book you were speaking about, which Prodder & Wiggs are to publish – *The Secret Nine*. Every time I sit down to write it a girl keeps trying to sneak in.'

'Into the room?'

'Into the story.'

'You don't want a love interest in your sort of book,' said Mr McKinnon, shaking his head. 'It delays the action.'

'I know it does. And every day I have to keep shooing this infernal female out. An awful girl, McKinnon. A soppy, soupy, treacly, drooping girl with a roguish smile. This morning she tried to butt in on the scene where Lester Gage is trapped in the den of the mysterious leper.'

'No!'

'She did, I assure you. I had to rewrite three pages before I could get her out of it. And that's not the worst. Do you know, McKinnon, that at this moment I am actually living the plot of a typical Leila May Pinckney novel in just the setting she always used! And I can see the happy ending coming nearer every day! A week ago a girl was knocked down by a car at my door and I've had to put her up, and every day I realize more clearly that sooner or later I shall ask her to marry me.'

'Don't do it,' said Mr McKinnon, a stout bachelor. 'You're too young to marry.'

'So was Methuselah,' said James, a stouter. 'But all the same I know I'm going to do it. It's the influence of this awful house weighing upon me. I feel like an eggshell in a maelstrom. I am being sucked on by a force too strong for me to resist. This morning I found myself kissing her dog!'

'No!'

'I did! And I loathe the little beast. Yesterday I got up at dawn and plucked a nosegay of flowers for her, wet with the dew.'

'Rodman!'

'It's a fact. I laid them at her door and went downstairs kicking myself all the way. And there in the hall was the apple-cheeked housekeeper regarding me archly. If she didn't murmur "Bless their sweet young hearts!" my ears deceived me.'

'Why don't you pack up and leave?'

'If I do I lose the five thousand pounds.'

'Ah!' said Mr McKinnon.

'I can understand what has happened. It's the same with all haunted houses. My aunt's subliminal ether vibrations have woven themselves into the texture of the place, creating an atmosphere which forces the ego of all who come in contact with it to attune themselves to it. It's either that or something to do with the fourth dimension.'

Mr McKinnon laughed scornfully.

'Tut-tut!' he said again. 'This is pure imagination. What has happened is that you've been working too hard. You'll see this precious atmosphere of yours will have no effect on me.'

'That's exactly why I asked you to come down. I hoped you might break the spell.'

'I will that,' said Mr McKinnon jovially.

The fact that the literary agent spoke little at lunch caused James no apprehension. Mr McKinnon was ever a silent tren-cherman. From time to time James caught him stealing a glance at the girl, who was well enough to come down to meals now, limping pathetically; but he could read nothing in his face. And yet the mere look of his face was a consolation. It was so solid, so matter of fact, so exactly like an unemotional coconut.

'You've done me good,' said James with a sigh of relief, as he escorted the agent down the garden to his car after lunch. 'I felt all along that I could rely on your rugged common sense. The whole atmosphere of the place seems different now.'

Mr McKinnon did not speak for a moment. He seemed to be plunged in thought.

'Rodman,' he said, as he got into his car, 'I've been thinking over that suggestion of yours of putting a love interest into *The Secret Nine*. I think you're wise. The story needs it. After all, what is there greater in the world than love? Love – love – aye, it's the sweetest word in the language. Put in a heroine and let her marry Lester Gage.'

'If,' said James grimly, 'she does succeed in worming her way in she'll jolly well marry the mysterious leper. But look here, I don't understand—'

'It was seeing that girl that changed me,' proceeded Mr McKinnon. And as James stared at him aghast, tears suddenly filled his hard-boiled eyes. He openly snuffled. 'Aye, seeing her sitting there under the roses, with all that smell of honeysuckle and all. And the birdies singing so sweet in the garden and the sun lighting up her bonny face. The puir wee lass!' he muttered, dabbing at his eyes. 'The puir bonny wee lass! Rodman,' he said, his voice quivering, 'I've decided that we're being hard on Prodder & Wiggs. Wiggs has had sickness in his home lately. We mustn't be hard on a man who's had sickness in his home, hey, laddie? No, no! I'm going to take back that contract and alter it to a flat 12 per cent. and no advance royalties.'

'What!'

'But you shan't lose by it, Rodman. No, no, you shan't lose by it, my manny. I am going to waive my commission. The puir bonny wee lass!'

The car rolled off down the road. Mr McKinnon, seated in the back, was blowing his nose violently.

'This is the end!' said James.

★   ★   ★

It is necessary at this point to pause and examine James Rodman's position with an unbiased eye. The average man, unless he puts himself in James's place, will be unable to appreciate it. James, he will feel, was making a lot of fuss about nothing. Here he was, drawing daily closer and closer to a charming girl with big blue eyes, and surely rather to be envied than pitied.

But we must remember that James was one of Nature's bachelors. And no ordinary man, looking forward dreamily to a little home of his own with a loving wife putting out his slippers and changing the gramophone records, can realize the intensity of the instinct for self-preservation which animates Nature's bachelors in times of peril.

James Rodman had a congenital horror of matrimony. Though a young man, he had allowed himself to develop a great many habits which were as the breath of life to him; and these habits, he knew instinctively, a wife would shoot to pieces within a week of the end of the honeymoon.

James liked to breakfast in bed; and, having breakfasted, to smoke in bed and knock the ashes out on the carpet. What wife would tolerate this practice?

James liked to pass his days in a tennis shirt, grey flannel trousers and slippers. What wife ever rests until she has inclosed her husband in a stiff collar, tight boots and a morning suit and taken him with her to *thés musicales*?

These and a thousand other thoughts of the same kind flashed through the unfortunate young man's mind as the days went by, and every day that passed seemed to draw him nearer to the brink of the chasm. Fate appeared to be taking a malicious pleasure in making things as difficult for him as possible. Now that the girl was well enough to leave her bed, she spent her time sitting in a chair on the sun-sprinkled porch, and James had to read to her – and poetry, at that; and not the jolly, wholesome sort of poetry the boys are turning out nowadays, either – good, honest stuff about sin and gas works and decaying corpses – but the old-fashioned kind with rhymes in it, dealing almost exclusively with love. The weather, moreover, continued superb. The honeysuckle cast its sweet scent on the gentle breeze; the roses over the porch stirred and nodded; the flowers in the garden were lovelier than ever; the birds sang their little throats sore. And every evening there was a magnificent sunset. It was almost as if Nature were doing it on purpose.

At last James intercepted Doctor Brady as he was leaving after one of his visits and put the thing to him squarely:

'When is that girl going?'

The doctor patted him on the arm.

'Not yet, Rodman,' he said in a low, understanding voice. 'No need to worry yourself about that. Mustn't be moved for days and days and days – I might almost say weeks and weeks and weeks.'

'Weeks and weeks!' cried James.

'And weeks,' said Doctor Brady. He prodded James roguishly in the abdomen. 'Good luck to you, my boy, good luck to you,' he said.

It was some small consolation to James that the mushy physician immediately afterward tripped over William on his way down the path and broke his stethoscope. When a man is up against it like James every little helps.

★   ★   ★

He was walking dismally back to the house after this conversation when he was met by the apple-cheeked housekeeper.

'The little lady would like to speak to you, sir,' said the apple-cheeked exhibit, rubbing her hands.

'Would she?' said James hollowly.

'So sweet and pretty she looks, sir – oh, sir, you wouldn't believe! Like a blessed angel sitting there with her dear eyes all a-shining.'

'Don't do it!' cried James with extraordinary vehemence. 'Don't do it!'

He found the girl propped up on the cushions and thought once again how singularly he disliked her. And yet, even as he thought this, some force against which he had to fight madly was whispering to him, 'Go to her and take that little hand! Breathe into that little ear the burning words that will make that little face turn away crimsoned with blushes!' He wiped a bead of perspiration from his forehead and sat down.

'Mrs Stick-in-the-Mud – what's her name? – says you want to see me.'

The girl nodded.

'I've had a letter from Uncle Henry. I wrote to him as soon as I was better and told him what had happened, and he is coming here tomorrow morning.'

'Uncle Henry?'

'That's what I call him, but he's really no relation. He is my guardian. He and daddy were officers in the same regiment, and when daddy was killed, fighting on the Afghan frontier, he died in Uncle Henry's arms and with his last breath begged him to take care of me.'

James started. A sudden wild hope had waked in his heart. Years ago, he remembered, he had read a book of his aunt's entitled *Rupert's Legacy*, and in that book—

'I'm engaged to marry him,' said the girl quietly.

'Wow!' shouted James.

'What?' asked the girl, startled.

'Touch of cramp,' said James. He was thrilling all over. That wild hope had been realized.

'It was daddy's dying wish that we should marry,' said the girl.

'And dashed sensible of him, too; dashed sensible,' said James warmly.

'And yet,' she went on, a little wistfully, 'I sometimes wonder—'

'Don't!' said James. 'Don't! You must respect daddy's dying wish. There's nothing like daddy's dying wish; you can't beat it. So he's coming here tomorrow, is he? Capital, capital! To lunch, I suppose? Excellent! I'll run down and tell Mrs Who-Is-It to lay in another chop.'

It was with a gay and uplifted heart that James strolled the garden and smoked his pipe next morning. A great cloud seemed to have rolled itself away from him. Everything was for the best in the best of all possible worlds. He had finished *The Secret Nine* and shipped it off to Mr McKinnon, and now as he strolled there was shaping itself in his mind a corking plot about a man with only half a face who lived in a secret den and terrorized London with a series of shocking murders. And what made them so shocking was the fact that each of the victims, when discovered, was found to have only half a face too. The rest had been chipped off, presumably by some blunt instrument.

The thing was coming out magnificently, when suddenly his attention was diverted by a piercing scream. Out of the bushes fringing the river that ran beside the garden burst the apple-cheeked housekeeper.

'Oh, sir! Oh, sir! Oh, sir!'

'What is it?' demanded James irritably.

'Oh, sir! Oh, sir! Oh, sir!'

'Yes, and then what?'

'The little dog, sir! He's in the river!'

'Well, whistle him to come out.'

'Oh, sir, do come quick! He'll be drowned!'

James followed her through the bushes, taking off his coat as he went. He was saying to himself, 'I will not rescue this dog. I do not like the dog. It is high time he had a bath, and in any case it would be much simpler to stand on the bank and fish for him with a rake. Only an ass out of a Leila J. Pinckney book would dive into a beastly river to save—'

At this point he dived. Toto, alarmed by the splash, swam rapidly for the bank, but James was too quick for him. Grasping him firmly by the neck, he scrambled ashore and ran for the house, followed by the housekeeper.

The girl was seated on the porch. Over her there bent the tall soldierly figure of a man with keen eyes and greying hair. The housekeeper raced up.

'Oh, miss! Toto! In the river! He saved him! He plunged in and saved him!'

The girl drew a quick breath.

'Gallant, damme! By Jove! By gad! Yes, gallant, by George!' exclaimed the soldierly man.

The girl seemed to wake from a reverie.

'Uncle Henry, this is Mr Rodman. Mr Rodman, my guardian, Colonel Carteret.'

'Proud to meet you, sir,' said the colonel, his honest blue eyes glowing as he fingered his short crisp moustache. 'As fine a thing as I ever heard of, damme!'

'Yes, you are brave – brave,' the girl whispered.

'I am wet – wet,' said James, and went upstairs to change his clothes.

★   ★   ★

When he came down for lunch, he found to his relief that the girl had decided not to join them, and Colonel Carteret was silent and preoccupied. James, exerting himself in his capacity of host, tried him with the weather, golf, India, the Government, the high cost of living, first-class cricket, the modern dancing craze, and murderers he had met, but the other still preserved that strange, absent-minded silence. It was only when the meal was concluded and James had produced cigarettes that he came abruptly out of his trance.

'Rodman,' he said, 'I should like to speak to you.'

'Yes?' said James, thinking it was about time.

'Rodman,' said Colonel Carteret, 'or rather, George – I may call you George?' he added, with a sort of wistful diffidence that had a singular charm.

'Certainly,' replied James, 'if you wish it. Though my name is James.'

'James, eh? Well, well, it amounts to the same thing, eh, what, damme, by gad?' said the colonel with a momentary return of his bluff soldierly manner. 'Well, then, James, I have something that I wish to say to you. Did Miss Maynard – did Rose happen to tell you anything about myself in – er – in connection with herself?'

'She mentioned that you and she were engaged to be married.'

The colonel's tightly drawn lips quivered. 'No longer,' he said.

'What?'

'No, John, my boy.'

'James.'

'No, James, my boy, no longer. While you were upstairs changing your clothes she told me – breaking down, poor child, as she spoke – that she wished our engagement to be at an end.'

James half rose from the table, his cheeks blanched.

'You don't mean that!' he gasped.

Colonel Carteret nodded. He was staring out of the window, his fine eyes set in a look of pain.

'But this is nonsense!' cried James. 'This is absurd! She – she mustn't be allowed to chop and change like this. I mean to say, it – it isn't fair—'

'Don't think of me, my boy.'

'I'm not – I mean, did she give any reason?'

'Her eyes did.'

'Her eyes did?'

'Her eyes, when she looked at you on the porch, as you stood there – young, heroic – having just saved the life of the dog she loves. It is you who won that tender heart, my boy.'

'Now listen,' protested James, 'you aren't going to sit there and tell me that a girl falls in love with a man just because he saves her dog from drowning?'

'Why, surely,' said Colonel Carteret, surprised. 'What better reason could she have?' He sighed. 'It is the old, old story, my boy. Youth to youth. I am an old man. I should have known – I should have foreseen – yes, youth to youth.'

'You aren't a bit old.'

'Yes, yes.'

'No, no.'

'Yes, yes.'

'Don't keep on saying yes, yes!' cried James, clutching at his hair. 'Besides, she wants a steady old buffer – a steady, sensible man of medium age – to look after her.'

Colonel Carteret shook his head with a gentle smile.

'This is mere quixotry, my boy. It is splendid of you to take this attitude; but no, no.'

'Yes, yes.'

'No, no.' He gripped James's hand for an instant, then rose and walked to the door. 'That is all I wished to say, Tom.'

'James.'

'James. I just thought that you ought to know how matters stood. Go to her, my boy, go to her, and don't let any thought of an old man's broken dream keep you from pouring out what is in your heart. I am an old soldier, lad, an old soldier. I have learned to take the rough with the smooth. But I think – I think I will leave you now. I should – should like to be alone for a while. If you need me you will find me in the raspberry bushes.'

He had scarcely gone when James also left the room. He took his hat and stick and walked blindly out of the garden, he knew not whither. His brain was numbed. Then, as his powers of reasoning returned, he told himself that he should have foreseen this ghastly thing. If there was one type of character over which Leila J. Pinckney had been wont to spread herself, it was the pathetic guardian who loves his ward but relinquishes her to the younger man. No wonder the girl had broken off the engagement. Any elderly guardian who allowed himself to come within a mile of Honeysuckle Cottage was simply asking for it. And then, as he turned to walk back, a sort of dull defiance gripped James. Why, he asked, should he be put upon in this manner? If the girl liked to throw over this man, why should he be the goat?

He saw his way clearly now. He just wouldn't do it, that was all. And if they didn't like it they could lump it.

Full of a new fortitude, he strode in at the gate. A tall, soldierly figure emerged from the raspberry bushes and came to meet him.

'Well?' said Colonel Carteret.

'Well?' said James defiantly.

'Am I to congratulate you?'

James caught his keen blue eye and hesitated. It was not going to be so simple as he had supposed.

'Well – er—' he said.

Into the keen blue eyes there came a look that James had not seen there before. It was the stern, hard look which – probably – had caused men to bestow upon this old soldier the name of Cold-Steel Carteret.

'You have not asked Rose to marry you?'

'Er – no; not yet.'

The keen blue eyes grew keener and bluer.

'Rodman,' said Colonel Carteret in a strange, quiet voice, 'I have known that little girl since she was a tiny child. For years she has been all in all to me. Her father died in my arms and with his last breath bade me see that no harm came to his darling. I have nursed her through mumps, measles – aye, and chicken pox – and I live but for her happiness.' He paused, with a significance that made James's toes curl. 'Rodman,' he said, 'do you know what I would do to any man who trifled with that little girl's affections?' He reached in his hip pocket and an ugly-looking revolver glittered in the sunlight. 'I would shoot him like a dog.'

'Like a dog?' faltered James.

'Like a dog,' said Colonel Carteret. He took James's arm and turned him toward the house. 'She is on the porch. Go to her. And if—' He broke off. 'But tut!' he said in a kindlier tone. 'I am doing you an injustice, my boy. I know it.'

'Oh, you are,' said James fervently.

'Your heart is in the right place.'

'Oh, absolutely,' said James.

'Then go to her, my boy. Later on you may have something to tell me. You will find me in the strawberry beds.'

It was very cool and fragrant on the porch. Overhead, little breezes played and laughed among the roses. Somewhere in the distance sheep bells tinkled, and in the shrubbery a thrush was singing its even-song.

Seated in her chair behind a wicker table laden with tea things, Rose Maynard watched James as he shambled up the path.

'Tea's ready,' she called gaily. 'Where is Uncle Henry?' A look of pity and distress flitted for a moment over her flower-like face. 'Oh I – I forgot,' she whispered.

'He is in the strawberry beds,' said James in a low voice.

She nodded unhappily.

'Of course, of course. Oh, why is life like this?' James heard her whisper.

He sat down. He looked at the girl. She was leaning back with closed eyes, and he thought he had never seen such a little squirt in his life. The idea of passing his remaining days in her society revolted him. He was stoutly opposed to the idea of marrying anyone; but if, as happens to the best of us, he ever were compelled to perform the wedding glide, he had always hoped it would be with some lady golf champion who would help him with his putting, and thus, by bringing his handicap down a notch or two, enable him to save something from the wreck, so to speak. But to link his lot with a girl who read his aunt's books and liked them; a girl who could tolerate the presence of the dog Toto; a girl who clasped her hands in pretty, childish joy when she saw a nasturtium in bloom – it was too much. Nevertheless, he took her hand and began to speak.

'Miss Maynard – Rose—'

She opened her eyes and cast them down. A flush had come into her cheeks. The dog Toto at her side sat up and begged for cake, disregarded.

'Let me tell you a story. Once upon a time there was a lonely man who lived in a cottage all by himself—'

He stopped. Was it James Rodman who was talking this bilge?

'Yes?' whispered the girl.

'– but one day there came to him out of nowhere a little fairy princess. She—'

He stopped again, but this time not because of the sheer shame of listening to his own voice. What caused him to interrupt his tale was the fact that at this moment the tea table suddenly began to rise slowly in the air, tilting as it did so a considerable quantity of hot tea on to the knees of his trousers.

'Ouch!' cried James, leaping.

The table continued to rise, and then fell sideways, revealing the homely countenance of William, who, concealed by the cloth, had been taking a nap beneath it. He moved slowly forward, his eyes on Toto. For many a long day William had been desirous of putting to the test, once and for all, the problem of whether Toto was edible or not. Sometimes he thought yes, at other times no. Now seemed an admirable opportunity for a definite decision. He advanced on the object of his experiment, making a low whistling noise through his nostrils, not unlike a boiling kettle. And Toto, after one long look of incredulous horror, tucked his shapely tail between his legs and, turning, raced for safety. He had laid a course in a bee line for the open garden gate, and William, shaking a dish of marmalade off his head a little petulantly, galloped ponderously after him. Rose Maynard staggered to her feet.

'Oh, save him!' she cried.

Without a word James added himself to the procession. His interest in Toto was but tepid. What he wanted was to get near enough to William to discuss with him that matter of the tea on his trousers. He reached the road and found that the order of the runners had not changed. For so small a dog, Toto was moving magnificently. A cloud of dust rose as he skidded round the corner. William followed. James followed William.

And so they passed Farmer Birkett's barn, Farmer Giles' cow shed, the place where Farmer Willetts' pigsty used to be before the big fire, and the Bunch of Grapes public house, Jno Biggs propr., licensed to sell tobacco, wines and spirits. And it was as they were turning down the lane that leads past Farmer Robin- son's chicken run that Toto, thinking swiftly, bolted abruptly into a small drain pipe.

'William!' roared James, coming up at a canter. He stopped to pluck a branch from the hedge and swooped darkly on.

William had been crouching before the pipe, making a noise like a bassoon into its interior; but now he rose and came beamingly to James. His eyes were aglow with chumminess and affection; and placing his forefeet on James's chest, he licked him three times on the face in rapid succession. And as he did so, something seemed to snap in James. The scales seemed to fall from James's eyes. For the first time he saw William as he really was, the authentic type of dog that saves his master from a frightful peril. A wave of emotion swept over him.

'William!' he muttered. 'William!'

William was making an early supper off a half brick he had found in the road. James stooped and patted him fondly.

'William,' he whispered, 'you knew when the time had come to change the conversation, didn't you, old boy!' He straightened himself. 'Come, William,' he said. 'Another four miles and we reach Meadowsweet Junction. Make it snappy and we shall just catch the up express, first stop London.'

William looked up into his face and it seemed to James that he gave a brief nod of comprehension and approval. James turned. Through the trees to the east he could see the red roof of

Honeysuckle Cottage, lurking like some evil dragon in ambush.

Then, together, man and dog passed silently into the sunset.

That (concluded Mr Mulliner) is the story of my distant cousin James Rodman. As to whether it is true, that, of course, is an open question. I, personally, am of opinion that it is. There is no doubt that James did go to live at Honeysuckle Cottage and, while there, underwent some experience which has left an ineradicable mark upon him. His eyes today have that unmistakable look which is to be seen only in the eyes of confirmed bachelors whose feet have been dragged to the very brink of the pit and who have gazed at close range into the naked face of matrimony.

And, if further proof be needed, there is William. He is now James's inseparable companion. Would any man be habitually seen in public with a dog like William unless he had some solid cause to be grateful to him, – unless they were linked together by some deep and imperishable memory? I think not. Myself, when I observe William coming along the street, I cross the road and look into a shop window till he has passed. I am not a snob, but I dare not risk my position in Society by being seen talking to that curious compound.

Nor is the precaution an unnecessary one. There is about William a shameless absence of appreciation of class distinctions which recalls the worst excesses of the French Revolution. I have seen him with these eyes chivvy a pomeranian belonging to a Baroness in her own right from near the Achilles Statue to within a few yards of the Marble Arch.

And yet James walks daily with him in Piccadilly. It is surely significant.

Neil Gaiman

Click-Clack

the Rattlebag

'CLICK-CLACK THE RATTLEBAG'

NEIL GAIMAN (BRITISH, 1960–)

First published in the collection *Impossible Monsters* in 2013.

I am very partial to the boy's admonition that Click-Clacks look like 'what you aren't paying attention to'. That's a good summing up of the modus operandi of many ghost stories: they sneak up on you. In this story Neil Gaiman does some especially skilful sneaking.

CLICK-CLACK THE RATTLEBAG
Neil Gaiman

'Before you take me up to bed, will you tell me a story?'

'Do you actually need me to take you up to bed?' I asked the boy.

He thought for a moment. Then, with intense seriousness, 'Yes, actually I think you do. It's because of, I've finished my homework, and so it's my bedtime, and I am a bit scared. Not very scared. Just a bit. But it is a very big house, and lots of times the lights don't work and it's a sort of dark.'

I reached over and tousled his hair.

'I can understand that,' I said. 'It is a very big old house.' He nodded. We were in the kitchen, where it was light and warm. I put down my magazine on the kitchen table. 'What kind of story would you like me to tell you?'

'Well,' he said, thoughtfully. 'I don't think it should be *too* scary, because then when I go up to bed, I will just be thinking about monsters the whole time. But if it isn't just a *little* bit scary then I won't be interested. And you make up scary stories, don't you? I know she says that's what you do.'

'She exaggerates. I write stories, yes. Nothing that's been published, yet, though. And I write lots of different kinds of stories.'

'But you *do* write scary stories?'

'Yes.'

The boy looked up at me from the shadows by the door, where he was waiting. 'Do you know any stories about Click-Clack the Rattlebag?'

'I don't think so.'

'Those are the best sorts of stories.'

'Do they tell them at your school?'

He shrugged. 'Sometimes.'

'What's a Click-Clack the Rattlebag story?'

He was a precocious child, and was unimpressed by his sister's boyfriend's ignorance. You could see it on his face. 'Everybody knows them.'

'I don't,' I said, trying not to smile.

He looked at me as if he was trying to decide whether or not I was pulling his leg. He said, 'I think maybe you should take me up to my bedroom, and then you can tell me a story before I go to sleep, but a very not-scary story because I'll be up in my bedroom then, and it's actually a bit dark up there, too.'

I said, 'Shall I leave a note for your sister, telling her where we are?'

'You can. But you'll hear when they get back. The front door is very slammy.'

We walked out of the warm and cosy kitchen into the hallway

of the big house, where it was chilly and draughty and dark. I flicked the light-switch, but nothing happened.

'The bulb's gone,' the boy said. 'That always happens.'

Our eyes adjusted to the shadows. The moon was almost full, and blue-white moonlight shone in through the high windows on the staircase, down into the hall. 'We'll be all right,' I said.

'Yes,' said the boy, soberly. 'I am very glad you're here.' He seemed less precocious now. His hand found mine, and he held onto my fingers comfortably, trustingly, as if he'd known me all his life. I felt responsible and adult. I did not know if the feeling I had for his sister, who was my girlfriend, was love, not yet, but I liked that the child treated me as one of the family. I felt like his big brother, and I stood taller, and if there was something unsettling about the empty house I would not have admitted it for worlds.

The stairs creaked beneath the threadbare stair-carpet.

'Click-Clacks,' said the boy, 'are the best monsters ever.'

'Are they from television?'

'I don't think so. I don't think any people know where they come from. Mostly they come from the dark.'

'Good place for a monster to come.'

'Yes.'

We walked along the upper corridor in the shadows, walking from patch of moonlight to patch of moonlight. It really was a big house. I wished I had a flashlight.

'They come from the dark,' said the boy, holding onto my hand. 'I think probably they're made of dark. And they come in when you don't pay attention. That's when they come in. And then they take you back to their . . . not nests. What's a word that's like *nests*, but not?'

'House?'

'No. It's not a house.'

'Lair?'

He was silent. Then, 'I think that's the word, yes. Lair.' He squeezed my hand. He stopped talking.

'Right. So they take the people who don't pay attention back to their lair. And what do they do then, your monsters? Do they suck all the blood out of you, like vampires?'

He snorted. 'Vampires don't suck all the blood out of you. They only drink a little bit. Just to keep them going, and, you know, flying around. Click-Clacks are much scarier than vampires.'

'I'm not scared of vampires,' I told him.

'Me neither. I'm not scared of vampires either. Do you want to know what Click-Clacks do? They drink you,' said the boy.

'Like a Coke?'

'Coke is very bad for you,' said the boy. 'If you put a tooth in Coke, in the morning, it will be dissolved into nothing. That's how bad coke is for you and why you must always clean your teeth, every night.'

I'd heard the Coke story as a boy, and had been told, as an adult, that it wasn't true, but was certain that a lie which promoted dental hygiene was a good lie, and I let it pass.

'Click-Clacks drink you,' said the boy. 'First they bite you, and then you go all *ishy* inside, and all your meat and all your brains and everything except your bones and your skin turns into a wet, milk-shakey stuff and then the Click-clack sucks it out through the holes where your eyes used to be.'

'That's disgusting,' I told him. 'Did you make it up?'

We'd reached the last flight of stairs, all the way in to the big house.

'No.'

'I can't believe you kids make up stuff like that.'

'You didn't ask me about the rattlebag,' he said.

'Right. What's the rattlebag?'

'Well,' he said, sagely, soberly, a small voice from the darkness beside me, 'once you're just bones and skin, they hang you up on a hook, and you rattle in the wind.'

'So what do these Click-Clacks look like?' Even as I asked him, I wished I could take the question back, and leave it unasked. I thought: *Huge spidery creatures. Like the one in the shower that morning.* I'm afraid of spiders.

I was relieved when the boy said, 'They look like what you aren't expecting. What you aren't paying attention to.'

We were climbing wooden steps now. I held on to the railing on my left, held his hand with my right, as he walked beside me. It smelled like dust and old wood, that high in the house. The boy's tread was certain, though, even though the moonlight was scarce.

'Do you know what story you're going to tell me, to put me to bed?' he asked. 'It doesn't actually have to be scary.'

'Not really.'

'Maybe you could tell me about this evening. Tell me what you did?'

'That won't make much of a story for you. My girlfriend just moved in to a new place on the edge of town. She inherited it from an aunt or someone. It's very big and very old. I'm going to spend my first night with her, tonight, so I've been waiting for an hour or so for her and her housemates to come back with the wine and an Indian takeaway.'

'See?' said the boy. There was that precocious amusement again. But all kids can be insufferable sometimes, when they think they know something you don't. It's probably good for them. 'You know all that. But you don't think. You just let your brain fill in the gaps.'

He pushed open the door to the attic room. It was perfectly dark, now, but the opening door disturbed the air, and I heard things rattle gently, like dry bones in thin bags, in the slight wind. Click. Clack. Click. Clack. Like that.

I would have pulled away, then, if I could, but small, firm fingers pulled me forward, unrelentingly, into the dark.

They

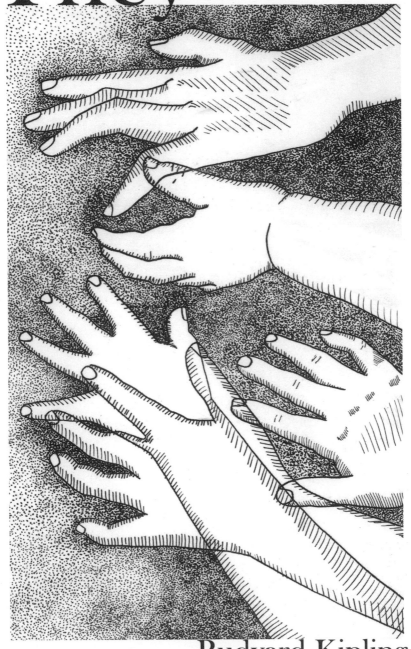

Rudyard Kipling

'THEY'

RUDYARD KIPLING (BRITISH, 1865–1936)

First published in *Scribner's Magazine* in 1904.

I have an ambivalent relationship with Kipling's work, as he can sometimes be a too-forthright champion of colonialism and empire. But he is also a marvellous and sympathetic writer, and this story is a very personal one, as Kipling's young daughter Josephine had died in 1899. It is set in Sussex, where Kipling lived, and the mysterious house is based on his own, Bateman's.

THEY
Rudyard Kipling

One view called me to another; one hill top to its fellow, half across the county, and since I could answer at no more trouble than the snapping forward of a lever, I let the county flow under my wheels. The orchid-studded flats of the East gave way to the thyme, ilex, and grey grass of the Downs; these again to the rich cornland and fig-trees of the lower coast, where you carry the beat of the tide on your left hand for fifteen level miles; and when at last I turned inland through a huddle of rounded hills and woods I had run myself clean out of my known marks. Beyond that precise hamlet which stands godmother to the capital of the United States, I found hidden villages where bees, the only things awake, boomed in eighty-foot lindens that overhung grey Norman churches; miraculous brooks diving under stone bridges built for heavier traffic than would ever vex them again; tithe-barns larger than their churches, and an old smithy that cried out aloud how it had once been a hall of the Knights of the Temple. Gipsies I found on a common where the gorse, bracken, and heath fought it out together up a mile of Roman road; and a little farther on I disturbed a red fox rolling dog-fashion in the naked sunlight.

As the wooded hills closed about me I stood up in the car to take the bearings of that great Down whose ringed head is a landmark for fifty miles across the low countries. I judged that the lie of the country would bring me across some westward-running road that went to his feet, but I did not allow for the confusing veils of the woods. A quick turn plunged me first into a green cutting brim-full of liquid sunshine, next into a gloomy tunnel where last year's dead leaves whispered and scuffled about my tyres. The strong hazel stuff meeting overhead had not been cut for a couple of generations at least, nor had any axe helped the moss-cankered oak and beech to spring above them. Here the road changed frankly into a carpeted ride on whose brown velvet spent primrose-clumps showed like jade, and a few sickly, white-stalked bluebells nodded together. As the slope favoured I shut off the power and slid over the whirled leaves, expecting every moment to meet a keeper; but I only heard a jay, far off, arguing against the silence under the twilight of the trees.

Still the track descended. I was on the point of reversing and working my way back on the second speed ere I ended in some swamp, when I saw sunshine through the tangle ahead and lifted the brake.

It was down again at once. As the light beat across my face my forewheels took the turf of a great still lawn from which sprang horsemen ten feet high with levelled lances, monstrous peacocks, and sleek round-headed maids of honour – blue, black, and glistening – all of clipped yew. Across the lawn – the marshalled woods besieged it on three sides – stood an ancient house of lichened and weather-worn stone, with mullioned windows and roofs of rose-red tile. It was flanked by semi-circular walls, also rose-red, that closed the lawn on the fourth side, and at their feet a box hedge grew man-high. There were doves on the roof about the slim brick chimneys, and I caught a glimpse of an octagonal dove-house behind the screening wall.

Here, then, I stayed; a horseman's green spear laid at my breast; held by the exceeding beauty of that jewel in that setting.

'If I am not packed off for a trespasser, or if this knight does not ride a wallop at me,' thought I, 'Shakespeare and Queen Elizabeth at least must come out of that half-open garden door and ask me to tea.'

A child appeared at an upper window, and I thought the little thing waved a friendly hand. But it was to call a companion, for presently another bright head showed. Then I heard a laugh among the yew-peacocks, and turning to make sure (till then I had been watching the house only) I saw the silver of a fountain behind a hedge thrown up against the sun. The doves on the roof cooed to the cooing water; but between the two notes I caught the utterly happy chuckle of a child absorbed in some light mischief.

The garden door – heavy oak sunk deep in the thickness of the wall – opened further: a woman in a big garden hat set her foot slowly on the time-hollowed stone step and as slowly walked across the turf. I was forming some apology when she lifted up her head and I saw that she was blind.

'I heard you,' she said. 'Isn't that a motor car?'

'I'm afraid I've made a mistake in my road. I should have turned off up above – never dreamed –' I began.

'But I'm very glad. Fancy a motor car coming into the garden! It will be such a treat –' She turned and made as though looking about her. 'You – you haven't seen anyone, have you – perhaps?'

'No one to speak to, but the children seemed interested at a distance.'

'Which?'

'I saw a couple up at the window just now, and I think I heard a little chap in the grounds.'

'Oh, lucky you!' she cried, and her face brightened. 'I hear them, of course, but that's all. You've seen them and heard them?'

'Yes,' I answered. 'And if I know anything of children, one of them's having a beautiful time by the fountain yonder. Escaped, I should imagine.'

'You're fond of children?'

I gave her one or two reasons why I did not altogether hate them.

'Of course, of course,' she said. 'Then you understand. Then you won't think it foolish if I ask you to take your car through the gardens, once or twice – quite slowly. I'm sure they'd like to see it. They see so little, poor things. One tries to make their life pleasant, but –' she threw out her hands towards the woods. 'We're so out of the world here.'

'That will be splendid,' I said. 'But I can't cut up your grass.'

She faced to the right. 'Wait a minute,' she said. 'We're at the

South gate, aren't we? Behind those peacocks there's a flagged path. We call it the Peacocks' Walk. You can't see it from here, they tell me, but if you squeeze along by the edge of the wood you can turn at the first peacock and get on to the flags.'

It was sacrilege to wake that dreaming house-front, with the clatter of machinery, but I swung the car to clear the turf, brushed along the edge of the wood and turned in on the broad stone path where the fountain-basin lay like one star-sapphire.

'May I come too?' she cried. 'No, please don t help me. They'll like it better if they see me.'

She felt her way lightly to the front of the car, and with one foot on the step she called: 'Children, oh, children! Look and see what's going to happen!'

The voice would have drawn lost souls from thc Pit, for the yearning that underlay its sweetness, and I was not surprised to hear an answering shout behind the yews. It must have been the child by the fountain, but he fled at our approach, leaving a little toy boat in the water. I saw the glint of his blue blouse among the still horsemen.

Very disposedly we paraded the length of the walk and at her request backed again. This time the child had got the better of his panic, but stood far off and doubting.

'The little fellow's watching us,' I said. 'I wonder if he'd like a ride.'

'They're very shy still. Very shy. But, oh, lucky you to be able to see them! Let's listen.'

I stopped the machine at once, and the humid stillness, heavy with the scent of box, cloaked us deep. Shears I could hear where some gardener was clipping; a mumble of bees and broken voices that might have been the doves.

'Oh, unkind!' she said weariedly.

'Perhaps they're only shy of the motor. The little maid at the window looks tremendously interested.'

'Yes?' She raised her head. 'It was wrong of me to say that. They are really fond of me. It's the only thing that makes life worth living – when they're fond of you, isn't it? I daren't think what the place would be without them. By the way, is it beautiful?'

'I think it is the most beautiful place I have ever seen.'

'So they all tell me. I can feel it, of course, but that isn't quite the same thing.'

'Then have you never –?' I began, but stopped abashed.

'Not since I can remember. It happened when I was only a few months old, they tell me. And yet I must remember something, else how could I dream about colours. I see light in my dreams, and colours, but I never see *them*. I only hear them just as I do when I'm awake.'

'It's difficult to see faces in dreams. Some people can, but most of us haven't the gift, I went on, looking up at the window where the child stood all but hidden.

'I've heard that too,' she said. 'And they tell me that one never sees a dead person's face in a dream. Is that true?'

'I believe it is – now I come to think of it.'

'But how is it with yourself – yourself?' The blind eyes turned towards me.

'I have never seen the faces of my dead in any dream,' I answered.

'Then it must be as bad as being blind.'

The sun had dipped behind the woods and the long shades were possessing the insolent horsemen one by one. I saw the light die from off the top of a glossy-leaved lance and all the brave hard green turn to soft black. The house, accepting another day at end, as it had accepted an hundred thousand gone, seemed to settle deeper into its rest among the shadows.

'Have you ever wanted to?' she said after the silence.

'Very much sometimes,' I replied. The child had left the window as the shadows closed upon it.

'Ah! So've I, but I don't suppose it's allowed... Where d'you live?'

'Quite the other side of the county – sixty miles and more, and I must be going back. I've come without my big lamp.'

'But it s not dark yet. I can feel it.'

'I'm afraid it will be by the time I get home. Could you lend me someone to set me on my road at first? I've utterly lost myself.'

'I'll send Madden with you to the cross-roads. We are so out of the world, I don't wonder you were lost! I'll guide you round to the front of the house; but you will go slowly, won't you, till you're out of the grounds? It isn't foolish, do you think?'

'I promise you I'll go like this,' I said, and let the car start herself down the flagged path.

We skirted the left wing of the house, whose elaborately cast lead guttering alone was worth a day's journey; passed under a great rose-grown gate in the red wall, and so round to the high front of the house which in beauty and stateliness as much excelled the back as that all others I had seen.

'Is it so very beautiful?' she said wistfully when she heard my raptures. And you like the lead-figures too? There's the old azalea garden behind. They say that this place must have been made for children. Will you help me out, please? I should like to come with you as far as the cross-roads, but I mustn't leave them. Is that you, Madden? I want you to show this gentleman the way to the cross-roads. He has lost his way but – he has seen them.'

A butler appeared noiselessly at the miracle of old oak that must be called the front door, and slipped aside to put on his hat. She stood looking at me with open blue eyes in which no sight lay, and I saw for the first time that she was beautiful.

'Remember,' she said quietly, 'if you are fond of them you will come again,' and disappeared within the house.

The butler in the car said nothing till we were nearly at the lodge gates, where catching a glimpse of a blue blouse in the shrubbery I swerved amply lest the devil that leads little boys to play should drag me into child-murder.

'Excuse me,' he asked of a sudden, 'but why did you do that, Sir?'

'The child yonder.'

'Our young gentleman in blue?'

'Of course.'

'He runs about a good deal. Did you see him by the fountain, Sir?'

'Oh, yes, several times. Do we turn here?'

'Yes, Sir. And did you 'appen to see them upstairs too?'

'At the upper window? Yes.'

'Was that before the mistress come out to speak to you, Sir?'

'A little before that. Why d'you want to know?'

He paused a little. 'Only to make sure that – that they had seen the car, Sir, because with children running about, though I'm sure you're driving particularly careful, there might be an accident. That was all, Sir. Here are the cross-roads. You can't miss your way from now on. Thank you, Sir, but that isn't *our* custom, not with –'

'I beg your pardon,' I said, and thrust away the British silver.

'Oh, it's quite right with the rest of 'em as a rule. Good-bye, Sir.'

He retired into the armour-plated conning tower of his caste and walked away. Evidently a butler solicitous for the honour of his house and interested, probably through a maid, in the nursery.

Once beyond the signposts at the cross-roads I looked back, but the crumpled hills interlaced so jealously that I could not see where the house had lain. When I asked its name at a cottage along the road the fat woman who sold sweetmeats there gave me to understand that people with motor cars had small right to live – much less to 'go about talking like carriage folk'. They were not a pleasant-mannered community.

When I retraced my route on the map that evening I was little wiser. Hawkin's Old Farm appeared to be the Survey title of the place, and the old County Gazetteer, generally so ample, did not allude to it. The big house of those parts was Hodnington Hall,

Georgian with early Victorian embellishments, as an atrocious steel engraving attested. I carried my difficulty to a neighbour – a deep-rooted tree of that soil – and he gave me a name of a family which conveyed no meaning.

A month or so later – I went again, or it may have been that my car took the road of her own volition. She over-ran the fruitless Downs, threaded every turn of the maze of lanes below the hills, drew through the high-walled woods, impenetrable in their full leaf, came out at the cross-roads where the butler had left me, and a little farther on developed an internal trouble which forced me to turn her in on a grass way-waste that cut into a summer-silent hazel wood. So far as I could make sure by the sun and a six-inch Ordnance map, this should be the road flank of that wood which I had first explored from the heights above. I made a mighty serious business of my repairs and a glittering shop of my repair kit, spanners, pump, and the like, which I spread out orderly upon a rug. It was a trap to catch all childhood, for on such a day, I argued, the children would not be far off. When I paused in my work I listened, but the wood was so full of the noises of summer (though the birds had mated) that I could not at first distinguish these from the tread of small cautious feet stealing across the dead leaves. I rang my bell in an alluring manner, but the feet fled, and I repented, for to a child a sudden noise is very real terror. I must have been at work half an hour when I heard in the wood the voice of the blind woman crying: 'Children, oh, children! Where are you?' and the stillness made slow to close on the perfection of that cry.

She came towards me, half feeling her way between the tree boles, and though a child it seemed clung to her skirt, it swerved into the leafage like a rabbit as she drew nearer.

'Is that you?' she said, 'from the other side of the county?'

'Yes, it's me from the other side of the county.'

'Then why didn't you come through the upper woods? They were there just now.'

'They were here a few minutes ago. I expect they knew my car had broken down, and came to see the fun.'

'Nothing serious, I hope? How do cars break down?'

'In fifty different ways. Only mine has chosen the fifty-first.'

She laughed merrily at the tiny joke, cooed with delicious laughter, and pushed her hat back.

'Let me hear,' she said.

'Wait a moment,' I cried, 'and I'll get you a cushion.'

She set her foot on the rug all covered with spare parts, and stooped above it eagerly. 'What delightful things!' The hands through which she saw glanced in the chequered sunlight. 'A box here – another box! Why you've arranged them like playing shop!'

'I confess now that I put it out to attract them. I don't need half those things really.'

'How nice of you! I heard your bell in the upper wood. You say they were here before that?'

'I'm sure of it. Why are they so shy? That little fellow in blue who was with you just now ought to have got over his fright. He's been watching me like a Red Indian.'

'It must have been your bell,' she said. 'I heard one of them go

261

past me in trouble when I was coming down. They're shy – so shy even with me.' She turned her face over her shoulder and cried again: 'Children, oh, children! Look and see!'

'They must have gone off together on their own affairs,' I suggested, for there was a murmur behind us of lowered voices broken by the sudden squeaking giggles of childhood. I returned to my tinkerings and she leaned forward, her chin on her hand, listening interestedly.

'How many are they?' I said at last. The work was finished, but I saw no reason to go.

Her forehead puckered a little in thought. 'I don't quite know,' she said simply. 'Sometimes more – sometimes less. They come and stay with me because I love them, you see.'

'That must be very jolly,' I said, replacing a drawer, and as I spoke I heard the inanity of my answer.

'You – you aren't laughing at me,' she cried. 'I – I haven't any of my own. I never married. People laugh at me sometimes about them because – because –'

'Because they're savages,' I returned. 'It's nothing to fret for. That sort laugh at everything that isn't in their own fat lives.'

'I don't know. How should I? I only don't like being laughed at about *them*. It hurts; and when one can't see…I don't want to seem silly,' her chin quivered like a child's as she spoke, 'but we blindies have only one skin, I think. Everything outside hits straight at our souls. It's different with you. You've such good defences in your eyes – looking out – before anyone can really pain you in your soul. People forget that with us.'

262

I was silent reviewing that inexhaustible matter – the more than inherited (since it is also carefully taught) brutality of the Christian peoples, beside which the mere heathendom of the West Coast nigger is clean and restrained. It led me a long distance into myself.

'Don't do that!' she said of a sudden, putting her hands before her eyes.

'What?'

She made a gesture with her hand.

'That! It's – it's all purple and black. Don't! That colour hurts.'

'But, how in the world do you know about colours?' I exclaimed, for here was a revelation indeed.

'Colours as colours?' she asked.

'No. *Those* Colours which you saw just now.'

'You know as well as I do,' she laughed, 'else you wouldn't have asked that question. They aren't in the world at all. They're in *you* – when you went so angry.'

'D'you mean a dull purplish patch, like port wine mixed with ink?' I said.

'I've never seen ink or port wine, but the colours aren't mixed. They are separate – all separate.'

'Do you mean black streaks and jags across the purple?'

She nodded. 'Yes – if they are like this,' and zig-zagged her finger again, 'but it's more red than purple – that bad colour.'

'And what are the colours at the top of the – whatever you see?'

Slowly she leaned forward and traced on the rug the figure of the Egg itself.

'I see them so,' she said, pointing with a grass stem, 'white, green, yellow, red, purple, and when people are angry or bad, black across the red – as you were just now.'

'Who told you anything about it – in the beginning?' I demanded.

'About the Colours? No one. I used to ask what colours were when I was little – in table-covers and curtains and carpets, you see – because some colours hurt me and some made me happy. People told me; and when I got older that was how I saw people.' Again she traced the outline of the Egg which it is given to very few of us to see.

'All by yourself?' I repeated.

'All by myself. There wasn't anyone else. I only found out afterwards that other people did not see the Colours.'

She leaned against the tree bole plaiting and unplaiting chance-plucked grass stems. The children in the wood had drawn nearer. I could see them with the tail of my eye frolicking like squirrels.

'Now I am sure you will never laugh at me,' she went on after a long silence. 'Nor at *them*.'

'Goodness! No!' I cried, jolted out of my train of thought. 'A man who laughs at a child – unless the child is laughing too – is a heathen!'

'I didn't mean that, of course. You'd never laugh *at* children, but I thought – I used to think – that perhaps you might laugh about *them*. So now I beg your pardon...What are you going to laugh at?'

I had made no sound, but she knew.

'At the notion of your begging my pardon. If you had done your duty as a pillar of the State and a landed proprietress you ought to have summoned me for trespass when I barged through your woods the other day. It was disgraceful of me – inexcusable.'

She looked at me, her head against the tree trunk – long and steadfastly – this woman who could see the naked soul.

'How curious,' she half whispered. 'How very curious.'

'Why, what have I done?'

'You don't understand . . . and yet you understood about the Colours. Don't you understand?'

She spoke with a passion that nothing had justified, and I faced her bewilderedly as she rose. The children had gathered them-selves in a roundel behind a bramble bush. One sleek head bent over something smaller, and the set of the little shoulders told me that fingers were on lips. They, too, had some child's tremendous secret. I alone was hopelessly astray there in the broad sunlight.

'No,' I said, and shook my head as though the dead eyes could note. 'Whatever it is, I don't understand yet. Perhaps I shall later – if you'll let me come again.'

'You will come again,' she answered. 'You will surely come again and walk in the wood.'

'Perhaps the children will know me well enough by that time to let me play with them – as a favour. You know what children are like.'

'It isn't a matter of favour but of right,' she replied, and while I wondered what she meant, a dishevelled woman plunged round the bend of the road, loose-haired, purple, almost lowing with agony as she ran. It was my rude, fat friend of the sweetmeat shop. The blind woman heard and stepped forward. 'What is it, Mrs Madehurst?' she asked.

The woman flung her apron over her head and literally grovelled in the dust, crying that her grandchild was sick to death, that the local doctor was away fishing, that Jenny the mother was at her wits' end, and so forth, with repetitions and bellowings.

'Where's the next nearest doctor?' I asked between paroxysms.

'Madden will tell you. Go round to the house and take him with you. I'll attend to this. Be quick!' She half supported the fat woman into the shade. In two minutes I was blowing all the horns of Jericho under the front of the House Beautiful, and Madden, in the pantry, rose to the crisis like a butler and a man.

A quarter of an hour at illegal speeds caught us a doctor five miles away. Within the half-hour we had decanted him, much interested in motors, at the door of the sweetmeat shop, and drew up the road to await the verdict.

'Useful things cars,' said Madden, all man and no butler. 'If I'd had one when mine took sick she wouldn't have died.'

'How was it?' I asked.

'Croup. Mrs Madden was away. No one knew what to do. I drove eight miles in a tax cart for the doctor. She was choked when we came back. This car'd ha' saved her. She'd have been close on ten now.'

'I'm sorry,' I said. 'I thought you were rather fond of children from what you told me going to the cross-roads the other day.'

'Have you seen 'em again, Sir – this mornin'?'

'Yes, but they're well broke to cars. I couldn't get any of them within twenty yards of it.'

He looked at me carefully as a scout considers a stranger – not as a menial should lift his eyes to his divinely appointed superior.

'I wonder why,' he said just above the breath that he drew.

We waited on. A light wind from the sea wandered up and down the long lines of the woods, and the wayside grasses, whitened already with summer dust, rose and bowed in sallow waves.

A woman, wiping the suds off her arms, came out of the cottage next the sweetmeat shop.

'I've be'n listenin' in de back-yard,' she said cheerily. 'He says Arthur's unaccountable bad. Did ye hear him shruck just now? Unaccountable bad. I reckon t'will come Jenny's turn to walk in de wood nex' week along, Mr Madden.'

'Excuse me, Sir, but your lap-robe is slipping,' said Madden deferentially. The woman started, dropped a curtsey, and hurried away.

'What does she mean by "walking in the wood"?' I asked.

'It must be some saying they use hereabouts. I'm from Norfolk myself,' said Madden. 'They're an independent lot in this county. She took you for a chauffeur, Sir.'

I saw the Doctor come out of the cottage followed by a draggle-tailed wench who clung to his arm as though he could make treaty for her with Death. 'Dat sort,' she wailed – 'dey're just as much to us dat has 'em as if dey was lawful born. Just as much – just as much! An' God he'd be just as pleased if you saved 'un, Doctor.

Don't take it from me. Miss Florence will tell ye de very same. Don't leave 'im, Doctor!'

'I know, I know,' said the man; 'but he'll be quiet for a while now. We'll get the nurse and the medicine as fast as we can.' He signalled me to come forward with the car, and I strove not to be privy to what followed; but I saw the girl's face, blotched and frozen with grief, and I felt the hand without a ring clutching at my knees when we moved away.

The Doctor was a man of some humour, for I remember he claimed my car under the Oath of Aesculapius, and used it and me without mercy. First we convoyed Mrs Madehurst and the blind woman to wait by the sick bed till the nurse should come. Next we invaded a neat county town for prescriptions (the Doctor said the trouble was cerebrospinal meningitis), and when the County Institute, banked and flanked with scared market cattle, reported itself out of nurses for the moment we literally flung ourselves loose upon the county. We conferred with the owners of great houses – magnates at the ends of overarching avenues whose big-boned womenfolk strode away from their tea-tables to listen to the imperious Doctor. At last a white-haired lady sitting under a cedar of Lebanon and surrounded by a court of magnificent Borzois – all hostile to motors – gave the Doctor, who received them as from a princess, written orders which we bore many miles at top speed, through a park, to a French nunnery, where we took over in exchange a pallid-faced and trembling Sister. She knelt at the bottom of the tonneau telling her beads without pause till, by short cuts of the Doctor's invention, we had her to the sweetmeat shop once more. It was a long afternoon crowded with mad episodes that rose and dissolved like the dust of our wheels; cross-sections of remote and incomprehensible lives through which we raced at right angles; and I went home in the dusk, wearied out, to dream of the clashing horns of cattle; round-eyed nuns walking in a garden of graves; pleasant tea-parties beneath shaded trees; the carbolic-scented, grey-painted corridors of the County Institute; the steps of shy children in the wood, and the hands that clung to my knees as the motor began to move.

*   *   *

I had intended to return in a day or two, but it pleased Fate to hold me from that side of the county, on many pretexts, till the elder and the wild rose had fruited. There came at last a brilliant day, swept clear from the south-west, that brought the hills within hand's reach – a day of unstable airs and high filmy clouds. Through no merit of my own I was free, and set the car for the third time on that known road. As I reached the crest of the Downs I felt the soft air change, saw it glaze under the sun; and, looking down at the sea, in that instant beheld the blue of the Channel turn through polished silver and dulled steel to dingy pewter. A laden collier hugging the coast steered outward for deeper water, and, across copper-coloured haze, I saw sails rise one by one on the anchored fishing-fleet. In a deep dene behind me an eddy of sudden wind drummed through sheltered oaks, and spun aloft the first dry sample of autumn leaves. When I reached the beach road the sea-fog fumed over the brickfields, and the tide was telling all the groins of the gale beyond Ushant. In less than an hour summer England vanished in chill grey. We were again the shut island of the North, all the ships of the world bellowing at our perilous gates; and between their outcries ran the piping of bewildered gulls. My cap dripped moisture, the folds of the rug held it in pools or sluiced it away in runnels, and the salt-rime stuck to my lips.

Inland the smell of autumn loaded the thickened fog among the trees, and the drip became a continuous shower. Yet the late flowers – mallow of the wayside, scabious of the field, and dahlia of the garden – showed gay in the mist, and beyond the sea's breath there was little sign of decay in the leaf. Yet in the villages the house doors were all open, and bare-legged, bare-headed children sat at ease on the damp doorsteps to shout 'pip-pip' at the stranger.

I made bold to call at the sweetmeat shop, where Mrs Madehurst met me with a fat woman's hospitable tears. Jenny's child, she said, had died two days after the nun had come. It was, she felt, best out of the way, even though insurance offices, for reasons which she did not pretend to follow, would not willingly insure such stray lives. 'Not but what Jenny didn't tend to Arthur as though he'd come all proper at de end of de first year – like Jenny herself.' Thanks to Miss Florence, the child had been buried with a pomp which, in Mrs Madehurst's opinion, more than covered the small irregularity of its birth. She described the coffin, within and without, the glass hearse, and the evergreen lining of the grave.

'But how's the mother?' I asked.

'Jenny? Oh, she'll get over it. I've felt dat way with one or two o' my own. She'll get over. She's walkin' in de wood now.'

'In this weather?'

Mrs Madehurst looked at me with narrowed eyes across the counter.

'I dunno but it opens de 'eart like. Yes, it opens de 'eart. Dat's where losin' and bearin' comes so alike in de long run, we do say.'

Now the wisdom of the old wives is greater than that of all the Fathers, and this last oracle sent me thinking so extendedly as I went up the road, that I nearly ran over a woman and a child at the wooded corner by the lodge gates of the House Beautiful.

'Awful weather!' I cried, as I slowed dead for the turn.

'Not so bad,' she answered placidly out of the fog. 'Mine's used to 'un. You'll find yours indoors, I reckon.'

Indoors, Madden received me with professional courtesy, and kind inquiries for the health of the motor, which he would put under cover.

I waited in a still, nut-brown hall, pleasant with late flowers and warmed with a delicious wood fire – a place of good influence and great peace. (Men and women may sometimes, after great effort, achieve a creditable lie; but the house, which is their temple, can-not say anything save the truth of those who have lived in it.) A child's cart and a doll lay on the black-and-white floor, where a rug had been kicked back. I felt that the children had only just hurried away – to hide themselves, most like – in the many turns of the great adzed staircase that climbed statelily out of the hall, or to crouch at gaze behind the lions and roses of the carven gallery above. Then I heard her voice above me, singing as the blind sing – from the soul:

In the pleasant orchard-closes.

And all my early summer came back at the call.

In the pleasant orchard-closes,
God bless all our gains say we –
But may God bless all our losses,
Better suits with our degree.

She dropped the marring fifth line, and repeated –

Better suits with our degree!

I saw her lean over the gallery, her linked hands white as pearl against the oak.

'Is that you – from the other side of the county?' she called.

'Yes, me – from the other side of the county,' I answered, laughing.

'What a long time before you had to come here again.' She ran down the stairs, one hand lightly touching the broad rail. 'It's two months and four days. Summer's gone!'

'I meant to come before, but Fate prevented.'

'I knew it. Please do something to that fire. They won't let me play with it, but I can feel it's behaving badly. Hit it!'

I looked on either side of the deep fireplace, and found but a half-charred hedge-stake with which I punched a black log into flame.

'It never goes out, day or night,' she said, as though explaining. 'In case anyone comes in with cold toes, you see.'

'It's even lovelier inside than it was out,' I murmured. The red light poured itself along the age-polished dusky panels till the Tudor roses and lions of the gallery took colour and motion. An old eagle-topped convex mirror gathered the picture into its mysterious heart, distorting afresh the distorted shadows, and curving the gallery lines into the curves of a ship. The day was shutting down in half a gale as the fog turned to stringy scud. Through the uncurtained mullions of the broad window I could see valiant horsemen of the lawn rear and recover against the wind that taunted them with legions of dead leaves.

'Yes, it must be beautiful,' she said. 'Would you like to go over it? There's still light enough upstairs.'

I followed her up the unflinching, wagon-wide staircase to the gallery whence opened the thin fluted Elizabethan doors.

'Feel how they put the latch low down for the sake of the children.' She swung a light door inward.

'By the way, where are they?' I asked. 'I haven't even heard them today.'

She did not answer at once. Then, 'I can only hear them,' she replied softly. 'This is one of their rooms – everything ready, you see.'

She pointed into a heavily timbered room. There were little low gate tables and children's chairs. A doll's house, its hooked front half open, faced a great dappled rocking-horse, from whose padded saddle it was but a child's scramble to the broad window-seat overlooking the lawn. A toy gun lay in a corner beside a gilt wooden cannon.

'Surely they've only just gone,' I whispered. In the failing light a door creaked cautiously. I heard the rustle of a frock and the patter of feet – quick feet through a room beyond.

'I heard that,' she cried triumphantly. 'Did you? Children, oh, children! Where are you?'

The voice filled the walls that held it lovingly to the last perfect note, but there came no answering shout such as I had heard in the garden. We hurried on from room to oak-floored room; up a step here, down three steps there; among a maze of passages; always mocked by our quarry. One might as well have tried to work an unstopped warren with a single ferret. There were bolt-holes innumerable – recesses in walls, embrasures of deep slitten windows now darkened, whence they could start up behind us; and abandoned fireplaces, six feet deep in the masonry, as well as the tangle of communicating doors. Above all, they had the twilight for their helper in our game. I had caught one or two joyous chuckles of evasion, and once or twice had seen the silhouette of a child's frock against some darkening window at the end of a passage; but we returned empty-handed to the gallery, just as a middle-aged woman was setting a lamp in its niche.

'No, I haven't seen her either this evening, Miss Florence,' I heard her say, 'but that Turpin he says he wants to see you about his shed.'

'Oh, Mr Turpin must want to see me very badly. Tell him to come to the hall, Mrs Madden.'

I looked down into the hall whose only light was the dulled fire, and deep in the shadow I saw them at last. They must have slipped down while we were in the passages, and now thought themselves perfectly hidden behind an old gilt leather screen. By child's law, my fruitless chase was as good as an introduction, but since I had taken so much trouble I resolved to force them to come forward later by the simple trick, which children detest, of pretending not to notice them. They lay close, in a little huddle, no more than shadows except when a quick flame betrayed an outline.

'And now we'll have some tea,' she said. 'I believe I ought to have offered it you at first, but one doesn't arrive at manners somehow when one lives alone and is considered – h'm – peculiar.' Then with very pretty scorn, 'Would you like a lamp to see to eat by?'

'The firelight's much pleasanter, I think.' We descended into that delicious gloom and Madden brought tea.

I took my chair in the direction of the screen ready to surprise or be surprised as the game should go, and at her permission, since a hearth is always sacred, bent forward to play with the fire.

'Where do you get these beautiful short faggots from?' I asked idly. 'Why, they are tallies!'

'Of course,' she said. 'As I can't read or write I'm driven back on the early English tally for my accounts. Give me one and I'll tell you what it meant.'

I passed her an unburned hazel-tally, about a foot long, and she ran her thumb down the nicks.

'This is the milk-record for the home farm for the month of April last year, in gallons,' said she. 'I don't know what I should have done without tallies. An old forester of mine taught me the system. It's out of date now for everyone else; but my tenants respect it. One of them's coming now to see me. Oh, it doesn't matter. He has no business here out of office hours. He's a greedy, ignorant man – very greedy or – he wouldn't come here after dark.'

'Have you much land then?'

'Only a couple of hundred acres in hand, thank goodness. The other six hundred are nearly all let to folk who knew my folk before me, but this Turpin is quite a new man – and a highway robber.'

'But are you sure I shan't be –?'

'Certainly not. You have the right. He hasn't any children.'

'Ah, the children!' I said, and slid my low chair back till it nearly touched the screen that hid them. 'I wonder whether they'll come out for me.'

There was a murmur of voices – Madden's and a deeper note – at the low, dark side door, and a ginger-headed, canvas-gaitered giant of the unmistakable tenant-farmer type stumbled or was pushed in.

'Come to the fire, Mr Turpin,' she said.

'If – if you please, Miss, I'll – I'll be quite as well by the door.' He clung to the latch as he spoke like a frightened child. Of a sudden I realized that he was in the grip of some almost over-powering fear.

'Well?'

'About that new shed for the young stock – that was all. These first autumn storms settin' in…but I'll come again, Miss.' His teeth did not chatter much more than the door latch.

'I think not,' she answered levelly. 'The new shed – m'm. What did my agent write you on the 15th?'

'I – fancied p'raps that if I came to see you – ma – man to man like, Miss. But –'

His eyes rolled into every corner of the room wide with hor-ror. He half opened the door through which he had entered, but I noticed it shut again – from without and firmly.

'He wrote what I told him,' she went on. 'You are overstocked already. Dunnett's Farm never carried more than fifty bullocks – even in Mr Wright's time. And *he* used cake. You've sixty-seven and you don't cake. You've broken the lease in that respect. You're dragging the heart out of the farm.'

'I'm – I'm getting some minerals – superphosphates – next week. I've as good as ordered a truck-load already. I'll go down to the station tomorrow about 'em. Then I can come and see you man to man like, Miss, in the daylight…That gentleman's not going away, is he?' He almost shrieked.

I had only slid the chair a little farther back, reaching behind me to tap on the leather of the screen, but he jumped like a rat.

'No. Please attend to me, Mr Turpin.' She turned in her chair and faced him with his back to the door. It was an old and sordid little piece of scheming that she forced from him – his plea for the new cow-shed at his landlady's expense, that he might with the covered manure pay his next year's rent out of the valuation after, as she made clear, he had bled the enriched pastures to the bone. I could not but admire the intensity of his greed, when I saw him out-facing for its sake whatever terror it was that ran wet on his forehead.

I ceased to tap the leather – was, indeed, calculating the cost of the shed – when I felt my relaxed hands taken and turned softly between the soft hands of a child. So at last I had triumphed. In a moment I would turn and acquaint myself with those quick-footed wanderers...

The little brushing kiss fell in the centre of my palm – as a gift on which the fingers were, once, expected to close: as the all-faithful half-reproachful signal of a waiting child not used to neglect even when grown-ups were busiest – a fragment of the mute code devised very long ago.

Then I knew. And it was as though I had known from the first day when I looked across the lawn at the high window.

I heard the door shut. The woman turned to me in silence, and I felt that she knew.

What time passed after this I cannot say. I was roused by the fall of a log, and mechanically rose to put it back. Then I returned to my place in the chair very close to the screen.

'Now you understand,' she whispered, across the packed shadows.

'Yes, I understand – now. Thank you.'

I – I only hear them.' She bowed her head in her hands. 'I have no right, you know – no other right. I have neither borne nor lost – neither borne nor lost!'

'Be very glad then,' said I, for my soul was torn open within me.

'Forgive me!'

She was still, and I went back to my sorrow and my joy.

'It was because I loved them so,' she said at last, brokenly. '*That* was why it was, even from the first – even before I knew that they – they were all I should ever have. And I loved them so!'

She stretched out her arms to the shadows and the shadows within the shadow.

'They came because I loved them – because I needed them. I – I must have made them come. Was that wrong, think you?'

'No – no.'

'I – I grant you that the toys and – and all that sort of thing were nonsense, but – but I used to so hate empty rooms myself when I was little.' She pointed to the gallery. 'And the passages all empty...And how could I ever bear the garden door shut? Suppose –'

'Don't! For pity's sake, don't!' I cried. The twilight had brought a cold rain with gusty squalls that plucked at the leaded windows.

'And the same thing with keeping the fire in all night. *I* don't think it so foolish – do you?'

I looked at the broad brick hearth, saw, through tears I believe, that there was no unpassable iron on or near it, and bowed my head.

'I did all that and lots of other things – just to make believe. Then they came. I heard them, but I didn't know that they were not mine by right till Mrs Madden told me – '

'The butler's wife? What?'

'One of them – I heard – she saw. And knew. Hers! *Not* for me. I didn t know at first. Perhaps I was jealous. Afterwards, I began to understand that it was only because I loved them, not because – .... Oh, you *must* bear or lose, she said piteously. There is no other way – and yet they love me. They must! Don't they?'

There was no sound in the room except the lapping voices of the fire, but we two listened intently, and she at least took comfort from what she heard. She recovered herself and half rose. I sat still in my chair by the screen.

'Don't think me a wretch to whine about myself like this, but – but I'm all in the dark, you know, and *you* can see.'

In truth I could see, and my vision confirmed me in my resolve, though that was like the very parting of spirit and flesh. Yet a little longer I would stay since it was the last time.

'You think it is wrong, then?' she cried sharply, though I had said nothing.

'Not for you. A thousand times no. For you it is right...I am grateful to you beyond words. For me it would be wrong. For me only...'

'Why?' she said, but passed her hand before her face as she had done at our second meeting in the wood. 'Oh, I see,' she went on simply as a child. 'For you it would be wrong.' Then with a little indrawn laugh, 'And, d'you remember, I called you lucky – once – at first. You who must never come here again!'

She left me to sit a little longer by the screen, and I heard the sound of her feet die out along the gallery above.

A. M. Burrage

Playmates

'PLAYMATES'

A. M. BURRAGE (ALFRED MCLELLAND BURRAGE, BRITISH,
1889–1956)

First published in Burrage's 1927 collection *Some Ghost Stories*.

A. M. Burrage was a copiously productive writer of stories for boys and of romantic fiction for women's magazines. He is best remembered for his horror stories and for his unusually frank First World War memoir, *War is War*. 'Playmates' is an empathetic study of the gap between the perceptions of children and adults and of the resilience of children, even in very unusual circumstances.

PLAYMATES

A. M. Burrage

Although everybody who knew Stephen Everton agreed that he was the last man under Heaven who ought to have been allowed to bring up a child, it was fortunate for Monica that she fell into his hands; else she had probably starved or drifted into some refuge for waifs and strays. True her father, Sebastian Threlfall the poet, had plenty of casual friends. Almost everybody knew him slightly, and right up to the time of his fatal attack of *delirium tremens* he contrived to look one of the most interesting of the regular frequenters of the Café Royal. But people are generally not hasty to bring up the children of casual acquaintances, particularly when such children may be suspected of having inherited more than a fair share of human weaknesses.

Of Monica's mother literally nothing was known. Nobody seemed able to say if she were dead or alive. Probably she had long since deserted Threlfall for some consort able and willing to provide regular meals.

Everton knew Threlfall no better than a hundred others knew

him, and was ignorant of his daughter's existence until the father's death was a new topic of conversation in literary and artistic circles. People vaguely wondered what would become of 'the kid', and while they were still wondering, Everton quietly took possession of her.

Who's Who will tell you the year of Everton's birth, the names of his *Almae Matres* (Winchester and Magdalen College, Oxford), the titles of his books and of his predilections for skating and mountaineering; but it is necessary to know the man a little less superficially. He was then a year or two short of fifty and looked ten years older. He was a tall, lean man, with a delicate pink complexion, an oval head, a Roman nose, blue eyes which looked out mildly through strong glasses, and thin straight lips drawn tightly over slightly protruding teeth. His high forehead was bare, for he was bald to the base of his skull. What remained of his hair was a neutral tint between black and grey, and was kept closely cropped. He contrived to look at once prim and irascible, scholarly and acute; Sherlock Holmes, perhaps, with a touch of old-maidishness.

The world knew him for a writer of books on historical crises. They were cumbersome books with cumbersome titles, written by a scholar for scholars. They brought him fame and not a little money. The money he could have afforded to be without, since he was modestly wealthy by inheritance. He was essentially a cold-blooded animal, a bachelor, a man of regular and temperate habits, fastidious, and fond of quietude and simple comforts.

Nobody is ever likely to know why Everton adopted the orphan daughter of a man whom he knew but slightly and neither liked nor respected. He was no lover of children, and his humours were sardonic rather than sentimental. I am only hazarding a guess when I suggest that, like so many childless men, he had theories of his own concerning the upbringing of children, which he wanted to see tested. Certain it is that Monica's childhood, which had been extraordinary enough before, passed from the tragic to the grotesque.

Everton took Monica from the Bloomsbury 'apartments' house, where the landlady, already nursing a bad debt, was wondering how to dispose of the child. Monica was then eight years old, and a woman of the world in her small way. She had lived with drink and poverty and squalor; had never played a game nor had a playmate; had seen nothing but the seamy side of life; and had learned skill in practising her father's petty shifts and mean contrivances. She was grave and sullen and plain and pale, this child who had never known childhood. When she spoke, which was as seldom as possible, her voice was hard and gruff. She was, poor little thing, as unattractive as her life could have made her.

She went with Everton without question or demur. She would no more have questioned anybody's ownership than if she had been an inanimate piece of luggage left in a cloak-room. She had belonged to her father. Now that he was gone to his own place she was the property of whomsoever chose to claim her. Everton took her with a cold kindness in which was neither love nor pity; in return she gave him neither love nor gratitude, but did as she was desired after the manner of a paid servant.

Everton disliked modern children, and for what he disliked in them he blamed modern schools. It may have been on this account that he did not send Monica to one; or perhaps he wanted to see how a child would contrive its own education. Monica could already read and write and, thus equipped, she had the run of his large library, in which was almost every conceivable kind of book from heavy tomes on abstruse subjects to trashy modern novels bought and left there by Miss Gribbin. Everton barred nothing, recommended nothing, but watched the tree grow naturally, untended and unpruned.

Miss Gribbin was Everton's secretary. She was the kind of hatchet-faced, flat-chested, middle-aged sexless woman who could safely share the home of a bachelor without either of them being troubled by the tongue of Scandal. To her duties was now added the instruction of Monica in certain elementary subjects. Thus Monica learned that a man named William the Conqueror arrived in England in 1066; but to find out what manner of man this William was, she had to go to the library and read the conflicting accounts of him given by the several historians. From Miss Gribbin she learned bare irrefutable facts; for the rest she was left to fend for herself. In the library she found herself surrounded by all the realms of reality and fancy, each with its door invitingly ajar.

Monica was fond of reading. It was, indeed, almost her only recreation, for Everton knew no other children of her age, and treated her as a grown-up member of the household. Thus she read everything from translations of the *Iliad* to Hans Andersen, from the Bible to the love-gush of the modern female fictionmongers.

Everton, although he watched her closely, and plied her with innocent-sounding questions, was never allowed a peep into her mind. What muddled dreams she may have had of a strange world surrounding the Hampstead house – a world of gods and fairies and demons, and strong silent men making love to sloppyminded young women – she kept to herself. Reticence was all that she had in common with normal childhood, and Everton noticed that she never played.

Unlike most young animals, she did not take naturally to playing. Perhaps the instinct had been beaten out of her by the realities of life while her father was alive. Most lonely children improvise their own games and provide themselves with a vast store of make-believe. But Monica, as sullen-seeming as a caged animal, devoid alike of the naughtiness and the charms of child-hood, rarely crying and still more rarely laughing, moved about the house sedate to the verge of being wooden. Occasionally Everton, the experimentalist, had twinges of conscience and grew half afraid...

★   ★   ★

When Monica was twelve Everton moved his establishment from Hampstead to a house remotely situated in the middle of Suffolk, which was part of a recent legacy. It was a tall, rectangular, Queen Anne house standing on a knoll above marshy fields and wind-bowed beech woods. Once it had been the manor house, but now little land went with it. A short drive passed between rank evergreens from the heavy wrought-iron gate to a circle of grass and flower beds in front of the house. Behind was an acre and a half of rank garden, given over to weeds and marigolds. The rooms were high and well lighted, but the house wore an air of depression as if it were a live thing unable to shake off some ancient fit of melancholy,

Everton went to live in the house for a variety of reasons. For the most part of a year he had been trying in vain to let or sell it, and it was when he found that he would have no difficulty in disposing of his house at Hampstead that he made up his mind. The old house, a mile distant from a remote Suffolk village, would give him all the solitude he required. Moreover he was anxious about his health – his nervous system had never been strong – and his doctor had recommended the bracing air of East Anglia.

He was not in the least concerned to find that the house was too big for him. His furniture filled the same number of rooms as it had filled at Hampstead, and the others he left empty. Nor did he increase his staff of three indoor servants and gardener. Miss Gribbin, now less dispensable than ever, accompanied him; and with them came Monica to see another aspect of life, with the same wooden stoicism which Everton had remarked in her upon the occasion of their first meeting.

As regarded Monica, Miss Gribbin's duties were then becoming more and more of a sinecure. 'Lessons' now occupied no more than half an hour a day. The older Monica grew, the better she was able to grub for her education in the great library. Between Monica and Miss Gribbin there was neither love nor sympathy, nor was there any affectation of either. In their common duty to Everton they owed and paid certain duties to each other. Their intercourse began and ended there.

Everton and Miss Gribbin both liked the house at first. It suited the two temperaments which were alike in their lack of festivity. Asked if she too liked it, Monica said simply 'Yes,' in a tone which implied stolid and complete indifference.

All three in their several ways led much the same lives as they had led at Hampstead. But a slow change began to work in Monica, a change so slight and subtle that weeks passed before Everton or Miss Gribbin noticed it. It was late on an afternoon in early spring when Everton first became aware of something unusual in Monica's demeanour.

He had been searching in the library for one of his own books – *The Fall of the Commonwealth of England* – and having failed to find it went in search of Miss Gribbin and met Monica instead at the foot of the long oak staircase. Of her he casually inquired about the book, and she jerked up her head brightly, to answer him with an unwonted smile:

'Yes, I've been reading it. I expect I left it in the schoolroom. I'll go and see.'

It was a long speech for her to have uttered, but Everton scarcely noticed that at the time, His attention was directed elsewhere.

'*Where* did you leave it?' he demanded.

'In the schoolroom,' she repeated.

'I know of no schoolroom,' said Everton coldly. He hated to hear anything mis-called, even were it only a room. 'Miss Gribbin generally takes you for your lessons in either the library or the dining-room. If it is one of those rooms, kindly call it by its proper name.'

Monica shook her head.

'No, I mean the schoolroom – the big empty room next to the library. That's what it's called.'

Everton knew the room. It faced north, and seemed darker and more dismal than any other room in the house. He had wondered idly why Monica chose to spend so much of her time in a room bare of furniture, with nothing better to sit on than uncovered boards or a cushionless window-seat; and put it down to her genius for being unlike anybody else.

'Who calls it that?' he demanded.

'It's its name,' said Monica smiling.

She ran upstairs, and presently returned with the book, which she handed to him with another smile. He was already wondering at her. It was surprising and pleasant to see her run, instead of the heavy and clumsy walk which generally moved her when she went to obey a behest. And she had smiled two or three times in the short space of a minute. Then he realized that for some little while she had been a brighter, happier creature than she had ever been at Hampstead.

'How did you come to call that room the schoolroom?' he asked, as he took the book from her hand.

'It *is* the schoolroom,' she insisted, seeking to cover her evasion by laying stress on the verb.

That was all he could get out of her. As he questioned further the smiles ceased and the pale, plain little face became devoid of any expression. He knew then that it was useless to press her, but his curiosity was aroused. He inquired of Miss Gribbin and the servant, and learned that nobody was in the habit of calling the long, empty apartment the schoolroom.

Clearly Monica had given it its name. But why? She was so altogether remote from school and schoolrooms. Some germ of imagination was active in her small mind. Everton's interest was stimulated. He was like a doctor who remarks in a patient some abnormal symptom.

'Monica seems a lot brighter and more alert than she used to be,' he remarked to Miss Gribbin.

'Yes,' agreed the secretary. 'I have noticed that. She is learning to play.'

'To play what? The piano?'

'No, no. To play childish games. Haven't you heard her dancing about and singing?'

Everton shook his head and looked interested.

'I have not,' he said. 'Possibly my presence acts as a check upon her – er – exuberance.'

'I hear her in that empty room which she insists upon calling the schoolroom. She stops when she hears my step. Of course, I have not interfered with her in any way, but I could wish that she would not talk to herself. I don't like people who do that. It is somehow – uncomfortable.'

'I didn't know she did,' said Everton slowly.

'Oh, yes, quite long conversations. I haven't actually heard what she talks about, but sometimes you would think she was in the midst of a circle of friends.'

'In that same room?'

'Generally,' said Miss Gribbin, with a nod.

Everton regarded his secretary with a slow, thoughtful smile.

'Development,' he said, 'is always extremely interesting. I am glad the place seems to suit Monica. I think it suits all of us.'

There was a doubtful note in his voice as he uttered the last words, and Miss Gribbin agreed with him with the same lack of conviction in her tone. As a fact, Everton had been doubtful of late if his health had been benefited by the move from Hampstead. For the first week or two his nerves had been the better for the change of air; but now he was conscious of the beginning of a relapse. His imagination was beginning to play him tricks, filling his mind with vague, distorted fancies. Sometimes when he sat up late, writing – he was given to working at night on strong coffee – he became a victim of the most distressing nervous symptoms, hard to analyse and impossible to combat, which invariably drove him to bed with a sense of defeat.

That same night he suffered one of the variations of this common experience.

It was close upon midnight when he felt stealing over him a sense of discomfort which he was compelled to classify as fear. He was working in a small room leading out of the drawing-room which he had selected for his study. At first he was scarcely aware of the sensation. The effect was always cumulative; the burden was laid upon him straw by straw.

It began with his being oppressed by the silence of the house. He became more and more acutely conscious of it, until it became like a thing tangible, a prison of solid walls growing around him.

The scratching of his pen at first relieved the tension. He wrote words and erased them again for the sake of that comfortable sound. But presently that comfort was denied him, for it seemed to him that this minute and busy noise was attracting attention to himself. Yes, that was it. He was being watched.

Everton sat quite still, the pen poised an inch above the half-covered sheet of paper. This was become a familiar sensation. He was being watched. And by what? And from what corner of the room?

He forced a tremulous smile to his lips. One moment he called himself ridiculous; the next, he asked himself hopelessly how a man could – argue with his nerves. Experience had taught him that the only cure – and that a temporary one – was to go to bed. Yet he sat on, anxious to learn more about himself, to coax his vague imaginings into some definite shape.

Imagination told him that he was being watched, and although he called it imagination he was afraid. That rapid beating against his ribs was his heart, warning him of fear. But he sat rigid, anxious to learn in what part of the room his fancy would place these imaginary 'watchers' – for he was conscious of the gaze of more than one pair of eyes being bent upon him.

At first the experiment failed. The rigidity of his pose, the hold he was keeping upon himself, acted as a brake upon his mind. Presently he realized this and relaxed the tension, striving to give his mind that perfect freedom which might have been demanded by a hypnotist or one experimenting in telepathy.

Almost at once he thought of the door. The eyes of his mind veered round in that direction as the needle of a compass veers to the magnetic north. With these eyes of his imagination he saw the door. It was standing half open, and the aperture was thronged with faces. What kind of faces he could not tell. They were just faces; imagination left it at that. But he was aware that these spies were timid; that they were in some ways as fearful of him as he was of them; that to scatter them he had but to turn his head and gaze at them with the eyes of his body.

The door was at his shoulder. He turned his head suddenly and gave it one swift glance out of the tail of his eye.

However imagination deceived him, it had not played him false about the door. It was standing half open although he could have sworn that he had closed it on entering the room. The aperture was empty. Only darkness, solid as a pillar, filled the space between floor and lintel. But although he saw nothing as he turned his head, he was dimly conscious of something vanishing, a scurrying noiseless and incredibly swift, like the flitting of trout in clear, shallow water.

Everton stood up, stretched himself, and brought his knuckles up to his strained eyes. He told himself that he must go to bed. It was bad enough that he must suffer these nervous attacks; to encourage them was madness.

But as he mounted the stairs he was still conscious of not being alone. Shy, timorous, ready to melt into the shadows of the walls if he turned his head, *they* were following him, whispering noise-lessly, linking hands and arms, watching him with the fearful, awed curiosity of – Children.

★　★　★

The Vicar had called upon Everton. His name was Parslow, and he was a typical country parson of the poorer sort, a tall, rugged, shabby, worried man in the middle forties, obviously embarrassed by the eternal problem of making ends meet on an inadequate stipend.

Everton received him courteously enough, but with a certain coldness which implied that he had nothing in common with his visitor. Parslow was evidently disappointed because 'the new people' were not church-goers nor likely to take much interest in the parish. The two men made half-hearted and vain attempts to find common ground. It was not until he was on the point of leaving that the Vicar mentioned Monica.

'You have, I believe, a little girl?' he said.

'Yes. My small ward.'

'Ah! I expect she finds it lonely here. I have a little girl of the same age. She is at present away at school, but she will be home soon for the Easter holidays. I know she would be delighted if your little – er – ward would come down to the Vicarage and play with her sometimes.'

The suggestion was not particularly welcome to Everton, and his thanks were perfunctory. This other small girl, although she was a vicar's daughter, might carry the contagion of other modern children and infect Monica with the pertness and slanginess which he so detested. Altogether he was determined to have as little to do with the Vicarage as possible.

Meanwhile the child was becoming to him a study of more and more absorbing interest. The change in her was almost as marked as if she had just returned after having spent a term at school. She astonished and mystified him by using expressions which she could scarcely have learned from any member of the household. It was not the jargon of the smart young people of the day which slipped easily from her lips, but the polite family slang of his own youth. For instance, she remarked one morning that Mead, the gardener, was a whale at pruning vines.

A whale! The expression took Everton back a very long way down the level road of the spent years; took him, indeed, to a nursery in a solid respectable house in a Belgravian square, where he had heard the word used in that same sense for the first time. His sister Gertrude, aged ten, notorious in those days for picking up loose expressions, announced that she was getting to be a whale at French. Yes, in those days an expert was a 'whale' or a 'don', not, as he is today, a 'stout fellow'. But who was a 'whale' nowadays? It was years since he had heard the term.

'Where did you learn to say that?' he demanded in so strange a tone that Monica stared at him anxiously.

'Isn't it right?' she asked eagerly. She might have been a child at a new school, fearful of not having acquired the fashionable phraseology of the place.

'It is a slang expression,' said the purist coldly. 'It used to mean a person who was proficient in something. How did you come to hear it?'

She smiled without answering, and her smile was mysterious, even coquettish after a childish fashion. Silence had always been her refuge, but it was no longer a sullen silence. She was changing rapidly, and in a manner to bewilder her guardian. He failed in an effort to cross-examine her, and, later in the day, consulted Miss Gribbin.

'That child,' he said, 'is reading something that we know nothing about.'

'Just at present,' said Miss Gribbin, 'she is glued to Dickens and Stevenson.'

'Then where on earth does she get her expressions?'

'I don't know,' the secretary retorted testily, 'any more than I know how she learned to play Cat's Cradle.'

'What? That game with string? Does she play that?'

'I found her doing something quite complicated and elaborate the other day. She wouldn't tell me how she learned to do it. I took the trouble to question the servants, but none of them had shown her.'

Everton frowned.

'And I know of no book in the library which tells how to perform tricks with string. Do you think she has made a clandestine friendship with any of the village children?'

Miss Gribbin shook her head.

'She is too fastidious for that. Besides, she seldom goes into the village alone.'

There, for the time, the discussion ended. Everton, with all the curiosity of the student, watched the child as carefully and closely as he was able without at the same time arousing her suspicions. She was developing fast. He had known that she must develop, but the manner of her doing so amazed and mystified him, and, likely as not, denied some preconceived theory. The untended plant was not only growing but showed signs of pruning. It was as if there were outside influences at work on Monica which could have come neither from him nor from any other member of the household.

Winter was dying hard, and dark days of rain kept Miss Gribbin, Monica and Everton within doors. He lacked no opportunities of keeping the child under observation, and once, on a gloomy after-noon, passing the room which she had named the schoolroom, he paused and listened until he became suddenly aware that his conduct bore an unpleasant resemblance to eavesdropping. The psychologist and the gentleman engaged in a brief struggle in which the gentleman temporarily got the upper hand. Everton approached the door with a heavy step and flung it open.

The sensation he received, as he pushed open the door, was vague but slightly disturbing, and it was by no means new to him. Several times of late, but generally after dark, he had entered an empty room with the impression that it had been occupied by others until the very moment of his crossing the threshold. His coming disturbed not merely one or two, but a crowd. He felt rather than heard them scattering, flying swiftly and silently as shadows to incredible hiding-places, where they held breath and watched and waited for him to go. Into the same atmosphere of tension he now walked, and looked about him as if expecting to see more than only the child who held the floor in the middle of the room, or some tell-tale trace of other children in hiding. Had the room been furnished he must have looked involuntarily for shoes protruding from under tables or settees, for ends of garments unconsciously left exposed.

The long room, however, was empty save for Monica from wainscot to wainscot and from floor to ceiling. Fronting him were the long high windows starred by fine rain. With her back to the white filtered light Monica faced him, looking up to him as he entered. He was just in time to see a smile fading from her lips. He also saw by a slight convulsive movement of her shoulders that she was hiding something from him in the hands clasped behind her back.

'Hullo,' he said, with a kind of forced geniality, 'what are you up to?'

She said: 'Nothing,' but not as sullenly as she would once have said it.

'Come,' said Everton, 'that is impossible. You were talking to yourself, Monica. You should not do that. It is an idle and very, very foolish habit. You will go mad if you continue to do that.'

She let her head droop a little.

'I wasn't talking to myself,' she said in a low, half playful but very deliberate tone.

'That's nonsense. I heard you.'

'I wasn't talking to myself.'

301

'But you must have been. There is nobody else here.'

'There isn't – now.'

'What do you mean? Now?'

'They've gone. You frightened them, I expect.'

'What do you mean?' he repeated, advancing a step or two towards her. 'And whom do you call "they"?'

Next moment he was angry with himself. His tone was so heavy and serious and the child was half laughing at him. It was as if she were triumphant at having inveigled him into taking a serious part in her own game of make-believe.

'You wouldn't understand,' she said.

'I understand this – that you are wasting your time and being a very silly little girl. What's that you're hiding behind your back?'

She held out her right hand at once, unclenched her fingers and disclosed a thimble. He looked at it and then into her face.

'Why did you hide that from me?' he asked. 'There was no need.'

She gave him a faint secretive smile – that new smile of hers – before replying.

'We were playing with it. I didn't want you to know.'

'*You* were playing with it, you mean. And why didn't you want me to know?'

'About them. Because I thought you wouldn't understand. You *don't* understand.'

He saw that it was useless to affect anger or show impatience. He spoke to her gently, even with an attempt at displaying sympathy.

'Who are "they"?' he asked.

'They're just them. Other girls.'

'I see. And they come and play with you, do they? And they run away whenever I'm about, because they don't like me. Is that it?'

She shook her head.

'It isn't that they don't like you. I think they like everybody. But they're so shy. They were shy of me for a long, long time. I knew they were there, but it was weeks and weeks before they'd come and play with me. It was weeks before I even saw them.'

'Yes? Well, what are they like?'

'Oh, they're just girls. And they're awfully, awfully nice. Some are a bit older than me and some are a bit younger. And they don't dress like other girls you see today. They're in white with longer skirts and they wear sashes.'

Everton inclined his head gravely. 'She got that out of the illustrations of books in the library,' he reflected.

'You don't happen to know their names, I suppose?' he asked, hoping that no quizzical note in his voice rang through the casual but sincere tone which he intended.

'Oh, yes. There's Mary Hewitt – I think I love her best of all – and Elsie Power and – '

'How many of them altogether?'

'Seven. It's just a nice number. And this is the schoolroom where we play games. I love games. I wish I'd learned to play games before.'

'And you've been playing with the thimble?'

'Yes. Hunt-the-thimble they call it. One of us hides it, and then the rest of us try to find it, and the one who finds it hides it again.'

'You mean you hide it yourself, and then go and find it.' The smile left her face at once, and the look in her eyes warned him that she was done with confidences.

'Ah!' she exclaimed. 'You don't understand after all. I somehow knew you wouldn't.'

Everton, however, thought he did. His face wore a sudden smile of relief.

'Well, never mind,' he said. 'But I shouldn't play too much if I were you.'

With that he left her. But curiosity tempted him, not in vain, to linger and listen for a moment on the other side of the door which he had closed behind him. He heard Monica whisper:

'Mary! Elsie! Come on. It's all right. He's gone now.'

At an answering whisper, very unlike Monica's, he started violently and then found himself grinning at his own discomfiture. It was natural that Monica, playing many parts, should try to change her voice with every character. He went downstairs sunk in a brown study which brought him to certain interesting conclusions. A little later he communicated these to Miss Gribbin.

'I've discovered the cause of the change in Monica. She's invented for herself some imaginary friends – other little girls, of course.'

Miss Gribbin started slightly and looked up from the newspaper which she had been reading.

'Really?' she exclaimed. 'Isn't that rather an unhealthy sign?'

'No, I should say not. Having imaginary friends is quite a common symptom of childhood, especially among young girls. I remember my sister used to have one, and was very angry when none of the rest of us would take the matter seriously. In Monica's case I should say it was perfectly normal – normal, but interesting. She must have inherited an imagination from that father of hers, with the result that she has seven imaginary friends, all properly named, if you please. You see, being lonely, and having no friends of her own age, she would naturally invent more than one "friend". They are all nicely and primly dressed, I must tell you, out of Victorian books which she has found in the library.'

'It can't be healthy,' said Miss Gribbin, pursing her lips. 'And I can't understand how she has learned certain expressions and a certain style of talking and games – '

'All out of books. And pretends to herself that "they" have taught her. But the most interesting part of the affair is this: it's given me my first practical experience of telepathy, of the existence of which I have hitherto been rather sceptical. Since Monica invented this new game, and before I was aware that she had done so, I have had at different times distinct impressions of there being a lot of little girls about the house.'

Miss Gribbin started and stared. Her lips parted as if she were about to speak, but it was as if she had changed her mind while framing the first word she had been about to utter.

'Monica,' he continued smiling, 'invented these "friends", and has been making me telepathically aware of them, too. I have lately been most concerned about the state of my nerves.'

Miss Gribbin jumped up as if in anger, but her brow was smooth and her mouth dropped at the corners.

'Mr Everton,' she said, 'I wish you had not told me all this.' Her lips worked. 'You see,' she added unsteadily, 'I don't believe in telepathy.'

★   ★   ★

Easter, which fell early that year, brought little Gladys Parslow home for the holidays to the Vicarage. The event was shortly afterwards signalized by a note from the Vicar to Everton, inviting him to send Monica down to have tea and play games with his little daughter on the following Wednesday.

The invitation was an annoyance and an embarrassment to Everton. Here was the disturbing factor, the outside influence, which might possibly thwart his experiment in the upbringing of Monica. He was free, of course, simply to decline the invitation so coldly and briefly as to make sure that it would not be repeated; but the man was not strong enough to stand on his own feet impervious to the winds of criticism. He was sensitive and had little wish to seem churlish, still less to appear ridiculous. Taking the line of least resistance he began to reason that one child, herself no older than Monica, and in the atmosphere of her own home, could make but little impression. It ended in his allowing Monica to go.

Monica herself seemed pleased at the prospect of going but expressed her pleasure in a discreet, restrained, grown-up way.

Miss Gribbin accompanied her as far as the Vicarage doorstep, arriving with her punctually at half past three on a sullen and muggy afternoon, and handed her over to the woman-of-all-work who answered the summons at the door.

Miss Gribbin reported to Everton on her return. An idea which she conceived to be humorous had possession of her mind, and in talking to Everton she uttered one of her infrequent laughs.

'I only left her at the door,' she said, 'so I didn't see her meet the other little girl. I wish I'd stayed to see that. It must have been funny.'

She irritated Everton by speaking exactly as if Monica were a captive animal which had just been shown, for the first time in its life, another of its own kind. The analogy thus conveyed to Everton was close enough to make him wince. He felt something like a twinge of conscience, and it may have been then that he asked himself for the first time if he were being fair to Monica.

It had never once occurred to him to ask himself if she were happy. The truth was that he understood children so little as to suppose that physical cruelty was the one kind of cruelty from which they were capable of suffering. Had he ever before troubled to ask himself if Monica were happy, he had probably given the question a curt dismissal with the thought that she had no right to be otherwise. He had given her a good home, even luxuries, together with every opportunity to develop her mind. For companions she had himself, Miss Gribbin, and, to a limited extent, the servants...

Ah, but that picture, conjured up by Miss Gribbin's words with their accompaniment of unreasonable laughter! The little creature meeting for the first time another little creature of its own kind and looking bewildered, knowing neither what to do nor what to say. There was pathos in that – uncomfortable pathos for Everton. Those imaginary friends – did they really mean that Monica had needs of which he knew nothing, of which he had never troubled to learn?

He was not an unkind man, and it hurt him to suspect that he might have committed an unkindness. The modern children whose behaviour and manners he disliked, were perhaps only obeying some inexorable law of evolution. Suppose in keeping Monica from their companionship he were actually flying in the face of Nature? Suppose, after all, if Monica were to be natural, she must go unhindered on the tide of her generation?

He compromised with himself, pacing the little study. He would watch Monica much more closely, question her when he had the chance. Then, if he found she was not happy, and really needed the companionship of other children, he would see what could be done.

But when Monica returned home from the Vicarage it was quite plain that she had not enjoyed herself. She was subdued, and said very little about her experience. Quite obviously the two little girls had not made very good friends. Questioned, Monica confessed that she did not like Gladys – much. She said this very thoughtfully with a little pause before the adverb.

'Why don't you like her?' Everton demanded bluntly.

'I don't know. She's so funny. Not like other girls.'

'And what do you know about other girls?' he demanded, faintly amused.

'Well, she's not a bit like – '

Monica paused suddenly and lowered her gaze.

'Not like your "friends", you mean?' Everton asked.

She gave him a quick, penetrating little glance and then lowered her gaze once more.

'No,' she said, 'not a bit.'

She wouldn't be, of course. Everton teased the child with no more questions for the time being, and let her go. She ran off at once to the great empty room, there to seek that uncanny companionship which had come to suffice her.

For the moment Everton was satisfied. Monica was perfectly happy as she was, and had no need of Gladys or, probably, any other child friends. His experiment with her was shaping successfully. She had invented her own young friends, and had gone off eagerly to play with the creations of her own fancy.

This seemed very well at first. Everton reflected that it was just what he would have wished, until he realized suddenly with a little shock of discomfort that it was not normal and it was not healthy.

★ ★ ★

Although Monica plainly had no great desire to see any more of Gladys Parslow, common civility made it necessary for the Vicar's little daughter to be asked to pay a return visit. Most likely Gladys Parslow was as unwilling to come as was Monica to entertain her. Stern discipline, however, presented her at the appointed time on an afternoon pre-arranged by correspondence, when Monica received her coldly and with dignity, tempered by a sort of grown-up graciousness.

Monica bore her guest away to the big empty room, and that was the last of Gladys Parslow seen by Everton or Miss Gribbin that afternoon. Monica appeared alone when the gong sounded for tea, and announced in a subdued tone that Gladys had already gone home.

'Did you quarrel with her?' Miss Gribbin asked quickly.

'No-o.'

'Then why has she gone like this?'

'She was stupid,' said Monica, simply. 'That's all.'

'Perhaps it was you who was stupid. Why did she go?'

'She got frightened.'

'Frightened!'

'She didn't like my friends.'

Miss Gribbin exchanged glances with Everton.

'She didn't like a silly little girl who talks to herself and imagines things. No wonder she was frightened.'

'She didn't think they were real at first, and laughed at me,' said Monica, sitting down.

'Naturally!'

'And then when she saw them – '

Miss Gribbin and Everton interrupted her simultaneously,

repeating in unison and with well-matched astonishment, her two last words.

'And when she saw them,' Monica continued, unperturbed, 'she didn't like it. I think she was frightened. Anyhow, she said she wouldn't stay and went straight off home. I think she's a stupid girl. We all had a good laugh about her after she was gone.'

She spoke in her ordinary matter-of-fact tones, and if she were secretly pleased at the state of perturbation into which her last words had obviously thrown Miss Gribbin she gave no sign of it. Miss Gribbin immediately exhibited outward signs of anger.

'You are a very naughty child to tell such untruths. You know perfectly well that Gladys couldn't have *seen* your "friends". You have simply frightened her by pretending to talk to people who weren't there, and it will serve you right if she never comes to play with you again.'

'She won't,' said Monica. 'And she *did* see them, Miss Gribbin.'

'How do you know?' Everton asked.

'By her face. And she spoke to them too, when she ran to the door. They were very shy at first because Gladys was there. They wouldn't come for a long time, but I begged them, and at last they did.'

Everton checked another outburst from Miss Gribbin with a look. He wanted to learn more, and to that end he applied some show of patience and gentleness.

'Where did they come from?' he asked. 'From outside the door?'

'Oh, no. From where they always come.'

311

'And where's that?'

'I don't know. They don't seem to know themselves. It's always from some direction where I'm not looking. Isn't it strange?'

'Very! And do they disappear in the same way?'

Monica frowned very seriously and thoughtfully.

'It's so quick you can't tell where they go. When you or Miss Gribbin come in –'

'They always fly on our approach, of course. But why?'

'Because they're dreadfully, dreadfully shy. But not so shy as they were. Perhaps soon they'll get used to you and not mind at all.'

'That's a comforting thought!' said Everton with a dry laugh.

When Monica had taken her tea and departed, Everton turned to his secretary.

'You are wrong to blame the child. These creatures of her fancy are perfectly real to her. Her powers of suggestion have been strong enough to force them to some extent on me. The little Parslow girl, being younger and more receptive, actually *sees* them. It is a clear case of telepathy and auto-suggestion. I have never studied such matters, but I should say that these instances are of some scientific interest.'

Miss Gribbin's lips tightened and he saw her shiver slightly.

'Mr Parslow will be angry,' was all she said.

'I really cannot help that. Perhaps it is all for the best. If Monica does not like his little daughter they had better not be brought together again.'

For all that, Everton was a little embarrassed when on the

following morning he met the Vicar out walking. If the Rev Parslow knew that his little daughter had left the house so unceremoniously on the preceding day, he would either wish to make an apology, or perhaps require one, according to his view of the situation. Everton did not wish to deal in apologies one way or the other, he did not care to discuss the vagaries of children, and altogether he wanted to have as little to do with Mr Parslow as was conveniently possible. He would have passed with a brief acknowledgement of the Vicar's existence, but, as he had feared, the Vicar stopped him.

'I had been meaning to come and see you,' said the Rev Parslow.

Everton halted and sighed inaudibly, thinking that perhaps this casual meeting out of doors might after all have saved him something.

'Yes?' he said.

'I will walk in your direction if I may.' The Vicar eyed him anxiously. 'There is something you must certainly be told. I don't know if you guess, or if you already know. If not, I don't know how you will take it. I really don't.'

Everton looked puzzled. Whichever child the Vicar might blame for the hurried departure of Gladys, there seemed no cause for such a portentous face and manner.

'Really?' he asked. 'Is it something serious?'

'I think so, Mr Everton. You are aware, of course, that my little girl left your house yesterday afternoon with some lack of ceremony.'

'Yes, Monica told us she had gone. If they could not agree it was surely the best thing she could have done, although it may sound inhospitable of me to say it. Excuse me, Mr Parslow, but I hope you are not trying to embroil me in a quarrel between children?'

The Vicar stared in his turn.

'I am not,' he said, 'and I am unaware that there was any quarrel. I was going to ask you to forgive Gladys. There was some excuse for her lack of ceremony. She was badly frightened, poor child.'

'Then it is my turn to express regret. I had Monica's version of what happened. Monica has been left a great deal to her own resources, and, haying no playmates of her own age, she seems to have invented some.'

'Ah!' said the Rev Parslow, drawing a deep breath.

'Unfortunately,' Everton continued, 'Monica has an uncomfortable gift for impressing her fancies on other people. I have often thought I felt the presence of children about the house, and so, I am almost sure, has Miss Gribbin. I am afraid that when your little girl came to play with her yesterday afternoon, Monica scared her by introducing her invisible "friends" and by talking to imaginary and therefore invisible little girls.'

The Vicar laid a hand on Everton's arm.

'There is something more in it than that. Gladys is not an imaginative child; she is, indeed, a practical little person. I have never yet known her to tell me a lie. What would you say, Mr Everton, if I were to tell you that Gladys positively asserts that she *saw* those other children?'

Something like a cold draught went through Everton. An ugly

suspicion, vague and almost shapeless, began to move in dim recesses of his mind. He tried to shake himself free of it, to smile and to speak lightly.

'I shouldn't be in the least surprised. Nobody knows the limits of telepathy and auto-suggestion. If I can feel the presence of children whom Monica has created out of her own imagination, why shouldn't your daughter, who is probably more receptive and impressionable than I am, be able to see them?'

The Rev Parslow shook his head.

'Do you really mean that?' he asked. 'Doesn't it seem to you a little far-fetched?'

'Everything we don't understand must seem far-fetched. If one had dared to talk of wireless thirty years ago – '

'Mr Everton, do you know that your house was once a girl's school?'

Once more Everton experienced that vague feeling of discomfiture.

'I didn't know,' he said, still indifferently.

'My aunt, whom I never saw, was there. Indeed she died there. There were seven who died. Diphtheria broke out there many years ago. It ruined the school which was shortly afterwards closed. Did you know that, Mr Everton? My aunt's name was Mary Hewitt – '

'Good God!' Everton cried out sharply. 'Good God!'

'Ah!' said Parslow. 'Now do you begin to see?'

Everton, suddenly a little giddy, passed a hand across his forehead.

'That is – one of the names Monica told me,' he faltered. 'How could she know?'

'How indeed? Mary Hewitt's great friend was Elsie Power. They died within a few hours of each other.'

'That name too... she told me... and there were seven. How could she have known? Even the people around here wouldn't have remembered names after all these years.'

'Gladys knew them. But that was only partly why she was afraid. Yet I think she was more awed than afraid, because she knew instinctively that the children who came to play with little Monica, although they were not of this world, were good children, blessed children.'

'What are you telling me?' Everton burst out.

'Don't be afraid, Mr Everton. You are not afraid, are you? If those whom we call dead still remain close to us, what more natural than these children should come back to play with a lonely little girl who lacked human playmates? It may seem inconceivable, but how else explain it? How could little Monica have invented those two names? How could she have learned that seven little girls once died in your house? Only the very old people about here remember it, and even they could not tell you how many died or the name of any one of the little victims. Haven't you noticed a change in your ward since first she began to – imagine them, as you thought?'

Everton nodded heavily.

'Yes,' he said, almost unwittingly, 'she learned all sorts of tricks of speech, childish gestures she never had before, and games . . . I couldn't understand. Mr Parslow, what in God's name am I to do?'

The Rev Parslow still kept a hand on Everton's arm.

'If I were you I should send her off to school. It may not be very good for her.'

'Not good for her! But the children, you say – '

'Children? I might have said angels. *They* will never harm her. But Monica is developing a gift of seeing and conversing with – with beings that are invisible and inaudible to others. It is not a gift to be encouraged. She may in time see and converse with others – wretched souls who are not God's children. She may lose the faculty if she mixes with others of her age. Out of her need, I am sure, these came to her.'

'I must think,' said Everton.

He walked on dazedly. In a moment or two the whole aspect of life had changed, had grown clearer, as if he had been blind from birth and was now given the first glimmerings of light. He looked forward no longer into the face of a blank and featureless wall, but through a curtain beyond which life manifested itself vaguely but at least perceptibly. His footfalls on the ground beat out the words: 'There is no death. There is no death.'

★ ★ ★

That evening after dinner he sent for Monica and spoke to her in an unaccustomed way. He was strangely shy of her, and his hand, which he rested on one of her slim shoulders, lay there awkwardly.

'Do you know what I'm going to do with you, young woman?' he said. 'I'm going to pack you off to school.'

'O-oh!' she stared at him, half smiling. 'Are you really?'

'Do you want to go?'

She considered the matter, frowning and staring at the tips of her fingers.

'I don't know. I don't want to leave *them*.'

'Who?' he asked.

'Oh, you know!' she said, and turned her head half shyly.

'What? Your – friends, Monica?'

'Yes.'

'Wouldn't you like other playmates?'

'I don't know. I love *them*, you see. But they said – they said I ought to go to school if you ever sent me. They might be angry with me if I was to ask you to let me stay. They wanted me to play with other girls who aren't – what aren't like they are. Because you know, they are *different* from children that everybody can see. And Mary told me not to – not to encourage anybody else who was different, like them.'

Everton drew a deep breath.

'We'll have a talk tomorrow about finding a school for you, Monica,' he said. 'Run off to bed, now. Good night, my dear.'

He hesitated, then touched her forehead with his lips. She ran from him, nearly as shy as Everton himself, tossing back her long hair, but from the door she gave him the strangest little brimming glance, and there was that in her eyes which he had never seen before.

Late that night Everton entered the great empty room which Monica had named the schoolroom. A flag of moonlight from the window lay across the floor, and it was empty to the gaze. But the deep shadows hid little shy presences of which some unnamed and undeveloped sense in the man was acutely aware.

'Children!' he whispered. 'Children!'

He closed his eyes and stretched out his hands. Still they were shy and held aloof, but he fancied that they came a little nearer.

'Don't be afraid,' he whispered. 'I'm only a very lonely man. Be near me after Monica is gone.'

He paused, waiting. Then as he turned away he was aware of little caressing hands upon his arm. He looked around at once, but the time had not yet come for him to see. He saw only the barred window, the shadows on either wall and the flag of moonlight.

A. S.
Byatt

The
July
Ghost

'THE JULY GHOST'

A. S. BYATT (DAME ANTONIA SUSAN DUFFY, BRITISH, 1936–)

First published in *Firebird I* in 1982.

'The July Ghost' is a quiet story full of immense emotions and misguided good intentions. It is the best evocation of bereavement I have read, and the most precise observation on the helplessness of other people in the presence of grief. Byatt's son, Charles, died in a car accident at the age of eleven, in 1972.

THE JULY GHOST
A. S. Byatt

'I think I must move out of where I'm living,' he said. 'I have this problem with my landlady.'

He picked a long, bright hair off the back of her dress, so deftly that the act seemed simply considerate. He had been skilful at balancing glass, plate and cutlery, too. He had a look of dignified misery, like a dejected hawk. She was interested.

'What sort of problem? Amatory, financial, or domestic?'

'None of those, really. Well, not financial.'

He turned the hair on his finger, examining it intently, not meeting her eye.

'Not financial. Can you tell me? I might know somewhere you could stay. I know a lot of people.'

'You would.' He smiled shyly. 'It's not an easy problem to describe. There's just the two of us. I occupy the attics. Mostly.'

He came to a stop. He was obviously reserved and secretive. But he was telling her something. This is usually attractive.

'Mostly?' Encouraging him.

'Oh, it's not like *that*. Well, not... Shall we sit down?'

★　★　★

They moved across the party, which was a big party, on a hot day. He stopped and found a bottle and filled her glass. He had not needed to ask what she was drinking. They sat side by side on a sofa: he admired the brilliant poppies bold on her emerald dress, and her pretty sandals. She had come to London for the summer to work in the British Museum. She could really have managed with microfilm in Tucson for what little manuscript research was needed, but there was a dragging love affair to end. There is an age at which, however desperately happy one is in stolen moments, days, or weekends with one's married professor, one either prises him loose or cuts and runs. She had had a sub at both, and now considered she had successfully cut and run. So it was nice to be immediately appreciated. Problems are capable of solution. She said as much to him, turning her soft face to his ravaged one, swinging the long bright hair. It had begun a year ago, he told her in a rush, at another party actually; he had met this woman, the landlady in question, and had made, not immediately, a kind of *faux pas*, he now saw, and she had been very decent, all things considered, and so...

He had said, 'I think I must move out of where I'm living.' He had been quite wild, had nearly not come to the party, but could not go on drinking alone. The woman had considered him coolly and asked, 'Why?' One could not, he said, go on in a place where one had once been blissfully happy, and was now miserable, however convenient the place. Convenient, that was, for work, and friends, and things that seemed, as he mentioned them, ashy and insubstantial compared to the memory and the hope of opening the door and finding Anne outside it, laughing and breathless, waiting to be told what he had read, or thought, or eaten, or felt that day. Someone I loved left, he told the woman. Reticent on that occasion too, he bit back the flurry of sentences about the total unexpectedness of it, the arriving back and finding only an envelope on a clean table, and spaces in the bookshelves, the record stack, the kitchen cupboard. It must have been planned for weeks, she must have been thinking it out while he rolled on her, while she poured wine for him, while... No, no. Vituperation is undignified and in this case what he felt was lower and worse than rage: just pure, child-like loss. 'One ought not to mind places,' he said to the woman. 'But one does,' she had said. 'I know.'

She had suggested to him that he could come and be her lodger, then; she had, she said, a lot of spare space going to waste, and her husband wasn't there much. 'We've not had a lot to say to each other, lately.' He could be quite self-contained, there was a kitchen and a bathroom in the attics; she wouldn't bother him. There was a large garden. It was possibly this that decided him: it was very hot, central London, the time of year when a man feels he would give anything to live in a room opening on to grass and trees, not a high flat in a dusty street. And if Anne came back, the door would be locked and mortice-locked. He could stop thinking about Anne coming back. That was a decisive move: Anne thought he wasn't decisive. He would live without Anne.

★   ★   ★

For some weeks after he moved in he had seen very little of the woman. They met on the stairs, and once she came up, on a hot Sunday, to tell him he must feel free to use the garden. He had offered to do some weeding and mowing and she had accepted. That was the weekend her husband came back, driving furiously up to the front door, running in, and calling in the empty hall, 'Imogen, Imogen!' To which she had replied, uncharacteristically, by screaming hysterically. There was nothing in her husband, Noel's, appearance to warrant this reaction; their lodger, peering over the banister at the sound, had seen their upturned faces in the stairwell and watched hers settle into its usual prim and placid expression as he did so. Seeing Noel, a balding, fluffy-templed, stooping thirty-five or so, shabby corduroy suit, cotton polo neck, he realized he was now able to guess her age, as he had not been. She was a very neat woman, faded blonde, her hair in a knot on the back of her head, her legs long and slender, her eyes downcast. Mild was not quite the right word for her, though. She explained then that she had screamed because Noel had come home unexpectedly and startled her: she was sorry. It seemed a reasonable explanation. The extraordinary vehemence of the screaming was probably an echo in the stairwell. Noel seemed wholly downcast by it, all the same.

*   *   *

He had kept out of the way, that weekend, taking the stairs two at a time and lightly, feeling a little aggrieved, looking out of his kitchen window into the lovely, overgrown garden, that they were lurking indoors, wasting all the summer sun. At Sunday lunch-time he had heard the husband, Noel, shouting on the stairs.

'I can't go on, if you go on like that. I've done my best, I've tried to get through. Nothing will shift you, will it, you won't *try*, will you, you just go on and on. Well, I have my life to live, you can't throw a life away...can you?'

He had crept out again on to the dark upper landing and seen her standing, half-way down the stairs, quite still, watching Noel wave his arms and roar, or almost roar, with a look of impassive patience, as though this nuisance must pass off. Noel swallowed and gasped; he turned his face up to her and said plaintively,

'You do see I can't stand it? I'll be in touch, shall I? You must want...you must need...you must...'

She didn't speak.

'If you need anything, you know where to get me.'

'Yes.'

'Oh, well...' said Noel, and went to the door. She watched him, from the stairs, until it was shut, and then came up again, step by step, as though it was an effort, a little, and went on coming, past her bedroom, to his landing, to come in and ask him, entirely naturally, please to use the garden if he wanted to, and please not to mind marital rows. She was sure he understood...things were

327

difficult...Noel wouldn't be back for some time. He was a journalist: his work took him away a lot. Just as well. She committed herself to that 'just as well'. She was a very economical speaker.

*   *   *

So he took to sitting in the garden. It was a lovely place: a huge, hidden, walled south London garden, with old fruit trees at the end, a wildly waving disorderly buddleia, curving beds full of old roses, and a lawn of overgrown, dense rye-grass. Over the wall at the foot was the Common, with a footpath running behind all the gardens. She came out to the shed and helped him to assemble and oil the lawnmower, standing on the little path under the apple branches while he cut an experimental serpentine across her hay. Over the wall came the high sound of children's voices, and the thunk and thud of a football. He asked her how to raise the blades: he was not mechanically minded.

'The children get quite noisy,' she said. 'And dogs. I hope they don't bother you. There aren't many safe places for children, round here.'

He replied truthfully that he never heard sounds that didn't concern him, when he was concentrating. When he'd got the lawn into shape, he was going to sit on it and do a lot of reading, try to get his mind in trim again, to write a paper on Hardy's poems, on their curiously archaic vocabulary.

'It isn't very far to the road on the other side, really,' she said. 'It just seems to be. The Common is an illusion of space, really.

Just a spur of brambles and gorse-bushes and bits of football pitch between two fast four-laned main roads. I hate London commons.'

'There's a lovely smell, though, from the gorse and the wet grass. It's a pleasant illusion.'

'No illusions are pleasant,' she said, decisively, and went in. He wondered what she did with her time: apart from little shopping expeditions she seemed to be always in the house. He was sure that when he'd met her she'd been introduced as having some profession: vaguely literary, vaguely academic, like everyone he knew. Perhaps she wrote poetry in her north-facing living-room. He had no idea what it would be like. Women generally wrote emotional poetry, much nicer than men, as Kingsley Amis has stated, but she seemed, despite her placid stillness, too spare and too fierce – grim? – for that. He remembered the screaming. Perhaps she wrote Plath-like chants of violence. He didn't think that quite fitted the bill, either. Perhaps she was a freelance radio journalist. He didn't bother to ask anyone who might be a common acquaintance. During the whole year, he explained to the American at the party, he hadn't actually *discussed* her with anyone. Of course he wouldn't, she agreed vaguely and warmly. She knew he wouldn't. He didn't see why he shouldn't, in fact, but went on, for the time, with his narrative.

⋆   ⋆   ⋆

They had got to know each other a little better over the next few weeks, at least on the level of borrowing tea, or even sharing pots of it. The weather had got hotter. He had found an old-fashioned deck-chair, with faded striped canvas, in the shed, and had brushed it over and brought it out on to his mown lawn, where he sat writing a little, reading a little, getting up and pulling up a tuft of couch grass. He had been wrong about the children not bothering him: there was a succession of incursions by all sizes of children looking for all sizes of balls, which bounced to his feet, or crashed in the shrubs, or vanished in the herbaceous border, black and white footballs, beach-balls with concentric circles of primary colours, acid yellow tennis balls. The children came over the wall: black faces, brown faces, floppy long hair, shaven heads, respectable dotted sun-hats and camouflaged cotton army hats from Milletts. They came over easily, as though they were used to it, sandals, training shoes, a few bare toes, grubby sunburned legs, cotton skirts, jeans, football shorts. Sometimes, perched on the top, they saw him and gestured at the balls; one or two asked permission. Sometimes he threw a ball back, but was apt to knock down a few knobby little unripe apples or pears. There was a gate in the wall, under the fringing trees, which he once tried to open, spending time on rusty bolts only to discover that the lock was new and secure, and the key not in it.

The boy sitting in the tree did not seem to be looking for a ball. He was in a fork of the tree nearest the gate, swinging his legs, doing something to a knot in a frayed end of rope that was attached to the branch he sat on. He wore blue jeans and training shoes, and a brilliant tee shirt, striped in the colours of the spectrum, arranged in the right order, which the man on the grass found visually pleasing. He had rather long blond hair, falling over his eyes, so that his face was obscured.

'Hey, you. Do you think you ought to be up there? It might not be safe.'

The boy looked up, grinned, and vanished monkey-like over the wall. He had a nice, frank grin, friendly, not cheeky.

He was there again, the next day, leaning back in the crook of the tree, arms crossed. He had on the same shirt and jeans. The man watched him, expecting him to move again, but he sat, immobile, smiling down pleasantly, and then staring up at the sky. The man read a little, looked up, saw him still there, and said,

'Have you lost anything?'

The child did not reply: after a moment he climbed down a little, swung along the branch hand over hand, dropped to the ground, raised an arm in salute, and was up over the usual route over the wall.

Two days later he was lying on his stomach on the edge of the lawn, out of the shade, this time in a white tee shirt with a pattern of blue ships and water-lines on it, his bare feet and legs stretched in the sun. He was chewing a grass stem, and studying the earth, as though watching for insects. The man said, 'Hi, there,' and the boy looked up, met his look with intensely blue eyes under long lashes, smiled with the same complete warmth and openness, and returned his look to the earth.

He felt reluctant to inform on the boy, who seemed so harmless and considerate: but when he met him walking out of the kitchen door, spoke to him, and got no answer but the gentle smile before the boy ran off towards the wall, he wondered if he should speak to his landlady. So he asked her, did she mind the children coming in the garden. She said no, children must look for balls, that was part of being children. He persisted – they sat there, too, and he had met one coming out of the house. He hadn't seemed to be doing any harm, the boy, but you couldn't tell. He thought she should know.

He was probably a friend of her son's, she said. She looked at him kindly and explained. Her son had run off the Common with some other children, two years ago, in the summer, in July, and had been killed on the road. More or less instantly, she had added drily, as though calculating that just *enough* information would preclude the need for further questions. He said he was sorry, very sorry, feeling to blame, which was ridiculous, and a little injured, because he had not known about her son, and might inadvertently have made a fool of himself with some casual reference whose ignorance would be embarrassing.

What was the boy like, she said. The one in the house? 'I don't – talk to his friends. I find it painful. It could be Timmy, or Martin. They might have lost something, or want...'

He described the boy. Blond, about ten at a guess, he was not very good at children's ages, very blue eyes, slightly built, with a rainbow-striped tee shirt and blue jeans, mostly though not always – oh, and those football practice shoes, black and green. And the other tee shirt, with the ships and wavy lines. And an extraordinarily nice smile. A really *warm* smile. A nice-looking boy.

He was used to her being silent. But this silence went on and on and on. She was just staring into the garden. After a time, she said, in her precise conversational tone,

'The only thing I want, the only thing I want at all in this world, is to see that boy.'

She stared at the garden and he stared with her, until the grass began to dance with empty light, and the edges of the shrubbery wavered. For a brief moment he shared the strain of not seeing the boy. Then she gave a little sigh, sat down, neatly as always, and passed out at his feet.

After this she became, for her, voluble. He didn't move her after she fainted, but sat patiently by her, until she stirred and sat up; then he fetched her some water, and would have gone away, but she talked.

'I'm too rational to see ghosts, I'm not someone who would see anything there was to see, I don't believe in an after-life, I don't see how anyone can, I always found a kind of satisfaction for myself in the idea that one just came to an end, to a sliced-off stop. But that was myself; I didn't think *he* – not *he* – I thought ghosts were – what people *wanted* to see, or were afraid to see...and after he died, the best hope I had, it sounds silly, was that I would go mad enough so that instead of waiting every day for him to come home from school and rattle the letter-box I might actually have the illusion of seeing or hearing him come in. Because I can't stop my body and mind waiting, every day, every day, I can't let go. And his bedroom, sometimes at night I go in, I think I might just for a moment forget he *wasn't* in there sleeping, I think I would pay almost anything – anything at all – for a moment of seeing him like I used to. In his pyjamas, with his – his – his hair... ruffled, and, his... you said, his... that *smile.*

'When it happened, they got Noel, and Noel came in and shouted my name, like he did the other day, that's why I screamed, because it – seemed the same – and then they said, he is dead, and I thought coolly, *is* dead, that will go on and on and on till the end of time, it's a continuous present tense, one thinks the most ridiculous things, there I was thinking about grammar, the verb to be, when it ends to be dead... And then I came out into the garden, and I half saw, in my mind's eye, a kind of ghost of his face, just the eyes and hair, coming towards me – like every day waiting for him to come home, the way you think of your son, with such pleasure, when he's – not there – and I – I thought – no, I won't *see* him, because he is dead, and I won't dream about him because he is dead, I'll be rational and practical and continue to live because one must, and there was Noel...

'I got it wrong, you see, I was so *sensible*, and then I was so shocked because I couldn't get to want anything – I couldn't *talk* to Noel—I – I – made Noel take away, destroy, all the photos, I – didn't dream, you can will not to dream, I didn't... visit a grave, flowers, there isn't any point. I was so sensible. Only my body wouldn't stop waiting and all it wants is to – to see that boy. *That* boy. That boy you – saw.'

★   ★   ★

He did not say that he might have seen another boy, maybe even a boy who had been given the tee shirts and jeans afterwards. He did not say, though the idea crossed his mind, that maybe what he had seen was some kind of impression from her terrible desire to see a boy where nothing was. The boy had had nothing terrible, no aura of pain about him: he had been, his memory insisted, such a pleasant, courteous, self-contained boy, with his own purposes. And in fact the woman herself almost immediately raised the possibility that what he had seen was what she desired to see, a kind of mix-up of radio waves, like when you overheard police messages on the radio, or got BBC 1 on a switch that said ITV. She was thinking fast, and went on almost immediately to say that perhaps his sense of loss, his loss of Anne, which was what had led her to feel she could bear his presence in her house, was what had brought them – dare she say – near enough, for their wavelengths to mingle, perhaps, had made him susceptible ... You mean, he had said, we are a kind of emotional vacuum, between us, that must be filled. Something like that, she had said, and had added, 'But I don't believe in ghosts.'

Anne, he thought, could not be a ghost, because she was elsewhere, with someone else, doing for someone else those little things she had done so gaily for him, tasty little suppers, bits of research, a sudden vase of unusual flowers, a new bold shirt, unlike his own cautious taste, but suiting him, suiting him. In a sense, Anne was worse lost because voluntarily absent, an absence that could not be loved because love was at an end, for Anne.

'I don't suppose you will, now,' the woman was saying. 'I think talking would probably stop any – mixing of messages, if that's what it is, don't you? But – if – *if* he comes again' – and here for the first time her eyes were full of tears – 'if – you must promise, you will *tell* me, you must promise.'

⋆　⋆　⋆

He had promised, easily enough, because he was fairly sure she was right, the boy would not be seen again. But the next day he was on the lawn, nearer than ever, sitting on the grass beside the deck-chair, his arms clasping his bent, warm brown knees, the thick, pale hair glittering in the sun. He was wearing a football shirt, this time, Chelsea's colours. Sitting down in the deck-chair, the man could have put out a hand and touched him, but did not: it was not, it seemed, a possible gesture to make. But the boy looked up and smiled, with a pleasant complicity, as though they now understood each other very well. The man tried speech: he said, 'It's nice to see you again,' and the boy nodded acknowledgement of this remark, without speaking himself. This was the beginning of communication between them, or what the man supposed to be communication. He did not think of fetching the woman. He became aware that he was in some strange way *enjoying the boy's company*. His pleasant stillness – and he sat there all morning, occasionally lying back on the grass, occasionally staring thoughtfully at the house—was calming and comfortable. The man did quite a lot of work – wrote about three reasonable pages on Hardy's original air-blue gown – and looked up now and then to make sure the boy was still there and happy.

★   ★   ★

He went to report to the woman – as he had after all promised to do – that evening. She had obviously been waiting and hoping – her unnatural calm had given way to agitated pacing, and her eyes were dark and deeper in. At this point in the story he found in himself a necessity to bowdlerize for the sympathetic American, as he had indeed already begun to do. He had mentioned only a child who had 'seemed like' the woman's lost son, and he now ceased to mention the child at all, as an actor in the story, with the result that what the American woman heard was a tale of how he, the man, had become increasingly involved in the woman's solitary grief, how their two losses had become a kind of *folie à deux* from which he could not extricate himself. What follows is not what he told the American girl, though it may be clear at which points the bowdlerized version coincided with what he really believed to have happened. There was a sense he could not at first analyse that it was improper to talk about the boy – not because he might not be believed; that did not come into it; but because something dreadful might happen.

'He sat on the lawn all morning. In a football shirt.'

'Chelsea?'

'Chelsea.'

'What did he do? Does he look happy? Did he speak?' Her desire to know was terrible.

'He doesn't speak. He didn't move much. He seemed – very calm. He stayed a long time.'

'This is terrible. This is ludicrous. There *is no boy.*'

'No. But l saw him.'

'Why you?'

'I don't know.' A pause. 'I do *like* him.'

'He is – was – a most likeable boy.'

*   *   *

Some days later he saw the boy running along the landing in the evening, wearing what might have been pyjamas, in peacock towelling, or might have been a track suit. Pyjamas, the woman stated confidently, when he told her: his new pyjamas. With white ribbed cuffs, weren't they? and a white polo neck? He corroborated this, watching her cry – she cried more easily now – finding her anxiety and disturbance very hard to bear. But it never occurred to him that it was possible to break his promise to tell her when he saw the boy. That was another curious imperative from some undefined authority.

They discussed clothes. If there were ghosts, how could they appear in clothes long burned, or rotted, or worn away by other people? You could imagine, they agreed, that something of a person might linger – as the Tibetans and others believe the soul lingers near the body before setting out on its long journey. But clothes? And in this case so many clothes? I must be seeing your memories, he told her, and she nodded fiercely, compressing her lips, agreeing that this was likely, adding, 'I am too rational to go mad, so I seem to be putting it on you.'

He tried a joke. 'That isn't very kind to me, to imply that madness comes more easily to me.'

'No, sensitivity. I am insensible. I was always a bit like that, and this made it worse. I am the *last* person to see any ghost that was trying to haunt me.'

'We agreed it was your memories I saw.'

'Yes. We agreed. That's rational. As rational as we can be, considering.'

*   *   *

All the same, the brilliance of the boy's blue regard, his gravely smiling salutation in the garden next morning, did not seem like anyone's tortured memories of earlier happiness. The man spoke to him directly then:

'Is there anything I can *do* for you? Anything you want? Can I help you?'

The boy seemed to puzzle about this for a while, inclining his head as though hearing was difficult. Then he nodded, quickly and perhaps urgently, turned, and ran into the house, looking back to make sure he was followed. The man entered the living room through the french windows, behind the running boy, who stopped for a moment in the centre of the room, with the man blinking behind him at the sudden transition from sunlight to comparative dark. The woman was sitting in an armchair, looking at nothing there. She often sat like that. She looked up, across the boy, at the man; and the boy, his face for the first time anxious, met the man's eyes again, asking, before he went out into the house.

'What is it? What is it? Have you seen him again? Why are you...?'

'He came in here. He went – out through the door.'

'I didn't see him.'

'No.'

'Did he – oh, this is so *silly* – did he see me?'

He could not remember. He told the only truth he knew.

'He brought me in here.'

'Oh, what can I do, what am I going to *do*? If I killed myself – I have thought of that – but the idea that I should be with him is an illusion I... this silly situation is the nearest I shall ever get. To him. He was *in here with me?*'

'Yes.'

And she was crying again. Out in the garden he could see the boy, swinging agile on the apple branch.

⋆   ⋆   ⋆

He was not quite sure, looking back, when he had thought he had realized what the boy had wanted him to do. This was also, at the party, his worst piece of what he called bowdlerization, though in some sense it was clearly the opposite of bowdlerization. He told the American girl that he had come to the conclusion that it was the woman herself who had wanted it, though there was in fact, throughout, no sign of her wanting anything except to see the boy, as she said. The boy, bolder and more frequent, had appeared several nights running on the landing, wandering in and out of bathrooms and bedrooms, restlessly, a little agitated, questing almost, until it had 'come to' the man that what he required was to be re-engendered, for him, the man, to give to his mother another child, into which he could peacefully vanish. The idea was so clear that it was like another imperative, though he did not have the courage to ask the child to confirm it. Possibly this was out of delicacy – the child was too young to be talked to about sex. Possibly there were other reasons. Possibly he was mistaken: the situation was making him hysterical, he felt action of some kind was required and must be possible. He could not spend the rest of the summer, the rest of his life, describing non-existent tee shirts and blond smiles.

★　★　★

He could think of no sensible way of embarking on his venture, so in the end simply walked into her bedroom one night. She was lying there, reading; when she saw him her instinctive gesture was to hide, not her bare arms and throat, but her book. She seemed, in fact, quite unsurprised to see his pyjamaed figure, and, after she had recovered her coolness, brought out the book definitely and laid it on the bedspread.

'My new taste in illegitimate literature. I keep them in a box under the bed.'

Ena Twigg, Medium. The Infinite Hive. The Spirit World. Is There Life After Death?

'Pathetic,' she proffered.

He sat down delicately on the bed.

'Please, don't grieve so. Please, let yourself be comforted. Please...'

He put an arm round her. She shuddered. He pulled her closer. He asked why she had had only the one son, and she seemed to understand the purport of his question, for she tried, angular and chilly, to lean on him a little, she became apparently compliant. 'No real reason,' she assured him, no material reason. Just her husband's profession and lack of inclination: that covered it.

'Perhaps,' he suggested, 'if she would be comforted a little, perhaps she could hope, perhaps...'

For comfort then, she said, dolefully, and lay back, pushing Ena Twigg off the bed with one fierce gesture, then lying placidly. He got in beside her, put his arms round her, kissed her cold cheek, thought of Anne, of what was never to be again. Come on, he said to the woman, you must live, you must try to live, let us hold each other for comfort.

She hissed at him 'Don't *talk*' between clenched teeth, so he stroked her lightly, over her nightdress, breasts and buttocks and long stiff legs, composed like an effigy on an Elizabethan tomb. She allowed this, trembling slightly, and then trembling violently: he took this to be a sign of some mixture of pleasure and pain, of the return of life to stone. He put a hand between her legs and she moved them heavily apart; he heaved himself over her and pushed, unsuccessfully. She was contorted and locked tight: frigid, he thought grimly, was not the word. *Rigor mortis,* his mind said to him, before she began to scream.

He was ridiculously cross about this. He jumped away and said quite rudely, 'Shut up,' and then ungraciously, 'I'm sorry.' She stopped screaming as suddenly as she had begun and made one of her painstaking economical explanations.

'Sex and death don't go. I can't afford to let go of my grip on myself. I hoped. What you hoped. It was a bad idea. I apologize.'

'Oh, never mind,' he said and rushed out again on to the landing, feeling foolish and almost in tears for warm, lovely Anne.

★   ★   ★

The child was on the landing, waiting. When the man saw him, he looked questioning, and then turned his face against the wall and leant there, rigid, his shoulders hunched, his hair hiding his expression. There was a similarity between woman and child. The man felt, for the first time, almost uncharitable towards the boy, and dial felt something else.

'Look, I'm sorry. I tried. I did try. Please turn round.'

Uncompromising, rigid, clenched back view.

'Oh well,' said the man, and went into his bedroom.

★   ★   ★

So now, he said to the American woman at the party, I feel a fool, I feel embarrassed, I feel we are hurting, not helping each other, I feel it isn't a refuge. Of course you feel that, she said, of course you're right – it was temporarily necessary, it helped both of you, but you've got to live your life. Yes, he said, I've done my best, I've tried to get through, I have my life to live. Look, she said, I want to help, I really do, I have these wonderful friends I'm renting this flat from, why don't you come, just for a few days, just for a break, why don't you? They're real sympathetic people, you'd like them, I like them, you could get your emotions kind of straightened out. She'd probably be glad to see the back of you, she must feel as bad as you do, she's got to relate to her situation in her own way in the end. We all have.

He said he would think about it. He knew he had elected to tell the sympathetic American because he had sensed she would be – would offer – a way out. He had to get out. He took her home from the party and went back to his house and landlady without seeing her into her flat. They both knew that this reticence was promising – that he hadn't come in then, because he meant to come later. Her warmth and readiness were like sunshine, she was open. He did not know what to say to the woman.

* * *

In fact, she made it easy for him: she asked, briskly, if he now found it perhaps uncomfortable to stay, and be replied that he had felt he should move on, he was of so little use . . . Very well, she had agreed, and had added crisply that it had to be better for everyone if 'all this' came to an end. He remembered the firmness with which she had told him that no illusions were pleasant. She was strong: too strong for her own good. It would take years to wear away that stony, closed, simply surviving insensibility. It was not his job. He would go. All the same, he felt bad.

* * *

He got out his suitcases and put some things in them. He went down to the garden, nervously, and put away the deck-chair. The garden was empty. There were no voices over the wall. The silence was thick and deadening. He wondered, knowing be would not see the boy again, if anyone else would do so, or if, now he was gone, no one would describe a tee shirt, a sandal, a smile, seen, remembered, or desired. He went slowly up to his room again.

* * *

The boy was sitting on his suitcase, arms crossed, face frowning and serious. He held the man's look for a long moment, and then the man went and sat on his bed. The boy continued to sit. The man found himself speaking.

'You do see I have to go? I've tried to get through. I can't get through. I'm no use to you, am I?'

The boy remained immobile, his head on one side, considering. The man stood up and walked towards him.

345

'Please. Let me go. What are we, in this house? A man and a woman and a child, and none of us can get through. You can't want that?'

He went as close as he dared. He had, he thought, the intention of putting his hand on or through the child. But could not bring himself to feel there was no boy. So he stood, and repeated,

'I can't get through. Do you want me to stay?'

Upon which, as he stood helplessly there, the boy turned on him again the brilliant, open, confiding, beautiful desired smile.

The Open Window

Laura

Saki

'LAURA'

'THE OPEN WINDOW'

Saki (Hector Hugh Monro, British, 1870–1916)

Both stories were first published in the 1914 collection *Beasts and Super-Beasts*.

Saki's dark and mischievous stories satirise Edwardian culture and the class system. Saki was born in Burma and was sent to live in England after his mother died (she was frightened by a charging cow). He began his writing career as a journalist and was a foreign correspondent stationed in Warsaw, the Balkans and Russia. He fought in the First World War, though he was officially overage, and died in France during the Battle of Ancre.

LAURA
Saki

'You are not really dying, are you?' asked Amanda.

'I have the doctor's permission to live till Tuesday,' said Laura.

'But today is Saturday; this is serious!' gasped Amanda.

'I don't know about it being serious; it is certainly Saturday,' said Laura.

'Death is always serious,' said Amanda.

'I never said I was going to die. I am presumably going to leave off being Laura, but I shall go on being something. An animal of some kind, I suppose. You see, when one hasn't been very good in the life one has just lived, one reincarnates in some lower organism. And I haven't been very good, when one comes to think of it. I've been petty and mean and vindictive and all that sort of thing when circumstances have seemed to warrant it.'

'Circumstances never warrant that sort of thing.' said Amanda hastily.

'If you don't mind my saying so,' observed Laura, 'Egbert is a circumstance that would warrant any amount of that sort of thing. You're married to him – that's different; you've sworn to love, honour, and endure him: I haven't.'

'I don't see what's wrong with Egbert,' protested Amanda.

'Oh, I dare say the wrongness has been on my part,' admitted Laura dispassionately; 'he has merely been the extenuating circumstance. He made a thin, peevish kind of fuss, for instance, when I took the collie puppies from the farm out for a run the other day.

'They chased his young broods of speckled Sussex and drove two sitting hens off their nests, besides running all over the flower beds. You know how devoted he is to his poultry and garden.

'Anyhow, he needn't have gone on about it for the entire evening and then have said, "Let's say no more about it" just when I was beginning to enjoy the discussion. That's where one of my petty vindictive revenges came in,' added Laura with an unrepentant chuckle; 'I turned the entire family of speckled Sussex into his seedling shed the day after the puppy episode.'

'How could you?' exclaimed Amanda.

'It came quite easy,' said Laura; 'two of the hens pretended to be laying at the time, but I was firm.'

'And we thought it was an accident!'

'You see,' resumed Laura, 'I really have some grounds for supposing that my next incarnation will be in a lower organism. I shall be an animal of some kind. On the other hand, I haven't been a bad sort in my way, so I think I may count on being a nice animal, some thing elegant and lively, with a love of fun. An otter, perhaps.'

'I can't imagine you as an otter,' said Amanda.

'Well, I don't suppose you can imagine me as an angel, if it comes to that,' said Laura.

Amanda was silent. She couldn't.

'Personally I think an otter life would be rather enjoyable,' continued Laura; 'salmon to eat all the year around, and the satisfaction of being able to fetch the trout in their own homes without having to wait for hours till they condescend to rise to the fly you've been dangling before them; and an elegant svelte figure – '

'Think of the otter hounds,' interposed Amanda, 'how dreadful to be hunted and harried and finally worried to death!'

'Rather fun with half the neighbourhood looking on, and anyhow not worse than this Saturday-to-Tuesday business of dying by inches; and then I should go on into something else. If I had been a moderately good otter I suppose I should get back into human shape of some sort; probably something rather primitive – a little brown, unclothed Nubian boy, I should think.'

'I wish you would be serious,' sighed Amanda; 'you really ought to be if you're only going to live till Tuesday.'

As a matter of fact Laura died on Monday.

'So dreadfully upsetting,' Amanda complained to her uncle-in-law, Sir Lulworth Quayne. 'I've asked quite a lot of people down for golf and fishing, and the rhododendrons are just looking their best.'

'Laura always was inconsiderate,' said Sir Lulworth; 'she was born during Goodwood week, with an Ambassador staying in the house who hated babies.'

'She had the maddest kind of ideas,' said Amanda; 'do you know if there was any insanity in her family? '

'Insanity? No, I never heard of any. Her father lives in West Kensington, but I believe he's sane on all other subjects.'

'She had an idea that she was going to be reincarnated as an otter,' said Amanda.

'One meets with those ideas of reincarnation so frequently, even in the West,' said Sir Lulworth, 'that one can hardly set them down as being mad. And Laura was such an unaccountable person in this life that I should not like to lay down definite rules as to what she might be doing in an after state.'

'You think she really might have passed into some animal form?' asked Amanda. She was one of those who shape their opinions rather readily from the standpoint of those around them.

Just then Egbert entered the breakfast-room, wearing an air of bereavement that Laura's demise would have been insufficient, in itself, to account for.

'Four of my speckled Sussex have been killed,' he exclaimed; 'the very four that were to go to the show on Friday. One of them was dragged away and eaten right in the middle of that new carnation bed that I've been to such trouble and expense over. My best flower bed and my best fowls singled out for destruction; it almost seems as if the brute that did the deed had special knowledge how to be as devastating as possible in a short space of time.'

'Was it a fox, do you think?' asked Amanda.

'Sounds more like a polecat,' said Sir Lulworth.

'No,' said Egbert, 'there were marks of webbed feet all over the place, and we followed the tracks down to the stream at the bottom of the garden; evidently an otter.'

Amanda looked quickly and furtively across at Sir Lulworth.

Egbert was too agitated to eat any breakfast, and went out to superintend the strengthening of the poultry yard defences.

'I think she might at least have waited till the funeral was over,' said Amanda in a scandalised voice.

'It's her own funeral, you know,' said Sir Lulworth; 'it's a nice point in etiquette how far one ought to show respect to one's own mortal remains.'

Disregard for mortuary convention was carried to further lengths next day; during the absence of the family at the funeral ceremony the remaining survivors of the speckled Sussex were massacred. The marauder's line of retreat seemed to have embraced most of the flower beds on the lawn, but the strawberry beds in the lower garden had also suffered.

'I shall get the otter hounds to come here at the earliest possible moment,' said Egbert savagely.

'On no account! You can't dream of such a thing!' exclaimed Amanda. 'I mean, it wouldn't do, so soon after a funeral in the house.'

'It's a case of necessity,' said Egbert; 'once an otter takes to that sort of thing it won't stop.'

'Perhaps it will go elsewhere now that there are no more fowls left,' suggested Amanda.

'One would think you wanted to shield the beast,' said Egbert.

'There's been so little water in the stream lately,' objected

Amanda; 'it seems hardly sporting to hunt an animal when it has so little chance of taking refuge anywhere.'

'Good gracious!' fumed Egbert, 'I'm not thinking about sport. I want to have the animal killed as soon as possible.'

Even Amanda's opposition weakened when, during church time on the following Sunday, the otter made its way into the house, raided half a salmon from the larder and worried it into scaly fragments on the Persian rug in Egbert's studio.

'We shall have it hiding under our beds and biting pieces out of our feet before long,' said Egbert, and from what Amanda knew of this particular otter she felt that the possibility was not a remote one.

On the evening preceding the day fixed for the hunt Amanda spent a solitary hour walking by the banks of the stream, making what she imagined to be hound noises. It was charitably supposed by those who overheard her performance, that she was practising for farmyard imitations at the forthcoming village entertainment.

It was her friend and neighbour, Aurora Burret, who brought her news of the day's sport.

'Pity you weren't out; we had quite a good day. We found it at once, in the pool just below your garden.'

'Did you – kill?' asked Amanda.

'Rather. A fine she-otter. Your husband got rather badly bitten in trying to "tail it". Poor beast, I felt quite sorry for it, it had such a human look in its eyes when it was killed. You'll call me silly, but do you know who the look reminded me of? My dear woman, what is the matter?'

When Amanda had recovered to a certain extent from her attack of nervous prostration Egbert took her to the Nile Valley to recuperate. Change of scene speedily brought about the desired recovery of health and mental balance. The escapades of an adventurous otter in search of a variation of diet were viewed in their proper light. Amanda's normally placid temperament re-asserted itself. Even a hurricane of shouted curses, coming from her husband's dressing-room, in her husband's voice, but hardly in his usual vocabulary, failed to disturb her serenity as she made a leisurely toilet one evening in a Cairo hotel.

'What is the matter? What has happened?' she asked in amused curiosity.

'The little beast has thrown all my clean shirts into the bath! Wait till I catch you, you little – '

'What little beast?' asked Amanda, suppressing a desire to laugh; Egbert's language was so hopelessly inadequate to express his outraged feelings.

'A little beast of a naked brown Nubian boy,' spluttered Egbert.

And now Amanda is seriously ill.

THE OPEN WINDOW
Saki

'My aunt will be down presently, Mr Nuttel,' said a very self-possessed young lady of fifteen; 'in the meantime you must try and put up with me.'

Framton Nuttel endeavoured to say the correct something which should duly flatter the niece of the moment without unduly discounting the aunt that was to come. Privately he doubted more than ever whether these formal visits on a succession of total strangers would do much towards helping the nerve cure which he was supposed to be undergoing.

'I know how it will be,' his sister had said when he was preparing to migrate to this rural retreat; 'you will bury yourself down there and not speak to a living soul, and your nerves will be worse than ever from moping. I shall just give you letters of introduction to all the people I know there. Some of them, as far as I can remember, were quite nice.'

Framton wondered whether Mrs Sappleton, the lady to whom

he was presenting one of the letters of introduction, came into the nice division.

'Do you know many of the people round here?' asked the niece, when she judged that they had had sufficient silent communion.

'Hardly a soul,' said Framton. 'My sister was staying here, at the rectory, you know, some four years ago, and she gave me letters of introduction to some of the people here.'

He made the last statement in a tone of distinct regret.

'Then you know practically nothing about my aunt?' pursued the self-possessed young lady.

'Only her name and address,' admitted the caller. He was wondering whether Mrs Sappleton was in the married or widowed state. An undefinable something about the room seemed to suggest masculine habitation.

'Her great tragedy happened just three years ago,' said the child; 'that would be since your sister's time.'

'Her tragedy?' asked Framton; somehow in this restful country spot tragedies seemed out of place.

'You may wonder why we keep that window wide open on an October afternoon,' said the niece, indicating a large French window that opened on to a lawn.

'It is quite warm for the time of the year,' said Framton; 'but has that window got anything to do with the tragedy?'

'Out through that window, three years ago to a day, her husband and her two young brothers went off for their day's shooting. They never came back. In crossing the moor to their favourite snipe-shooting ground they were all three engulfed in

a treacherous piece of bog. It had been that dreadful wet summer, you know, and places that were safe in other years gave way
suddenly without warning. Their bodies were never recovered.
That was the dreadful part of it.' Here the child's voice lost its
self-possessed note and became falteringly human. 'Poor aunt
always thinks that they will come back some day, they and the
little brown spaniel that was lost with them, and walk in at that
window just as they used to do. That is why the window is kept
open every evening till it is quite dusk. Poor dear aunt, she has
often told me how they went out, her husband with his white
waterproof coat over his arm, and Ronnie, her youngest brother,
singing, 'Bertie, why do you bound?' as he always did to tease her,
because she said it got on her nerves. Do you know, sometimes on
still, quiet evenings like this, I almost get a creepy feeling that they
will all walk in through that window –'

She broke off with a little shudder. It was a relief to Framton
when the aunt bustled into the room with a whirl of apologies for
being late in making her appearance.

'I hope Vera has been amusing you?' she said.

'She has been very interesting,' said Framton.

'I hope you don't mind the open window,' said Mrs Sappleton
briskly; 'my husband and brothers will be home directly from
shooting, and they always come in this way. They've been out for
snipe in the marshes today, so they'll make a fine mess over my
poor carpets. So like you men-folk, isn't it?'

She rattled on cheerfully about the shooting and the scarcity
of birds, and the prospects for duck in the winter. To Framton,

it was all purely horrible. He made a desperate but only partially successful effort to turn the talk on to a less ghastly topic; he was conscious that his hostess was giving him only a fragment of her attention, and her eyes were constantly straying past him to the open window and the lawn beyond. It was certainly an unfortunate coincidence that he should have paid his visit on this tragic anniversary,

'The doctors agree in ordering me complete rest, an absence of mental excitement, and avoidance of anything in the nature of violent physical exercise,' announced Framton, who laboured under the tolerably wide-spread delusion that total strangers and chance acquaintances are hungry for the least detail of one's ailments and infirmities, their cause and cure. 'On the matter of diet they are not so much in agreement,' he continued.

'No?' said Mrs Sappleton, in a voice which only replaced a yawn at the last moment. Then she suddenly brightened into alert attention – but not to what Framton was saying.

'Here they are at last!' she cried. 'Just in time for tea, and don't they look as if they were muddy up to the eyes!'

Framton shivered slightly and turned towards the niece with a look intended to convey sympathetic comprehension. The child was staring out through the open window with dazed horror in her eyes. In a chill shock of nameless fear Framton swung round in his seat and looked in the same direction.

In the deepening twilight three figures were walking across the lawn towards the window; they all carried guns under their arms, and one of them was additionally burdened with a white coat hung over his shoulders. A tired brown spaniel kept close at their heels. Noiselessly they neared the house, and then a hoarse young voice chanted out of the dusk: 'I said, Bertie, why do you bound?'

Framton grabbed wildly at his stick and hat; the hall-door, the gravel-drive, and the front gate were dimly noted stages in his headlong retreat. A cyclist coming along the road had to run into the hedge to avoid imminent collision.

'Here we are, my dear,' said the bearer of the white mackintosh, coming in through the window; 'fairly muddy, but most of it's dry. Who was that who bolted out as we came up?'

'A most extraordinary man, a Mr Nuttel,' said Mrs Sappleton; 'could only talk about his illnesses, and dashed off without a word of good-bye or apology when you arrived. One would think he had seen a ghost.'

'I expect it was the spaniel,' said the niece calmly; 'he told me he had a horror of dogs. He was once hunted into a cemetery somewhere on the banks of the Ganges by a pack of pariah dogs, and had to spend the night in a newly dug grave with the creatures snarling and grinning and foaming just above him. Enough to make any one lose their nerve.'

Romance at short notice was her speciality.

The
Specialist's
Hat

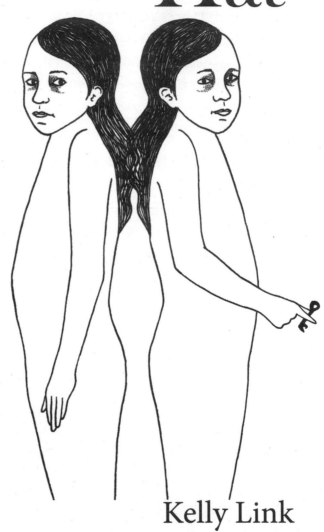

Kelly Link

KELLY LINK (AMERICAN, 1969–)

First published in *Event Horizon* in 1998.

'The Specialist's Hat' is the best spooky-babysitter story ever written. Kelly Link is a master of a deadpan humour that deftly prevents us from understanding the awfulness of the events that befall her characters until it is extremely too late. I was torn between this story and another of Link's masterpieces, 'Stone Animals' (which features a haunted toothbrush), but 'The Specialist's Hat' is perfect, so here it is.

THE SPECIALIST'S HAT

Kelly Link

'When you're Dead,' Samantha says, 'you don't have to brush your teeth.'

'When you're Dead,' Claire says, 'you live in a box, and it's always dark, but you're not ever afraid.'

Claire and Samantha are identical twins. Their combined age is twenty years, four months, and six days. Claire is better at being Dead than Samantha.

The babysitter yawns, covering up her mouth with a long white hand. 'I said to brush your teeth and that it's time for *bed*,' she says. She sits cross-legged on the flowered bedspread between them. She has been teaching them a card game called Pounce, which involves three decks of cards, one for each of them. Samantha's deck is missing the Jack of Spades and the Two of Hearts, and Claire keeps on cheating. The babysitter wins anyway. There are still flecks of dried shaving cream and toilet paper on her arms. It is hard to tell how old she is – at first they thought she must be a grownup, but now she hardly looks older than them. Samantha has forgotten the babysitter's name.

Claire's face is stubborn. 'When you're Dead,' she says, 'you stay up all night long.'

'When you're dead,' the babysitter snaps, 'it's always very cold and damp, and you have to be very, very quiet or else the Specialist will get you.'

'This house is haunted,' Claire says.

'I know it is,' the babysitter says. 'I used to live here.'

Something is creeping up the stairs,
Something is standing outside the door,
Something is sobbing, sobbing in the dark;
Something is sighing across the floor.

Claire and Samantha are spending the summer with their father, in the house called Eight Chimneys. Their mother is dead. She has been dead for exactly 282 days.

Their father is writing a history of Eight Chimneys, and of the poet, Charles Cheatham Rash, who lived here at the turn of the century, and who ran away to sea when he was thirteen, and who returned when he was thirty-eight. He married, fathered a child, wrote three volumes of bad, obscure poetry, and an even worse and more obscure novel, *The One Who Is Watching Me Through the Window,* before disappearing again in 1907, this time for good. Samantha and Claire's father says that some of the poetry is actually quite readable, and at least the novel isn't very long.

When Samantha asked him why he was writing about Rash, he replied that no one else had, and why didn't she and Samantha go play outside. When she pointed out that she *was* Samantha, he just scowled and said how could he be expected to tell them apart when they both wore blue jeans and flannel shirts, and why couldn't one of them dress all in green and the other pink?

Claire and Samantha prefer to play inside. Eight Chimneys is as big as a castle, but dustier and darker than Samantha imagines a castle would be. The house is open to the public, and during the day people – families – driving along the Blue Ridge Parkway will stop to tour the grounds and the first story; the third story belongs to Claire and Samantha. Sometimes they play explorers, and sometimes they follow the caretaker as he gives tours to visitors. After a few weeks, they have memorized his lecture, and they mouth it along with him. They help him sell postcards and copies of Rash's poetry to the tourist families who come into the little gift shop. When the mothers smile at them, and say how sweet they are, they stare back and don't say anything at all. The dim light in the house makes the mothers look pale and flickery and tired. They leave Eight Chimneys, mothers and families, looking not quite as real as they did before they paid their admissions, and of course Claire and Samantha will never see them again, so maybe they aren't real. Better to stay inside the house, they want to tell the families, and if you must leave, then go straight to your cars.

The caretaker says the woods aren't safe.

Their father stays in the library on the second story all morning, typing, and in the afternoon he takes long walks. He takes his pocket recorder along with him, and a hip flask of Old Kentucky, but not Samantha and Claire.

The caretaker of Eight Chimneys is Mr Coeslak. His left leg is noticeably shorter than his right. Short black hairs grow out of his ears and his nostrils, and there is no hair at all on top of his head, but he's given Samantha and Claire permission to explore the whole of the house. It was Mr Coeslak who told them that there are copperheads in the woods, and that the house is haunted. He says they are all, ghosts and snakes, a pretty bad-tempered lot, and Samantha and Claire should stick to the marked trails, and stay out of the attic.

Mr Coeslak can tell the twins apart, even if their father can't; Claire's eyes are grey, like a cat's fur, he says, but Samantha's are *gray*, like the ocean when it has been raining.

Samantha and Claire went walking in the woods on the second day that they were at Eight Chimneys. They saw something. Samantha thought it was a woman, but Claire said it was a snake. The staircase that goes up to the attic has been locked. They peeked through the keyhole, but it was too dark to see anything.

And so he had a wife, and they say she was real pretty. There was another man who wanted to go with her, and first she wouldn't, because she was afraid of her husband, and then she did. Her husband found out, and they say he killed a snake and got some of this snake's blood and put it in some whiskey and gave it to her. He had learned

this from an island man who had been on a ship with him. And in about six months snakes created in her and they got between her meat and the skin. And they say you could just see them running up and down her legs. They say she was just hollow to the top of her body, and it kept on like that till she died. Now my daddy said he saw it.
– An Oral History of Eight Chimneys

Eight Chimneys is over two hundred years old. It is named for the eight chimneys which are each big enough that Samantha and Claire can both fit in one fireplace. The chimneys are red brick, and on each floor there are eight fireplaces, making a total of twenty-four. Samantha imagines the chimney stacks stretching like stout red tree trunks, all the way up through the slate roof of the house. Beside each fireplace is a heavy black firedog, and a set of wrought iron pokers shaped like snakes. Claire and Samantha pretend to duel with the snake-pokers before the fireplace in their bedroom on the third floor. Wind rises up the back of the chimney. When they stick their faces in, they can feel the air rushing damply upward, like a river. The flue smells old and sooty and wet, like stones from a river.

Their bedroom was once the nursery. They sleep together in a poster bed which resembles a ship with four masts. It smells of mothballs. Charles Cheatham Rash slept here when he was a little boy, and also his daughter. She disappeared when her father did. It might have been gambling debts. They may have moved to New Orleans. She was fourteen years old, Mr Coeslak said. What was her name, Claire asked. What happened to her mother, Samantha wanted to know. Mr Coeslak closed his eyes in an almost wink. Mrs Rash had died the year before her husband and daughter disappeared, he said, of a mysterious wasting disease. He can't remember the name of the poor little girl, he said.

Eight Chimneys has exactly 100 windows, all still with the original wavery panes of hand-blown glass. With so many windows, Samantha thinks, Eight Chimneys should always be full of light, but instead the trees press close against the house, so that the rooms on the first and second story – even the third-story rooms – are green and dim, as if Samantha and Claire are underwater. This is the light that makes the tourists into ghosts. In the morning, and again towards evening, a fog settles in around the house. Sometimes it is grey like Claire's eyes, and sometimes it is more gray, like Samantha's.

I met a woman in the wood,
Her lips were two red snakes.
She smiled at me, her eyes lewd
And burning like a fire.

A few nights ago, the wind was sighing in the nursery chimney. Their father had already tucked them in, and turned off the light. Claire dared Samantha to stick her head into the fireplace, in the dark, and so she did. The cold, wet air licked at her face, and it almost sounded like voices talking low, muttering. She couldn't quite make out what they were saying.

Their father has been drinking steadily since they arrived at

Eight Chimneys. He never mentions their mother. One evening they heard him shouting in the library, and when they came downstairs, there was a large sticky stain on the desk, where a glass of whiskey had been knocked over. It was looking at me, he said, through the window. It had orange eyes.

Samantha and Claire refrained from pointing out that the library is on the second story.

At night, their father's breath has been sweet from drinking, and he is spending more and more time in the woods, and less in the library. At dinner, usually hot dogs and baked beans from a can, which they eat off of paper plates in the first floor dining room, beneath the Austrian chandelier (which has exactly 632 leaded crystals shaped like teardrops), their father recites the poetry of Charles Cheatham Rash, which neither Samantha nor Claire cares for.

He has been reading the ship diaries which Rash kept, and he says that he has discovered proof in them that Rash's most famous poem, 'The Specialist's Hat', is not a poem at all, and in any case, Rash didn't write it. It is something that one of the men on the whaler used to say, to conjure up a whale. Rash simply copied it down and stuck an end on it and said it was his.

The man was from Mulatuppu, which is a place neither Samantha nor Claire has ever heard of. Their father says that the man was supposed to be some sort of magician, but he drowned shortly before Rash came back to Eight Chimneys. Their father says that the other sailors wanted to throw the magician's chest overboard, but Rash persuaded them to let him keep it until

he could be put ashore, with the chest, off the coast of North
Carolina.

The specialist's hat makes a noise like an agouti;
The specialist's hat makes a noise like a collared peccary;
The specialist's hat makes a noise like a white-lipped peccary;
The specialist's hat makes a noise like a tapir;
The specialist's hat makes a noise like a rabbit;
The specialist's hat makes a noise like a squirrel;
The specialist's hat makes a noise like a curassow;
The specialist's hat moans like a whale in the water;
The specialist's hat moans like the wind in my wife's hair;
The specialist's hat makes a noise like a snake;
I have hung the hat of the specialist upon my wall.

The reason that Claire and Samantha have a babysitter is that
their father met a woman in the woods. He is going to meet her,
tonight, and they are going to have a picnic supper and look at
the stars. This is the time of year when the Perseids can be seen,
falling across the sky on clear nights. Their father said that he has
been walking with the woman every afternoon. She is a distant
relation of Rash, and besides, he said, he needs a night off, and
some grownup conversation.

Mr Coeslak won't stay in the house after dark, but he agreed to
find someone to look after Samantha and Claire. Then their father
couldn't find Mr Coeslak, but the babysitter showed up precisely at
seven o'clock. The babysitter, whose name neither twin quite caught,

wears a blue cotton dress with short floaty sleeves. Both Samantha and Claire think she is pretty in an old-fashioned sort of way.

They were in the library with their father, looking up Mulatuppu in the red leather atlas, when she arrived. She didn't knock on the front door, she simply walked in, and up the stairs, as if she knew where to find them.

Their father kissed them goodbye, a hasty smack, told them to be good and he would take them into town on the weekend to see the Disney film. They went to the window to watch as he walked out of the house and into the woods. Already it was getting dark, and there were fireflies, tiny yellow-hot sparks in the air. When their father had quite disappeared into the trees, they turned around and stared at the babysitter instead. She raised one eyebrow. 'Well,' she said. 'What sort of games do you like to play?'

Widdershins around the chimneys,
once, twice, again.
The spokes click like a clock on the bicycle;
they tick down the days of the life of a man.

First they played Go Fish, and then they played Crazy Eights, and then they made the babysitter into a mummy by putting shaving cream from their father's bathroom on her arms and legs, and wrapping her in toilet paper. She is the best babysitter they have ever had.

At nine-thirty, she tried to put them to bed. Neither Claire nor Samantha wanted to go to bed, so they began to play the Dead

375

game. The Dead game is a let's pretend that they have been playing every day for 274 days now, but never in front of their father
or any other adult. When they are Dead, they are allowed to do
anything they want to. They can even fly, by jumping off the nursery beds, and just waving their arms. Someday this will work, if
they practice hard enough.

The Dead game has three rules.

One. Numbers are significant. The twins keep a list of
important numbers in a green address book that belonged to
their mother. Mr Coeslak's tour has been a good source of significant amounts and tallies: they are writing a tragical history
of numbers.

Two. The twins don't play the Dead game in front of grownups.
They have been summing up the babysitter, and have decided that
she doesn't count. They tell her the rules.

Three is the best and most important rule. When you are Dead,
you don't have to be afraid of anything. Samantha and Claire
aren't sure who the Specialist is, but they aren't afraid of him.

To become Dead, they hold their breath while counting to 35,
which is as high as their mother got, not counting a few days.

'You never lived here,' Claire says. 'Mr Coeslak lives here.'

'Not at night,' says the babysitter. 'This was my bedroom when
I was little.'

'Really?' Samantha says. Claire says, 'Prove it.'

The babysitter gives Samantha and Claire a look, as if she is
measuring them: how old; how smart; how brave; how tall. Then
she nods. The wind is in the flue, and in the dim nursery light they

can see the little strands of fog seeping out of the fireplace. 'Go stand in the chimney,' she instructs them. 'Stick your hand as far up as you can, and there is a little hole on the left side, with a key in it.'

Samantha looks at Claire, who says, 'Go ahead.' Claire is fifteen minutes and some few uncounted seconds older than Samantha, and therefore gets to tell Samantha what to do. Samantha remembers the muttering voices, and then reminds herself that she is Dead. She goes over to the fireplace and ducks inside.

When Samantha stands up in the chimney, she can only see the very edge of the room. She can see the fringe of the mothy blue rug, and one bed leg, and beside it, Claire's foot, swinging back and forth like a metronome. Claire's shoelace has come undone, and there is a Band-Aid on her ankle. It all looks very pleasant and peaceful from inside the chimney, like a dream, and for a moment, she almost wishes she didn't have to be Dead. But it's safer, really. She sticks her left hand up as far as she can reach, trailing it along the crumbly wall, until she feels an indentation. She thinks about spiders and severed fingers, and rusty razorblades, and then she reaches inside. She keeps her eyes lowered, focused on the corner of the room, and Claire's twitchy foot.

Inside the hole, there is a tiny cold key, its teeth facing outward. She pulls it out, and ducks back into the room. 'She wasn't lying,' she tells Claire.

'Of course I wasn't lying,' the babysitter says. 'When you're Dead, you're not allowed to tell lies.'

'Unless you want to,' Claire says.

Dreary and dreadful beats the sea at the shore.
Ghastly and dripping is the mist at my door.
The clock in the hall is chiming one, two, three, four.
The morning comes not, no, never, no more.

Samantha and Claire have gone to camp for three weeks every summer since they were seven. This year their father didn't ask them if they wanted to go back, and after discussing it, they decided that it was just as well. They didn't want to have to explain to all their friends how they were half-orphans now. They are used to being envied, because they are identical twins. They don't want to be pitiful.

It has not even been a year, but Samantha realizes that she is forgetting what her mother looked like. Not her mother's face so much as the way she smelled, which was something like grass, and something like Chanel No. 5, and like something else too. She can't remember whether her mother had gray eyes, like her, or grey eyes, like Claire. She doesn't dream about her mother anymore, but she does dream about Prince Charming, a bay whom she once rode in the horse show at her camp. In the dream, Prince Charming did not smell like a horse at all. He smelled like Chanel No. 5. When she is Dead, she can have all the horses she wants, and they all smell like Chanel No. 5.

★   ★   ★

'Where does the key go to?' Samantha says.

The babysitter holds out her hand. 'To the attic. You don't

really need it, but taking the stairs is easier than the chimney. At least the first time.'

'Aren't you going to make us go to bed?' Claire says.

The babysitter ignores Claire. 'My father used to lock me in the attic when I was little, but I didn't mind. There was a bicycle up there and I used to ride it around and around the chimneys until my mother let me out again. Do you know how to ride a bicycle?'

'Of course,' Claire says.

'If you ride fast enough, the Specialist can't catch you.'

'What's the Specialist?' Samantha says. Bicycles are okay, but horses can go faster.

'The Specialist wears a hat,' says the babysitter. 'The hat makes noises.'

She doesn't say anything else.

When you're dead, the grass is greener
Over your grave. The wind is keener.
Your eyes sink in, your flesh decays. You
Grow accustomed to slowness; expect delays.

The attic is somehow bigger and lonelier than Samantha and Claire thought it would be. The babysitter's key opens the locked door at the end of the hallway, revealing a narrow set of stairs. She waves them ahead and upwards.

It isn't as dark in the attic as they had imagined. The oaks that block the light and make the first three stories so dim and green and mysterious during the day, don't reach all the way up. Extravagant moonlight, dusty and pale, streams in the angled dormer windows. It lights the length of the attic, which is wide enough to hold a softball game in, and lined with trunks where Samantha imagines people could sit, could be hiding and watching. The ceiling slopes down, impaled upon the eight thick-waisted chimney stacks. The chimneys seem too alive, somehow, to be contained in this empty, neglected place; they thrust almost angrily through the roof and attic floor. In the moonlight, they look like they are breathing. 'They're so beautiful,' she says.

'Which chimney is the nursery chimney?' Claire says.

The babysitter points to the nearest righthand stack. 'That one,' she says. 'It runs up through the ballroom on the first floor, the library, the nursery.'

Hanging from a nail on the nursery chimney is a long, black object. It looks lumpy and heavy, as if it were full of things. The babysitter takes it down, twirls it on her finger. There are holes in the black thing, and it whistles mournfully as she spins it. 'The Specialist's hat,' she says.

'That doesn't look like a hat,' says Claire. 'It doesn't look like anything at all.' She goes to look through the boxes and trunks that are stacked against the far wall.

'It's a special hat,' the babysitter says. 'It's not supposed to look like anything. But it can sound like anything you can imagine. My father made it.'

'Our father writes books,' Samantha says.

'My father did too.' The babysitter hangs the hat back on the nail. It curls blackly against the chimney. Samantha stares at it. It nickers at her. 'He was a bad poet, but he was worse at magic.'

Last summer, Samantha wished more than anything that she could have a horse. She thought she would have given up anything for one – even being a twin was not as good as having a horse. She still doesn't have a horse, but she doesn't have a mother either, and she can't help wondering if it's her fault. The hat nickers again, or maybe it is the wind in the chimney.

'What happened to him?' Claire asks.

'After he made the hat, the Specialist came and took him away. I hid in the nursery chimney while it was looking for him, and it didn't find me.'

'Weren't you scared?'

There is a clattering, shivering, clicking noise. Claire has found the babysitter's bike and is dragging it towards them by the handlebars. The babysitter shrugs. 'Rule number three,' she says.

Claire snatches the hat off the nail. 'I'm the Specialist!' she says, putting the hat on her head. It falls over her eyes, the floppy shapeless brim sewn with little asymmetrical buttons that flash and catch at the moonlight like teeth. Samantha looks again, and sees that they are teeth. Without counting, she suddenly knows that there are exactly fifty-two teeth on the hat, and that they are the teeth of agoutis, of curassows, of white-lipped peccaries, and of the wife of Charles Cheatham Rash. The chimneys are moaning, and Claire's voice booms hollowly beneath the hat. 'Run away, or I'll catch you and eat you!'

Samantha and the babysitter run away, laughing, as Claire

mounts the rusty, noisy bicycle and pedals madly after them. She rings the bicycle bell as she rides, and the Specialist's hat bobs up and down on her head. It spits like a cat. The bell is shrill and thin, and the bike wails and shrieks. It leans first towards the right, and then to the left. Claire's knobby knees stick out on either side like makeshift counterweights.

Claire weaves in and out between the chimneys, chasing Samantha and the babysitter. Samantha is slow, turning to look behind. As Claire approaches, she keeps one hand on the handle-bars, and stretches the other hand out towards Samantha. Just as she is about to grab Samantha, the babysitter turns back and plucks the hat off Claire's head.

'Shit!' the babysitter says, and drops it. There is a drop of blood forming on the fleshy part of the babysitter's hand, black in the moonlight, where the Specialist's hat has bitten her.

Claire dismounts, giggling. Samantha watches as the Specialist's hat rolls away. It gathers speed, veering across the attic floor, and disappears, thumping down the stairs. 'Go get it,' Claire says. 'You can be the Specialist this time.'

'No,' the babysitter says, sucking at her palm. 'It's time for bed.'

When they go down the stairs, there is no sign of the Specialist's hat. They brush their teeth, climb into the ship-bed, and pull the covers up to their necks. The babysitter sits between their feet. 'When you're Dead,' Samantha says, 'do you still get tired and have to go to sleep? Do you have dreams?'

'When you're Dead,' the babysitter says, 'everything's a lot easier. You don't have to do anything that you don't want to. You don't have to have a name, you don't have to remember. You don't even have to breathe.'

She shows them exactly what she means.

★   ★   ★

When she has time to think about it (and now she has all the time in the world to think), Samantha realizes, with a small pang, that she is now stuck, indefinitely between ten and eleven years old, stuck with Claire and the babysitter. She considers this. The number 10 is pleasing and round, like a beach ball, but all in all, it hasn't been an easy year. She wonders what 11 would have been like. Sharper, like needles, maybe. She has chosen to be Dead instead. She hopes that she's made the right decision. She wonders if her mother would have decided to be Dead, instead of dead, if she could have.

Last year, they were learning fractions in school when her mother died. Fractions remind Samantha of herds of wild horses, piebalds and pintos and palominos. There are so many of them, and they are, well, fractious and unruly. Just when you think you have one under control, it throws up its head and tosses you off. Claire's favorite number is 4, which she says is a tall, skinny boy. Samantha doesn't care for boys that much. She likes numbers. Take the number 8, for instance, which can be more than one thing at once. Looked at one way, 8 looks like a bent woman with curvy hair. But if you lay it down on its side, it looks like a snake curled with its tail in its mouth. This is sort of like the difference between being Dead and being dead. Maybe when Samantha is tired of one, she will try the other.

On the lawn, under the oak trees, she hears someone calling her name. Samantha climbs out of bed and goes to the nursery window. She looks out through the wavy glass. It's Mr Coeslak. 'Samantha, Claire!' he calls up to her. 'Are you all right? Is your father there?' Samantha can almost see the moonlight shining through him. 'They're always locking me in the tool room,' he says. 'Are you there, Samantha? Claire? Girls?'

The babysitter comes and stands beside Samantha. The babysitter puts her finger to her lip. Claire's eyes glitter at them from the dark bed. Samantha doesn't say anything, but she waves at Mr Coeslak. The babysitter waves too. Maybe he can see them waving, because after a little while, he stops shouting and goes away. 'Be careful,' the babysitter says. '*He'll* be coming soon. It will be coming soon.'

She takes Samantha's hand, and leads her back to the bed, where Claire is waiting. They sit and wait. Time passes, but they don't get tired, they don't get any older.

Who's there?
Just air.

The front door opens on the first floor, and Samantha, Claire, and the babysitter can hear someone creeping, creeping up the stairs. 'Be quiet,' the babysitter says. 'It's the Specialist.'

Samantha and Claire are quiet. The nursery is dark and the

wind crackles like a fire in the fireplace.

'Claire, Samantha, Samantha, Claire?' The Specialist's voice is blurry and wet. It sounds like their father's voice, but that's because the hat can imitate any noise, any voice. 'Are you still awake?'

'Quick,' the babysitter says. 'It's time to go up to the attic and hide.'

Claire and Samantha slip out from under the covers and dress quickly and silently. They follow her. Without speech, without breathing, she pulls them into the safety of the chimney. It is too dark to see, but they understand the babysitter perfectly when she mouths the word, *Up*. She goes first, so they can see where the fingerholds are, the bricks that jut out for their feet. Then Claire. Samantha watches her sister's foot ascend like smoke, the shoe-lace still untied.

'Claire? Samantha? Goddammit, you're scaring me. Where are you?' The Specialist is standing just outside the half-open door. 'Samantha? I think I've been bitten by something. I think I've been bitten by a goddamn snake.' Samantha hesitates for only a second. Then she is climbing up, up, up the nursery chimney.

TINY GHOSTS

Amy Giacalone

So I was sitting in the bath when the tiny ghosts started showing up, and I'm not going to tell you anything too specific about my bath because I don't believe in pornography. Because right away you're thinking it's bubbly and sexy and ooh-la-la, but that's not the kind of bath I take. I take oatmeal baths. You can buy the oatmeal bath packets from Walmart for $4.99 on sale, they come in a box of eight, and Walmart's all that's around for shopping. So I take an oatmeal bath with Epsom salts for my arthritis, and the water's the color of street slush in the winter. Little blobs of oatmeal float around sometimes and I smush them in my fingers. It's weirdly satisfying and I don't mind mentioning it.

I take my baths in the upstairs bathroom, which is not attached to the bedroom, since it's an older house. I light a candle that smells like peach pie. I pour myself a cup of wine. I don't like wine-glasses, too delicate, so it's just in a cup, which is good enough for me. We buy Sutterhome White Zinfandel, which is $3.50 a bottle.

In town we can get it from CVS for $4.99, that's why we really do have to drive out to the Walmart, it's like that with everything. I like my bathwater really hot, as hot as I can get it to go. I have my bath copy of *Jane Eyre*. The good copy is hardcover, and this one's a fat paperback. It's got warbly pages from the bathwater. I never start at the beginning of it anymore, not particularly. Usually I just flip to any spot I feel like reading.

It's a very complicated book, and I'm proud to say I've read it many times, because I'm a good reader. My bath is comfortable, and the room looks nice because I have a very nice house, and I can't help but notice for a second that things are perfect. You know, you have to work hard all the time just to get things perfect for even a second. It's very satisfying to be me.

Well, I'm only about halfway through my Bath Night when my husband, Gary, gets home, this is still before the tiny ghosts, now, and I hear him come up the stairs. And he just comes on in, like he does. He opens the door, and I pop up straight in the bath, and he comes over and kisses me on top of my head. He has to bend all the way over to do it, and then we start to talk:

'Hey.'

'Hey.'

'How was your night?'

'Good. Yours?'

'Well, it's still going on.' I have wrinkled hands always, but especially now from the bath water, and I reach over my shoulder for some wine.

And he says, 'Mind if I pee?' and I say, 'Yeah, sure,' and I pull back the shower curtain while I take a sip, so he has his privacy.

'You're reading *Jane Eyre* again?' Gary asks.

'It's my favorite,' I tell him.

'Huh,' he says, 'I was just talking to Pete. Now, he's a guy who really knows how to *read*. Reads a book a week. Big ones, too. Very impressive.'

Now, it's pretty nice with the curtain pulled. Dark. It's like a tiny room that's all bath, which is an idea I don't mind saying I like. I picture myself in the tiny room and I wonder how I'd get into it, probably a tiny door. Tiny door? Sure, a tiny door. And then I see myself very tiny, and I get in through a tiny door and dive right into the bath. Gary flushes. He washes his hands. He pulls back the shower curtain and then I'm my real size again. He picks up my book.

'Pete should read *Jane Eyre*,' I say, because it's a great book. Anyone would like it. But guess what my husband says?

'Nah, he only likes new books. Hip ones.'

'*Jane Eyre* is a hip book!'

'Oh, I know that.' Gary blushes and now of course he's back-tracking. 'That's not what I meant. I meant like whatever the newest book is on the new book list.'

So I say, 'Humph,' which is what I think of that, and I say, 'You know, I'm trying to enjoy my bath.'

Gary comes over and kisses me on the head again. 'Okay. You know I didn't mean that, about your book. I'm sure Pete would like it a lot.' And then he leaves, and he didn't mean it, but he made me feel like an old fuddy-duddy, sitting in the fuddy-duddy bath with my fuddy-duddy bath book. And that's when the tiny ghosts start showing up.

First, a tiny door opens up. The tiny door's in the corner by my feet, where the tub meets the wall, and there's a tiny ledge. It's not like a fancy door. Just a regular, brown door with a knob. And a little person walks out! And he just stands there. He's kind of clear, like a shadow, and he's wearing cargo shorts, flipflops, and a t-shirt. Maybe the size of my hand. He has tiny black hair and a tiny beard. He's carrying a tiny towel.

Of course, I pull my feet back, fast, which splashes. I cover up my chest area with my knees. I think I'm probably imagining things, but I'm a pretty steady person, and it isn't like me to imagine this hard. And he talks to me!

'Oh, hey.' He holds up one hand. He's waving. He looks around.

'Hey?' I say. I'm holding my two knees tight.

'What are you doing here?' he asks, like I'm interfering with his night and not the other way around.

So I go, 'Taking a bath?'

He doesn't say anything, just puts his hands in his pockets, and nods. 'Okay,' he says, and turns back to the door.

'Wait! What are you doing here?' I ask, pretty quick, since I want to know, and I think he's leaving.

'I thought I'd take a bath. Didn't know you were still using the tub.'

'I'm sorry. What?'

'Bath.' He says slowly, like I'm stupid, and he makes a circle

with his hand, indicating the tub I'm sitting in. 'But it's no problem,' he says, 'I'll come back later.'

'What?'

'See ya.'

I talk fast: 'I'm sorry...' I say, and I hesitate at what I should
call him. Mister? Sir? Little guy? I go with: 'I'm sorry...you there.
You're a...? Not to be rude, but what are you?'

'Ghost.'

'A tiny ghost?'

'No, a big one. Asshole.'

'Excuse me?'

'Kay, bye.' He waves again, and goes out the tiny door, and I'm
alone again.

Wait. What? I lean over and open the tiny door, which is still
there, but the ghost is gone. I'm all thumbs because the door knob
is so tiny, and for a second I think that maybe my hand will go
right through it if it's a ghost door after all, but no. I open it just
fine, and I have to lean all the way over to peek inside. All there
is, is a long, black, tiny hallway. It's cold in there. I can feel a little
chill coming out.

So of course I shut the little door and get my butt out of that
bath. I wrap myself in two big towels, one is a dress, and the other
I twist my hair up in, but kind of crazy since I'm shaking all over.
I flip on the light switch. I blow out the peach pie candle and
'Ga-ry!' is what I start yelling.

He's yelling, too: 'Hey! Hey-o! Look out, Angie! Where're you
at?' I hear his footsteps coming towards the bathroom. I open

the door and we almost smack right into each other, we're going so fast.

'Honey,' he says, 'I think I'm hallucinating something.'

And then we both start babbling and waving our hands and we're saying the same thing. Gary's going on and on about a tiny door, and a tiny ghost, too.

So we sit up all night together, right in the middle of the bed. We can't fall asleep. We don't even try to talk to each other, we just sit and stare out in different directions. Soon, we're laying down, but it's laying down like a couple of kittens. In the middle of the bed, all curled up around each other.

At about two o'clock, I get hungry. I don't put my feet on the floor, because I'm afraid a tiny ghost is going to scurry out. I bend down by my nightstand and open the bottom drawer on it. I keep a box of saltines there.

'Don't drop any crumbs,' Gary says.

'Huh?'

He shakes my saltine box. 'Crumbs will just attract them.'

'Like with mice?'

He shrugs, and I have to admit, in my mind it's like we have mice instead of tiny ghosts, too.

Then again, maybe the saltines do attract them, I don't know. Because a tiny door opens in the bedroom, right above Gary's dresser. A little brown door, and out come six—*six*—tiny ghosts! It's a tiny ghost gang. They're mostly woman-ghosts, but there's a couple men in the group, too. They're loud like teenagers, laughing, and slapping each other on the back. They say things like:

'Is this the place?'

'Yeah.'

'Oh my god, this room is ugly as hell.'

Now, our bedroom is *not* ugly as hell, to give you some idea of how wrong these tiny ghosts are. Our bedroom is actually very nice, with flower wallpaper and a matching flower bedspread that I found on sale.

Gary loops his arms around my waist, tight, like we're about to jump off a plane together. He whispers, 'That's the ghost I told you about,' meaning one of the ghosts that just walked in.

'Which one?'

'The noisy one.'

Well, they're all noisy at first, so I don't know what he's talking about until the *really* noisy one speaks up. She talks right to my husband, like she knows him.

'Hey, Gary,' she waves, elbowing one of the ghosts next to her. She has long black hair that's full of waves and little braids. She's wearing jeans and a black leather jacket. 'Is this your special lady?' She points to me.

Gary squeezes me so tight it hurts. 'This is my wife.'

The noisy ghost laughs. 'Then I guess she's the one responsible for this lousy wallpaper.'

'Lousy!' I say, my mouth dropping open, but she's laughing.

'Hey, Gary, what's your lady's name?'

But I answer, not him, because now I'm pretty mad at her for insulting my nice bedroom, so I say, 'I'm Angie.'

She loves it. She cracks up at that, like my name is a joke that I wouldn't understand. 'Classic,' she says.

'Why?' I say. 'What's your name?'

And she spreads her arms wide, like she's asking for a hug. 'I'm Mystica.'

'Humph,' I say. 'Doesn't sound like you're in much of a position to be making fun of names, then.'

Then Mystica does something that really freaks us out. She jumps to the bed. I mean, she *jumps*. Practically flies. Of course, I shriek, and I climb right over my husband and I duck behind him like he's a shield. Gary's a good man. He holds out an arm to protect me, and sticks his chin out. 'I didn't know you could *do* that!' I say. 'I didn't know she could do that!'

'Listen,' Mystica says, stepping closer to us, pointing at us with her arm straight out in front of her. 'I own this house now. These are my friends, and I'm in charge. You don't want to mess with me.'

When she sees that we're scared, and of course we are, she smiles and flies back to the dresser. And it's so weird when she does it, she stays facing us, flying backwards like she's being sucked back into the door. 'Let's get out of here,' she says to her friends, and they file out the tiny, brown door behind her.

At five'o'clock, we know Al's is going to open up again soon, and Gary decides to tiptoe over to the closet. The coast is clear. He throws me a pair of my jeans and a Cardinals sweatshirt and some underwear. I have to be honest, we don't look our best. Up all night isn't a good look, and my hair dried kind of fuzzy from the bath. I try to smooth it down with some Jergens lotion, which I have on my nightstand. The Jergens I buy because I like the smell, even though it's a whopping $6.99, even at Walmart, and it never goes on sale.

So we creep out of the house. We only see one tiny ghost on the way out. She's on the kitchen counter, making herself a giant piece of toast. She gives us the finger, the *middle* finger, when we walk past. I make a mental note to put the bread in the fridge, and, oh yeah, a slice of toast is food for how many tiny ghosts? I picture her cutting it into twenty pieces, and twenty tiny ghosts dig in. It gives me the chills, and I'm glad when we're safely in the truck.

'What's up, early birds?' Marsh is whistling when we get there. His place smells like French fries and chicken nuggets, and it's such a good smell I get hungry right away. He pours a silver pre-wrapped coffee packet into the machine and closes it. He flips a switch, and an orange light goes on, for brewing.

Marsh himself is a pretty little guy. I mean, he's not tiny ghost tiny, but he's a smallish man. 'Bad night?' he asks, when he takes a look at us. I'll be honest, I don't feel great. My hair's a mess and I don't live in a nice house anymore. I live in a haunted house. I've always thought of myself as more of a Jane Eyre, but right about now I feel like the crazy lady locked upstairs. And it bugs me to have Marsh knowing about it.

'We couldn't sleep,' Gary tells him.

'You guys okay?'

'Nope. Our house is haunted.'

I jump in, defensive, 'But haunted by *tiny* ghosts.'

'Really,' Marsh says, raising his eyebrows. 'What do you mean, tiny?'

Gary says, 'About the size of my hand.'

Marsh pours the coffee, and we tell him everything we know about the tiny ghosts so far, while we order and eat our breakfasts. Marsh can't believe it. I say, 'They're jerks,' a few times, to Gary and Marsh both. I say it so many times, I'm afraid they've stopped listening to me. 'They're jerks, they're little, tiny jerks. That's all they are.'

But the Saturday crowd comes into Al's pretty early, and after there's just crumbs on our plates, and we're both looking jittery from the no sleep and all the coffee on top of it, we realize we've got to leave eventually. I look around and nobody else has anything on their mind but breakfast. They're all doing great. Me and Gary are the ones who have to go back home, whether we like it or not. Back to our tiny ghost house.

The tiny ghosts stick around for months. *Months!* Think about how long that is. We learn the names of a few of the tiny ghosts, and recognize them on sight. The blonde one, the one that was making toast, is named Olivia, and the first tiny ghost that interrupted my bath? His name is Chad. As far as we can tell, there are at least a dozen of them, living in tunnels that wind around our house. The tiny doors appear for days at a time, disappear for longer.

We try to get rid of them. Gary comes home with a gray plastic Walmart bag full of mousetraps and bug spray.

'It's *not like mice*,' I say to him, for the millionth time.

He sets the mousetraps up all around the usual places where the tiny ghosts pop out. He sprays the walls down with ant and roach repellant. But when Mystica sees it, she just laughs. 'Oh, please,' she says, hopping right over the mousetraps, the kind of big jump she's so good at, where she hangs suspended in the air for whole seconds. 'A for effort, Gary,' she says.

The same with the BB gun, and time we try to light them on fire. Nothing works. Although we do leave a scorch mark above the kitchen sink, which we'll have to paint over. Which is actually going to cost a fair amount, since we have to do the whole wall. And every time the tiny ghosts win, we start to feel dumber. They don't like my hair, the way I talk, the way I decorate.

Finally, we give up. We even try to make friends with them. We're friendly people. Even to people that are already dead, even if we're not sure they were ever people at all. Even if they're the meanest not-people we've ever met and they're hurting our feelings every day. And what do you know? That doesn't work, either.

Alright. I can tell you what did work, if you want. How we got rid of them, although I doubt you'll believe it.

It starts one day, with me trying to be nice. 'I love what you've done with your hair,' I say to Mystica. Her hair is all looped up on top of her head, she's wearing tall boots and lipstick. Me and Gary are in the TV room. We're watching TV.

And she goes, '*Thanks*,' rolling her eyes, 'I've been *dying* for you to notice. I *live* for your approval.'

And it occurs to me: Mystica doesn't live or die at all. She doesn't worry. She doesn't have dreams. She's nothing like me, because I dream of the geraniums I'll plant next spring, and I worry that we'll get a late frost, and they'll all die. Those are real dreams and worries. So I say, 'Shut up.'

Mystica likes that. She laughs at first, then she jumps over to the coffee table. She stands between me and Gary. She goes, 'You're nothing, Angie. You're worthless. You're not very interesting, and you have an ugly house. You're a boring, stupid bitch.'

And for a minute, I go back to feeling like she's right. I look around my uninteresting, worthless house. My life here with my husband. I think, yeah. I am, actually, a boring, stupid b-word.

But then, I look at Gary. He's frowning, and he glances at me. He shakes his head, 'No. Not true.' He's got his arms crossed over his belly, and his hairline is receding a little, and I love him. And I think about all of the things that I like about our house and our life together. I think about how it's blue, pretty blue. With a clean, squishy carpet and two copies of *Jane Eyre,* which is a hip enough book for me. I think about how nice it is to open up the windows for fresh air. And I think that Mystica has no place in this house.

So then, I do something that's a little weird but I don't mind mentioning it. I lean forward, and I roar at Mystica. Like a roar, like how a lion roars. It's not something I've ever done in my life, and I expect her to make fun of me, like she always does, but I don't really care what she thinks about me anymore.

She pulls back for a second, and her eyes open wide. 'Hey,' she says.

'You're just a ghost!' I say. 'Get out of here! This is *my* house!'

For a second, it seems like she's going to get even meaner. But then, 'Rawwwr!' That's Gary next to me. He does the same thing. 'Beat it!' He points to the door she came out of. 'Go back to your little ghost-hole.'

Mystica doesn't know what to do with that. So I roar again. And so does Gary. We're roaring, it's like a jungle in there, and the most amazing thing happens. Mystica leaves. Right back out the tiny door. And of course, we're cracking up, because we just made lion noises. Gary puts his arm around me, and I give him a kiss on the cheek.

So that's it. From then on, the tiny ghosts come out every once in a while, but we just roar at them like lions. We start collecting lion stuff. Lion figurines. Gary buys me a Lion King sweatshirt, which he ordered online for $19.50, and I wear it whenever I want. Because this is my house, and my life, and I do what I want. Tell *that* to your tiny ghosts.

Rebecca Curtis

The Pink
House

'THE PINK HOUSE'

REBECCA CURTIS (AMERICAN, 1976–)

First published in the *New Yorker* in 2014.

From an interview with Rebecca Curtis by Willing Davidson in the *New Yorker*:

There's something lively about ghost stories – ha! – because the story contains built-in excitement and horror. Of course, you still need to create conflict and a plot, if you're a traditionalist, but you're starting on stilts, maybe, because you have a dramatic element that a normal, two-people-drinking-coffee-and-complaining-about-their-bunions story doesn't have.

Rebecca Curtis is a New York-based fiction writer whose work has appeared in *McSweeney's*, *Harper's* and *n+1*.

THE PINK HOUSE
Rebecca Curtis

'But it's tawdry,' the woman said.

'Petty. I still can't figure out what happened...'

She was tall, pale, and had dark hair and a heart-shaped face. She looked to be in her early thirties. 'I made a series of mistakes,' she said, 'due to being hasty, or influenced by who knows? And each led to the next, and they seem to have ruined this man's life— my ex-boyfriend's—or else changed it completely. And the initial mistake was that, when I moved from Manhattan to a bleak town upstate, I took a house sight unseen.'

'That doesn't sound so bad,' someone said.

'Yes,' a man, a novelist, said, and nodded. 'If you didn't like it when you got there, you could have just switched houses.'

'But I didn't,' the woman said. 'I didn't realize the truth about the house until too late, and then I stayed. I was too lazy to move, or else sick in the head.'

The woman sat down at the table. It was the first time she had that evening. Rain smashed sideways against the bungalow's steel siding. The rain had begun halfway through dinner. Then thin straws of lightning appeared beyond the dark windows, and hail fell on the tin roof. The woman had served jumbo shrimp sautéed in garlic butter; chicken quesadillas with goat Cheddar cheese; refried black beans, sautéed onions and peppers; a pear-and-bitter-greens salad; and flourless chocolate cake with raspberry-vodka sauce. Everyone had drunk Lone Star beer. Her guests were a Korean-American crime-noir novelist, a Lebanese fantasy writer, a Thai journalist, and three Brazilian painters. None of the seven people around the table knew one another well; they'd all been flown to this mountain town on the Mexican border by a foundation that was putting them up and paying them to practice their respective arts for six weeks. They were all unsuccessful, middle-aged, and hard up for cash. None of them knew who'd selected them for the residency, or why. The woman had agreed to host a dinner, because her bungalow was the largest. Three of the group were divorced; four never married. Over dinner, they'd discussed politics and failed relationships, then moved on to ghost stories. The guests were full, tipsy and reluctant to go out into the rain. They'd heard about the boot steps on the stairs of the old Virginia fort, and the Northern California gold-rush-era hotel where female guests woke with hand-shaped bruises around their necks. A ghost story about a man's life getting ruined seemed better. They leaned forward.

The novelist opened a bottle of wine and poured it into glasses. 'Tawdry,' he said 'I like it.'

The woman spread her hands. 'The mistakes were trivial.'

'It's always like that,' a painter said. He smiled. 'Everything on earth is trivial. Also tawdry.'

'You think you ruined a mans life,' the novelist said. 'But all women think that.'

A few people laughed.

'Maybe I didn't,' the woman said. 'That would make me happy.'

'Tell us and we'll judge.'

She sipped her wine.

⋆　⋆　⋆

'The year I met this man, I was twenty-five and lived in New York City, where I'd moved to become a writer. But no journal responded to the stories I mailed them—I knew myself they were no good—and I spent all my time tutoring and proctoring exams for a test-prep company. Most days, I taught at the test-prep center, others I travelled to Riverdale or White Plains to sit in grand dining rooms with people my own age and show them how to combine tricky if-then statements so as to improve their scores on the law- and business-school entrance exams. The students' parents paid the company exorbitant sums, but my checks were so small I barely made rent. I had three dollars a day for food; every day I bought a bagel and a small carton of milk to go in my oatmeal. When I was accepted to a Master of Fine Arts program in Syracuse, I was thrilled, even though I was rejected from the fiction track and accepted only for poetry, and even though the city was a frigid, depressed backwater, because the program offered me a fellowship with a stipend.

'When time came to secure housing, I was too broke to make the trip to Syracuse, so I called the program secretary and asked if she knew of any apartments. She demurred, but called back the next day; a student was vacating an apartment. Several others had lived there before him, and had also broken the lease; she didn't know why. It was cheap, and close to campus. The apartment was a two-bedroom for four hundred and thirty-five dollars a month; how could I go wrong?

'Here comes the tawdry part of the story. I couldn't afford a U-Haul. I didn't know how I'd manage the move—but at the last minute my father called me. He'd recently bought a trailer. He offered to drive with my mother from Maine, where they lived, to Manhattan with the trailer hitched to their station wagon, and pick me up on a Friday morning in August; if we left early, he said, we'd beat weekend traffic. They'd have me in Syracuse by 2 P.M., and they could drive the eight hours from Syracuse back to Maine that same day, My father guessed, he said gruffly, that I was broke. He was embarrassed to offer this help; he guessed that, since I had some pride, I'd refuse.

'My parents and I were not close. They were typical New England parents; they showed my sister and me little affection, and we showed them little back. My father always told me that if I accepted any assistance from him after he'd paid for college I'd be a loser. My mother was a housewife who believed that all non-Catholics and women who had premarital sex would burn in agonizing flames forever after death. As a kid, I wished I felt a sense of kinship with my parents, but I never did. Like many people, I suppose, I fantasized that I'd discover I was adopted, and had 'real' parents somewhere far away who were intelligent, well-read, sophisticated, and cared about improving the world. But because I resembled my parents physically— my father's eyebrows, my mother's round face, their pink skin—I knew I was not adopted.

'I'm an ingrate, I know, but my parents' control of my sisters and my bodies and movements, when we were kids—over the organization of the clothes in our closets; the minute of our return, should we go out to see a movie—was so total that after I left home the idea of their entering any space of mine was repulsive. They left a scent behind them. Maybe all parents do. It didn't help that my mother had a habit of 'fixing' whatever room she entered—rearranging pillows on beds, dusting windowsills, and finding hidden spots of mold—and my father of 'checking': he opened cupboards and desk drawers when he thought no one was looking, and he always peeked under loose couch cushions for lost change. So I didn't want to accept my parents' help. But my father had said that they'd drop me off in Syracuse and leave immediately, and so I slyly felt that I'd get something for nothing.

'My father warned me that I must have my boxes on the sidewalk in front of my apartment by 9 A.M. that Friday. He didn't want to spend money on a hotel, or stay overnight in Syracuse. Of course, I swore I'd be ready at nine. But I managed to fuck things up. I'd been dating a handsome black banker-by-day who did standup at night—one of several handsome black men I'd dated that summer—and when he suggested we have dinner on the eve of my departure I agreed, because I suspected romantic pickings would be slim in Syracuse; besides, I enjoyed his company. After dinner, we went to a bar with an outdoor patio and had drinks; the time when I should have gone home to pack came and went. I thought, Ah, how important is packing? I can stuff things in boxes between 1 and 3 A.M.! We had such fun that the banker suggested we continue to date once I was in Syracuse; he could drive up, he said, and I could bus down to see him. But I was intoxicated, also caddish, and replied, "That's silly—it's too far to drive."

'His face flushed. He had full cheeks; he looked down at his tie; I guessed I'd offended him. To apologise, I added, "You'll have girlfriends here, and I'll be busy with coursework and people I meet in Syracuse." He flushed deeper. A drink later, I asked if he'd come up to my place; I loved his humor, and thought it would be nice to have one last roll with him. It'd be quick, I figured, and I could pack once he'd left. When we reached my tiny fourth-floor studio and started making out on my moldy old futon, he asked, out of nowhere, if I'd ever slept with other black men; I said I had; we were already undressed; he said, half comic, half angry, "You like black cock?" I hesitated. To me, the question seemed odd, since it was evident that I did. Who, I wondered, wouldn't like such a good thing?'

The woman looked around the table.

The rain was still beating against the tin roof. A painter got up and poured wine. The journalist took a bite of chocolate cake. He said, 'This relates to the ghost story?'

She nodded. 'Yes.'

He waved his arm. 'Then go on.'

'In retrospect,' the woman said, 'I should have said something sensitive, like, "I like *your* black cock," or "I like *you*," but I just nodded. He said, "Say it," and so I said, "I like black cock," and he proceeded to love me so vehemently that afterward I fell asleep without setting my alarm or peeing, as all women must after sex.

'When I woke, it was nine and my parents were waiting; my father was irate. He asked why I wasn't ready, and I told him I'd overslept; he swore and hit the trailer. My mother made him sit in the car with her while my pale, skinny sister helped me pack and carry boxes down the stairs. On the road, my father sped. The day was sunny, and, once we were out of the city, hay fields stretched beyond the highway. It looked as if we might still beat the weekend traffic. My father even turned on his radio station that played the Beach Boys, and hummed. My mother watched pine trees pass by, read her study-group Bible, and chewed chocolate truffles; my sister read a fantasy novel.

'Eventually, my mother touched my father's thigh. She murmured, "We'll get home tonight, don't worry."

'Just then, I felt a horrible pain in my crotch. Or, more precisely, in my urinary tract. I knew why I had it. I also knew that my parents would know, and how angry they'd be. As subtly as possible, I stuffed my fist in my crotch. I held my book in my lap. But the pain got worse. After an hour, I tapped my mother's shoulder, and whispered that I needed a clinic. I begged her not to say why.

'She stared at me; her eyes narrowed.

'My father asked what was wrong; my mother announced that I had a U.T.I. My father cursed and said we couldn't stop, or we'd never make Syracuse in time. My sister, who was thirteen, asked what a U.T.I. was.

'My mother, her lips curled in disgust, informed her that a U.T.I. was a disease that married women got; my sister remarked that I wasn't married; no one replied.

'In the next town we found a clinic, but there was a line; getting medicine took three hours. When I returned to the car, no one spoke. We pulled onto the highway, and hit traffic. It was dusk when the hills of Syracuse came into view.

'On the street that was to be mine, rusted filing cabinets sat in overgrown yards. My address was a tall, narrow Victorian with a second-level porch that tilted downward as if it might fall off; the house was deep, Pepto-Bismol pink.

'The front door was locked. But I spied a rickety wooden staircase in back, so I walked up the driveway and climbed it; the second-story back door opened to a dusty kitchen. Dirty mops and old buckets littered the floor. In the bathroom, nails and asbestos poked through the exposed attic roof beams. A claw-footed tub stood mid-room; its bottom was stained a radiant orange-green. The toilet sat below a rusty old-fashioned standing tank that almost reached the ceiling.

'On my return to the car, I passed two black boys tossing a foot-ball in my neighbor's driveway and, seated in a lawn chair nearby, a middle-aged man with an unusual look. He had a normal, if markedly masculine, body: dark chest hair burst out of the top of his blue-checkered button-down shirt. What was unusual was his large egg-shaped head and a forehead that encompassed nearly half his oddly appealing face. He had almond-shaped brown eyes, olive skin, wide cheeks, and fierce eyebrows. He frowned slightly as he wrote in the book—a thick manuscript—in his lap. As I passed him, he looked up. His hand raised in a small wave. I said hello, without intending to chat, but once I'd spoken the man greeted me and said, "So you're the new girl."

'I nodded.

'His long legs stretched in font of the old chair. His khaki pants were wrinkled, his leather shoes scuffed. He gestured toward the car.

'"Them, too?"

'I explained that my family was helping me move, and leaving that night.

'"So it's just you," he said. "Good."

'When I asked him whether he lived in the adjacent house, he shrugged and gestured toward the kids.

'"Tom takes people in," he said.

'I decided that meant he was homeless.

'I'd just said, "Nice to meet you," and started moving toward my parents' wagon when he pointed at my house and said, lightly, "You know, that house is haunted."

'Once he said it, it made sense—I'm not one to believe in ghosts, and, as far as I knew, I had never seen one; but the apartment felt stuffy. If it was haunted, though, I didn't care. What unsettled me was the man's intimate demeanor and offerings about the house I hadn't inhabited yet.

'"Oh, really?" I said.

'"Don't worry." His hand moved across the manuscript. "He can't do anything to you unless you give him permission."

'What do you mean, "give him permission"?' I asked.

'The man shrugged. The evening breeze blew his curly dark hair. My father honked the car horn.

'The man looked down at his papers with embarrassment. "Oh, you know," he said. "Summon him with a Ouija board, ask him to tell you secrets, take his stuff. That's true with any ghost. They can never affect you unless you address them and invite them to appear." He smiled disarmingly.

'I thanked him for the advice. He remained there, reading his manuscript, while my family and I carried boxes into the house. My parents seemed not to see him. At one point, a middle-aged black man opened the back door of the neighboring house, peered across the driveway, ignored the man, and told the kids to come inside. Only my little sister noticed the man. She looked at him once, jerked her head down—she had a tic—and asked who he was; I told her that he was a vagrant.

'My sister said, "Weird neighborhood."

'My father reassembled my futon while my sister and I carried in boxes, and I was feeling pleased that my parents were helping me move in but curious why they weren't hurrying home, when my father announced that we should get food. My mother said they weren't staying: the apartment was disgusting, and I had only one bed; she wanted a hotel. My father replied, No way in hell was he spending money when he'd driven nine hundred miles to save me money; they could use my bed.

'I knew they could afford a hotel, because my mother collected designer clothes and bought herself ruby and emerald bracelets on a regular basis. I felt humiliated that I had the U.T.I.; I wanted to be alone. Mostly, I did not want them to sleep in my house— for their presence in it to infect my new life in Syracuse, however absurd that sounds. I wanted them to leave. I almost offered to pay for a hotel. But I knew hew ungrateful my feelings were— undaughterly and unnatural. They'd done me a favor. Of course they could have my bed, I said.

'We drove to get takeout Chinese, then brought it back and ate it straight from the cartons, in silence, while sitting on the living-room floor.

'Eventually, I spoke. Perhaps I couldn't take the silence.

'I said casually, "The house has a ghost."

'My sister pushed a carton of greasy noodles toward the center of the room.

'My father put a piece of broccoli in his mouth, then a piece of long red beef, and chewed. He stared at me.

'My mother gazed at the windowsills. On one were three dead flies. "There's no such thing as ghosts," she said, "Except for the Holy Ghost, who lives with God and is part of him. Once we die on earth, we're done here. After people die, they go to Heaven to be with God. Unless they go to"—she looked at me—"Hell."

'My father pulled my sister's lo mein toward him, stabbed a chicken gristle-blob with his fork, and ate it.

'"This Chinese food is delicious!" he yelled. "I bet the ghost would like some! Rachel, what do you think?"

'My sister stored at him. Our father was a duplicitous, lascivious, agnostic Yankee skinflint who could go from jovial to enraged in a second. He liked to joke.

'I felt nervous and repeated the man's superstition—the ghost couldn't affect us unless we invited it to appear.

'My father held out both hands palms up. "In that case," he yelled, "I invite the ghost to have his way with whoever he finds in the house!" He lowered his voice. "I can speak generously because I'm pretty sure the ghost will choose one of my young attractive daughters."

'My mother wailed my father's name. My sister looked at the floor.

'"Or my attractive wife," he added.

'He hummed "Runaround Sue."

'I arranged the futon for my parents, made a blanket-bed on the dining-room floor for my sister, and slept on the floor myself, using a sweatshirt as a pillow. I felt bad that my sister had come on this journey and learned what a U.T.I. was. Through the night, a breeze moved the bedroom door, which my parents had left ajar, back and forth, and the creaking woke me; several times I dreamed that a man, my father, left the bedroom and stood, half menacingly, half perplexedly, over my sister's form. I thought, Please don't let it take her; if it has to take anyone, let it take me.

She hasn't done anything; let it leave her alone. It seemed as if I'd just thought this when I woke. Everyone else was up.

'While I slept, my mother had scrubbed and mopped the entire flat. It was "filthy," she said, "disgusting." Before they left, my father handed me two quarters, which he'd discovered in a bedroom closet, and a man's ring, which he happened to find atop the old toilet tank. "Pretty grody up there," he said.

'The ring was large and had a blue-green stone shaped like an elephant, outlined in silver. Trunk and tail were tucked; the torso was an octagon. My mother said the stone was a Paraiba tourmaline, nice but occluded. A shame, she said; it weighed at least thirty carats. She showed me a dark blot in the elephant's torso and said, "Flawed." I dropped the ring onto the necklace I always wore, a simple chain with some charms—a rose quartz, a silver goat head—and forgot about it.

* * *

'I settled into Syracuse. Because of precipitation from the Great Lakes, snow arrived in September and stayed through May. I learned that its population declined in the seventies and eighties, when General Electric moved west and that, owing to industrial contamination, its lake, Onondaga, was among the most polluted in the world. Personally, I thrived: I started classes, ran in the local park, and read copious books, especially the absurd dead Russian writers.

'One night, soon after moving into the house, I put on tight pants, a top that showed my midriff, and a thin leather jacket, and went to the neighborhood bar, Taps. Once there, I did something uncharacteristic: I picked out a man I normally wouldn't have chosen.'

The woman rose and put plates in the sink. 'For some reason,' she said, 'I'm not attracted to men who are Christian or "white." Perhaps it's self-loathing.'

The rain poured down.

The fantasy writer sipped his wine. 'I'll take a piece of chocolate torte,' he said. 'But one without raspberries.'

She flicked the raspberries off a slice and served it to him.

'The bar was a former funeral parlor, long and dark, with no windows. But it had pool tables, cheap drinks, and free popcorn. It was owned by a Greek family who had lived in town a long time. Locals liked it, and graduate students went there to shoot pool and discuss literature. The man—I'll call him Paul—was a year ahead of me, the program's best writer. He already had a literary agent; his professors predicted that he'd be famous.

'I heard this before we met, from other students; also that he was engaged.

'I introduced myself to Paul. When he asked where I'd moved from, I said Manhattan. He appraised my outfit and said that I wouldn't like Syracuse. When I asked why he said I was a "sophisticated city type."

'I told him I'd grown up in Maine, bought the jacket at an outlet.

'"But you wear jewels," he said, and pointed to the ring on the chain around my neck.

418

'I laughed and said it was flawed.

'He plucked it from my shirt and mock-examined it, said he didn't see any flaws.

'When I looked at him, I was repulsed. I feel like a traitor, even now, saying this. Others found him handsome, but I was repulsed. He had silky blond hair, green eyes, a cherubic face, and rosy skin. Usually, I don't feel comfortable around pink-skinned Christian men; they seem porcine, stupid, and swollen. I like tall, dark, big men; Paul was five feet eight and skinny. Yet I was drawn to him. He made me feel as if we shared a secret and he'd never judge me for anything. He'd boxed in college, but was so gentle, I'd later learn, that when he found a spider in a house he carried it outside. His mother had multiple sclerosis and was in love with him. She tied pink ribbons around her slender waist whenever he visited, and repeatedly told him that he was the kind of boy she wished she'd met at his age. He wrote by hand, in cursive sentences that wound on for pages, riffs that "rolled like music," our teachers said, and loved gerunds. His fiancée had lupus and lived in Virginia, where he was from, because of her job.

'That night, we played pool. Afterward, I invited him to my flat to play chess.'

The woman paused.

'I have morals. But they're my own. If I make a promise, I keep it. If someone else breaks promises, that's their business.

'What I regret is that I spent six years with a man I wasn't physically attracted to. I'm not sure why, or why'—the woman shrugged—'he liked me. It was cold in Syracuse. The program was small. He was smart and kind. Even after smoking twelve joints, he told charming anecdotes. After we'd dated awhile, he called off his engagement.

'I went to lengths to please him. He liked my apartment, but said my living room needed a couch; I got a tutoring job and bought a couch. He said my living room needed a TV; I bought a twenty-five-inch tube with a built-in VHS player. At yard sales, I scored coffee tables and lamps. Soon Paul was spending most of his time at my apartment. I'd always preferred solitude, but his presence made me happy. And he taught me how to write. In our first year together, he produced stories our teachers called masterpieces, and under his tutelage my writing improved so much that I was allowed to switch to the fiction track. We discussed our writing and our childhoods, dreams, and plans. I felt that I could be myself around him. He loved my cooking—he didn't know that I had bought a tin of MSG at Price Chopper, and stirred tablespoons into my curries before I served them.

'One night toward the end of my first year at Syracuse, Paul stayed home to work, and I wrote until late. I felt so content—in my work and life—that I slept with the lights off.

'Usually, I leave the lights on when I sleep. It's ridiculous, but I'm afraid of the dark, if I'm alone.

'That night, I turned them off. I fell asleep with the bedroom door ajar. At 3 A.M., I woke, The room was dark. But I could see the outline of my bureau, and, in the light from the window, the outline of the bedroom door. Then the doorknob moved.

'Nothing moved outside the door. But its knob turned back

and forth, I could see the knob turning. It jerked all the way left, clicked, then turned right.

'I was terrified. I lay rigid, watching the knob turn for several minutes, until it stopped. Then I flicked the lights on and called Paul. Almost every night after that, he stayed at my house. When he didn't, I left the lights on.

'Weeks later, a student who'd lived in the apartment before me told Paul why he'd left. He'd been lying in bed late at night, in the room now my bedroom, and the knob of the door—which he'd closed fully—had turned suddenly, and continued to twist. The student, a self-proclaimed goatfucker from Nevada, leaped out of bed, took his nunchakus out of his underwear drawer, brandished it, and yelled, "Whaddya want, Motherfucker?"

'O.K., I thought A ghost who turns doorknobs. So what? I wasn't thrilled to live in a haunted apartment. But it was big and cheap, and I'd had a good time there so far.

★　★　★

'One odd thing happened my second year in the program. I was at Taps, chatting with the owner's son, the bartender—a Greek tough, mid-thirties, gold chains, hairy chest—when he pointed to the ring on my necklace and asked where I'd got it.

'When I explained, the bartender asked where I lived. Then he asked to see the ring, and examined it. A guy had died in my apartment, he said. The ring was his.

'The bartender had been a kid when the guy died, he said. He, the bartender, had hung out at the bar a lot, done his homework there, helped his dad, and he'd liked the ring because it was an elephant, and the guy, a regular, had let him play with it. The guy was no one special, the bartender said. He'd come from the Midwest to help with construction at the power plant. The guy was a self-taught type: he welded, built furniture, made the ring himself. Sat at the bar every night, drinking seltzer and reading physics textbooks. The guy died, the bartender said, because there was an accident at the plant. Some workers were exposed to too much radiation. One thing that made the guy weird, the bartender said: he'd refused treatment. The "treatment" was a crock—the guys who accepted it all died anyway, but in the hospital. This guy died in his apartment, while taking a bath.

'The bartender gave me the ring back, wrung out his rag, and said I shouldn't wear it.

'When I asked why not, he blushed. He said that it was probably just superstition, but in Greek culture they believed the dead were attached to objects they'd interacted with, and that when you wore their things you attracted their spirit.

'He walked to the end of the bar. Added, "Plus, you look stupid wearing a man's ring."

'So I stuck the ring in a drawer and forgot about it.

★   ★   ★

'I didn't think about Syracuse much. I was busy taking classes, reading books. The economy was depressed—in the square,

422

boutiques stood empty. But people still came down from Canada to go to the mall. The park nearby had a lot of rapes in it, but only at night. It was pretty, and had a rose garden.

'I sometimes saw the homeless guy, who I assumed lived with my neighbor—he was always wearing the same khaki pants and blue checkered shirt, sitting in the lawn chair reading papers or tomes—but he spoke to me only once after the day I moved in. He'd been sweeping the neighbor's driveway. I might have been staring at him, because the hair on his big head was so wild and curly, and he looked funny pushing a broom in khakis. Possibly I was lonely. When he saw me watching him, he smiled and said, "How's the writing?"

'I said, "Fine."

'He said, "Good."

'He indicated the broom: "Doing a little yard work. Tom expects everyone who hangs around to pitch in."

'I didn't think sweeping a blacktop was work, but I nodded.

'The guy pushed the broom brusquely. Dust flew into the air. Then he walked over, asked where I was from, where I went jogging, what books I liked. Eventually, he offered, "I've been working on my manuscript."

'"That's good," I mumbled.

'"It's about my life," he said.

'I said I bet it was interesting. I guessed it was about hopping trains, carrying food sacks on sticks, whatever hobo stuff hobos did.

'"Well, I don't know about *that*," he said. "But I've had interesting jobs."

'I nodded, asked where he was from.

'"Nebraska," he said.

'I had little interest in the Midwest, which I thought of as a wasteland of flat-faced, goiter-ridden white people. He didn't look like a Midwesterner, not with his olive skin and nearly black hair. He'd folded his muscular arm across his chest, and was peering inscrutably at my apartment's porch. He was standing quite close to me, I realized.

'He said, "You ever been?"

'I shook my head.

'"It's *beautiful*," he said. Then he added that his fiancée, the best girl in the world, was there, and that he was returning soon.

'I felt irrationally peeved and blurted out, "If you really like her, why are you here and she's there?"

'He looked down at his scuffed shoes, and his cheeks reddened. He explained that there were things he "had to do" in Syracuse, but that he was going back once he finished his work. He *hoped* she'd wait for him. He smiled at me and said, "Do you think time and space matter?"

'I wasn't sure what to say, it seemed such a stupid question.

'"Yes," I said.

'He smiled. "Then maybe they do," he said gently. "For you."

'He pulled a photograph from his pocket. It was color, but so faded that I couldn't see an image—just a form.

'I said she was pretty.

'For lack of better topics, and because I'm interested in these things—how people develop emotions and make the absurd

424

decision to spend their whole life with one probably actually disgusting and not very intelligent person—I asked how they'd met, and he told me that she was a freshman in high school when he was a senior, and that she'd been dating his younger brother. His eyebrows lifted "You can't tell by looking at me," he said, "But my brother has blond hair and blue eyes. I'm the dark one in my family." He frowned. He'd had to do a lot of work to get his fiancée away from his brother, he said, because she'd found his brother incredibly handsome. When I asked what he'd done, he said, "Oh, just the usual: took her out a lot, invented surprise-adventure treats, and told her a lot of bad jokes. Persistence."

'He peered off into the woods behind my house.

'That was the last time I saw him.

* * *

'When Paul graduated from the program, he said he might move to D.C. and work as a reporter. I was devastated, because I'd imagined he would stay in Syracuse. When I suggested it, he looked away. He said since I didn't plan to be with him long-term there was no reason for him to stay.

'I'd told him frankly, when it came up, that I had no interest in marrying him. I had no interest in marriage at all. I suppose that, like many people, I lacked a good model. Marriage seemed a bad deal: the man cheated, and the woman got fat. Also, I'd never met anyone I liked enough to want to marry; also, I wasn't attracted to Paul.

'I knew I was selfish to want him to stay, just to help me with my work. But whenever I wrote a story he knew whether it was good or bad, and, when it was bad, he told me exactly how to fix it. Also, I'd never had the kind of friendship and support I got from him.

'We stood in my dining room. He asked me, point blank, if I wanted to be with him long-term. I knew that if I said "No," or "Not sure," he'd leave.

'I hesitated.

'He turned away.

'I panicked.

'"Wait," I said.

'My mother was cold but whenever she wanted someone to do something for her she gave gifts.

'Paul waited.

'I went into my bedroom and grabbed the tourmaline. The stone sparkled. I had some jewellers' boxes, and I slipped the ring in one. I brought the box to Paul and held it out.

'I said that I'd been meaning to give it to him, as a symbol of my fondness for him, and that I hoped he'd stay.

'He seemed impressed. He put it on. He said he'd stay.

'I suggested we get a nicer apartment. But Paul decided that he liked my flat. So he moved into the pink house.

★   ★   ★

'Paul quite smoking weed. He swore off Taps and spent days in the second bedroom—now his office—but his novel never progressed. He had taken a position working in the warehouse at the air-conditioner factory in town, and he complained that it took all his energy. But he also stayed up every night until 4 A.M. watching movies, and each morning when I opened the freezer I found that a large carton of Breyer's ice cream that had been full the night before was now half empty. We went on walks together during which he didn't speak, or else ranted about the crooked Republican government. When his mother called, he didn't pick up. I guessed that his pot-smoking habit had masked depression; or that living with me depressed him; or that depression was the inevitable result of living in Syracuse.

'He claimed he was "fine"; but sometimes he said his head hurt, and that he couldn't concentrate; however, this seemed natural for a writer. We seldom had sex; but that was natural, I guessed, for a couple who'd moved in together.

'I'd thought Paul and I were similar—agnostic, liberal. But one afternoon, a few months after moving in, he asked how many men I'd slept with in my life. I trusted him, so I gave an honest answer. That is, an honest estimate. He'd never said he thought having sex was immoral, so I was shocked by his response: he wiped his brow and said, "Really?" Then his eyes glistened. I was concerned. It was his birthday and we'd invited friends over for the evening. I'd baked a cake, and guests were about to arrive.

'I asked what was wrong, "Are you O.K.?" I said, and tried to hug him.

'Abruptly he said he had to go buy beer for our guests. I said I'd bought beer; he answered that I hadn't bought enough. When

427

our guests arrived, Paul hadn't returned. Eventually, someone reported that he was at the bar, on a bender.

'I forgave him for that night, or he me—but I felt betrayed. I'd seldom experienced such revulsion directed my way, and I felt vulnerable, as I had when I was a child. I saw him now as I had initially— his face and body so viscerally pink, like underdone pork loin.

'When I stopped sleeping with him, he didn't seem to care. I thought he'd cheat on me, but he left the house now only to work at the factory.

'I thought he'd leave. But he didn't. I'd published some stories in national magazines—almost entirely because of his encouragement, plot ideas, edits, and, often, insertions of missing paragraphs—and Paul soon informed me excitedly that I was now eligible to apply for tenure-track teaching jobs. I must apply, he said. If *he* could, he would. It was an honor, the chance of a lifetime.

'All year, Paul had worked and paid our rent. Because of this, he said, he'd been unable to write. If I got a tenure-track job, I thought, I could support us, and Paul could finish his novel. So I applied for jobs. Paul organized the whole thing, printing out the list from the M.L.A. Web site highlighting ads I qualified for, and circling the best positions.

'To please him, I applied to schools in Ohio, Utah, Iowa, and even Minnesota. But not Nebraska—I wouldn't go there, I said.

'"But it's the best job," he said. The teaching load was low, the salary high. So I applied.

'Ultimately, I got several offers, but the job in Nebraska was the best.

'When the time to move came, we hadn't slept together in a year. I told Paul we should break up. To my surprise, he asked me to give him another chance. He'd change in Nebraska, he said.

'In the end, I acceded, because I was afraid to move to Nebraska by myself. Even If he'd become unfamiliar—morose, silent, unable to read—he was familiar— his scent, body, posture, gestures, voice. He was my friend.

'But in Nebraska we grew further apart. Paul loved the friendliness of the people and the fields and trees. I hated the flatness of the Nebraskans' faces and of the terrain. He'd studied the town's layout before we moved, scoured rental ads, and chosen a stone "worker's house" for us that I found ugly and he adored. The university gave him classes to teach, and he loved doing it; I saw teaching as a job. Evenings, we walked along the low, sluggish river that cut through town. The river was brown and smelled of industrial runoff and dead fish. Mosquitoes swarmed along the levee, and as we walked we dripped sweat. Sand islands in the river had signs with skulls on them that read, "Toxic, No Fishing," and on larger ones old men sat in lawn chairs, rods in the water. I found this tragic. Paul said mildly, "People need to eat."

'He taught his classes, I mine. He worked in his home office, I in mine. We slept in the same bed like brother and sister. Sometimes he offered me a back rub or touched my shoulder in the night, and I rejected him. I'm ashamed now.

'He stacked neighbors' wood for fun, swept their driveways.

There was one old woman down the block whose lawn he mowed for free, and whose weeds he trimmed. Only now can I see how terrible my attitude was, but I told him that he didn't need to play grandson to every prairie hag. He reprimanded me calmly, saying he did it because he liked doing it, and wanted to. She wasn't old, he said; she wasn't even sixty.

'Only once did he seem his former self—he read a book and talked to me about it. It was a true-crime novel. He bought—but failed to read—biographies, histories, pop science. His head hurt too much, he admitted, to read.

'I almost never went into his office, because I respected his privacy. But one time I did, and I saw a piece of paper that said "KILL YOURSELF" in black letters, taped to the wall above his desk. When I told him I'd seen the sign and was concerned, he laughed and said it was a joke. "Don't go in my office," he said.

'He still stayed up watching movies most nights. Once, he told me that he'd written a novel but it was worthless, and he'd thrown it out. I know now that various things cause depression, But, at the time, I was baffled; he seemed so different.

'We lived in Nebraska for two years. Once, we had it out. "I see the way you look at me," he said. He wasn't stupid. He knew I'd "settled." Did I ever think maybe *he'd* settled for *me*? I was critical, self-righteous, and a jerk. I was no beauty. There hadn't been many options in Syracuse for him, either, he said.

'"You were *engaged*," I said.

'He blinked. Flicked his ear as If brushing off a fly. "True," he said.

430

★   ★   ★

'I still recall the last time we had sex, because it occurred in an odd way. He touched my shoulder in the night, and, as usual, I rolled away; I don't want to disgust you with sordid information, but, because it sticks in my memory and is potentially relevant to the story, I have to say. A minute later, I was pushed onto my back and held down; I told him to cut it out, and he ignored me; he was slender, but a boxer, and much stronger than me. It's going to sound like a terrible romance novel, but he forced me, held me down, looked right at me the whole time, and basically made me want things I didn't even know I wanted. It was a different style, I guess you could say. Anyway, I was half-horrified and half-exalted afterward, thinking that my whole life had changed, thinking, Maybe this could work, our lives could change, we could be happy, I've been such a fool this whole time. I was thinking these things when he said casually, lying apart from me now, "That was for him, by the way."

'I was still catatonic, and unsure what he meant, when he added, "Because he still likes you, even though you're being such a cunt."

'I lay there for a minute.

'I said, "It's not O.K. to call me a cunt."

'He settled onto his side and looked at me calmly, fully naked, completely unembarrassed. "You're right," he said. He added reasonably, "It's also not O.K. to be a cunt."

*　*　*

'When I said we should separate, his first words were "I want the house."

'He also said, when I asked, that I couldn't have the ring back. It was tacky of me to ask. He gently pointed that out.

'I left Nebraska; he stayed.

'I moved to Brooklyn. I heard through acquaintances that he continued to teach, and also got a job at a foundry. For years I thought of him as a failure. A debacle. I don't know why I judge people this way. He didn't publish. I saw pictures of him on Facebook with various younger women, possibly students. I was glad he was dating.

'After I moved to Brooklyn, I started substitute teaching at private high schools. One needed a gym teacher, and so I became one.' She shrugged. 'I realized I liked being a gym teacher. I wasn't writing. The truth is, without Paul's help I can't finish a story. I dated now and then, men I liked well enough, no burning love. It's only recently—' the woman looked up and brushed her hair behind her ear; her skin was plump, but when she smiled tiny lines appeared under her eyes—'that I fell in love and understood what people mean when they talk about wanting to be with someone forever.'

'What happened?' the fantasy writer asked.

She shrugged. 'I don't know if he loves me.'

The guests fidgeted.

'Last fall,' she continued, 'I went to Paul's Facebook page and saw a picture of him with a woman: she had a wrinkled face, watery blue eyes, and gray hair. In the picture next to her, Paul's face looked larger. He was thirty-five; his arms gripped the woman tightly. She was probably sixty. I recognized her: it was the woman who'd lived down the block from us in Nebraska, whose lawn he'd mowed. That surprised me. But they looked happy. So I thought, Well, they get along. The profile—it was his profile photo—said "Married, to Erendita Dantine."'

The woman got up and cleared some plates, then sat down.

'I make too much out of nothing, maybe. But here's the end: though I'd published nothing in years, I was invited to Syracuse to give a reading. The morning after, I walked to my old neighborhood and knocked on the door of my former apartment. When a young woman answered, I said I'd lived there once, described the doorknob's turning in the night, and asked if anything similar had happened to her. She didn't know what I was talking about.

'I had time before my flight, so I went to Taps. The owner's son was still bartending, though his face was beefy now, and he had a paunch; his old dad was with him. I ordered a vodka-soda and chatted. Neither of them remembered me. Eventually, I said I used to live nearby, in the pink house, where a man had died.

'"Otensky," the owner said.

'I remembered that the bartender had said his father knew him well; I asked the owner to tell me about him.

'He told me what I already knew: that he'd been a regular. That he'd come to town to work at the FitzPatrick plant, but once he saved enough money he was going back to where he was from. The owner paused. "Midwest somewhere. Oklahoma, Wyoming . . ."

'I said, "Nebraska?"

'That was it, he said. "The guy had a cute fiancée. Showed everybody her picture. Came here to make quick dough, go home, and buy her a house." But there was an accident; the man's crew was exposed to dangerous levels of radioactive chemicals. The victims were offered treatment, but the guy declined. "Maybe he was smart," the owner said. "The other guys still died." He'd heard from locals who'd visited them in the hospital—the skin slid off their faces like putty.

'I asked the owner what the guy was like before he died, and the owner said that he only came in a couple of times after the accident, but that he said something about finding a way out. He'd seen medical doctors, naturopathic doctors, homeopathic ones, and finally a Santería. Said he paid her up the wazoo, and that they'd worked out a special deal with the universe. He said he'd gotten permission to do something extraordinary.

'I asked what the thing was; he shook his head.

'The owner's son walked outside to smoke.

'The owner polished the counter, became expressive. He said that the guy, Otensky, didn't drink. He just ordered tonics with Rosie's and read books about quantum mechanics. He bragged that he was smarter than most men, though he'd never been to college. He was a rabbi's son. The bar owner told me that after the accident, before the radiation affected him, he said, "I can do what God tells us we can't. Do you know why?" When the owner asked why, he said, "Because there is no God. There's only matter, energy, subatomic particles, and vectors." He told the owner that man could do almost anything he wanted through physics, and that thought and matter were intertwined. He said that a person's whole spirit could be contained within one bit of flesh from the inside of his cheek.

'The owner leaned forward. "He got crazy," he said. He shrugged. "He claimed that through a combination of"—he paused—"quantum entanglement, infrared energy, crystals, and welding tools, he'd welded a piece of himself into the stone in his ring, and that he was going to mail the ring to his fiancée. He told me that he was going to write to her, "I'm going to try to come back to you," and tell her to take the ring and find a man she liked, and tell him to put it on.'

'I said that was crazy, which it was.

'The owner smiled. "Guy had a big head," he said. "Brilliant man, kinda crazy, big head."

'I was at the door when the owner said, "The wife had a weird name. Emeralda. Topaz, something like that."'

The people at the dinner table stared blankly at one another.

The crime-noir novelist said, 'Was the name Erendita?'

The woman nodded.

The novelist pushed his dessert plate away. 'So, the fiancée had the same name as the woman your ex-boyfriend married,' he said. 'But that's just coincidence.'

The people at the table yawned. They felt that the story was overlong, and unsatisfying.

'I don't understand,' a painter said.

'Let's see if I got this,' the fantasy writer said. 'You and your boyfriend liked each other at first. After living together, you got sick of each other and treated each other like shit. Then you broke up. That's all relationships. Isn't it?'

'What are you saying?' the crime-noir novelist asked. 'Are you saying this guy melted, hung around as a ghost in a lawn chair in Syracuse *for thirty years*, somehow took possession of your boyfriend, and persuaded you to be his paying escort back to Nebraska? So he could get with his old lady?'

The woman shrugged.

'Hmm,' the crime-noir novelist said. 'It's kind of a stretch.'

Two painters chatted rapidly in Portuguese. They laughed. One turned to the woman and smiled. She said, apologetically, 'Stupid story.'

The woman nodded.

'And the ring?' the crime-noir novelist said. 'The stupid elephant ring? What was the deal with that?'

The woman didn't know. After she gave it to Paul, she said, he always wore it.

'Interesting,' the crime-noir novelist said. 'I guess.'

'There's one more thing,' the woman said. 'He published a novel this summer. That's why I can't tell you his real name. It's been on the best-seller list for fifteen weeks.'

'Guy's a writer,' the crime-noir novelist said.

'It's good,' the woman said. 'I'm happy for him. But the prose is odd. It's like the writing of someone who didn't go beyond eighth grade. Short, simple sentences. Very declarative.'

The crime-noir novelist raised his eyebrows.

'But every hundred pages or so—' she looked up forlorn-ly—'there's one sentence that goes on for three pages, full of modifying clauses and gerunds.'

The fantasy writer laughed. 'Now you're saying—what? Two authors, one body?'

She shrugged. 'I don't know. Say it's possible. The original owner. And a guest.'

The journalist smiled. 'So, if there *was* a ghost, the ghost didn't choose you.'

The fantasy writer spread his hands. 'Trivial crap,' he said. 'It's pointless to unpack these things. Every man makes his own path. This guy, Paul, fucked up by sleeping with you. Excuse my honesty. Sure, he got depressed. No man really wants to find out his girlfriend's a ho-bag. But what's to worry about? He wrote a best-selling novel. So what if he had to pump old pussy to do it? Even if a man gets half of what he was meant to get, and becomes half of what he was meant to be, that's good. Who cares how it happens? I hope some dead fuck helps me get where I'm going, too.'

The people at the table sighed and shifted in their seats. The night outside was still—the rain had stopped—but in the nearby trailer park a mutt howled. In the yard, the dark stubby shapes of three javelinas trotted through a stand of prickly-pear cactuses. One grunted softly and kicked an empty can, and in the lights of the bungalow's porch it flashed like a star.

August 2026, There Will Come Soft Rains

Ray Bradbury

'AUGUST 2026: THERE WILL COME SOFT RAINS'
RAY BRADBURY (AMERICAN, 1920–2012)
First published in 1950 in *Collier's* magazine. In the original version the
day described in the story is 28 April 1985.

Perhaps this is not a ghost story at all, but I like to think it is. It is a story of the ghost of a house and the ghost of a civilisation. It is a warning and a parable. Of all the stories in this book, it is the most possible. We don't usually think of Ray Bradbury as a realist, but as time passes, his work acquires unfortunate shadings as reality catches up with it. His own house in Los Angeles was recently demolished, alas.

AUGUST 2026:THERE WILL COME SOFT RAINS
Ray Bradbury

In the living-room the voice-clock sang. *Tick-tock, seven o'clock, time to get up, time to get up, seven o'clock!* as if it were afraid that nobody would. The morning house lay empty. The clock ticked on, repeating its sounds into the emptiness. *Seven-nine, breakfast time, seven-nine!*

In the kitchen the breakfast stove gave a hissing sigh and ejected from its warm interiors eight pieces of perfectly browned toast, eight eggs sunny-side up, sixteen slices of bacon, two coffees, and two cool glasses of milk.

'Today is August 4, 2026,' said a second voice from the kitchen ceiling, 'in the city of Allendale, California.' It repeated the date three times for memory's sake. 'Today is Mr Featherstone's birthday. Today is the anniversary of Tilita's marriage. Insurance is payable, as are the water, gas, and light bills.'

Somewhere in the walls, relays clicked, memory tapes glided under electric eyes.

Eight-one, tick-tock, eight-one o'clock, off to school, off to work, run, run, eight-one! But no doors slammed, no carpets took the soft tread of rubber heels. It was raining outside. The weather box on the front door sang quietly: 'Rain, rain, go away; rubbers, raincoats for today...' And the rain tapped on the empty house, echoing.

Outside, the garage chimed and lifted its door to reveal the waiting car. After a long wait the door swung down again.

At eight-thirty the eggs were shrivelled and the toast was like stone. An aluminium wedge scraped them into the sink, where hot water whirled them down a metal throat which digested and flushed them away to the distant sea. The dirty dishes were dropped into a hot washer and emerged twinkling dry.

Nine-fifteen, sang the clock, *time to clean.*

Out of warrens in the wall, tiny robot mice darted. The rooms were a-crawl with the small cleaning animals, all rubber and metal. They thudded against chairs, whirling their moustached runners, kneading the rug nap, sucking gently at hidden dust. Then, like mysterious invaders, they popped into their burrows. Their pink electric eyes faded. The house was clean.

Ten o'clock. The sun came out from behind the rain. The house stood alone in a city of rubble and ashes. This was the one house left standing. At night the ruined city gave off a radioactive glow which could be seen for miles.

Ten-fifteen. The garden sprinklers whirled up in golden founts, filling the soft morning air with scatterings of brightness. The water pelted window-panes, running down the charred west side where the house had been burned evenly free of its white paint.

The entire west face of the house was black, save for five places. Here the silhouette in paint of a man mowing a lawn. Here, as in a photograph, a woman bent to pick flowers. Still farther over, their images burned on wood in one titanic instant, a small boy, hands flung into the air; higher up, the image of a thrown ball, and opposite him a girl, hands raised to catch a ball which never came down.

The five spots of paint – the man, the woman, the children, the ball – remained. The rest was a thin charcoaled layer.

The gentle sprinkler rain filled the garden with falling light.

Until this day, how well the house had kept its peace! How carefully it had inquired, 'Who goes there? What's the password?' and, getting no answer from lonely foxes and whining cats, it had shut up its windows and drawn shades in an old-maidenly pre-occupation with self-protection which bordered on a mechanical paranoia.

It quivered at each sound, the house did. If a sparrow brushed a window, the shade snapped up. The bird, startled, flew off! No, not even a bird must touch the house!

The house was an altar with ten thousand attendants, big, small, servicing, attending, in choirs. But the gods had gone away, and the ritual of the religion continued senselessly, uselessly.

Twelve noon.

A dog whined, shivering, on the front porch.

The front door recognized the dog voice and opened. The dog, once huge and fleshy, but now gone to bone and covered with sores, moved in and through the house, tracking mud. Behind it whirred angry mice, angry at having to pick up mud, angry at inconvenience.

For not a leaf fragment blew under the door but what the wall-panels flipped open and the copper scrap rats flashed swiftly out. The offending dust, hair or paper, seized in miniature steel jaws, was raced back to the burrows. There, down tubes which fed into the cellar, it was dropped into the sighing vent of an incinerator which sat like evil Baal in a dark corner.

The dog ran upstairs, hysterically yelping to each door, at last realizing, as the house realized, that only silence was here.

It sniffed the air and scratched the kitchen door. Behind the door, the stove was making pancakes which filled the house with a rich baked odour and the scent of maple syrup.

The dog frothed at the mouth, lying at the door, sniffing, its eyes turned to fire. It ran wildly in circles, biting at its tail, spun in a frenzy, and died. It lay in the parlour for an hour.

Two o'clock, sang a voice.

Delicately sensing decay at last, the regiments of mice hummed out as softly as blown grey leaves in an electrical wind.

Two-fifteen.

The dog was gone.

In the cellar, the incinerator glowed suddenly and a whirl of sparks leaped up the chimney.

Two thirty-five.

Bridge tables sprouted from patio walls. Playing-cards fluttered on to pads in a shower of pips: Martinis manifested on an oaken bench with egg-salad sandwiches. Music played.

But the tables were silent and the cards untouched.

At four o'clock the tables folded like great butterflies back through the panelled walls.

★   ★   ★

Four-thirty.

The nursery walls glowed.

Animals took shape: yellow giraffes, blue lions, pink antelopes, lilac panthers cavorting in crystal substance. The walls were glass. They looked out upon colour and fantasy. Hidden films clocked through well-oiled sprockets, and the walls lived. The nursery floor was woven to resemble a crisp, cereal meadow. Over this ran aluminium roaches and iron crickets, and in the hot, still air butterflies of delicate red tissue wavered among the sharp aromas of animal spoors! There was the sound like a great matted yellow hive of bees within a dark bellows, the lazy bumble of a purring lion. And there was the patter of okapi feet and the murmur of a fresh jungle rain, like other hoofs, falling upon the summer-starched grass. Now the walls dissolved into distances of parched weed, mile on mile, and warm, endless sky. The animals drew away into thornbrakes and water-holes.

It was the children's hour.

★   ★   ★

Five o'clock. The bath filled with clear hot water.

Six, seven, eight o'clock. The dinner dishes manipulated like magic tricks, and in the study a *click.* In the metal stand opposite the hearth where a fire now blazed up warmly, a cigar popped out, half an inch of soft grey ash on it, smoking, waiting.

Nine o'clock. The beds warmed their hidden circuits, for nights were cool here.

Nine-five. A voice spoke from the study ceiling: 'Mrs McClellan, which poem would you like this evening?'

The house was silent.

The voice said at last, 'Since you express no preference, I shall select a poem at random.' Quiet music rose to back the voice. 'Sara, Teasdale. As I recall, your favourite . . .

'There will come soft rains and the smell of the ground,
The swallows circling with their shimmering sound;

And frogs in the pools singing at night,
And wild plum-trees in tremulous white;

Robins will wear their feathery fire,
Whistling their whims on a low fence-wire;

And not one will know of the war, not one
Will care at last when it is done.

Not one would mind, neither bird nor tree,

If mankind perished utterly;

And Spring herself, when she woke at dawn,
Would scarcely know that we were gone.'

The fire burned on the stone hearth and the cigar fell away
into a mound of quiet ash on its tray. The empty chairs faced each
other between the silent walls, and the music played.

At ten o'clock the house began to die.

The wind blew. A falling tree-bough crashed through the
kitchen window. Cleaning solvent, bottled, shattered over the
stove. The room was ablaze in an instant!

'Fire!' screamed a voice. The house-lights flashed, water-
pumps shot water from the ceilings. But the solvent spread on the
linoleum, licking, eating, under the kitchen door, while the voices
took it up in chorus: 'Fire, fire, fire!'

The house tried to save itself. Doors sprang tightly shut, but
the windows were broken by the heat, and the wind blew and
sucked upon the fire.

The house gave ground as the fire in ten billion angry sparks
moved with flaming ease from room to room and then up the
stairs. While scurrying water-rats squeaked from the walls, pis-
tolled their water, and ran for more. And the wall-sprays let down
showers of mechanical rain.

But too late. Somewhere, sighing, a pump shrugged to a
stop. The quenching rain ceased. The reserve water supply

447

which had filled baths and washed dishes for many quiet days was gone.

The fire crackled up the stairs. It fed upon the Picassos and Matisses in the upper halls, like delicacies, baking off the oily flesh, tenderly crisping the canvases into black shavings.

Now the fire lay in beds, stood in windows, changed the colours of drapes!

And then, reinforcements.

From attic trap-doors, blind robot faces peered down with faucet mouths gushing green chemical.

The fire backed off, as even an elephant must at the sight of a dead snake. Now there were twenty snakes whipping over the floor, killing the fire with a clear, cold venom of green froth.

But the fire was clever. It had sent flame outside the house, up through the attic to the pumps there. An explosion! The attic brain which directed the pumps was shattered into bronze shrapnel on the beams.

The fire rushed back into every closet and felt the clothes hung there.

The house shuddered, oak bone on bone, its bared skeleton cringing from the heat, its wire, its nerves revealed as if a surgeon had torn the skin off to let the red veins and capillaries quiver in the scalded air. Help, help! Fire! Run, run! Heat snapped mirrors like the first brittle winter ice. And the voices wailed Fire, fire, run, run, like a tragic nursery rhyme, a dozen voices, high, low, like children dying in a forest, alone, alone. And the voices fading as the wires popped their sheathings like hot chestnuts. One, two, three, four, five voices died.

In the nursery the jungle burned. Blue lions roared, purple giraffes bounded off. The panthers ran in circles, changing colour, and ten million animals, running before the fire, vanished off towards a distant steaming river...

Ten more voices died. In the last instant under the fire avalanche, other choruses, oblivious, could be heard announcing the time, playing music, cutting the lawn by remote control mower, or setting an umbrella frantically out and in the slamming and opening front door, a thousand things happening, like a clock-shop when each clock strikes the hour insanely before or after the other, a scene of maniac confusion, yet unity; singing, screaming, a few last cleaning mice darting bravely out to carry the horrid ashes away! And one voice, with sublime disregard for the situation, read poetry aloud in the fiery study, until all the film-spools burned, until all the wires withered and the circuits cracked.

The fire burst the house and let it slam flat down, puffing out skirts of spark and smoke.

In the kitchen, an instant before the rain of fire and timber, the stove could be seen making breakfasts at a psychopathic rate, ten dozen eggs, six loaves of toast, twenty dozen bacon strips, which, eaten by fire, started the stove working again, hysterically hissing!

The crash. The attic smashing into kitchen and parlour. The parlour into cellar, cellar into sub-cellar. Deep freeze, arm-chair, film tapes, circuits, beds, and all like skeletons thrown in a cluttered mound deep under.

449

Smoke and silence. A great quantity of smoke.

Dawn showed faintly in the east. Among the ruins, one wall stood alone. Within the wall, a last voice said, over and over again and again, even as the sun rose to shine upon the heaped rubble and steam:

'Today is August 5, 2026, today is August 5, 2026, today is...'